Modern Latin Am

Modern
Latin
American
Fiction

A Survey

Edited by
John King

faber and faber

LONDON · BOSTON

First published in 1987
by Faber and Faber Limited
3 Queen Square London WC1N 3AU

Typeset by Goodfellow & Egan Cambridge
Printed in Great Britain by Cox and Wyman
All rights reserved

British Library Cataloguing in Publication Data
Modern Latin American fiction.
1. Spanish American fiction—20th
century—History and criticism
I. King, John
863   PQ7082.N7

ISBN 0-571-14508-6

Contents

v

Introduction

This book is intended as an introductory survey of the wealth and diversity which is modern Latin American fiction. Although it first reached an international readership in the 1960s, it is only in the past few years that North American and British publishing houses have consistently made available a range of texts from Latin America and that the media has registered the 'emergence' of a distinctive and dynamic body of literature. Milan Kundera, the Czech writer, articulated a now widely held view when he stated: 'To speak of the end of the novel is a local preoccupation of West European writers, notably the French – it's absurd to talk about it to a writer from my part of Europe, or from Latin America. How can one possibly mumble about the death of the novel and have on one's bookshelf *One Hundred Years of Solitude* by Gabriel García Márquez?' ('Kundera on the Novel', *New York Times Book Review*, 8 January 1978.)

With this increased, but often unfocused attention, there has been an unfortunate tendency to label texts as simply 'Latin American' or 'magical realist' when in fact they are from diverse countries and cultures. Anthony Burgess, for example, in a recent review of Mario Vargas Llosa's *The War of the End of the World* wrote with scorn of a 'Latin freakshow': 'There is a danger that the Great Contemporary Latin American Novel will soon be laying down (if it has not done so already) rigid rules in respect of its content, length and style. Apparently it has to be bulky, baroque, full of freaks and cripples with names hard to fix in one's mind, crammed with wrongs done to peasants by the state or the land owners, seasoned with grotesque atrocities, given to apocalyptic visions, ending up with resignation at the impossibility of anything ever going right for South America.' ('Latin Freakshow', *Observer*, 19 May 1985)

By offering the reader an analysis of the development of Latin American fiction which concentrates both on themes and on the work of representative writers this book hopes to undermine such stereotypes. It would be impossible to map the whole field in one short study and so the emphasis is placed on those works that are readily available in English editions. The contributors include scholars from North America and Britain as well as some of the Latin American writers themselves. Most of the essays have been specifically written for this volume.

A number of contributors take the 1920s to mark the emergence of modern fiction in Latin America. However, talk of beginnings must be imprecise since the whole process of cultural production is one of both continuities and breaks with the past. Mario Vargas Llosa describes how fiction was largely outlawed in Spanish America until after the Wars of Independence in the early nineteenth century, and how the dominant European form of the realist novel never got a firm hold after this date. It was not established because the material conditions in which the rise of the novel in Europe took place were almost totally absent in nineteenth-century Latin America. *One Hundred Years of Solitude* explores these circumstances. How can one expect, García Márquez asks, the stability of the realist text, the complex psychological development of character and personal relationships operating within an ordered historical and social framework, when, during this period countries such as Colombia were economically under-developed, controlled by neo-imperialism and had a dynamic popular culture that was oral rather than written.

Many of the writers studied in this volume, therefore, draw not on any tradition of realist fiction, but rather on earlier, often dissimilar forms such as the romances of chivalry. Vargas Llosa draws a persuasive parallel between the earliest Spanish chroniclers trying to come to terms with the diversity and difference of America and resorting to analogies which blend fantasy and reality, and contemporary novelists who, faced with the same narrative problems, adopt similar strategies. As Edwin Williamson points out, conquistadores and explorers used the exhilarating fantasies of the romances to express the marvels they found in the New World. Little wonder that the realist novel sold America short, for 'it remained a misfit in an environment that had once lent itself so well to far more robust flourishes of the imagination'.

Novelists could draw on these legacies of conquest narratives, but they could also help to revive 'the vision of the vanquished', by exploring the pre-Columbian roots of Latin American civilization. Gordon Brotherston's essay analyses the many different ways in which Indian culture has been rescued from oblivion or a position of exotic 'otherness', and restored to a place of centrality in the culture of the continent.

In the 1920s, some writers began to break free of the legacy of anachronistic romanticism or positivist naturalism, exploring the revolution in a narrative form that was a feature of twentieth-century modernist fiction. Vanguard movements in Latin America grew up in the major cities, in particular São Paulo, Buenos Aires and Mexico City. Randal Johnson examines the work of Brazilian intellectuals in São

Paulo, who asserted cultural nationalism through the wilfully barbarous metaphor of cannibalism. John Gledson provides a context for this and other movements in his survey of Brazilian fiction, from the corrosive Machado de Assis at the end of the last century to the present day. Discussion of Brazilian fiction is often absent from studies of Latin American writing, and the present volume helps to rectify this imbalance by offering three major essays on the subject.

The chapters on Borges and Carpentier discuss further the impact of modernist ideas on Argentine cultural life and on the community of exiled writers living in Paris throughout this period. The 1920s was a period of experimentation and excitement, but it was the poets rather than the writers of fiction who assimilated most rapidly the lessons of the avant-garde. As Carlos Fuentes persuasively argues, it would take until the 1950s and early 1960s for the revolutions in narrative structure and narrative time to be assimilated fully by the novelists.

The 1930s witnessed few interesting developments in prose fiction in Spanish America. The avant-garde had run out of steam and even the rich vein of regionalist fiction that had appeared in the 1920s produced few worthy successors. In Brazil, however, a diverse and important body of literature was written in or about the north-east of the country. The most significant writer of this decade was undoubtedly Graciliano Ramos whose novels, such as *Barren Lives* and *São Bernardo*, would influence his own generation and also provide inspiration for the 'new wave' of Brazilian film-makers in the 1960s. The analysis of Brazilian fiction focuses on the undisputed master of modern Brazilian fiction, João Guimarães Rosa who, from the 1940s, as Charles Perrone points out, defied the frontier between 'regionalist' and 'universal' approaches to fiction and achieved an unparalleled transformation of Brazilian literary language.

In Spanish America, three writers in particular, Miguel Angel Asturias, Jorge Luis Borges and Alejo Carpentier began to write texts in the 1920s and 1930s, which would prove extremely infuential in the development of prose fiction. Asturias drew on pre-Columbian traditions in order to explore the myths and realities of the people of Guatemala. Borges asserted a self-confident cosmopolitanism and taught novelists to concentrate on form and intellectual coherence in writing. Carpentier defined and explored the 'magical realism' of the continent of Latin America.

Developments in the 1940s and 1950s cannot be as comprehensively covered in this book, since the works of a number of important writers, especially from the River Plate region – Juan Carlos Onetti and Mario Benedetti of Uruguay, and Eduardo Mallea, Leopoldo Marechal and Ernesto Sábato of Argentina – are not readily available to the English-speaking reader. The same is true of novels dealing with the historical impact of the Mexican Revolution, those by Agustin Yáñez and in particular by Juan Rulfo: Rulfo's *Pedro Páramo* (1955), a Faulknerian exploration of an impoverished, violent and abandoned rural countryside, remains, in Fuentes's terms, one of the great novels of the twentieth century.

The main body of this study concentrates on developments in literature since the late 1950s, a period which has been termed the 'boom' in Latin American fiction. Certainly the decade of the 1960s saw important changes in the cultural field, which had a far-reaching impact on writers and readers. The Cuban Revolution of 1959 had a profound political and symbolic influence in the continent. It was a nationalist, anti-imperialist revolution which seemed exemplary and demonstrated a need for commitment and for political clarity. Also, in the beginning the Cubans invited many members of the artistic community to the island, awarded literary prizes, and promoted discussion. The group of so-called 'boom' novelists was closely identified with this process. A number of intellectuals turned against Cuba in the late 1960s, as the regime clarified its objectives and directions. This tendency is analysed by Gerald Martin in his assessment of Mario Vargas Llosa's literary trajectory. Other writers, such as Cortázar, García Márquez and Mario Benedetti, remained committed to the ideals of the Revolution. In recent years, the debate over the nature of Cuba has become increasingly bitter and polarized.

The word 'boom', a North American marketing term, adequately describes the increased consumption of cultural production in the 1960s. It also implies successful marketing strategies, another feature of the period. Certainly in many areas of Latin America the 1960s heralded an era of modernization, and a certain 'democratization' of what had previously been considered high-brow culture. This process is especially apparent in the field of literature. Whereas in the late 1950s a writer might hope to sell one print run of 2,000 books, by the late 1960s successful writers sold tens of thousands of copies in a year. A Latin American readership had emerged, prepared to buy books by their own writers. Publishing houses, newspapers and weekly news journals both reflected and directed these tastes through a vigorous promotion of certain novels and novelists. In some cases, the author became a type of brand name, a mark of industrial quality by which new products could be sold. The enthusiasm spread to Europe and the United States and the writers became international stars.

Introduction

Yet an analysis of consumerism does not negate the fact that since the late 1950s, Latin America has produced a quality and a diversity of writing unparalleled in its history. This anthology includes critical assessments of five of the 'boom' writers – Julio Cortázar, Carlos Fuentes, Gabriel García Márquez, Mario Vargas Llosa and José Donoso – who, with the exception of Cortázar who died recently, are still writing at the height of their powers.

Consideration is also given to Guillermo Cabrera Infante and Manuel Puig, who have explored the influence of mass culture on the modernist novel. Stephanie Merrim's essay on this topic is complemented by an autobiographical essay by Manuel Puig in which he analyses his dual commitment to the cinema and to fiction. Similar points are covered in Cabrera Infante's interview with Jason Wilson.

In the 1960s, and even today, the 'boom' writers can be seen as a male club, a family, in Susan Bassnett's terms, made up entirely of fathers, brothers and sons. Her essay focuses on women writers who have, until very recently, been excluded from analyses of Latin American fiction. She argues persuasively that these women are not writing like the great 'masters' of the past, but are giving expression to women's points of view that have been hidden from history for so long.

The 1970s witnessed a sombre period of history, especially in the Southern Cone of Latin America. Military coups in Uruguay and Chile in 1973 and in Argentina in 1976, resulted in hundreds of thousands of deaths and millions were forced to live abroad. This is the theme of the essay by Augusto Roa Bastos, who has lived outside his country of birth, Paraguay, since 1947, due to the brutal dictatorship of General Stroessner. Roa's work provides a subtle and passionate insight into the many forms of exile suffered by Latin American writers. In other cases the painful and bewildering process of return after exile is a theme that recurs in much contemporary fiction from the Southern Cone.

I hope more Latin American writers will continue to become available to English readers. The texts are there, awaiting translators and publishers. Finally, I should like to thank all the contributors to this volume for their support in this collective enterprise.

John King
University of Warwick
February 1987

Editor's Note

Texts referred to in these essays are given first in English if a published translation exists, with the original Spanish or Portuguese title in brackets. If no published translation exists, the Spanish or Portuguese title is given with a literal English translation in brackets and quotes. Additional bibliographical details can be found in the Bibliography at the end of the book.

Latin America: Fiction and Reality

Mario Vargas Llosa

The historian who mastered the subject of the discovery and conquest of Peru by the Spaniards better than anyone else had a tragic story: he died without having written the book for which he had prepared himself all his life and whose theme he knew so well that he almost gave the impression of being omniscient.

His name was Raúl Porras Barrenechea. He was a small, pot-bellied man, with a large forehead and a pair of blue eyes which became impregnated with malice every time he mocked someone. He was the most brilliant teacher I have ever had. Only Marcel Bataillon, another historian, whom I had the chance to listen to at the Collège de France (in a course of lectures he gave on a Peruvian chronicler, by the way) seemed to be able to match Porras Barrenechea's eloquence and evocative power as well as his academic integrity. But not even the learned and elegant Bataillon could captivate an audience with the enchantment of Porras Barrenechea. In the big old house of San Marcos, the first university founded by the Spaniards in the New World, a place which had already begun to fall into an irreparable process of decay when I passed through it in the 1950s, the lectures on historical sources attracted such a vast number of listeners that it was necessary to arrive well in advance so as not to be left outside the classroom, listening together with dozens of students, literally hanging from the doors and windows.

Whenever Porras Barrenechea spoke, history became anecdote, gesture, adventure, colour, psychology. He depicted history as a series of murals which had the magnificence of a Renaissance painting and in which the determining factor of events was never the impersonal forces – the geographical imperative, the economic relations, divine providence – but the cast of certain outstanding individuals whose audacity, genius, charisma or contagious insanity had imposed on each era and society a certain orientation and shape.

As well as this concept of history, which the 'scientific' historians had already named as romantic in an effort to discredit it, Porras Barrenechea demanded knowledge and documentary precision, which none of his colleagues and critics at San Marcos has so far been able to equal. Those historians who dismissed Porras Barrenechea because he was interested in simple 'narrated' history instead of a social or economic interpretation have been less effective than he was in explaining to us that crucial event in the destiny of Europe and America: the destruction of the Inca Empire and the linking of its vast territories and peoples to the Western world. This was because for Porras Barrenechea, although history had to have a dramatic quality, architectonic beauty, suspense, richness and a wide range of human types and the excellence in style of a great fiction, everything in it also had to be scrupulously true, proven time after time.

In order to be able to narrate the discovery and conquest of Peru in this way, Porras Barrenechea, before anything else, had to evaluate very carefully all the witnesses and documents so as to establish the degree of credibility of each one of them. And in the numerous cases of deceitful testimonies, Porras Barrenechea had to find out the reasons that led the authors to conceal, misrepresent or overpaint the facts so that, knowing their peculiar limitations, those sources had a double meaning: what they revealed and what they distorted. For forty years Porras Barrenechea dedicated all his powerful intellectual energy to this heroic hermeneutic. All the works he published while he was alive constituted the preliminary work for what should have been his *magnum opus*. Once he was perfectly equipped to embark upon it, pressing on with assurance through the labyrinthine jungle of chronicles, letters, testaments, rhymes and ballads of the discovery and conquest which he had read, cleansed, confronted and almost memorized, sudden death put an end to his encyclopaedic information. As a result all those interested in that era and in the men who lived it, have had to keep on reading the old but so far unsurpassed *History of the Conquest* written by an American who never set foot on the country but who sketched it with extraordinary skill: William Prescott.

Dazzled by Porras Barrenechea's lectures, at one time I seriously considered the possibility of leaving aside literature so as to dedicate myself to history. Porras Barrenechea had asked me to work with him as an assistant in an ambitious project on the general history of Peru, under the auspices of the bookseller and publisher Juan Mejía Baca. It was Porras Barrenechea's task to write the volumes devoted to the Conquest and Emancipation. For four years, I spent three hours a day, five days a week in that dusty house on Colina Street, where the books, the card indexes and the notebooks had slowly invaded and devoured everything, except Porras Barrenechea's bed and the dining table. My job was to read and take notes on the chroniclers' various themes, but principally on the myths and legends which preceded and followed the discovery and conquest of Peru. That experience has become an unforgettable memory for me. Whoever is familiar with the chronicles of the conquest and discovery of America will understand why. They represent for us Latin Americans what the novels of chivalry represent for Europe: the beginning of literary fiction as we understand it today.

(Permit me, here, a long parenthesis.

As you probably know, the novel was forbidden in the Spanish Colonies by the Inquisition. The inquisitors considered this literary genre – the novel – to be as dangerous for the spiritual fate of the Indians as for the moral and political behaviour of society, in which, of course, they were absolutely right. We novelists must be grateful to the Spanish Inquisition for having discovered, before any critic did, the inevitable subversive nature of fiction. The prohibition included reading and publishing novels in the colonies. There was no way, naturally, to avoid a great number of novels being smuggled into our countries and we know, for example, that the first copies of *Don Quixote* entered America hidden in barrels of wine. We can only dream with envy about what kind of experience it was, in those times, in Spanish America, to read a novel: a sinful adventure in which, in order to abandon yourself to an imaginary world, you had to be prepared to face prison and humiliation.

Novels were not published in Spanish America until after the Wars of Independence. The first, *El Periquillo sarniento* ('The Itching Parrot'), appeared in Mexico only in 1816. Although novels were abolished for three centuries, the goal of the inquisitors – a society exonerated from the disease of fiction – was not achieved. They did not realize that the realm of fiction was larger and deeper than that of

4

the novel. Nor could they imagine that the appeti̇
– that is, for escaping objective reality through illusi̇
was so powerful and rooted in the human spirit, that, on̄
the vehicle of the novel was not available to satisfy it, the
thirst for fiction would infect – like a plague – all the other
disciplines and genres in which the written word could
freely flow. Repressing and censoring the literary genre
specifically invented to give 'the necessity of lying' a place
in the city, the inquisitors achieved the exact opposite of
their intentions: a world without novels, yes, but a
world into which fiction had spread and contaminated
practically everything: history, religion, poetry, science,
art, speeches, journalism, and the daily habits of people.

We are still victims in Latin America of what we could
call 'the revenge of the novel'. We still have great difficulty
in our countries in differentiating between fiction and
reality. We are traditionally accustomed to mix them in
such a way that this is, probably, one of the reasons why
we are so impractical and inept in political matters, for
instance. But some good also came from this novelization
of our whole life. Books like *One Hundred Years of Solitude*,
Cortázar's short stories and Roa Bastos's novels wouldn't
have been possible otherwise.

The tradition from which this kind of literature sprang –
in which we are exposed to a world totally reconstructed
and subverted by fantasy – started, without doubt, in
those chroniclers of the conquest and discovery that I
read and noted under the guidance of Porras Barrenechea.

I now close the parenthesis and return to my subject.)

History and Literature – truth and falsehood, reality and
fiction – mingle in these texts in a way that is often
inextricable. The thin demarcation line that separates
one from the other frequently fades away, so that both
worlds can entwine in a completeness which the more

ambiguous it is, the more seductive it becomes, because the likely and unlikely in it seem to be part of the same substance. Right in the middle of the most cruel battle, the Virgin appears, who, taking the believers' side, charges against the unlucky pagans. The shipwrecked conquistador Pedro Serrano actually lives out, on a tiny island in the Caribbean, the story of Robinson Crusoe, which a novelist only invented centuries later. The Amazons of Greek mythology materialize by the banks of the river baptized with their name, to wound Pedro de Orellana's followers with their arrows, one arrow landing in Fray Gaspar de Carvajal's buttocks, the man who meticulously narrated this event. Is that episode more fabulous than another, probably historically correct, in which the poor soldier Manso de Leguisamo loses in one night of dice-playing the solid gold wall of the Temple of the Sun in Cuzco which was given to him in the spoils of war? Or more fabulous perhaps than the unutterable outrages committed – always with a smile on his face – by the rebel Francisco de Carvajal, that octogenarian Devil of the Andes who merrily began to sing: 'Oh mother, my poor little curly hairs, the wind is taking them away one by one, one by one', as he was being taken to the gallows where he was to be quartered, beheaded and burnt?

The chronicle, a hermaphrodite genre, is distilling fiction in life all the time, as in Borges's tale *Tlön, Uqbar, Orbis Tertius*. Does this mean that its testimony must be challenged from a historical point of view and accepted only as literature? Not at all. Its exaggerations and fantasies often reveal more about the reality of the era than its truths. Astonishing miracles from time to time enliven the tedious pages of the *Crónica moralizada* ('The Exemplary Chronicle') of Padre Calancha, sulphurous outrages come from the male and female demons fastidiously catechized in the Indian villages by the extirpators of idolatries, like Padre Arriaga, to justify their devastation of idols, amulets, ornaments, handicrafts and tombs, and these teach us more about the innocence, fanaticism and stupidity of the time than the wisest of treaties. As long as one knows how to read them, everything is contained in these pages, written sometimes by men who hardly knew how to write and who were impelled by the unusual nature of contemporary events to try to communicate and register them for posterity, thanks to an intuition of the privilege they enjoyed: that of being the witnesses and actors of events that were changing the history of the world. Because they narrate these events under the passion of recently lived experience, they often relate things that to us seem like naïve or cynical fantasies. For the people of the time, these were not so, but phantoms that credulity, surprise, fear and hatred had endowed with a solidity and vitality often more powerful than beings made of flesh and blood.

The conquest of the Tahuantinsuyu – the Empire of the Incas – by a handful of Spaniards is a fact of history that even now, after having digested and ruminated over all the explanations, we find hard to unravel. The first wave of conquistadores, Pizarro and his companions, were fewer than two hundred (without counting the black slaves and the collaborating Indians); when the reinforcements started to arrive, this first wave had already dealt a mortal blow and had taken over an empire which ruled over at least twenty million people. This was not a primitive society, made up of barbaric tribes, like the ones the Spaniards had found in the Caribbean or in Darien, but a civilization which had reached a high level of social, military, agricultural and handicraft development which, in many senses, Spain

7

itself had not reached. The most remarkable aspects of this civilization, however, were not the paths that crossed the four *suyos* or regions of its vast territory, the temples and fortresses, the irrigation systems or the complex administrative organization, but something in which all the testimonies of these chronicles coincide: this civilization managed to eradicate hunger in that immense region, it was able to produce – and distribute all that which was produced – in such a way that all its subjects had enough to eat. Only a very small number of empires throughout the whole world have succeeded in achieving this.

Are the conquistadores' firearms, horses and armour enough to explain the immediate collapse of this Inca civilization at the first clash with the Spaniards? It is true that gunpowder, bullets and the charging of beasts that were unknown to them, paralysed the Indians with a religious terror and inspired in them the sensation that they were fighting not against men, but against gods who were invulnerable to the arrows and slings with which they fought. Even so, the numerical difference was such that the Quechua Ocean would have had to shake, in order to drown the invader. What prevented this from happening? What is the profound explanation for that defeat from which the Inca population never recovered? The answer may perhaps lie hidden in the moving account that appears in the chronicles of what happened in the Cajamarca Square the day Pizarro captured the Inca Atahualpa. We must, above all, read the accounts of those who were there, those who lived through the event or had direct testimony of it, like Pedro Pizarro. At the precise moment the Emperor is captured, before the battle begins, his armies give up the fight as if manacled by a magic force. The slaughter is indescribable, but only from one of the two sides: the Spaniards discharge their harquebuses, thrust their pikes and swords and charge their horses against a bewildered mass, who, having witnessed the capture of their god and master, seem unable to defend themselves or even run away. In the space of a few minutes, the army which had defeated Huáscar and which dominated all the northern provinces of the empire, disintegrates like ice in warm water.

The vertical and totalitarian structure of the Tahuantinsuyu was, without doubt, more harmful to its survival than all the conquistadores' firearms and iron weapons. As soon as the Inca, that figure which was the vortex towards which all the wills converged searching for inspiration and vitality, the axis around which the entire society was organized and upon which depended the life and death of every person – from the richest to the poorest – was captured, no one knew how to act. So they did the only thing they could do, with heroism, we must admit, but without breaking the thousand and one taboos and precepts which regulated their existence: they let themselves get killed. And that was the fate of dozens and perhaps hundreds of Indians stultified by the confusion and loss of leadership that they suffered when the Inca Emperor, the life force of their universe, was captured right before their eyes.

Those Indians who let themselves be knifed or blown up into pieces that sombre afternoon in the Cajamarca Square, lacked the ability to make their own decisions, either with the sanction of the authority or indeed against it, and were incapable of taking individual initiatives, of acting with a certain degree of independence according to the changing circumstances. Those one hundred and eighty Spaniards who had placed the Indians in ambush and were now slaughtering them, did possess this ability.

9

It was this difference, more than the numerical one or the weapons, that created an immense inequality between both civilizations. The individual had no importance and virtually no existence in that pyramidal and theocratic society, the achievement of which had always been collective and anonymous: carrying the gigantic stones of Machu Picchu citadel or of Ollantaytambo fortress up the steepest of peaks, directing water to all the slopes of the Cordillera hills by building terraces which even today enable irrigation to take place in the most desolate places, and making paths to unite regions separated by infernal geographies. A state religion that took away the individual's free will and crowned the authority's decision with the aura of a divine mandate turned the Tahuantinsuyu into a beehive: laborious, efficient, stoic. But its immense power was in fact very fragile; it rested completely on the sovereign-god's shoulders, the man whom the Indian had to serve and to whom he owed a total and selfless obedience.

It was religion, rather than force, that preserved the people's metaphysical docility toward the Inca. The social and political function of its religion is an aspect of the Tahuantinsuyu that has not been studied enough. The creed and the rite, as well as the prohibitions and the feasts, the values and the vices, all served to strengthen carefully the Emperor's absolute power, and to propitiate the expansionist and colonizing design of the Cuzco sovereigns. It was an essentially political religion, which on the one hand turned the Indians into diligent servants, and on the other was capable of receiving into its bosom, as minor gods, all the deities of the peoples that had been conquered – the idols of which were moved to Cuzco and enthroned by the Inca himself. The Inca religion was less cruel than the Aztec one, for it performed human sacrifices with a certain degree of moderation (if I can say this) making use only of the necessary cruelty to ensure the hypnosis and fear of the subjects towards the divine power incarnated in the temporary power of the Inca.

We cannot call into question the organizing genius of the Inca. The speed with which the Empire, in the short period of a century, grew from its nucleus in Cuzco to become a civilization which embraced three quarters of South America is incredible. And this was the result not only of the Quechuas' military efficiency but also of the Incas' ability to persuade the neighbouring peoples and cultures to join the Tahuantinsuyu. Once these became part of the Empire, the bureaucratic mechanism was immediately set in motion, enrolling the new servants in that system which dissolves individual life into a series of tasks and gregarian duties carefully programmed and supervised by the gigantic network of administrators whom the Inca sent to the furthest borders. Either to prevent or to extinguish rebelliousness there was a system called *mitimaes*, whereby villages and people were removed *en masse* to faraway places where, feeling misplaced and lost, these exiles naturally assumed an attitude of passivity and absolute respect, which, of course, represented the Inca system's ideal citizen.

Such a civilization was capable of fighting against the natural elements and defeating them; it was capable of consuming rationally what it produced, heaping together reserves for future times of poverty or disaster; and it was also able to evolve slowly and with care in the field of knowledge, inventing only that which could support it and hindering all that which in some way or another could undermine its foundations (as for example writing or any other form of expression liable to develop individual pride or a rebellious imagination). It was not capable, however, of facing the unexpected, that absolute novelty represented by that phalanx of armoured men on horseback who assaulted the Incas with weapons, transgressing all the war and peace patterns known to them.

When, after the initial confusion, resistance attempts started breaking out here and there, it was too late. The complicated machinery regulating the Empire had entered a process of decomposition. Leaderless with the murder of Huayna Cápac's two sons – Huáscar, whose killing was ordered by Atahualpa, and the latter, executed by Pizarro – the Inca system seems to fall into a monumental state of confusion and cosmic deviation, similar to the chaos which according to the Cuzquean sages, the Amautas, had prevailed in the world before the Tahuantinsuyu was founded by Manco Cápac and Mama Ocllo. While on the one hand, caravans of Indians loaded with gold and silver continued taking to the conquistador the treasures the Inca ordered to be brought to pay for his rescue, on the other, a group of Quechua generals, attempting to organize the resistance, fired at the wrong target, for they were venting their fury on the Indian cultures that had begun to collaborate with the Spaniards because of their grudge against their ancient masters.

Spain had already won the game, although the rebellious outbreaks (which were always localized and counterchecked by the servile obedience that great sectors of the Inca system transferred automatically from the Incas to their new masters) had multiplied in the following years, up to Manco Inca's insurrection. But not even these, notwithstanding their importance, represented a real danger to the Spanish rule.

Those who destroyed the Inca Empire and created that country which is called Peru – a country which four and a half centuries later has not yet managed to

12

heal the bleeding wounds of its birth – were men whom we can hardly admire. They were, it is true, uncommonly courageous, but, in opposition to what the edifying stories teach us, most of them lacked any idealism or higher purpose. They possessed only greed, hunger, and, in the best of cases, a certain vocation for adventure. The cruelty in which the Spaniards took pride – and which the chronicles depict to the point of making us shiver – was inscribed in the ferocious customs of the times and was, without doubt, equivalent to that of the people they subdued and almost extinguished (three centuries later the Inca population had been reduced from twenty million to only six).

But these semi-illiterate, implacable and greedy swordsmen who, even before having completely conquered the Inca Empire, were already savagely fighting among themselves, or fighting the 'pacifiers' sent against them by the faraway monarch to whom they had given a continent, represented a culture in which (we will never know if for the benefit or disgrace of mankind) something new, exotic, had germinated in the history of man. In this culture, although injustice and abuses had proliferated, often favoured by religion, little by little, in an unforeseen way, by the alliance of multiple factors – among them chance – a social space of human activities had grown neither legislated nor controlled by the powers. On the one hand, this would produce the most extraordinary economic, scientific and technical development human civilization has ever known since the times of cavemen with their clubs; on the other, this would give way to the creation of the individual as the sovereign source of values which society had to respect.

Those who, rightly so, are shocked by the abuses and crimes of the conquest, must bear in mind that the first

13

men to condemn them and ask that they be brought to an end were men like Padre Las Casas, who came to America with the conquistadores and abandoned their ranks in order to collaborate with the defeated ones, whose sufferance they denounced with an indignation and virulence that still moves us today. Padre Las Casas was the most active, although not the only one, of those nonconformists who rebelled against the abuses inflicted upon the Indians. They fought against their fellow men and against the policies of their own country in the name of a moral principle which to them was higher than any nation or state principle. This could not have been possible among the Inca or any of the other pre-Hispanic cultures. In these cultures, as in the other great civilizations of history foreign to the West, the individual could not morally question the social organism of which he was part, because he only existed as an integral atom of that organism, and because for him the reason of the state could not be separated from morality. The first culture to interrogate and question itself, the first to break up the masses into individual beings who, with time, gradually gained the right to think and act for themselves, was to become, thanks to that unknown exercise – freedom – the most powerful civilization in the world. It is useless to ask oneself whether it was good that it happened in this manner or whether it would have been better for humanity if the individual had never been born and the tradition of the ant-like societies had continued for ever.

The pages of the chronicles of the conquest and the discovery depict that crucial, bloody moment full of phantasmagoria and in which, disguised as a handful of invading treasure-hunters, killing and destroying, the Judaeo-Christian tradition, the Spanish language, Greece, Rome and the Renaissance, the notion of individual sovereignty,

and the chance of living sometime in freedom,
shores of the Empire of the Sun.

So it was that we, as Peruvians, were born. A
course, the Bolivians, Chileans, Ecuadorians, C
etc. Almost five centuries later this is still an u ....eu
business. We have not yet, properly speaking, seen the
light. We don't yet constitute real nations.

Our contemporary reality is still impregnated with the
violence and marvels that those first texts of our literature –
those novels disguised as history or historical books corrupted by fiction – told us about. At least one basic problem
is the same. Two cultures, one Western and modern, the
other aboriginal and archaic, hardly coexist, separated the
one from the other because of the exploitation and discrimination that the former exercises over the latter. Our country
– our countries – are in a deep sense more a fiction than a
reality. In the eighteenth century, in France, the name of
Peru rang with a golden echo, and an expression was then
born – *'ce n'est pas le Pérou'* – which is used when something
is not as rich and extraordinary as its legendary name
suggests. Well, *'Le Pérou, ce ne'est pas le Pérou'*. It never was,
at least for the great part of its inhabitants, that fabulous
country of legends and fictions, but rather an artificial
gathering of men from different languages, customs and
traditions whose only common denominator was having
been condemned by history to live together without knowing or loving each other.

The immense opportunities brought by the civilization
that discovered and conquered America have been benefi-
cial only to a minority – sometimes a very small one –
whereas the great majority manage to have only the negative share of the conquest; that is, contributing in
their serfdom and sacrifice, in their misery and neglect, to
the prosperity and refinement of the Westernized élites.

One of our worst defects – our best fictions – is to believe that our miseries have been imposed on us from abroad, that others have always had the responsibility for our problems, for instance, the conquistadores. There are countries in Latin America – Mexico is the best example – in which the 'Spaniards' are even now severely indicted for what 'they' did with the Indians. Did 'they' really do it? We did it. We are the conquistadores. They were our parents and grandparents who came to our shores and gave us the names we have and the language we speak. They gave us also the habit of passing to the devil the responsibility for any evil we do. Instead of making amends for what they did, by improving and correcting our relationship with our indigenous compatriots, mixing with them and amalgamating ourselves to form a new culture which would have been a kind of synthesis of the best of both, we – the Westernized Latin Americans – have persevered in the worst habits of our forebears, behaving towards the Indians during the nineteenth and twentieth centuries as the Spaniards behaved towards the Aztecs and the Incas. And sometimes even worse. We must remember that, in countries like Chile and Argentina, it was during the Republic, not during the Colony, that the native cultures were systematically exterminated. It is a fact that in many of our countries, as in Peru, we share, in spite of the pious and hypocritical 'indigenist' rhetoric of our men of letters and poltiticians, the mentality of the conquistadores.

Only in countries where the native population was small or non-existent, or where the aboriginals were practically liquidated, can we talk of integrated societies. In the others, a discreet, sometimes unconscious but very effective 'apartheid' prevails. There, integration is extremely slow and the price the native has to pay for it is high: renunciation of his culture – his language, his beliefs, his

16

traditions and customs – and adoption of that of his ancient masters.

Maybe there is no realistic way to integrate our societies other than by asking the Indians to pay that price; maybe, the ideal – that is, the preservation of the primitive cultures of America – is a utopia incompatible with this other and more urgent goal: the establishment of societies in which social and economic inequalities among citizens be reduced to human, reasonable limits and where everybody can enjoy, at least, a decent and free life. In any case, we have been unable to reach any of those ideals and are still, as when we had just entered Western history, trying to find what we are and what our future will be.

That is why it is very useful for we Latin Americans to review the literature that gives testimony to the discovery and the conquest. In the chronicles we not only dream about the time in which our fantasy and our realities seemed to be incestuously confused; in them we also learn about the roots of our problems and challenges that are still there, unanswered. And in these half-literary, half-historical pages we also perceive, formless, mysterious, fascinating, the promise of something new and formidable, something that if it ever would turn into reality, would enrich the world and improve civilization. Of this promise we have only had until now, sporadic manifestations – in our literature and in our art, for example. But it is not only in our fictions that we must strive to achieve; we must not stop until our promise passes from our dreams and words into our daily lives and becomes objective reality. We must not permit our countries to disappear, as did my dear teacher, the historian Porras Barrenechea, without writing in real life the definitive masterwork we have been preparing ourselves to accomplish since the three caravels stumbled on to our coasts.

17

Brazilian Fiction:
Machado de Assis to the Present

John Gledson

'When we learn from Stendhal that he wrote one of his books for only a hundred readers, we are both astonished and disturbed. The world will neither be astonished nor, probably, disturbed if the present book has not one hundred readers, like Stendhal's, nor fifty, nor twenty, nor even ten. Ten. Maybe five.'

These are the opening words of *Epitaph of a Small Winner* (*Memórias póstumas de Brás Cubas*), 1880, by Machado de Assis, the first indisputable masterpiece of Brazilian fiction. An appropriate way to begin, in more ways than one: and I want to use these words and the extraordinary figure of Machado himself to introduce the reader to something of the common situation of Brazilian fiction – an *entre-lugar*, or between-place, as one critic defines it. Of course there are risks in any such enterprise – that situation has changed a good deal since 1880 (and in the last few years in particular), and it can be distorting to see Brazil as something unique, when it is very like other places, notably the rest of Latin America. But the attempt seems preferable to a contextless series of great names; so before I highlight some of these later in this essay, I want to sketch out this larger map, using Machado as my base, but ranging speculatively over every period of literature since the late nineteenth century.

To whom was Machado addressing himself? To more

than five readers, no doubt: yet the fact remains, for all the irony, that audiences for fiction remain small in a country with a huge population (over 140 million). Roberto Schwarz, in the 1970s, reckoned on some fifty or sixty thousand as an optimistic upper limit, in a country where editions rarely exceed three thousand, and a novel is lucky to reach its fourth or fifth. Obviously, for most novelists and short-story writers, fiction cannot provide a living: they have other jobs, and very often, as in Machado's case, as civil servants and journalists. In turn, such dependence on the state in particular may limit their freedom to say all that they otherwise might, especially when governments turn repressive, as has happened with unhappy frequency, and never with more ferocity than during the worst period of the recent military regime, lasting from the mid 1960s to the mid 1970s.

It would be wrong to associate financial and intellectual freedom, however. Walnice Nogueira Galvão has noticed that two writers who made a substantial amount from their work, Jorge Amado and Erico Veríssimo, were also the first to publish protest novels, in 1973. What she noticed, too, was that Amado's novel, at any rate, was very bad, and, moreover, his critique of the regime did not go very far, or very deep. Having broken out of one dependent relationship, he had fallen into another, that of dependence on middle-class readers – and that middle-class was precisely the beneficiary of the repression, if anything wishing that the economic boom – the so-called 'miracle' – could take place with less brutality. The title of Amado's novel was *Teresa Batista, Tired of War* (*Cansada da guerra* – the English title was *Teresa Batista, Home from the Wars*).

It might seem that I am well on my way to defining less a between-place than a no-place. Certainly, fiction has always been the art of a small minority in Brazil, and with the growth of the cinema and above all of television, there is no reason to think that that situation will change. But it would be wrong to judge these matters solely in terms of audience size: and this is not just an assumption that 'literary quality' is the only criterion. This marginal and constrained situation does affect their writing, but in often unexpected ways. No one illustrates this better than Machado, who knew his audience very well indeed. As well as novelist and short-story writer, he was a journalist (at the period when newspapers were still the most advanced mass medium), a poet and a dramatist. From long training and experience (he began as a proof-reader in his teens) he knew exactly what his audience wanted. That is why he was able to offer them that, and something different. *Dom Casmurro* (1899) is perhaps the most intricate example of all: it is what Borges and Bioy Casares speculate about in the opening story of *Fictions (Ficciones)*, 'a novel in the first person, whose narrator would omit or disfigure the facts and indulge in various contradictions which would permit a few readers – a very few readers – to perceive an atrocious or banal reality'. Bento recounts his adolescent love affair and subsequent marriage to Capitu; slowly, we begin to realize that all is not well, until, after the drowning of his best friend Escobar, Bento accuses Capitu of having committed adultery with him, and decides that their child is in fact Escobar's. Many, if not most, readers have taken the novel to be a tragic love story, with Bento as its unfortunate hero. The truth, to use Borges's word, is more banal – perhaps, in the long run, more atrocious too. Bento is not a hero but a spoilt mother's boy, cornered by her pre-natal promise to make him a priest, who is out of his depth with a girl from lower down the social scale and so invents compensatory stories which, in clearing him or his mother of any blame, inevitably inculpate others. As we unravel the tangle of 'fact' and story, an unrivalled picture of a society and a mentality emerge: something which is equally true of his two earlier masterpieces, *Epitaph of a Small Winner* and *The Heritage of Quincas Borba/Philosopher or Dog? (Quincas Borba)*. The picture which emerges, etched with a sarcastic, deadpan humour, is certainly not a flattering one.

Machado presents his readers, in effect, with the choice between two books, the one immensely readable, interesting, amusing, the other much more unsettling, giving uncomfortable insights into Brazilian upper-class society and its dependence on slavery (abolished only in 1888), its repressiveness and callousness. With immense tact and daring, with a mixture of aggression and politeness which is the hallmark of his style, Machado kept his readers and was, in his own lifetime, a writer of considerable prestige. The only price he had to pay (and no doubt he was content to do so) was that part of his message went unperceived until long after his death.

In order to achieve this aim, Machado had not only to know his readers and to anticipate their reactions with unrivalled skill. He had also to experiment, using models like those of writers – Stendhal, Sterne, Xavier de Maistre – mentioned in the same prologue to *Epitaph of a Small Winner*, to produce something much more playful in form than anything either the 'solemn' or the 'frivolous', the twin pillars of public opinion, as he calls them, would recognize as a novel. He had, in fact, written much more conventional novels during the 1870s, up to only two years before the publication of *Small Winner*. His experimentation has led critics to exclaim at his modernity. To a great degree this is unhelpful, though no doubt our more sceptical reading habits are admirably suited to him. Even so, he is quite capable of outwitting us. Machado was responding to local impositions (though with a great deal more agility than his contemporaries), rejecting for very good reasons both the outdated Romanticism and the modish, determinist and often racially stereotyped Naturalism of his day. He had to find some other model, or stop writing.

Though it may seem peculiar to the literary crisis of his own time, Machado's situation in this respect too is paradigmatic, and marks many other writers, though in different ways. Of course, when modernism in its various forms appeared in Europe, it was imported just as Romanticism and Naturalism had been before. It was accompanied, in the 1920s, by a nationalism which ranged from the fascistic to the genuine exploration of a country still largely unknown outside the so-called Rio–São Paulo axis, which still today controls Brazil's cultural life. But if this conjunction of nationalism and modernist revolt was accidental, it was a happy accident. Not only did avant-garde forms suit the iconoclastic, satirical aims of the writers of the 1920s, they gave them an aesthetic justification for the unpopularity they lived with, or even courted for the sake of a future audience: 'the people will one day eat the high quality cookies I'm manufacturing for them today' as Oswald de Andrade, the most radical of the group, said. More than that, they felt, with a good deal of justification, that the discordant, irreverent style of much 'modern' writing suited Brazilian reality, itself so full of jarring contrasts and disharmonies. In other words, experimentalism was, for them as for Machado, a natural and necessary thing, an imposition of fundamentally realist aims (though they might not have put it that way). Conventional writers, like Jorge Amado, the most translated and commercially successful of Brazilian novelists,

risk relapsing into a kind of sub-literature. Experimentation need not be avant-garde: Graciliano Ramos, the
most important novelist of the 1930s, was in fact highly
suspicious of what he regarded as the élitist aestheticism
of the modernists, yet (like Machado's) each of his novels
is a changing response to reality, and that reality itself
forces on the honest writer a change in style and narrative
method. In the end, indeed, his concern for authenticity
forced him to abandon fiction altogether, for autobiography.

Experiment may be a necessity, but that does not make
it any more comfortable or less dangerous. Fascinating as
they are, Machado's last two novels, *Esau and Jacob (Esaú e
Jacó)* and *Counselor Ayres' Memorial (Memorial de Aires)*, the
first of them the most self-conscious of all his work, lack
the force and conviction of the three great works mentioned earlier; and Guimarães Rosa's masterpiece, *The
Devil to Pay in the Backlands (Grande sertão:veredas)* was
followed by short stories in which his extraordinary style
can come closer to preciosity than to grandeur (at least to
my taste). Conversely, Clarice Lispector, the author of
some marvellously intense short stories, finds it difficult to
sustain that intensity convincingly in the novels which she
nevertheless wrote and published. To that extent, it is
right to see Brazilian literature in its greatest and most
individual expression as a series of lonely, even tragic
figures, who have produced their most powerful work in a
struggle against considerable odds.

I hope that this does not conjure up an excessively
Romantic picture of writers who compensate for their
marginal position by contentment with superior isolation,
however; the real position is far more dialectically
complex than that (as talk of future audiences, for instance,
indicates), though no doubt the genuine precariousness of

their position can bring with it a heightened existential awareness. That, too, can be seen in Machado, whose mordant scepticism makes the Schopenhauerian pessimism by which he was undoubtedly influenced appear abstract and dogmatic. There is, too, a strong introspective vein in this writing, which can seem perverse to a European or North American reader agog for magical realism or social and political commitment.

It is realistic to say that artistic radicalism exists less for its own sake than as a way of marking out an audience: indeed, Brazilian writers have been nothing if not adaptable, perhaps because they can take so little for granted. Much recent fiction has in fact been criticized for its sensationalism of 'documentary' methods, borrowed from journalism or from television. No doubt rightly, in many cases; but the counterpart of this is an unselfconscious willingness to appropriate methods from other media, and not to regard 'literature' as an inviolable category. As a counterpart to this openness, and an indication of the importance of fiction in the Brazilian cultural context, it is worth pointing out how many of the best Brazilian films have been adaptations of novels, stories, or memoirs. A few will be mentioned in what follows.

Machado was a great precursor and a great example, but he was not what he also aspired to be, a great founder figure. (He was the first President of the Brazilian Academy of Letters which he intended to have a guiding role that it has never really earned.) This is no doubt in large measure the result of the nature of his realism, which is frequently not even seen for what it is: and for this, his strange relationship with his readers is largely responsible. For all the unsettling, sharply subversive nature of his underlying message, Machado was easily domesticated in the modernizing, superficially euphoric Brazil of the early twentieth century: he 'became' an elegant *fin-de-siècle* sceptic in the mould of Anatole France. Indeed, such was his need for respectability that he may even have collaborated in the creation of this travesty of himself. It has taken years of critical revaluation to establish the more complex figure, so deeply characteristic of his own milieu. Of course, there are limits to his realism, of which he was quite conscious: he rarely goes beyond the city of Rio, or beyond its upper and middle classes. To incorporate other dimensions, he has recourse to various tactics (of which one is an allegory that itself may well fly in the face of realism). When he comments on slavery, for instance, it is in short, if shocking episodes which unblinkingly reveal its horror – like that dealing with Prudêncio, Brás Cubas's whipping boy, who buys his own slave to whip when he is freed.

The lack of a great or even a solid and convincing traditional realism in Brazil, in the style of Dickens, Balzac or Pérez Galdós (a lack Brazil shares with the rest of Latin America) has meant that later writers have felt correspondingly less secure in their relation to reality, and suspicious of what ideological traps may lurk behind that apparently simple word: either that, of course, or they are over-secure, and so the unwitting dupes of the extraordinary number of more or less false myths which this vast, complex, racially mixed, socially divided country has been prone to since the early days of the conquest by Portugal.

The two most important prose writers of the early twentieth century, Lima Barreto and Euclides da Cunha, were anti-Machadian both in style and outlook. Da Cunha's *Rebellion in the Backlands (Os Sertões)* – the *sertões* are the drought-prone, backward interior of the northern part of the country – his account of the messianic Canudos revolt of 1895–7, led by Antônio Conselheiro, is written in an ornate prose, littered with scientific terms, with an assertive grandiloquence as different as possible from the more understated, surreptitiously complex Machado. *Rebellion in the Backlands* is not a novel (Euclides proclaimed, in fact, that he would never write one, though he succeeds in writing something fully as gripping, complete with plot and characters), but it is far more than a history book. The fanatical followers of the Conselheiro, emerging from the backward peasants of the interior of Bahia state, are taken by da Cunha to be the kernel of an emerging country ('the living rock of our race'), as well as a set of savage, regressive, mixed-race degenerates (Euclides was nothing if not the child of nineteenth-century positivism). From the conflict between these two – false – myths, and from his encounter with the *sertão* (albeit brief – he witnessed only the last three weeks of the military campaign against Canudos) sprang an opposition which has haunted many writers since, between the heavily populated and supposedly civilized coastal regions of Brazil and the almost unknown interior, inhabited not by romanticized Indians like those of José de Alencar (Machado's predecessor), but by less readily malleable peasants. It is a powerful dichotomy, which can be taken as a paradigm for Latin America as a whole, as Vargas Llosa's recent rewriting of Euclides in *The War at the End of the World* shows. *Rebellion in the Backlands* has set its stamp on much fiction in Brazil too, as we will see – on Graciliano Ramos and on Guimarães Rosa, for instance.

Lima Barreto, like Machado, wrote about Rio, and like him, he was mulatto. But there the resemblance ends. A tragic figure, who lost his sanity more than once and ended as a dipsomaniac, he was in furious revolt against the superficial values of a society hellbent on putting a European façade on a recalcitrant reality. His style, again, is anti-Machadean – plain and direct to the point of bluntness, it is aggressively non-literary by the standards of the day. His best novel, and the only one translated into English, is *The Patriot (Triste fim de Policarpo Quaresma)* in which he sets up a naïvely idealized vision of Brazil, incarnated in Quaresma, and gradually reveals the bureaucratic incompetence, intellectual sloth and fanaticism, rural backwardness, and finally violence and repression of his time and place. For all his shortcomings – the plot is the thinnest of threads on which to hang his polemic – he is a challenging writer, less easily assimilable by an official culture than Machado or Euclides.

Modernism in Brazil should not be confused with the movement of the same name in Spanish America and Spain, which took place a generation earlier, and enthusiastically embraced the modernization which Euclides and Lima Barreto saw as so destructive. The Brazilian variety, rather, was modernist in the Anglo-American sense and appeared in the 1920s. I have already commented on these writers' adoption of avant-garde techniques, which they thought admirably suited to Brazilian reality, and the optimistic, future-based élitism which sometimes characterizes them. Modernism, in fact, was even more of a minority affair than art usually is in Brazil: more good poetry than good fiction came out of it, and the best of the prose was poetic at least in some sense. One should not assume, in reading it, that writing for the future is a guarantee of success, any more than building for it has been in Brasília.

The two most interesting figures of the movement, its co-founders, are Oswald de Andrade and Mário de Andrade – both from São Paulo, then rapidly becoming the economic centre of the country, and its most go-ahead, 'modern' city. Both these writers (who were unrelated, and in fact in fundamental ways ideologically opposed – radical and reformist is a tempting if insufficient way of describing their positions) produced aggressively modernistic fictions; Oswald, *The Sentimental Memoirs of John Seaborne (Memórias sentimentais de João Miramar)* and *Seraphim Grosse Pointe (Serafim Ponte Grande)*, and Mário, *Macunaíma*. All these works defy classification as novels (Mário called his a rhapsody), though they do have plots of sorts. It would be going too far to say that they defy reading also, but the telegraphically short sections (chapters) of Oswald's works, and the jolting juxtapositions of slang, satirized pedantry, regionalisms and neologisms, the references to international culture and indigenous myth, etc., do without a doubt make them works for a minority: in 1970, *Macunaíma* was a collector's item – it had been out of print for some years. In one sense, though, the optimism of both writers has been vindicated: because of the success of a 1960s production of a play by Oswald, *The Candle King (O rei da vela)*, and his revaluation by the concretist poets in the 1960s, and because of a film of *Macunaíma* directed by Joaquim Pedro de Andrade (again no relation), brilliantly updated to the period of military repression in which it was made, all these works now have a secure place in the 'tradition' (if that is the right word). It would be quite wrong to put this down to accident, too; the world of the economic miracle, of impotent political protest, even the idealism and modishness of the 1960s, all brought these works back to life.

A healthy feature of some modernist writing – which could at times be naïvely, even jingoistically optimistic, was a debunking of nationalism. In the elaboration of *Macunaíma*, in fact, Mário used anthropological works on Amerindian mythology, but he uses them for an insidious critique of his own country. Macunaíma is a 'hero without a character', who easily changes shape and skin, thus contributing to the predominantly flippant and rumbustious tone of the work. But the price of these constant transformations gradually makes itself felt: it is the sacrifice of his identity, and so perhaps of that of the country he embodies, torn between past and present, between the jungle and the modern city represented by the São Paulo industrialist, Venceslau Pietro Pietra, alias the giant Piaimã. In many ways, this failure embedded in the book's plot prefigures that of Mário himself, one of the most genuinely heroic figures in Brazilian literature and culture. No one could have been more aware than he was of the need for culture to reach beyond a privileged minority, or have done more to spread that democratic ideal. In São Paulo in the 1930s, as Director of the city's Department of Culture, he tried to set up such rudimentary tools for this as lending libraries. He failed for reasons which would have given Lima Barreto sour satisfaction: the government changed, and he was removed from his post.

As the 1920s moved into the 1930s, a reaction set in against the more avant-garde elements of modernism: most obviously, from the north-east of the country, the traditional (and impoverished) sugar-cane growing area. The aims of this reaction were realist as well as regionalist: to what extent they succeeded is another matter. In part, this was a reaction in more senses than one, for these writers were influenced by the underlying paternalism and nostalgia for a relatively simple (if admittedly brutal) past expressed in Gilberto Freyre's fascinating account of colonial plantation society, *The Masters and the Slaves (Casa grande e senzala)*. This is most obviously so in José Lins do Rego's highly enjoyable *Plantation Boy (Menino de engenho)*, which more or less abandons the pretence of

29

being a novel after a melodramatic opening in which the hero's father kills his mother in an access of madness, and settles down to carry out its real aim, the depiction of life in such an intimate (at times shockingly intimate, as in the scenes of sexual initiation with animals, common in such a milieu) yet hierarchially organized world.

Lins do Rego continued his heroes' (in the plural, for he follows both the son of the master and the black plantation child) careers into the world of larger, mechanized plantations, and to the city itself, in a series of novels. In similar vein, Jorge Amado in his early works, written in the 1930s, dealt with the workers' struggle in the cocoa plantations of Bahia – in fact, he was the only writer of any standing to come close to socialist realism – *Red Harvest (Seara Vermelha)*. But it was his later novels, written in the 1960s and 1970s, which have been such runaway successes with the reading public – *Gabriela, Clove and Cinnamon (Gabriela, cravo e canela), Dona Flor and her Two Husbands (Dona Flor e seus dois maridos):* it may well be that he is more popular than the most widely read of the Spanish-Americans; some of his works have been turned into immensely successful television soap operas and films. It may seem perverse, then, that Brazilian critics of considerable sense and moderation, like Alfredo Bosi, as well as those of sharper pen, like Nogueira Galvão (cited earlier) and Carlos Guilherme Mota, should regard his work as beneath contempt. Their judgement is sound, and has nothing to do with intellectual snobbery; for beneath his populist optimism in the goodness and strength of the Brazilian people, his self-confident realism and anti-racialism, defence of the poor, of blacks and of women, lies a naïvely simplistic, stereotyped characterization, with transparently good and evil, perverse or sexually healthy, animal or intellectual qualities, and a series of demeaning sexual and racial sterotypes which mark him as a man of the past, and make his books either excessively, titillatingly, readable or unbearable. The film and television versions (for instance, of *Tent of Miracles (Tenda dos Milagres)*) are often much better, simply because they are reduced to plot.

The greatest writer of the north-eastern group was undoubtedly Graciliano Ramos: a friend of both Lins do Rego and Amado (whose Communist sympathies he shared in the 1930s and 1940s), he nevertheless achieves an intensity and depth which they could never aspire to. Like theirs, his aims were realist, but he lacked their ideologically underpinned confidence in the ease of achieving them. He was uneasily aware, too, like Euclides or Lima Barreto, that fiction might not be the ideal medium for confronting himself and his reader with an uncomfortable reality. Narrative stance always constituted a problem for him: his first three novels are in the first person, and struggle manfully to make the narration itself a realistic act (i.e. to make it possible that such a person would actually have written this, let alone have written in this way, as Bento is a realistic narrator in *Dom Casmurro*). Paulo Honório, the narrator of *São Bernardo* is an unscrupulous man who has fought his way up the social scale until he owns the farm which gives the novel its title, only to have his life ruined by his failure to understand his sensitive and educated wife, Margarida. At the beginning of the novel he ponders the possibility of using an amanuensis to dictate his thoughts to, only to conclude that such a person would distort them. Luis da Silva, the unattractive, resentful and guilt-ridden journalist hero of *Angústia* ('Anguish'), really descends below the level where he could realistically write his thoughts, and the novel is closer to stream of consciousness. Graciliano's most famous novel is the short

Barren Lives (Vidas sêcas), where he abandons these problems and adopts a clipped, unblinkingly objective and distanced third-person narration to describe the hardships of life for Fabiano, a cowhand, Sinhá Vitória, their two children and dog in the *sertão.* Most remarkably, he sets out to humanize these people whom life has brutalized to the point that they regard themselves at times as little better than animals, and shows them in their losing struggle for survival in a hostile natural and social enviroment. Most memorable, and most revealing, perhaps, are Fabiano's encounters with the authorities (whom he calls, indifferently, 'governo' (the government)), the resigned sense that he will always lose, and that useless violence would be the only result of any real rebellion, is brought out in actions which are hardly more than gestures. *Barren Lives* is a *tour de force* comparable to the stories of the Mexican Juan Rulfo *(The Burning Plain and Other Stories (El llano en llamas), Pedro Páramo)* which are set in a comparably impoverished and violent rural area: in both cases, one can do no other than refer to the dignity and honesty of the writing, and curiously enough, in both cases, this breakthrough to a harsh, uncompromising realism led to a cul-de-sac: neither ever published fiction again. Graciliano, however, did write a further, less acknowledged (and, unfortunately, still untranslated) masterpiece: his longest book, *Prison Memoirs (Memórias do cárcere),* published after his death in 1953, and recently successfully made into a film (it is worth mentioning that *São Bernardo* and *Barren Lives* have also produced two of the classics of the Brazilian cinema). The *Prison Memoirs* recount Graciliano's year-long imprisonment under the Vargas regime in 1936–7, and it is not inapt to call them a Brazilian *House of the Dead,* though they lack the ultimate faith in the goodness of the people of Dostoevsky's work.

The dominant theme (as, in a way, is also true of *Barren Lives*, significantly enough written after the experience of imprisonment) is the encounter of the writer with others of different classes and types: most dramatically on the penal colony island of Ilha Grande, where Graciliano was kept along with common criminals. He is never prone to over-simplify, or to turn others, much less himself, into heroes: rather it is the spectacle of the complex operation of power relationships which constitutes the fascination of this work: the *Prison Memoirs* explore depths of alienation and solidarity which most writers simply cannot touch with conviction, because they cannot write from experience, yet which in Brazil, partly because of the (often hidden) inheritance of slavery, are as rich and varied as they are depressing or encouraging as reflections on human nature. This persistent analysis often causes Graciliano to bring literature itself and the status of the writer, even of literacy itself, into question in his work. Writing may give power: but it may bring doubts, and so make one vulnerable to the whims of others who have simpler aims; as when one of the prison officers 'requests' Graciliano to write for him a laudatory speech with which he intends to honour the Governor of the penal colony (unpredictably perhaps, Graciliano manages to explain why this would not be a good idea).

As we approach our own time, discerning patterns of development within Brazilian fiction, whose hold on tradition has always been somewhat tenuous in any case, necessarily becomes more difficult. The establishment of a healthy readership and of a normal relationship with it on which such a tradition might depend has in any case been impeded by the military coup in 1964, and by the subsequent gradual imposition – and then gradual lifting – of strict censorship in the 1960s and 1970s; and, more insidiously, by the spread and misuse of the mass media, above all of television, which of course was manipulated by the military regime as by other interests. Within this relatively inimical environment, however, writers have continued, often with striking success, to present the Brazilian public with a somewhat more honest picture of itself, to continue that exploration of the relation between the individual and the collectivity, whether in an urban or a rural, present or historical setting, begun by such writers as Machado and Graciliano. Fiction retains, in spite of everything, an irreplaceable role, because – at its best – it lays its finger on experiences and truths which are simply unavailable elsewhere. It is significant that Brazilian writers (in contrast to the Spanish-American experience) have seldom taken easily to exile: their strength comes rather from their insistence on speaking from within.

The two writers who came to dominate the post-war period, Clarice Lispector and João Guimarães Rosa, strike one first of all by the intensity of their language. They are both experimenters, and they both lived, or at any rate wrote, dangerously. Lispector's world, at first sight, is individual to the point of idiosyncrasy. Her stories and novels tend to involve single characters, most often women, in encounters – often failed or flawed – with themselves, with members of their family, or with others as highly strung as they usually are. To my mind, her most successful works are her stories, and they are often quite literally unforgettable, staying on after they are read as part of the mind's furniture. Many, if not most, of the stories in *Family Ties (Laços de família)* and *The Foreign Legion (A Legião estrangeira)* are some of the most vivid accounts of growing up, of family tension and indifference, of the paradoxes of self-realization, one could hope to read. 'The imitation of the rose' to give one example, is an extremely moving portrait of a woman on the edge of a nervous breakdown, as her husband looks on, more embarrassed than truly sympathetic (perhaps partly because he resents what he supposes is her infertility). The crisis centres on a bunch of bud-roses, patently a symbol of some kind of unattainable perfection; but the effect of Clarice's writing doesn't depend just on such 'meanings' (never heavily insinuated, anyway), but also on her portrayal of people in a given social environment. Here, in fact, the roses become the centre of a battle. Not only does Laura feel that they are in some obscure way 'hers'; she also knows she ought to give them to the friend who has invited her and her husband for dinner. However, she cannot make up her mind to do so, partly because she doesn't know how to tell the maid to take them, never having been good at the requisite authoritative tone, a *sine qua non* of middle-class housewives.

Partly because these unobtrusive but pervasive sexual and social conditionings tend to be less important in her novels, they – *A paixão segundo G.H.* ('The Passion according to G.H.'), *The Apple in the Dark (A maçã no escuro)*, for instance – can be a good deal less successful. Again they centre on existential crisis, but the adjective takes on a more narrowly philosophical meaning. Clarice tries to universalize the same ingredients which work perfectly in her stories by means of a language which, taken to extremes, simply becomes too abstract and incapable of carrying her meaning, and of a philosophical or mythical superstructure which ultimately seems forced to the point of absurdity – the 'passion' of G.H., involving an encounter with a cockroach in her maid's room, is intended to be a parallel to that of Christ in some way.

With Guimarães Rosa, on the other hand, immersion in a given mythology comes first. Almost all his work is set in the *sertão*, and his version of it, however real it may also be, is also based on the literary precedent of Euclides da Cunha. The career of the protagonist of Rosa's fine early short story (also turned into a splendid film), 'A hora e vez de Augusto Matraga', reads very much like that of the Conselheiro, as described in *Rebellion in the Backlands*, before he took up his messianic role. Rosa's great novel, *The Devil to Pay in the Backlands* is both a cowboy story and an obsessive enquiry into the possibility of the existence of the Devil, all cast in a remarkable language which is near impossible to translate adequately, an amalgam of colloquial and dialect speech, of erudition and invention, which can be difficult even for Brazilians, though it is a climate most find it worthwhile adjusting themselves to.

Both Lispector and Guimarães Rosa were daring writers, both at the level of language, of plot, and of the analysis of moral and emotional situations: as such, they have added new dimensions to prose writing in Portuguese, and have provided an inspiration for younger writers, who have learnt ways of telling stories simply not open to them before in their own language. Without losing sight of their achievements, or returning to naïve realism, however, others have striven to put them to use in a less mythical, more social and historical setting: a tendency which has naturally increased with the ending of censorship, but which began much earlier, and even has precedents in such writers as Cornélio Pena and Lúcio Cardoso (*A menina morta* ('The Dead Girl'), *Cronica da casa assassinada* ('Annals of a Murdered House')) with detailed and subtle accounts of the declining oligarchy of the ex-coffee-growing areas of the state of Rio de Janeiro. Clarice herself, in fact, is witness of this same tendency, notably in her last short novel, published after her death (and again, turned into a successful film), *The Hour of the Star (A hora da estrela):* it is the story of Macabéa, a poor typist, and her absurd death under the wheels of a Mercedes when Madame Carlota, an ex-prostitute clairvoyante, has just predicted love and fortune for her. This is not to say that Clarice abandons existential enquiry: what is remarkable rather is her ability to increase its range to embrace an impoverishment which extends beyond money to the meaningless bits of information shorn of context which Macabéa picks up from 'Radio Cultura', to her awful macho boy friend Olímpico, and beyond.

Of a slightly younger generation is Autran Dourado, a novelist from Minas Gerais, who sets many of his stories in an isolated interior town called Duas Pontes (Two Bridges) – an apt name, for this is a microcosm which leads to many other places: his historical and psychological range is in fact deceptively broad. In one of the best of these, *The Voices of the Dead (Opera dos mortos)* which concentrates on a triangle of lonely people – the aristocratic Rosalina, final product of a once-powerful family; her servant, the dumb Quiquina; and the jack-of-all-trades Juca Passarinho (Joey Bird), we feel how the forces of history have conformed the tragic plot. From the brutal, slave-hunting grandfather to the idealistic reformist father who is cheated out of his political career by skulduggery, we follow a process which leaves little hope for a better future, or even for the real contact between classes on which such a future might be based: the 'opera' played out between the characters, for all its intensity, is very largely dumb show.

In a completely different mode, though of a similar period, is Dalton Trevisan, a short-story writer of elliptical and concise violence, who explores, this time in a contemporary urban context, the lives of ordinary people – who often turn out to be extraordinary, in frightening ways – in the provinces, in his case Curitiba, the capital of the southern state of Paraná. Antônio Callado, one of the few writers who managed to live in Brazil and publish politically controversial material in the worst periods of censorship, published his *Quarup* (the title derives from an Indian ceremony) in 1967. It is an ambitious and courageous attempt to come to grips with the political situation facing Brazil in the wake of the coup, and a semi-documentary account of the coup itself as it happened in the north-east, one of the areas in which repression was most thorough and violent from the beginning. His later *Bar Don Juan* (1972) which had the honour of being withdrawn from sale by the censors for its frank treatment of torture, is, however, a less successful attempt to portray the irresponsible romantic urban terrorists of the period.

Since the virtual lifting of censorship in the late 1970s, a huge number of novels, stories, memoirs and semi-documentaries has appeared: at this point, in fact, so vast is the material to be covered, so limited my own reading in relation to it, that it is necessary to drop all pretence of objectivity, and simply hope that the three novels I have chosen to represent the most recent period are as representative as they seem to me to be: I deal with them partly because I read them with great enjoyment, and partly because they are all available in English.

Darcy Ribeiro's *Maíra* is the work of an anthropologist – and ex-political exile, later Deputy Governor of the State of Rio – which returns, unexpectedly perhaps, to one of the oldest themes of Brazilian Romantic literature before Machado, the Indian. It does so, however, in a mood at once lyrical and despairing, aware both of the originality and beauty of Indian culture and the fact that it is condemned to extinction by a 'superior', 'Christian', 'civilization'. The conflict is played out in the mind of Isiaías/

Avá, a priest who is an Indian, but was taken as a child to be ordained in Rome, as well as in the jungle itself, prey to commercial development as well as to missionaries, Protestant and Catholic.

Ivan Angelo's *A Celebration (A festa)* is in a sense a successor to at least two other interesting novels about the crises facing successive generations of intellectuals, Cyro dos Anjos's *O amanuense Belmiro* ('Belmiro the Clerk'), 1937, and Fernando Sabino's *A Time to Meet (O encontro marcado)*, 1956. All three are set in Belo Horizonte, the capital of Minas Gerais, Brazil's third city, and (as Angelo himself realizes) a kind of central point between the developed coastal and southern parts of the country, and the poorer north and interior. But *A Celebration* goes beyond its predecessors not only in social but in temporal, historical range. It opens, in fact, with quotations from *Rebellion in the Backlands*, and describes in fictionally documentary terms the arrival of some 800 refugees from the drought which afflicted the north-eastern *sertão* in 1970. This arrival and the attempts of some well-intentioned people to do something for the *flagelados*, as they are called, are interpreted as part of a political conspiracy, and accordingly repressed by the police. Around this nucleus, and through flashbacks, we are shown the careers and fates of some twenty or thirty people of varying class, age, sex, sexuality, and political opinions. *A Celebration*, among its other virtues, is a very funny novel; and Angelo has not betrayed expectations with his second book, a collection of five interrelated short stories, *The Tower of Glass (A casa de vidro)*. The social range of both is impressive; for all that, as I have mentioned, some recent fiction has been criticized for being over documentary and journalistic in the worst sense, I wonder if Angelo's profession (he works in the press in São Paulo) has not allowed him to break new ground.

The most recent of the trio I have chosen is João Ubaldo Ribeiro's *Viva a povo brasileiro* ('Long Live the Brazilian People'). Already well known as the author of *Sergeant Getúlio (Sargento Getúlio)*, Ribeiro here attempts a grand, sweeping historical novel in the vein of García Márquez or Alejo Carpentier – and no doubt owes something to them, particularly the former. Although centred on the island of Itaperica in Bahia, he manages to take in the Dutch occupation of the seventeenth century, Independence in 1822, the Paraguayan war, Canudos – again . . . – and the military regime. As important, he moves between classes, taking in oppressed as well as oppressors, and if the historical message at times veers dangerously close to Jorge Amado's enthusiasm for the enduring virtues of the 'people' (though not as close as the novel's title perhaps suggests) this does not prevent *Viva o povo brasileiro* from being an exciting and vividly realized novel – above all, I am tempted to say, because it takes history seriously and not, as has also been the fashion in recent years, as a grotesque joke.

Maíra, *A Celebration* and *Viva o povo brasileiro* are very different novels; not that that should surprise anyone. That they are all serious, exciting works dealing with experiences beyond the daily ken of their readers, which have sold well and gone into fifth and sixth printings, is perhaps not saying that much. Yet all these factors put together, and the last in particular, do indicate cracks in the mould that I set at the beginning of this essay. The future gives cause for considerable optimism.

I should like to thank the following people (among others) whose writings and/or conversations have helped me in thinking about and writing this essay: Walnice Nogueira Galvão, José Guilherme Merquior, Silviano Santiago, Roberto Schwarz, David Treece.

Tupy or not Tupy:
Cannibalism and Nationalism in Contemporary Brazilian Literature and Culture

Randal Johnson

In the final sequence of Joaquim Pedro de Andrade's 1969 film version of Mário de Andrade's modernist novel *Macunaíma* (1928), the protagonist, abandoned and alone, wakes up one morning with a feeling of desire, something he has not felt for some time. To subdue the feeling, he goes to the nearby river for a cold swim. But there he sees a beautiful, nude woman beckoning from the icy water. Unbeknown to him, she is not a woman, but rather a man-eating *uiara*, or mermaid-like figure from indigenous mythology and folk legends. Unable to resist her call, Macunaíma throws himself in the water, where the cannibal/siren devours him. The image is particularly aggressive, as the final shot shows blood gushing up from under the water while Macunaíma's green jacket spreads over the surface.

The cannibalistic image is polyvalent. On one level, it represents a Brazilian being devoured by Brazil. But Macunaíma is more than just an average Brazilian. Through the course of the film he comes to represent, for better or worse, Brazil itself. So the cannibalistic consumption is actually a self-consumption, a metaphorical rendering of Brazil devouring its people and ultimately itself through the violence of an economic model imposed by relations of dependency with advanced industrial powers and enforced by a repressive military regime. The green jacket, soaked with blood, resembles the Brazilian flag as it

41

spreads across the water. The military have cynically repressed the Brazilian people in the name of 'development', but are themselves ultimately consumed by those they have repressed. Cannibalism thus becomes a complex metaphor that expresses not only the struggle of the weak against the strong, but also the symbol of all social relations.

Joaquim Pedro de Andrade's film is but one of a number of re-evaluations that occurred in the 1960s and 1970s of Brazilian modernism and more specifically the faction of modernism known as the *movimento antropófago* (cannibalist movement), initiated by Oswald de Andrade in 1928. Since the 1920s, cannibalism has become a major cultural metaphor in Brazil, constituting a reflection on the possibility of creating a genuine national culture, an attack on acritical imitation of foreign models, and a critical metaphor of cultural relations between First and Third World nations. In its more recent and militant manifestations, such as Andrade's film, it has served as a radical critique of the capitalist model imposed on Brazil by a ruling class more closely aligned with Europe and the United States than with the real needs of the Brazilian people and has thus represented an exemplary mode of symbolic struggle against neo-colonial dependency, conservative thought, and the authoritarianism of contemporary Brazilian society. This essay will examine the origins of the cannibalist metaphor in Brazil within the context of literary modernism, notably in the work of Oswald de Andrade and 1920s debates concerning cultural nationalism.

The cannibalist metaphor first appeared in Brazilian literature during the modernist movement of the 1920s, most forcefully in the *Manifesto Antropófago* published by Oswald de Andrade in the first number of his *Revista de*

Antropofagia (Cannibal Review) in May 1928. Brazilian modernism arose initially as a response to European pre- and post-World War I avant-garde artistic movements, as a reaction to the literary codes that had dominated Brazilian letters since the end of the nineteenth century, and as a cultural reflection of the socio-political and economic changes the country was undergoing in the first quarter of the century. The 'Week of Modern Art', a series of exhibitions of plastic arts, concerts, poetry and prose readings, and lectures on contemporary aesthetic theory held in São Paulo in February 1922, marks the official beginning of the movement, although it was in reality the culmination of a process of artistic and intellectual renovation that had begun in the previous decade.

In its attempt to bring Brazilian art into the twentieth century, the initial impulse of modernism was toward aesthetic renewal, but by 1924 the question of the creation of an authentically national art began to dominate literary debates, and artists began searching for proper cultural symbols. Oswald de Andrade's publication in 1924 of the *Manifesto de Poesia Pau-Brasil* (Manifesto of Brazil-Wood Poetry), the first elaboration of the ideas that formed the basis of *Antropofagia*, gave rise to the formation of rival groups, notably *Verde-Amarelo* (Green-Yellow), 1926, and its successor *Anta* (Tapir), 1927, both by Menotti del Picchia, Cassiano Ricardo, Cândido Motta Filho, and Plínio Salgado. *Antropofagia* was Oswald de Andrade's response to what he saw as the exacerbated, xenophobic nationalism of *Verde-Amarelo/Anta*. Despite programmatic and ultimately political differences, all these groups shared a concern with overcoming Brazil's cultural imitativeness and dependence on Europe.

Of course, the search for national cultural symbols goes back at least as far as nineteenth-century Romanticism, where Brazilian writers such as José de Alencar and Gonçalves Dias, influenced by Chateaubriand and others, developed an Indianist tendency in national literature, specifically by creating local versions of the noble savage, in reality little more than a European in native dress (for example Peri, in Alencar's *O Guarani*, 1857). But it was only in the twentieth century that artists and intellectuals gained an awareness of the true nature of relationships between their country and hegemonic powers and consciously sought to break the bonds of cultural dependency.

Pau-Brasil exemplifies the search for 'Brazil-ness' which permeated debates of the period.[1] Oswald de Andrade, one of the leaders of modernism most influenced by the European avant-garde, paradoxically 'discovered' Brazil during one of his many trips to Paris, and launched, in 1924, the *Manifesto da Poesia Pau-Brasil*.[2]

In writing the manifesto and his *Pau-Brasil* poetry, Oswald was deeply influenced by the primitivism that was in vogue in Paris at the time. It was not, however, simply one more example of imitation. Primitivism was something that could be drawn from Brazilian cultural history and did not need to be imported. Both the Brazilian and the European primitivists took advantage of the same sources and the same ambience in which attempts were made to rationalize the irrational and in which the dialogue concerning 'la pensée logique' and 'la pensée sauvage' began.[3]

With *Pau-Brasil* Oswald de Andrade attempted to reverse the historically imitative stance of Brazilian literature and the one-directional flow of artistic influence by creating a poetry for export, just as Brazil-wood was the nation's first export product. Oswald's movement was based on the idea that a native originality, still extant in popular manifestations of Brazilian culture, had been repressed and deformed by an erudite or élitist perspective ('o lado doutor', in Oswald's words) imported and imposed from Europe beginning with the first colonizers. Opposing élite forms of knowledge (rational and analytical) with popular forms (intuitive and synthetic), it sought a dialectical synthesis between antagonisms such as past and present, modernization and backwardness, country and city. To discover the true Brazil – and the mechanisms of that discovery are not made clear – one must break through artificial, imported ways of seeing and create an authentic national culture integrated with the national reality. 'Ver com olhos livres' ('See with open eyes'), says Oswald's manifesto.[4]

Although *Pau-Brasil* criticized imitation of European solutions, it was not xenophobic in its nationalism, nor was it opposed to modernization *per se*. The manifesto itself recognized that the French poet Blaise Cendrars had given Oswald an important suggestion: 'tendes as locomotivas cheias, ides partir' ('You have the train loaded, ready to leave'). It wanted to create a new kind of poetry based on intuitive perception of Brazilian reality. 'A poesia existe nos fatos' ('Poetry exists in facts'). The native originality Oswald sought was to be found in Brazilian cuisine, folklore, history, economics, ethnological formation, as well as in the peculiarly Brazilian version of the Portuguese language, with all its errors.[5] The originality was to be discovered by forgetting the thought schemes imposed through years of conditioning by a social and economic élite educated in Europe or according to European standards.

Pau-Brasil sought to take advantage of the benefits of technology, but put them to use in the creation of a national culture, to take advantage of what modern society had to offer, without rejecting the best of Brazilian traditions. It wanted to synthesize, as the manifesto puts it, the 'forest and the school'. More importantly, *Pau-Brasil* recognized the existence of a primitive, collective innocence and national purity that had been effaced by centuries of false interpretations and perspectives which derived from European and not Brazilian experience and which could only be overcome through knowledge which was at the same time emotional, intellectual, sentimental, and ingenuous.[6] *Pau-Brasil* poetry was to be 'Agile and candid. Like a child.'

Pau-Brasil is not of course without its contradictions. When Oswald de Andrade writes that his Pau-Brasil poetry is for export, he implicitly accepts the continuation of Brazil's historical role as an exporter of raw materials and of a certain 'exoticism' that has long fascinated Europeans.[7] Although it explicitly criticizes imitation of Europe, it is deeply influenced by the European avant-garde, especially Cubism and Expressionism (the first in its concern with reducing artistic form to its essential or minimal elements, the second with its psychological primitivism, valorizing 'raw states' of the collective national soul).[8] Although today *Pau-Brasil* is canonized as marking the beginning of the nationalist current in Brazilian modernist literature, at the time Oswald was harshly criticized for being too heavily influenced by European writers. One critic referred consistently to Oswald's movement as *Pau-Paris*.[9]

In opposition to Oswald's *Pau-Brasil*, which they saw as being excessively submissive to the European avant-garde, a group of modernists led by Menotti del Picchia, Cassiano Ricardo, and Plínio Salgado founded the *Verde-Amarelo* movement in 1926.[10] Although the group's only official manifesto was written only in 1929, after they themselves had declared the movement defunct, their writing in the pages of the *Correio Paulistano*, the official organ of São Paulo's conservative Republic Party, outlined their programme, They, like Oswald de Andrade, wanted to take advantage of modernism's achievements in terms of renovation of formal aspects of literature and to use them to create an authentically national literature based on what Cassiano was fond of calling Brazil's 'originality'.[11] They saw *Pau-Brasil*, albeit discovered in Paris, as a necessary first step itn the sense that it enumerated a series of motifs for the 'higher' task of nation building and the creation of a national literature.[12]

Like *Pau-Brasil*, *Verde-Amarelo* rejected rational categories and an analytical consciousness as means of understanding Brazilian reality, favouring, as did its Oswaldian counterpart, an intuitive, emotional, sentimental form of comprehension. They called for a kind of *bandeirismo mental*, exploring the depths of the Brazilian nation and integrating all its elements into a vast, organic, harmonious unity.[13] The difference is that Oswald sought to create a new critical consciousness through the dialectical resolution of subjacent antagonisms, while the *verde-amarelistas* saw Brazilian reality not in terms of historical existence, but rather in terms of a latent immanence or essence that could simply be absorbed by attentive writers.[14]

The difference between the two groups became clearer in 1927 with the adoption of the *Anta*, or Tapir, the totem of the Tupi Indians, as their major cultural symbol. With the *Anta*, proposed initially by Plínio Salgado, who in the 1930s was to lead a fascist-oriented political movement, the Ação Integralista Brasileira, a form of neo-Indianism was reintroduced to Brazilian literature. The concept the two groups (*Verde-Amarelo/Anta*, on the one hand, and *Pau-Brasil/Antropofagia*, on the other) had of the Indian is the key to understanding their ultimate differences.

Plínio Salgado introduced the *Anta* as a symbol in response to an article by fellow *verde-amarelista* Menotti del Picchia, who argued that the true roots of Brazil were not indigenous, but rather Lusitanian. Del Picchia had specifically rejected the image of the cannibal, 'eating British entrails . . . and dancing around their cadavers like the Tupinambá Indians around the body of Father Sardinha'.[15] The title of del Picchia's column, 'Let's Kill Peri', is indicative of his opposition to a neo-Indianism and his ultimate, if paradoxical, filiation with Europe.

Salgado agreed with del Picchia that they should destroy the Romantic image of Peri as a noble savage, but retain him as a symbol of an original American race that cannot be destroyed without destroying the Brazilian nationality itself. The Indian race had largely been eliminated by contact with Europeans, but just as the Tupi ritually consumed the blood of the totemic *Anta* prior to battle, the Europeans, through conquest, had absorbed the Indians' qualities. The Indian, although without a direct contribution to the constitution of Brazilian culture, served the important indirect function as a factor of integration and as a common denominator of the nation's people. 'We go from the Indian to the Universal,' writes Salgado, 'taking in along the way all of the ethnic, moral, geographic, and political elements that participated in the formation of our people's soul . . . The Indian is the starting point, for there is no other starting point.'[16] Influenced by Mexican José Vasconcelos's idea of the 'cosmic race', Salgado saw the Indian as the initial step in the formation of an organic, harmonious national unity. The conservative nature of Salgado's formulation is apparent, since it substitutes integration for conflict, peaceful assimilation for violence. The *Manifesto Nhengaçu Verde Amarelo* is explicit: 'We accept all conservative institutions, for it is within them that we will undertake the inevitable renovation of Brazil.'[17]

It was in response to *Verde-Amarelo/Anta* that Oswald de Andrade published his *Manifesto Antropófago* in 1928. He replaced Salgado's image of a passive, submissive Indian with the aggressive image of the cannibal as a symbol of cultural relationships, thus essentially reversing the meaning of Indian/European relationships as formulated by Salgado. Rather than having the colonizer absorb the values of the defeated foe, Oswald valorizes the cannibalization of the colonizer by the Indian. Initially, then, cannibalism is a form of resistance. Metaphorically speaking, it represents a new attitude toward cultural relationships with hegemonic powers. Imitation and influence in the traditional sense of the word are no longer possible. The *antropófagos* do not want to copy European culture, but rather to devour it, taking advantage of its positive aspects, rejecting the negative, and creating an original national culture that would be a source of artistic expression rather than a receptacle for forms of cultural expression elaborated elsewhere.

The *movimento antropófago* is thus a lucid response to the dilemma of Third World intellectuals whose education and, frequently, inclination is European and yet who want to free themselves from the bonds of European hegemony and create an art and a culture faithful to national reality. Unlike the sometimes xenophobic nationalism of Salgado and the *Verde-Amarelo* group, Oswald's movement recognizes the need for taking advantage of influences from wherever they may come and adapting them to Brazilian reality. Vera Chalmers refers to Oswald de Andrade's 'anthropophagic attitude' as a way of organizing elements already saturated with cultural signification. Imported cultural influences must be devoured, digested, and critically re-elaborated in terms of local conditions.[18]

The cannibal was not, of course, unique to Brazilian literature at the time. It had appeared in European avant-garde literature as early as 1902, and can be seen in the work of Jarry, Apollinaire, Cendrars, Marinetti, as well as the Dadaists. In 1920, Francis Picabia published the review *Cannibale* as part of the Dadaist programme. For Dada, cannibalism was an aggressive, anti-bourgeois element used to shock and insult. In Marinetti, cannibalism, through the absorption of primitive values, has a purely ritual sense. According to Heitor Martins, cannibalism is the ultimate degree of primitivism and is shocking 'to the Western spirit recently freed from Parnassian Hellenism and the sickly "finesse" of "art nouveau".'[19]

In Oswald de Andrade, the idea of the cannibal was used to scandalize, to threaten the imagination of the reader with the possibility of its permanent resurgence.[20] As Benedito Nunes puts it, the word *'antropofagia'* was used as a verbal weapon, as an instrument of personal aggression, and as an offensive arm with explosive reso-nances. 'It is a catalysing word, reactive and elastic, which mobilizes negations in a single negation, of which the practice of cannibalism, anthropophagic devouring, is a bloody symbol, a mixture of insult and sacrilege, of scorn and public flagellation, like the verbal substitute of physi-cal aggression against an enemy of many faces.'[21]

In Oswald de Andrade, cannibalism becomes the under-lying force of all social relationships. It is a new paradigm that expresses, in allegorical terms, the revolt of the colo-nized against the colonizer. As David George puts it, Oswaldian cannibalism is an attempt 'to eat, devour, and swallow the advantages of the colonizer without being destroyed culturally.'[22] The favoured weapons in this

Randal Johnson

metaphorical deglutition: corrosive humour, irreverence, parody and sarcasm. 'Tupy or not Tupy, that is the question', is Oswald's version of Hamlet's dilemma.

Benedito Nunes sees *Antropofagia* as at once an organic metaphor, a diagnosis, and a cure. As a metaphor it is inspired by the Tupy custom of cannibalizing their warrior-enemies as a means of absorbing their strengths. In Oswaldian terms it encompasses the consumption of everything that should be rejected, assimilated, and overcome in the creation of intellectual and cultural autonomy. The diagnosis is that Brazilian society has been traumatized by colonial repression and conditioning, the paradigm of which is the suppression of the original anthropophagical ritual by the Jesuits. Catechism is exemplary of a censorial action. The cure is to use that which was originally repressed – cannibalism – as a weapon against historically repressive society, political, and intellectual mind frames as a means of recovering the original and authentic bases of Brazilian society.[23]

The immediate enemies to be faced still, according to Benedito Nunes, are: the repressive colonial politico-religious apparatus under which Brazilian civilization took shape; patriarchal society and its moralism; the vacuous, imitative rhetoric of that society's intellectuals; and the Romantic Indianism that simply imitates the colonizer. Oswald rejects the cultural icons imposed by centuries of colonial rule and dependent relationships, replacing them with native symbols deriving from Amerindian civilizations.

He calls for a utopian return to a pre-Cabralian Golden Age of matriarchal society when man, rather than enslaving his enemies, ate them. It was a society based on natural communism, where a just distribution of material and spiritual goods was practised.[24] But even then, Oswald did

51

not reject all of the benefits of technological society. His programme was influenced by Lévy-Bruhl's concept of the primitive mind as being at a pre-logical stage as well as by Keyserling's idea that modern civilized man alienated by technology, not primitive man, is the true barbarian. Oswald accepts the advantages of technological society, but rejects the analytical consciousness of civilized man.

In the second phase, or 'dentição' of the *Revista de Antropofagia* (24 March 1929), one of the review's collaborators, using the pseudonym Japy-Mirim, writes: 'The anthropophagic descent is not a literary revolution. Nor a social one. Nor political. Nor religious. It is all of this at the same time. It gives man the true meaning of life, whose secret is – and the wise men ignore – the transformation of taboos into totems.' The influence of Freud is evident in this the proposed transformation. Antropophagy represented a metaphorical attack on all the taboos imposed by bourgeois consciousness, and sought a total and permanent liberation, in moral, religious, social, and political terms.

Antropofagia proposes a permanent revolution, the *Caraíba* revolution, which synthesizes then subsumes all previous revolutions:

> We want the Caraíba revolution. Greater than the French revolution. The unification of all effective revolts in the direction of Man. Without us Europe would not even have had its poor declaration of the rights of man . . .
>
> Filiation. Contact with Caraíba Brazil. *Ou Villegaignon print terre*. Montaigne. Natural man. Rousseau. From the French Revolution to Romanticism, to the Bolshevik Revolution, to the surrealist Revolution and to Keyserling's technological barbarian. We move forward.

Reversing traditional interpretations, the New World thus becomes the source of all revolutions and all theories of primitivism, the Caraíba revolution the synthesis, the beginning and the end, of all Western revolutions. It will transcend capitalism, fascism, and communism, returning mankind to a state of primitive yet bountiful innocence.

Of course Oswald de Andrade's programme is a utopian vision. Although he and other *antropófagos* did become politically involved in the 1930s, joining the Brazilian Communist Party, the concrete reality of contemporary Brazilian politics was somewhat alien to the immediate goals of the movement. While Oswald was talking about metaphorically devouring the philosophical bases of Western thought, Plínio Salgado and the *verde-amarelistas* actively participated in conservative politics and called on intellectuals to become involved in the political process. With the growth of Salgado's fascist movement in the 1930s and the subsequent advent of the *Estado Novo* (1937–45), the participants of *Verde-Amarelo/Anta*, with their authoritarian vision, were very close to the centre of power, while Oswald de Andrade maintained a distant, yet critical watch.

The most important literary work written in the spirit of and contemporary to *Antropofagia* was Mário de Andrade's *Macunaíma*, although its composition preceded the movement by almost two years.[25] *Macunaíma*, subtitled *The Hero Without a Character*, is an allegorical discussion of the nature of Brazilian civilization, the national psyche, and the relationship of Brazilian to European cultures. It orchestrates popular and folkloric motifs around a structural core formed by indigenous legends collected by German ethnologist Theodor Koch-Grünberg in the headwaters of the Orinoco in northern Brazil and southern

Venezuela early in this century.[26] The novel satirizes technological society, rhetorical forms of language, and Brazilian mores and customs. Although it is literally filled with cannibals of all sorts, especially the Italo-Brazilian industrialist Venceslau Pietro Pietra (also known as the man-eater Piaimã), cannibalism does not have in *Macunaíma* the programmatic or ontological sense it does in Oswald's movement.

But it is not that sense of *Antropofagia* that has remained alive in Brazilian culture. What has become the Oswaldian heritage is his corrosive, irreverent sense of humour, his use of satire and parody, and his critical vision of social relationships.[27] The most important re-evaluation of Oswald took place in the mid-1960s with José Celso Martinez Correa's staging of the modernist writer's play *The Candle King (O Rei da Vela)*, 1937, in São Paulo's Oficina theatre in 1967. The play, a virulent critique of capitalism, economic dependency, and authoritarianism, was re-created as a parody of all theatrical styles, as an aggressive attack on the hypocrisy of the national bourgeoisie's values and morality, and as a radical critique of the economic and political model then being imposed by the military regime.[28]

José Celso's version of *The Candle King* was followed two years later by Joaquim Pedro de Andrade's filmic adaptation of *Macunaíma*, which, unlike the original, uses cannibalism as the motivating force of the narrative and of all social relationships. The film not only criticizes the exploitative nature of Brazil's 'savage capitalism' and the country's relations of dependency with advanced industrial powers, but also criticizes the Left and its penchant for self-destruction, or self-cannibalism. Joaquim Pedro's film has been called an 'Oswaldian reading' of Mário de Andrade's novel, but is in fact a lucid reinterpretation of both Mário and Oswald in the light of Brazil's socio-economic and political situation in the late 1960s.[29]

The anthropophagic attitude continues to be seen in the work of writers such as Márcio Souza and Darcy Ribeiro. Souza's 1976 novel, *The Emperor of the Amazon (Galvez, Imperador do Acre)* is a provocative satire of Brazil's possession of the Acre territory by an army composed of decadent opera singers and prostitutes and led by Spaniard Luis Galvez Rodrigues de Aria.[30] The novel not only parodies the official historical version of the events, but also creates an allegory of economic and cultural imperialism. Almost all the major personages of the novel, allegorically of Brazilian history, are foreign. The character Sir Henry Lust, a British scientist who collects Indians' genital organs, is the perfect symbol of the castrating function of colonialism.

Darcy Ribeiro's 1982 'fable', *Utopia Selvagem: Saudades da inocência perdida* ('Savage Utopia: Longings for a Lost Innocence')[31] explicitly cites Oswald's *Manifesto Antropófago* in the creation of a vast allegorical satire of contemporary Brazilian society, of historical interpretations of Brazil, and of political relationships. In a true cannibalist attitude, Ribeiro self-reflexively weaves many different modes of literary discourse into an often hilarious, yet always critical, portrait of Brazil and its culture.

The impact of Oswald de Andrade and his *movimento antropófago* continues to be felt in Brazilian culture. It was perhaps Joaquim Pedro de Andrade who took the movement to its logical conclusion. In his film with the punning title *O Homem do Pau-Brasil* ('The Brazil-Wood Man'), 1982 – *'pau'*, in Portuguese, can refer to the male genital organ – which deals with the life and work of Oswald de Andrade, he creates a *tour de force* by having two people, a man and a woman, play the role of Oswald. They are frequently in the scene at the same time, with the woman representing his 'female' side. At the end of the film, she overcomes his dominance and commandeers his erect phallus before embarking on the path to the matriarchal, Caraíba revolution.

NOTES

1. For a thorough discussion of the question of *brasilidade*, or Brazilian-ness, see Eduardo Jardim de Moraes, *A Brasilidade Modernista: Sua Dimensão Filosófica*, Rio de Janeiro, Edições Graal, 1978, especially Chapter 3, pp. 71–109.

2. The *Manifesto da Poesia Pau-Brasil*, originally published in the *Correio da Manhã*, 18 March 1924, is reprinted in Oswald de Andrade, *Do Pau-Brasil à Antropofagia e às Utopias*, 2nd edn., Rio de Janeiro, Civilização Brasileira, 1978, pp. 3–10. For English translation, see 'Manifesto of Pau-Brasil Poetry', tr. Stella M. de Sá Rego, *Latin American Literary Review*, vol. XIV, no 27, January–June 1986, pp. 184–7. Citations in the text are from this translation. On *Pau-Brasil* see also Paulo Prado's introduction to Andrade's book of poetry, *Pau-Brasil*, in Oswald de Andrade, *Poesias Reunidas*, 3rd edn., Rio de Janeiro, Civilização Brasileira/MEC, 1972, pp. 5–9. Also Wilson Martins, *O Modernismo*, 4th edn., São Paulo, Cultrix, 1973, and Benedito Nunes, 'Antropofagia ao Alcance de Todos', in Oswald de Andrade, *Do Pau-Brasil à Antropofagia e às Utopias*, pp. xi–liii.

3. Benedito Nunes, 'Canibais Europeus e Antropófagos Brasileiros', *Minas Gerais (Suplemento Literário)*, 9 and 16 November 1968.

4. Moraes, pp. 83–9.

5. Nunes, 'Antropofagia ao Alcance de Todos', p. xix.

6. Martins, p. 91; Nunes, p. xix.

7. Aracy Amaral, *Tarsila: Sua Obra e Seu Tempo*, São Paulo,

Perspectiva/Universidade de São Paulo, 1975, p. 124.

8. Nunes, p. xix.

9. Menotti del Picchia, 'Feira de Sexta', *Correio Paulistano*, 28 January 1927. For an early critique of Oswald's imitation of Europe, see Tristão de Athayde (Alceu Amoroso Lima), 'Literatura suicida', 1925; rpt. in *Estudos Literários*, Rio de Janeiro, Aguilar, 1966, pp. 914–27; also in Gilberto Mendonça Teles, org., *Tristão de Athayde: Teoria, crítica e história literária*, Rio de Janeiro, Livros Técnicos e Científicos Editora em convênio com o Instituto Nacional do Livro, Ministerio da Educação e Cultura, 1980, pp. 345–61.

10. Literary critics have yet to study *Verde-Amarelo* and *Anta* in great depth. One possible reason for this is that it is difficult to recognize the fact that a major tendency in Brazilian modernism served as an ideological basis for a fascist movement in the 1930s and provided support for the authoritarian *Estado Novo*, declared by Getúlio Vargas in 1937. The two major studies on the movement, both by social scientists, are Gilberto Vasconcelos, *Ideologia Curupira: Análise do Discurso Integralista*, São Paulo, Brasiliense, 1979, and Mônica Pimenta Velloso, 'O Mito da Originalidade Brasileira: A trajetoria intelectual de Cassiano Ricardo (dos anos 20 ao Estado Novo)', M.A. thesis, Pontifícia Universidade Católica, Rio de Janeiro, 1983. The latter has unfortunately not yet been published.

11. In 1935 Ricardo published a book with the symptomatic title, *Brasil no Original* (São Paulo, Coleção Cultura da Bandeira), in which he analysed the nation's originality in the light of the experience of the *bandeirantes*, expeditions that left what is now the state of São Paulo to explore and exploit the interior of the country.

12. Cassiano Ricardo, 'Brasilidade', *Correio Paulistano*, 14 September 1926.

13. Cassiano Ricardo, 'Afirmação brasileira', 31 August 1926.

14. Velloso, p. 29.

15. Menotti del Picchia (Hélios), 'Crónica Social: Matemos Peri', *Correio Paulistano*, 5 January 1927. Sardinha was a

Catholic priest who was cannibalistically devoured by the
Tupinambá in the sixteenth century. Oswald de Andrade's
Manifesto Antropófago is dated 374 years after his
consumption.

16. Plínio Salgado, 'A Anta contra a Loba', *Correio Paulistano*,
    11 January 1927. For an insightful analysis of Salgado's
    Indianism, see Moraes, op.cit., Chapter IV, pp. 113–37.
17. Published originally in the *Correio Paulistano*, 17 May
    1929; reprinted in Gilberto Mendonça Teles, ed.,
    Vanguarda Européia e Modernismo Brasileiro, 3rd rev. edn.,
    Petrópolis, Vozes/MEC, 1976, pp. 301–7.
18. Vera M. Chalmers, *3 Linhas e 4 Verdades: o jornalismo
    de Oswald de Andrade*, São Paulo, Duas Cidades, 1976,
    p. 19.
19. Nunes, 'Canibais Europeus . . .'
20. Paradoxically, the first Brazilian writer to propose
    cannibalism in a programmatic sense was apparently
    Plínio Salgado, the leading figure of the *Anta* movement
    and subsequent founder of the fascist-oriented Ação
    Integralista Brasileira (Brazilian Integralist Party). See his
    letter ('Carta Antropófaga') to Menotti del Picchia in the
    Correio Paulistano, 18 February 1927. In this letter he
    proposes to 'make a barbecue of the ridiculous figures of
    the "boulevard", roasting them on a spit over the fire . . .
    What I propose is precisely anthropophagy, the devouring
    of everything that is ridiculous in the face of our barbarous
    nature. I'm hungry for Frenchmen! We want to roast all
    philosophers and make mush of all those who bother us
    with their "n'est pas moderne" . . .'
21. Nunes, 'Antropofagia ao Alcance de Todos', p. xxv.
22. David George, *Teatro e Antropofagia*, tr. Eduardo Brandão,
    São Paulo, Global Editora, 1985, p. 21.
23. Nunes, 'Antropofagia ao Alcance de Todos', p. xxvi.
24. David George, p. 22.
25. The novel, or 'rhapsody', as the author calls it, was written
    in seven days in 1926, revised in 1927, and finally published
    in 1928. Mário de Andrade, no relation to Oswald, lamented
    the coincidence with Oswald's movement.

26. For a thorough structural analysis of *Macunaíma*, see Haroldo de Campos, *Morfologia do Macunaíma*, São Paulo, Perspectiva, 1973.
27. Although São Paulo's Concretist poets have contributed much to the revitalization of Oswald de Andrade, their concern is more aesthetic than cultural. I have thus chosen not to include them in this essay.
28. For an insightful discussion of the play and José Celso's staging of *O Rei da Vela*, see David George, op. cit., pp. 33–60.
29. For a discussion of the novel and film, see Randal Johnson, *Literatura e Cinema: Macunaíma do Modernismo na Literatura ao Cinema Novo*, São Paulo, Thomaz A. Queiroz, 1982.
30. Márcio Souza, *Galvez, Imperador do Acre*, 7th edn., Rio de Janeiro: Civilização Brasileira, 1978. English translation published by Avon.
31. Darcy Ribeiro, *Utopia Selvagem: Saudades da inocência perdida*, Rio de Janeiro, Nova Fronteira, 1982.

The Latin American Novel
and its Indigenous Sources

Gordon Brotherston

A factor which strongly distinguishes the American novel, both Anglo and Latin, from its European counterpart and antecedents, is human geography. That is, literary difference has been signified not just because of the morphology and sheer scale of the New World landscape from Alaska to Patagonia, with its fictions of frontier, but because of the prior presence in it of people, languages, customs, roads, towns, and civilizations, and of a conscious history which long antedates Christendom. With its class-defined origins in Europe and corresponding norms of setting, character, and so on, the novel transplanted to America has not always wished to explore this order of its new environment. Conversely, it has been turned into a source of strength, especially in Latin America, the home of the continent's first urban societies, where in many areas the imported European language (Spanish, Portuguese) remains confined to an élite or a minority, and where even today native political resistance retains some territorial base and has not been vanquished militarily.

In this perspective the very first anticipations of narrative concern with the indigenous in Latin America can be found in early first hand accounts of European experience of the New World, like Bernal Díaz's *The Conquest of New Spain (Historia verdadera)* which deals with his and Cortés's entry into Aztec parts, and is a main ingredient in

Carlos Fuentes's masterpiece *Terra Nostra* (1975); or Alonso de Ercilla's sixteenth-century epic testimony to the resistance offered to the Spanish (as it had been previously to the Inca) by the Mapuche or Araucanians of Chile, *La araucana*, a touchstone for Ariel Dorfman's powerful indigenist study of the new novel, *Imaginación y violencia en América* ('Imagination and Violence in America', 1970). However, with the political independence gained from Spain and Portugal by the Latin American republics in the course of the nineteenth century, problems of epistemology and moral commitment to the native subject were radically reformulated, since only then could the Latin American novelist begin in principle to identify this human geography as his 'own'.

For the Latin American novelists who first focused on the native peoples living within the often still ill-defined boundaries of their respective countries, a certain conceptual filter was provided by the notions of natural man which Rousseau derived from previous ideals of the noble savage, a creature who was characteristically American in the first place, to judge from, say Montaigne's highly influential essays on the 'cannibal' Caribs, and on the Tupi whose home is Brazil, then also known as 'La France antarctique'. To this should be added the overtly Romantic weight of the novelist Chateaubriand, who embarked on his tribute to *Les Natchez* (a nation of the southern Mississippi massacred by French troops in 1727), in order to avenge and vindicate the virtue of 'primitive America'.

In line with this then dominant version of the American Indian, most Indianist novels, as they were called, that appeared in nineteenth-century Latin America focused precisely on its traditionally least urban parts: the forest cultures and 'green mansions' (to quote W. H. Hudson's romance) of lowland South America and the Caribbean.

This was true above all of Brazil, where *O Guaraní* ('The Guaraní') 1857, by José de Alencar celebrated the virtues of the Tupi-Guaraní, whose language once extended from the Amazon to Paraguay and was still widely spoken as a 'lingua geral' in Alencar's day. In Brazil, attentive as they were to the Indian, Alencar and several of his contemporaries (including even the adolescent Machado de Assis), styled themselves true Americanist: Alencar's next novel *Iracema*, 1866 (in English as *The Honey-lips*, 1886), proclaims the continent America as the anagram of the native heroine's name; and a third, a 'Tupi legend' named after its hero *Ubirajara*, yet more stringently obeys his own dictum that 'Knowledge of the native language is the best criterion by which to judge the national quality of a literature'. The customs and speech of the Indians were to become an authentic local source of inspiration, more authentic than those proper to the imported European language (in this case Portuguese), and hence were to provide models for social and political behaviour. In practice this meant a highly selective reading of native ethics and of the world view they were set into; and the programme made little headway, since even so the gulf between the desired source and bourgeois life in Rio de Janeiro simply remained too great. At the time this incongruity was neatly caught in Angelo Agostini's engravings of the 1880s, which depict Alencar and other Americanists as heads stuck on to jungle bodies. The significance of these pioneer Americanists lies rather in their having raised basic questions variously answered by the schools of novelists who succeeded them.

At this same early stage of events, nothing on quite the scale of the Brazilian Indianist enterprise can be found in Spanish America, perhaps because of the more powerful legacy there of a church and crown committed to converting and reducing the American heathen. This element is

certainly present in two much-cited Indianist pieces: the
Ecuadorian Juan León Mera's 'drama among savages'
Cumandá (1879); and Manuel de Jesús Galván's lament
over Spain's entry into his native Santo Domingo, *Enri-
quillo*, 1882 (translated into English by Robert Graves as
The Cross and the Sword, 1956) in which the hero having
become Christian reverts to his 'natural' state. In *Cumandá*,
in the Amazonian forest of Ecuador, a white landowner
Orozco whose cruelty provokes an Indian uprising in
which most of his family perishes, switches to being a
priest and hence is able to elicit a final tear of repentance
from the Indian leader Tibon. Meanwhile his son Carlos
falls in love with Cumandá, who looks like the Indians she
grew up with but turns out to be Carlos's sister, having
been snatched from the ruins of the family house by
Tibon's band. Doubly frustrated in his would-be communication with the native race, Carlos wanders through
America's wilds like Chateaubriand's hero René: natural
happiness is shown to be impossible for anyone who
belongs to the civilized world. In Orozco's Christian
victory over the Indians and in his son's romantic
estrangement from them, human incompatibility is proposed in terms at once moral and racial.

A more complex and contorted version of this same
literary dilemma arose in cases where the heathen Indians
in question were perceived less as hapless innocents of the
wild than as inheritors of the great ancient civilizations of
America, i.e. those of Middle America (Southern Mexico
and Central America), and the Inca empire Tahuantinsuyu
of the Andes (Bolivia, and non-Amazonian Peru and
Ecuador). In *Aves sin nido*, 1889 (*Birds without a Nest: A
story of Indian life and priestly oppression in Peru* as the
English translation has it), the Peruvian Clorinda Matto de
Turner begins by casting herself as the charitable Lucía

who, like Mera's repentant Orozco would save what she could of the Indian soul (to this end she also translated the Bible into Quechua). Yet her sense of the tremendous degradation undergone by these survivors of the noble Inca becomes so great that she is driven actually to desire their extinction:

> May it please God that one day, exercising His goodness, He may decree the extinction of the indigenous race, which after displaying imperial grandeur, swallows the filth of opprobrium. May it please God to extinguish them, for they cannot possibly recover their dignity or exercise their rights!

Matto de Turner was unquestionably a naïve writer. But her exposure of such violent inner ambiguities greatly illuminates the contradictions inherent in much early Indianist writing. These reappear in Alcides Arguedas's *Raza de bronce* ('Race of Bronze'), 1919, in especially interesting fashion since Arguedas can be seen emending his attitudes and style as an Indianist writer in successive versions of the novel. Arguedas was first attracted to the Indian as a magic figure, an avatar of the 'bronze race' of the Incas who carried within him the strangeness and exoticism of another ancient civilization, qualities made much of by the modernists who influenced the young Arguedas. But try as he would, he could not blot out the far more immediate spectacle of Indian peasantry and proletariat whom, in the successive versions of his novel, he came to find more and more 'abominable'. Consistent with this, the one white character in the novel sympathetic to the Indians, Suárez, an author with Modernist leanings who resembles the younger Arguedas, is made to appear increasingly ridiculous and futile.

All in all, and by its final version, *Raza de bronce* would then appear to be no less fatalist than Matto de Turner's *Birds without a Nest.* Yet in at least alluding to such matters as land-tenure systems, and by openly comparing the Andean Indian to the *mujik* of pre-Bolshevik Russia, this work of Arguedas's marks a shift away from previous Indianist models. It raises questions also anticipated in Mexico, in the singular novel *El Zarco, the Bandit (El zarco)*, 1901, by Manuel Ignacio Altamirano, himself an Aztec or Nahuatl-speaking Indian who rather than demur to imported creeds of fatalism devoted all his energy to fostering an image of the Indian who was not 'subject and servile, but enhanced by work and aware of his strengh and worth'. In other words, from being religous and moral, the Indian 'problem' was becoming social and political, though even so the factor of race was not fully resolved. This emphasis was favoured in the aftermath of the Mexican Revolution (1910–20), apologists of which went on to found the continentally-based Instituto Indigenista Interamericano; and it was modified again by the spread of socialist ideas in the Andean republics, notably in Juan Carlos Mariátegui's *Seven Interpretations of Peruvian Reality (Siete ensayos en torno a la realidad peruana)*, 1927. In line with this reappraisal of the role and the destiny of the Indian in Latin American society, the 'Indianist' novel became 'indigenist'. Significantly this new development was best represented in just those parts of the subcontinent which not only were undergoing the greatest ideological change but which, in the first place, have traditionally had the most concentrated native societies: Middle America and Tahuantinsuyu.

Endeavouring to avoid the false consciousness of their predecessors, indigenist novels focused preferentially on political struggles of the present. Examples are: *El indio*

('The Indian'), 1935, by the Mexican Gregorio López y Fuentes; *The Villagers (Huasipungo)*, 1934, by the Ecuadorian Jorge Icaza; and *Broad and Alien is the World (El mundo es ancho y ajeno)*, 1941, by the Peruvian Ciro Alegría. The first traces the experience of a Nahuatl-speaking village before, during and after the Mexican revolution, and in so doing anticipates Juan Rulfo's intense and laconic depiction of rural Comala, made into a ghost of its vivid native past by the land-owner of the title *Pedro Páramo* (1955). The other two feature the violent dispossession of Andean Indians from their lands, and may be said actually to have affected later patterns of legislation in Ecuador and Peru. Each in its own way, and territory, exposes the mechanism of white and capitalist oppression, sometimes in sickening detail of rape, plunder, and massacre; and each deplores the relegation of the Indian to the lowest levels of society, urging the need for immediate reform.

About the good intentions of these indigenist writers there can be little doubt. Yet the fact is that they for the most part continued to work within a positivist frame of reference, which, as Dorfman has acutely observed, left the Indians as mere objects of oppression, politically as devoid of strategy as of a conscious history of their own. And this is a tendency which continues still today in Western journalism and even in Marxist analysis, which will dub the Indian a 'peasant' sooner than credit him with his own named identity, be it Maya-Quiché, Quechua, or Guaraní. For all their sympathy and even intimacy with Indian life, most indigenist novels of this period may be said to have followed the programme of the highly influential Mexican Manuel Gamio, who recommended that the Indian problems of race, culture and language should be solved by miscegenation, education, and the eradication of native speech through the teaching of Spanish. The novelists in question sooner write *about* Indians from the outside, typically in debates between whites about their worth, of the sort that fill the pages of *Raza de bronce* and *El indio*, and hence fail to present reality within a native consciousness and perspective.

All this may be said to have changed with a further profound shift in the tradition of novels concerned with native Americans. In part synonymous with the 'new novel' of Latin America inaugurated (according to Dorfman) by Miguel Angel Asturias's epoch-making *Men of Maize (Hombres de maíz)*, 1949, this shift is best explained in terms of an increasing concern with representation, in both the political and the literary senses; failing faith in the universality of metropolitan Western values, including orthodox Marxist; and in particular, the exhumation, edition, and translation of classic Indian texts. In this new departure, which offered totally to resolve lingering dilemmas of 'race', and which shapes the novels of Asturias, Ermilo Abreu Gómez, José María Arguedas, Augusto Roa Bastos, Darcy Ribeiro and others, these native texts emerge as a prime influence and the key to a proper understanding of present-day native America, in each of the main cultural areas outlined so far: Middle America, Tahuantinsuyu, and lowland South America. They bring forward an element neglected by the Brazilian Americanists, avoided by Mera (who only as a scholar and critic took notice of native American literature), and emphatically rejected by the more positivist of the *indigenistas* (who at best saw native literature as the work of superstition).

In the case of the first of these three areas, Middle America, its very geography is defined by native literature, and stems from the existence there in pre-Columbian times of paginated books of paper and skin, and of a corresponding tradition of script. Formed from an elaborate calendar and ritual patterning of life, this script in its two main varieties, iconographic and Maya hieroglyphic, is the antecedent and palimpsest of huge numbers of alphabetic texts written out after the European invasion, in the two principal literary languages of the area: Nahuatl or Aztec; and Maya in its lowland and highland forms. A critic recently asked: 'How specifically indigenist can a writer be in a country like Mexico which has more than fifty Indian languages and, in a sense, cultures?' Part of the answer must lie in the logic of this deep and ancient literary tradition, as novelists who have drawn on it have shown. For example, using the Nahuatl scholarship of such compatriots as Angel María Garibay and Miguel León Portilla, and recent readings of surviving pre-Columbian books, Carlos Fuentes has been able to provide a Mexican version on the time and resonance of the Spanish invasion, at once calendrical and magic, in the central section of *Terra Nostra*. Again, acknowledging this same native legacy corrects too Old World a view of the submerged motifs in Juan Rulfo's narratives: the sacred maize field or *milpa* whose food sustains and is equivalent to man; and the Lord of Hell Mictlantecutli or 'presidente del infierno', present still today in shamanist images that directly echo the pre-Columbian books, on whom is modelled the lord of Comala, Pedro Páramo.

A similar continuity can be found in the Maya literary tradition, especially in lowland Yucatan where there has been an unbroken line of transcription from the hieroglyphs of the Classic period (AD 300 to 900), through the post-Classic hieroglyphic books, to the corpus of alphabetic Chilam Balam books which extends from the sixteenth to the present century, and which has been intimately connected in turn with the process of translation into Spanish and other languages. For the Latin

American novel an important moment was reached in 1930 with the Spanish translation of the Chilam Balam Book of the town Chumayel by Antonio Médiz Bolio, who used this text as the basis for his own Maya revivalist work *La tierra del faisán y del venado,* second edition 1934 ('The Land of the Pheasant and the Deer'); this translation also served Miguel Angel Asturias with material for his *Leyendas de Guatemala* ('Legends of Guatemala'), 1930, and was subsequently put into French by the Surrealist writer Benjamin Péret, 1955.

Above all, Médiz Bolio's translation became an ingredient of the brilliant novel by Ermilo Abreu Gómez, *Canek,* 1940, Canek being the name of a Maya rebel leader executed by the Spaniards in Merida (Yucatan) in 1761. In the novel Canek's cause is linked to the continuing struggle of the Maya throughout the nineteenth century, after Mexican Independence, in the so-called War of the Castes, for the legal right to land and some degree of cultural automomy. Throughout, the Maya *Book of Chumayel,* which Abreu Gómez was later to edit, palpably endows the text of *Canek* with its whole being, thus distinguishing it sharply from the same author's earlier folkloric cameos of Spanish colonial rule, in which Maya literature plays no part at all. The epigraphs, all from the *Book of Chumayel,* which introduce each of the five parts of the work and the narrative as a whole, point us to a close and sensitive reading of the Maya original, as a medium for understanding Maya behaviour and philosophy, and indeed correspond to the main chapters of that original. They include the political forecasts made in the sixteenth century by the 'prophets' Napuctun, Nahau Pech, and Chilam Balam himself, which in fact affected the course of the Maya and hence Mexican history that Abreu Gómez follows; the riddles asked of candidates for office under the 'katun' or calendrical system of government, through which Canek expresses his doctrine; the cosmogony which fundamentally undermines the Judaeo-Christian Genesis, being for that reason set out as allegory, and in disguise, like Canek's followers; and most fundamental of all, the basic claim to the land and water of Yucatan itself largely still occupied by Maya and first settled completely by them many centuries before Montejo, as the *Book of Chumayel* again takes good care to testify in its *katun* chronicles. Moreover, bibiographically exact as these echoes are, they contrive not at all to clutter Abreu Gómez's narrative, but rather to enhance its structure and drive.

When it comes to the highland Maya of Guatemala, where non-Indians constitute a minority of the population, we find similar examples both of major native texts and of novels that draw inventively upon them. Outstanding among the former is the *Popol vuh* of the Quiché-Maya, the 'Book of counsel' rightly considered the 'bible of America'; sweeping chronologically from the beginning of time to the arrival of Cortés's lieutenant Alvarado in Quich territory, this work traces the emergence of early life forms, reptile, bird, monkey, and recounts the catastrophes of the mud people and the machine-like doll people which preceded the making of contempory man from maize and the first *milpa*. Along with the *Chronicle* of the Cakchiquel neighbours of the Quiché, the *Popol vuh* may be accounted the prime source of Miguel Angel Asturias's *Men of Maize*; indeed, it can be shown to have completely altered that novelist's perspective on the native peoples of Guatemala. For early in his career, taking to an extreme indigenist policies learnt in post-revolutionary Mexico, he spoke of the need for immigration from Germanic Europe in the following terms:

This radical remedy will attack at its roots the illnesses that undermine the indigenous organism [i.e. the Maya]. The medical doctor has found a lack of red blood cells, defective diet, the deleterious action of our mountain and coastal climates, tropical diseases and many others that are unknown. The biologist has found a marked diminishment in the quantity of urea. The physiologist has found meager weight and size and a lack of energy. Psychiatry has found very significant defective traits of criminality, nearly total lack of personality, and a lack of intellectual and moral life. The jurist has found the most horrifying ignorance of the law. The clergy has found an absurd understanding of the rites and dogmas of his religion. The moralist has found selfishness, the custom of lying and general low standards. The economist has found poverty and exhaustion.

Then, at the Sorbonne in the late 1920s, Asturias worked with Georges Raynaud on a translation of the Quiché and the Cakchiquel texts, hitherto unknown to him, and all was changed dramatically. These classics enabled him to see the Maya as if for the first time. Treating their literature seriously enabled him to find reason in a behaviour and a mentality he had previously considered degenerate and sadly incoherent, notably in his characterization of the rebel Maya leader Gaspar Ilóm, inside whose head and body the novel opens:

Gaspar Ilóm lets them rob the land of Ilóm of the sleep of its eyes.

Gaspar Ilóm lets them tear out with an axe the eylids of the land of Ilóm . . .

Gaspar Ilóm lets them scorch the branches of the

eyelashes of the land of Ilóm with fires that turn the
moon the colour of an old ant . . .

This newly learnt intimacy continues throughout: with its
exuberant table manners, the feast which celebrates Ilóm's
(temporary) victory over the *ladinos* or 'Latins' owes much
to Maya concepts of the reciprocity between human and
vegetal flesh, as does the vision achieved by Ilóm's survivors in the episode, where after a rehearsal of the *Popol
vuh's* world ages 'maize awaits them in every form, in the
flesh of their children, who are of maize'. Above all, like
Canek and by reference to the same textual authority,
Asturias's novel asserts the Maya right to their land,
against a political system that has slaughtered them in tens
of thousands.

Other Mayanist novels that have appeared in the wake
of Abreu Gómez's and Asturias's monumental examples
include those of Rosario Castellanos. Shaping her childhood experience of Chiapas through reference to the
trinity of classic Maya texts, the *Book of Chumayel*, the
Popol vuh, and the Cakchiquel *Chronicle*, Castellanos succeeds in giving greater resonance to the legends remembered from that past and to the spiritual resistance they
sustain among the Tzeltal Maya in *The Nine Guardians*
(*Balún Canán*, 1957) and the Tzotzil Maya (*Oficio de tinie-
blas*, 1962). Then going beyond Mexico and Central America, Maya literature has the distinction of having served as
a source of inspiration for writers on a continental scale.
From the decidedly un-Indian Buenos Aires far in the
south of the continent, Jorge Luis Borges turned to the
Popol vuh in order to detail the vision of the imprisoned
Maya priest in 'The Handwriting of the God' (*El Aleph*,
1949). And from Cuba, Alejo Carpentier took the *Book of
Chumayel* and the *Popol vuh* as his guide (particularly the

cosmogony in the latter, which is deemed unique in its wariness of unfeeling technology), when tracing *The Lost Steps* of American man back to a dark interior of his continent: these native touchstones are critical to a proper understanding of the three-fold structure of the narrative, of its indigenous heroine Rosario and her manifold non-Western time, and of Carpentier's whole doctrine of the 'marvellous reality' *(lo real maravilloso)* of America.

Like Middle America, Tahuantinsuyu has its classic alphabetic texts, typically in Quechua, which in their way continue a tradition of pre-Columbian literacy, in this case one related to the *quipu* or string device used to administer and record in the Inca state; and again these classics have impinged on the novel writing in the area. Indeed, in Mario Unzueta's *Valle* ('Valley'), the novel in question has itself been a main means of diffusion for the Quechua text – a drama concerning Pizarro's murder of Atahualpa still performed in Bolivia, which belongs to the kingship cycle that originated under the Inca. Similarly, Jesús Lara's *Yanakuna*, 1952, interpolates texts which he himself has edited as a Quechua scholar. More intricately related with that source are the novels of the Peruvian José María Arguedas. Assessments of the conflict between the Indian and non-Indian worlds of his country, *Deep Rivers (Los ríos profundos)*, 1958, and *Todas las sangres* ('All the bloods'), 1964, win much of their energy from the ancestral songs in Quechua which Arguedas had anthologized early in his writing career (in *Canto Kechwa*, 1938) and which become the literal life-blood of Rendon Willka, the revolutionary hero of the latter novel, in his efforts to re-establish the traditional *ayllu* sytem of communal land ownership, just as his Bolivian namesake had historically founded an Andean Indian republic. Then, in his posthumous *El zorro de arriba y el zorro de abajo* ('The Fox from Above and the

Fox from Below'), 1969, which some critics have judged yet more epoch-making than Asturias's *Men of Maize*, the textual range of reference is decisively broadened to include the *Huarochiri Narrative* which Arguedas had translated into Spanish a few years before (*Dioses y hombres de Huarochiri*, 1966) and whose cosmogony is comparable with that found in the *Popol vuh*. At the outset and following the pattern of the original, the two foxes of the title discuss their respective parts of Peru, mountain and coast, diagnosing the hidden sicknesses of its inhabitants. Arguedas privileges their ability to perceive the underlying moral and economic geography of the country and their common preference for Huatyacuri, the hero from Above; and against their intelligence is set the brute power of the avalanche (*lloqlla*), like that of a world age, which brings Indians down to the coast, to cannery row, cultural loss, and confusion. In this framework, and by anticipating in the novel the defiant gesture of his own suicide, rein is given to the forces which today are furthering the military struggle first precipitated by Pizarro.

Returning finally to the South American lowlands with which we began, with its myriad rivers and languages, we find that it is only now that anything like a native literary tradition has been made perceptible from the outside, through the publication of such key texts as the Guaraní *Ayvu rapyta* ('Origin of human speech') and *Book of the Dead*; the Desana narrative which serves as the basis for Reichel Dolmatoff's aptly entitled *Amazonian Cosmos*; and above all *Watunna: an Orinoco Creation Cycle*, which stems from the Carib heartland where the Orinoco and Amazon conjoin, and which presents a cosmogony again readily comparable with that of the *Popol vuh*, along with a history that extends to Caracas, the 'lost kingdom' of Roraima, and Damab, the Carib sea. In the first instance these lowland

classics help to locate on native grounds novels that
antedate their publication, for example Rómulo Gallegos's
principal work *Canaima*, 1935, a Carib title synonymous
with the white exploitation and macho madness described
at length in *Watunna*; and *The Vortex* (*La vorágine*), 1924
by the Colombian José Eustacio Rivera which in similarly
dwelling on the threat to and the native 'solidarity' of the
rain forest includes the Mapiripana fragment of Amazonian cosmogony.

Among more recent novelists from this area, and following the trajectory of Asturias and Arguedas, Augusto Roa
Bastos has made himself increasingly familiar, in literary
terms, with the Guaraní heritage of his native Paraguay,
where that language remains commoner than Spanish.
Dissatisfied with what he calls the 'parla mestiza' of his
first work, he came to found the whole concept of *Son of
Man* (*Hijo de hombre*, 1960) on the conscious and persistent
opposition between the transcendence of Christianity and
the Guaraní *Book of the Dead*, refrains of which haunt the
opening pages of the novel and intimately sustain the
revolutionary hero Cristóbal Jara, in this a southern counterpart to Canek, Ilóm, and Willka. In the subsequent *I the
Supreme* (*Yo el Supremo*, 1974), Guaraní texts enter more
fully into a dialectical process proper, engendering thereby
a mordant and unrelenting humour. In one discussion,
between the supreme 'I' of the title, the dictator Dr Francia,
and two visiting Scots, the leitmotif is provided by a
raconteur dog who authoritatively contrasts the cosmogony of the South American shaman or *paye*, in particular
its notions of dual autogenesis and its Blue Jaguar, with
the biblical Genesis and even with the musings of
Nietzsche. In another vein, and from political exile, Roa
Bastos has denounced the horrific persecution of the
Guaraní from the days of the Jesuit Mission up to the

present, in his study *Las culturas condenadas* ('The Condemned Cultures'), 1978. At the same time, many hundreds of miles towards the north west and the mouth of the Amazon, the same dialectic between the Blue Jaguar of the Tupi-Guaraní and the pale angels of Christianity has appeared in the novel *Maíra*, 1978, by the Brazilian anthropologist Darcy Ribeiro. By intercalating experience of everyday Indian life with the passages from their classic texts, this work succeeds in affirming not just another way of life but the reason for it, one vastly richer than customary apologias for ours, and one in which spreading white economy and technology uncomfortably recall those doll-like monsters of a former and doomed world age. By the end we have learnt again what we already know, that in destroying the last green mansions of America we destroy ourselves.

In the wider spectrum of the Latin American novel in general, opinions have varied sharply about the worth and significance of its indigenous thread. And this has been so since Joaquim Nabuco suggested that Alencar's prose resembled the 'incomprehensible' chant of a shaman or *paye*, and taunted the whole Brazilian *escola americana* with the jibe, likewise a statement of exclusive political if not racist intent: 'we are Brazilians, not Guaraní'. Among the new novelists a notable division was caused by Julio Cortázar's angry response to the first published instalments of *El zorro de arriba* in which Arguedas characterized Cortázar and others as cosmopolitan and morally detached from the provincial America he cared so passionately for himself, along with Rulfo, Roa Bastos, and the Brazilian João Guimarães Rosa. More tenacious and consequential has been the criticism offered by the Peruvian Mario Vargas Llosa. Having implicitly made light of the nativism of Rómulo Gallegos when accepting the literary prize named after that figure, he has commented too, in the second case at some length, on each of the two pillars of indigenism in the new novel, Asturias, and his own compatriot Arguedas, consigning them both to a world of 'myth and dream' that is alien to 'progress and development within the democratic structures of Latin American society'. Indeed, in his most recent novel *The Real Life of Alejandro Mayta (Historia de Mayta,* 1984), Vargas Llosa detects a common enemy to the state in Quechua Indians and the cause of Trotsky.

And so the debate goes on, much affected by urgent ideological concern from within Latin America. Yet this should not obscure the more radical fact that over time indigenism has succeeded in adapting the imported form of the novel to a new environment, one possessed of its own lexis – *milpa, katun, ayllu, canaima, paye* – and the world view and time thereby implied. It has encouraged that switch in consciousness within once imperial Spanish and Portuguese discourse, that literary 'reversal of the Conquest' to use León-Portilla's phrase, wittily achieved, for example, by Gabriel García Márquez in *The Autumn of the Patriarch (El otoño del patriarca,* 1975), where a height of human solidarity corresponds to the 'we' of the Caribs who watch Columbus arrive. In short, it has afforded a first hint of the true matrix of Latin American culture.

Coming to Terms with Modernity:
Magical Realism and the Historical Process in the Novels of Alejo Carpentier

Edwin Williamson

For Alejo Carpentier, the art of narrative was strongly associated with mysterious, if not magical, powers. In an early novel he wrote of the Haitian shaman Mackandal's impact on his audience: 'It was a notorious fact that with his deep, grave voice he could get all he wanted from the negresses. And his skills as a narrator ... could impose silence on the men'. Mackandal's extraordinary power to seduce and marvel his listeners makes him the guardian, and in a sense the creator, of whatever cultural identity the black slaves might have in common. His stories recall for them their origins in Africa, revealing the power of their old gods and the majesty of their former kings; they serve as lifelines to a past which would otherwise be entirely lost to these uprooted people. So effectively does Mackandal bond the slaves into a community that he inspires them to rebel against their white masters, provoking the first movement for independence in Latin America.

Carpentier's fascination with Mackandal is symptomatic of the new mood of nationalism that emerged in Spanish America in the 1920s. A growing awareness of being dominated by Europe and the United States produced the conviction that the work of independence was not yet complete: Spanish America had still to find her true identity. Such a belief called into question the nature of the independence already won, and the special role the writer had played in its achievement.

The break with Spain had conferred upon intellectuals and writers a public authority unprecedented in colonial times. Under the empire, society had been dominated by the Church far more than in Spain itself. But once the imperial connection had been severed, writers were free to promote the new liberal ideology which provided the rationale for independence. They could become the high priests of the modern culture of the Enlightenment, bearers of the values of rationalist humanism. Not surprisingly, liberal reformers regarded their Spanish heritage with distaste: it was authoritarian, superstitious and irrational, scarcely capable any longer of civilizing the endemic barbarism of America, let alone carrying the new republics forward along the path of progress. Yet for all that, the vast majority of the people – white, half-caste, Indian and black – remained very much under the influence of the old beliefs, their imaginations fired still by fables and legends kept alive by a popular culture in which oral traditions, public festivals and religious pageants played their part as vigorously as in the past. Thus, in so far as he was a member of the enlightened minority which formed the intellectual leadership of the new republics, the writer's task was the opposite of Mackandal's: it was not to keep alive the old myths but rather to educate the people out of them, inventing new myths to take their place which would positively articulate their sense of being native-born Americans rather than transplanted Europeans. However, by the end of the nineteenth century the task of expressing the 'realities' of America remained unfulfilled: the old gods had not been successfully replaced and such new stories as had been invented – with rare exceptions – lacked the potency of the fables that

thrived among the common people. An important reason
for this insufficiency was that the rationalist ethos of the
liberal élites militated against the creation of powerful
myths, but perhaps also the medium in which the new
stories had largely been told – the European novel – was
itself unable to do justice to the cultural needs of the new
societies.

The birth of the novel in Spanish America coincided
with the first moves towards independence. Before 1816,
whatever was read in the way of narrative fiction had
largely been written in Spain, and from the earliest days of
the discovery and conquest a favourite form of fiction had
been the Spanish romance of chivalry. Here was a kind of
narrative that had proved its worth as an imaginary
correlative of the experiences afforded by America. Conquistadores and explorers had had recourse to the exhilarating fantasies of the romances in order to express the
marvels they encountered in the New World. Bernal Díaz
del Castillo, a soldier in Cortés's army, wrote in a famous
passage that when they beheld the Aztec capital of
Tenochtitlan 'we could compare it to nothing but the
enchanted scenes we had read of in *Amadis of Gaul*'. The
names of California and Patagonia were taken from
sixteenth-century chivalric romances. America possessed
the virtue of conjuring up the mythical and the legendary
in men's imaginations.

Analogously, the Wars of Independence could furnish
copious material with which to create the founding myths
of the new republics. There were heroes to be praised and
great deeds to be sung, yet the traditional instruments of
celebration, the epic and the romance, had fallen into
disuse. Instead, there was the novel, but the particular
difficulty with the novel was that it had originated precisely as a parodic rejection of the mythologizing resources

of romance and epic. In other words, it had arisen in circumstances peculiar to Europe: the novelist was inherently suspicious of ideals and fantasies, his voice was ironic, his point of view individualistic rather than communal. The very fabric from which the novel was made was shot with ambiguity and equivocation. Little wonder then that the novel had sold America short – it remained a misfit in an environment that had once lent itself so well to far more robust flourishes of the imagination.

The nationalist writers of the first decades of this century looked for ways of expanding the possibilities of the novel so as to give voice to their specific American identity. This made them receptive to the experimentalism of the modernist movement. Carpentier himself joined the avant-garde, nationalist *Grupo Minorista* in Havana and helped to found the *Revista de Avance* whose title proclaimed its commitment to new forms and new ideas. But at the same time, these Latin American writers looked to areas of national life which they took to be specifically American or at least non-European. In the process they noticed the existence of more humble counterparts – the oral storytellers who had survived in the hitherto despised plebeian subcultures of the continent. For instance, Carpentier himself was to recall how he had once come across an illiterate troubadour in Venezuela 'looking out to sea and reciting, with ceremonial fervour, the tales of Charlemagne and of the ruin of Troy'. Such primitive storytellers, employing techniques and material rooted in long-standing popular traditions, could not fail to appeal to cultivated writers seeking to connect more fully with the realities of America. The new nationalism therefore combined with modernist experimentalism to produce a current of nativist or *indigenista* writing whose aim was to

eschew foreign-derived models and create an autoctho-
nous culture in which tradition could be reconciled with
modernity.

Alejo Carpentier's first novel *Ecué-Yamba-O*, 1933, is an
example of the new nativist literature. Written during a
term of imprisonment in 1927 for signing a nationalist
manifesto against the dictator Machado, it is an evocation
of the life of poor Cuban blacks, and portrays both their
preservation of ethnic traditions and their conscious rejection of white culture through their voodoo cults. All the
same, Carpentier remains ambivalent about the blacks'
animistic religion, as if he could not quite shake off the
idea that it was barbarous and retrograde. Although he
admired the vitality of the blacks, he was still too much
under the influence of European culture himself to accept
voodoo and shamanism without reservation. *Ecué-Yamba-
O*, like other nativist writing, illustrates the new interest in
establishing an American identity. But Europe could not
simply be denied; it too had contributed to the creation
of America. Cultural nationalism, therefore, involved a
reassessment of Latin America's relations with Europe,
and in particular, it meant coming to terms once more with
the modern culture of the Enlightenment.

In Paris, where he lived from 1928 to 1939, Carpentier
became disillusioned with the effects of rationalist humanism on Europe. He frequented avant-garde circles and
was involved in the Surrealist movement. He found there
an interest in the primitive which equalled his own but
with the difference that it formed part of a much more
radical critique of European culture. Surrealism strengthened his belief that the rationalism of the Enlightenment
had alienated Europeans from the life of instinct, desire
and imagination. What is more, the rise of Fascism and
Nazism made him lose the traditional Latin American

reverence for European civilization: under the surface of enlightened humanism there lurked a barbarous urge to power, a hubris which had led Europeans to tear up their roots in nature in their wish to become masters of their own destiny. Still, the spiritual sickness of Europe could only instil pessimism in a Latin American, for this was the future that awaited the new republics if they continued to follow the path taken since Independence. Yet to change direction and recover their original optimism called for a new model of history, one less compromised with the fate of Europe.

It was his reading of Spengler's *Decline of the West* that took Carpentier a critical stage further in his re-evaluation of the historical process. Spengler's explanation of history in terms of cycles of cultural growth and degeneration enabled Carpentier to overcome his pessimism about the historical prospects for Latin America: if the loss of spirituality to which rationalist humanism appeared to lead was not an ineluctable destiny, then to approve the vitality of primitive cultures, as the nativist writers had done, was not necessarily reactionary; for these local cultures could now be seen not as vestiges of the past but as the seeds of a new, specifically American culture in the making. A visit to Haiti in 1943 confirmed his emerging historical optimism. He realized that the motive force behind the first successful movement for independence in Latin America had been the voodoo of the black slaves, not the ideas of the Enlightenment. Magic and religion – the repositories of authenticity and wholeness – were capable also of intervening positively in history as vehicles of freedom.

The combination of Spengler's model of history, the Surrealists' desire to recover psychic wholeness, and the Haitian experience, formed the basis of Carpentier's attempts to imagine an alternative destiny for Latin America. He envisaged the evolution of a new hybrid civilization formed from the races and cultures which had been thrown together in the New World. A favourite notion became that of the Caribbean as a new cradle of civilization such as the Mediterranean had once been thanks to an earlier fertile cross-breeding of different peoples. Carpentier's new-found optimism is evident in the prologue he wrote to his second novel *The Kingdom of this World* (*El reino de este mundo*), 1949, which was based on the story of Haiti's independence. It is a famous text because it introduced Carpentier's highly influential conception of *lo real maravilloso*, or the 'marvellous in the real', and this was to become the essential point of departure for discussion of Latin American 'magical realism'.

Like the Surrealists, Carpentier sought to redeem the mind from the dead hand of rationality by unblocking once more the sources of the marvellous. But Carpentier saw the Surrealists' attempts to do this 'as nothing more than a literary trick'. In America, on the other hand, the presence of thriving ethnic cultures, the mixture of mentalities, together with the extraordinarily diverse and imposing natural phenomena made it possible to experience the marvellous quite spontaneously in everyday life. As a result, the limits of the real could be expanded well beyond European expectations; the 'unperceived riches of reality' were accessible through miracles, illuminations and epiphanies. Carpentier, however, was very clear about one thing: the Surrealists had invoked the marvellous in a state of unbelief but 'the experience of the marvellous presupposes a faith'. The marvellous in literature entailed a belief in the supernatural: 'those who do not believe in saints cannot heal themselves by the miracles of saints, nor can those who are not Quixotes enter, body and soul, into

the world of Amadis of Gaul o...
tier's magical realism, therefore, ...
Enlightenment and pre-novelistic ...
terms, it sought to take the novel out o...
drawing-room, out of the cultivated Europ...
and thrust it into the wilderness of Americ...
might recuperate the mythological powers of ...
romance, those narrative forebears it had once des...,ed
through irony and burlesque in Europe. Carpentier put his
finger on that nostalgia for the freedom of romance which
underlies much of the exuberance of modern fiction in
Latin America (a nostalgia exemplified also by García
Márquez's professed admiration for *Amadis of Gaul* and
Vargas Llosa's for *Tirant lo Blanc*). Thus in his 1949
prologue, Carpentier was attempting to replenish the
powers of the novelist in Latin America so that he might
fulfil a role he had failed to perform adequately at Independence: he must assume the functions of a mythologist like
Mackandal, whose stories bonded his people into a community by sinking roots into the past, by creating a stock
of images that served to spell out a collective identity.

Yet, for all that, it was no easy matter to recover the faith
upon which the marvellous depended. Nor could the Latin
American writer repudiate the rationalist humanism of the
European Enlightenment altogether, for to call into question the basic ideology of Independence was to undermine
in some way his own *raison d'être*. By celebrating the
supernatural and the miraculous, then, magical realism
inevitably generated antinomies between faith and
reason, imagination and intellect, nature and culture. The
tensions they provoked can be observed, for example, in
the vindictive relish with which Carpentier describes the
thwarting of the rational designs of Europeans by the raw
power of nature in the New World. Similarly, they pervade

Alejo Carpentier

.uriant, baroque prose style; his language seems
to register the contrary impulses that set imagination
against reason, its involuted syntax coils round the sharp
edges of concepts and ideas as if to draw them into
equivocal and more mysterious terrain. Again, by bringing the past to bear so critically upon present and future,
magical realism undermined a sense of linear progress,
deepening the mystery of historical time. Much critical
attention has been devoted to the temporal patterns of
Carpentier's stories – the fragmentation and counter-
pointing, the cycles and spirals which sometimes give his
work a labyrinthine quality reminiscent of Borges.

The development of Carpentier's fiction, in fact, can be
seen as a struggle with the conflicts produced by his
original conception of magical realism. His career has
something of the character of a spiritual quest: each
successive novel takes up a problem left unresolved in the
previous one and either analyses it from a different perspective or attempts a new synthesis. The search is complex and cannot be discussed fully here. Instead, I shall
restrict myself to his major novels, focusing largely on
three aspects: the powers of the artist, the sexual politics of
the characters, and the meaning of history. Each, of course,
interlocks with the others: the artist's powers have a
distinct erotic quality and they compete with the power of,
say, the scientist or the politician in giving shape to
historical experience. But my reason for choosing these
three aspects is that their interplay reveals a pattern of
assumptions that underlies Carpentier's work from first to
last. As we have seen from his portrayal of Mackandal,
Carpentier associates imaginative power with virility, yet
the artist's imagination can find the psychic wholeness
which eludes the power of reason only by means of a
union with a feminine principle. The vital conjugation of

masculine and feminine occurs either in the sexual act or in the re-creation of the security of the womb. Outside these two poles of authentic satisfaction, there exists little else but the alienating vicissitudes of history. Carpentier conceives of human life as a journey between two timeless idylls – after the wholeness of the womb there is the quest through the labyrinthine circumstances of history for an equivalent plenitude of being in the future. And this, of course, is the archetypal psychic pattern that informs romance narrative. As Northrop Frye put it in his celebrated study of romance, *The Secular Scripture*:

> Reality for romance is an order of existence most readily associated with the word identity . . . [Identity] is existence before 'once upon a time', and subsequent to 'and they lived happily ever after'. What happens in between are adventures, or collisions with external circumstances, and the return to identity is a release from the tyranny of these circumstances. Illusion for romance, then, is an order of existence that is best called alienation. Most romances end happily, with a return to a state of identity, and begin with a departure from it. (p. 54)

It could be said that Carpentier's magical realism, his wish to re-enter 'the world of Amadis of Gaul or Tirant lo Blanc', his concern with identity and authenticity, reflect a desire to rediscover the imperatives of romance within the context of the modern novel.

Carpentier's account of the long process of Haiti's wars of independence in *The Kingdom of this World* eschews straight chronological narrative for a technique which allows the action to displace itself constantly, leaping over long spans of time from one event to the next, switching from one character to another, modulating the tempo of the narrative by contrasting violent episodes of rebellion with more circumscribed scenes that possess an emblematic quality. The meaning of things lies beyond any one point of view: the blacks may interpret events from a magical perspective but the novel never departs from the factual record on which a European might base his understanding of them.

At first sight, the action follows a negative, circular pattern as one tyranny is overthrown only to be replaced by another. Relations between master and slave appear to swing uncontrollably between two opposite extremes. On the one hand, there is bondage (symbolized by the black masseur Solimán's pent-up desire for the white body of his mistress Pauline Bonaparte) but on the other, pointlessly destructive revolt (Solimán's desire finds vicarious release in the emblematic scene where Mademoiselle Floridor – a failed actress who liked to declaim Racine in a transparent gown before the assembled company of her slaves – lies raped and murdered after one of the uprisings). Nevertheless, Carpentier orchestrates these violent oppositions and unexpected echoes through the character of Ti Noel, who alone is present for the duration of the novel. His consciousness progresses beyond the brutal polarities of bondage and revolt, as old values are changed and alien influences absorbed in a dialectical play of circumstances. The cycle of rebellions is initiated by the shaman Mackandal's legends and occult powers which promise the slaves a return to the idyll of an organic African society. Eventually, Ti Noel realizes that voodoo can offer no lasting refuge from the rationalizing power of whites or mulattos in some magically reborn neo-African kingdom. He therefore places his hopes in 'the kingdom of this world' rather than in a kingdom of heaven, and to that extent is capable of appreciating the universalizing, humanistic values of liberty, equality and fraternity which had emerged from the alien culture of his former white masters. However, the ending of the novel is ironic, for in committing himself to improve man's lot in this world, Ti Noel undermines the supernatural basis of voodoo; he is on the point, therefore, of starting down the road which leads to secular humanism, with all that that implies in the way of loss of psychic wholeness, erotic vitality and harmony with nature. The novel ends not with a synthesis but with a contradiction (even though the latter is spirited away by the great hurricane into which Ti Noel mysteriously vanishes). An authentic, organic community, such as the one evoked by Mackandal, is based on faith in a transcendental reality, but the struggle to improve things in this world produces a consciousness that excludes that kind of faith, and therefore makes such a community impossible.

Carpentier's next novel *The Lost Steps* (*Los pasos perdidos*), 1953, approaches this fundamental contradiction from the opposite direction. It is the story of a composer fleeing an empty existence in New York as a pedlar of music for commercial purposes by taking a journey with his mistress into the hinterland of a South American country on the pretext of collecting primitive instruments and pursuing research into the origins of music. As he strikes deeper into the wilderness, he imagines he is travelling back into the past. His quest takes on a larger significance: he is retracing the lost steps of mankind to a point where the work of so-called progress may be undone and the ills of modernity find a cure.

He is a man seeking to recover that faith upon which the sense of the marvellous depends. In the terms of the prologue to *The Kingdom of this World*, the anonymous narrator-protagonist, like Don Quixote, is trying to 'enter, body and soul, into the world of Amadis of Gaul or Tirant lo Blanc'. There is an explicit reference to the Quixote theme when he meets an indigenous woman called Rosario for the first time. Reminded suddenly of El Toboso, the day-dreaming composer starts to recite to himself the opening lines of *Don Quixote*, but, when he falters, Rosario inadvertently supplies him with the right word. He becomes smitten with this Dulcinea of the New World, for she embodies the soul of nature, the essence of womanhood. Unlike his wilful, sexually unreliable mistress whom he eventually abandons in disgust, Rosario poses no challenge to his authority; she even comes to refer to herself quite simply as Your Woman, for not the least virtue of this preternaturally compliant creature is that, combining the attributes of mother and lover as she does, she can make the jaded narrator feel like a Mackandal, an artist-shaman who, by possessing nature so completely, can transcend it and make the world a magical and enchanting place once again.

The Lost Steps is a modern novel trying to turn itself into a romance. The narrator-protagonist superimposes an episodic quest structure on his journey: he imagines himself to be recuperating by stages a lost consciousness, purging himself of the modern sickness by what he regards as successive trials and adventures. Increasingly, he reveals a penchant for allegory, capitalizing nouns in a perpetual straining after symbols and portents that might bestow higher meanings on ordinary experience. Finally, he reaches a remote settlement in a place he chooses to call The Valley Where Time Stands Still. He has found at last the Holy Grail of authentic consciousness – outside history – in a primitive, organic community where he seems able to fulfil all his creative needs.

In relating these adventures, Carpentier's always sonorous, complex prose style becomes as ornately gilded and curlicued as an altarpiece in a colonial church. Actually, there is something too knowingly operatic and overblown about the language. The narrative is presented in a manner that exposes it constantly to the possibility of irony. As a first-person narrator who is forever reflecting upon and speculatively interpreting his experiences, the protagonist blends equivocally with the author himself. However, the reader, finding himself swept up into a boundlessly subjective discourse, and therefore bereft of dependable guidelines, reacts by developing a sceptical attitude towards the narrator's judgements, matching them against events and noticing the way that the closer the composer comes to his Holy Grail the more reason there is to suspect that he may be deluding himself. In the event, the idyll does not last: the protagonist interrupts it to go back to civilization for a while (as he thinks) in order to carry out certain prosaic requirements. When he tries to return, he cannot find the entrance to the secret channel through which he might once again penetrate the womb of time: Rosario is lost, the promise of psychic wholeness gone. He leaves for New York with the bitter realization that, of all people, it is the artist who is 'forbidden to sever the bonds of time'. Still, the composer succumbs to this fate with the fear that the inescapable hammer-blows of Time might 'deafen him and deprive him of his voice'. As in *The Kingdom of this World*, there is the anxiety that the march of history will eventually emasculate the imagination.

It is difficult to determine Carpentier's intentions in the novel: was he lamenting the fate of the composer, or subtly mocking his folly in seeking a refuge from history? No doubt, as the allusion to Quixote would suggest, he remained ambivalent, torn between heart and head. Yet if

increasingly sceptical of the Revolution, seeing it fail to live up to its promise and believing it to be dehumanizing precisely because its lofty, abstract ideals seem unable to accommodate the small-scale needs of ordinary men and women. He begins to observe nature and to rediscover through eroticism and the imagination the particular contours of his individual personality.

The second part concerns the development of Esteban's thoughts on the destiny of man once he leaves France and returns to the Caribbean. As he contemplates the rich, intricate forms of nature in the tropics he believes he can perceive a deeper movement of time beneath the super-ficial agitation of human history. The Revolution is one of a number of mysterious Events that break surface in the ocean of history, carrying man forwards despite the apparent failure of the repeated attempts to improve his lot in this world. Historical progress is not a linear man-made development but takes instead the form of a spiral that turns about an invisible axis impelled by a mysterious power. In successive meditations, Esteban likens that transcendent power to a Tree, then an Anchor, finally seeing both images resolved in a great crucifix he finds in a hospital looking out on to the sea as if in a perpetual dialogue with the ocean of time.

The parity accorded by the structure of the novel to Victor and Esteban suggests that each is equally important but also equally lacking in his relation to history: Victor gets too close to events to understand their significance, while Esteban withdraws so far from them that he can no longer affect them directly. Still, by virtue of his spiritual illumin-ation (which contrasts ironically with the 'enlightenment' that inspired the French Revolution), Esteban becomes the vehicle through which the transcendent power that guides history revitalizes the spent resources of the human actors.

In the third part, Esteban meets his cousin Sofía once again in Cuba. She had formerly been Victor's lover but Esteban now falls in love with her himself. Yet that love is expressed ultimately through an act of self-sacrifice prefigured in the symbol of the crucifix: Esteban allows himself to be thrown into prison for alleged revolutionary activity and thus enables Sofía, the true revolutionary, to escape, carrying with her the ideals of a Revolution he himself no longer believes in. Esteban's sacrifice, then, is the pivot which turns the narrative from historical pessimism to a renewed optimism, infusing the exhausted ideals of a Victor Hugues with new promise. It reconciles the role of the artist with that of the politician, and dissolves the anxiety manifest in *The Lost Steps* that the imagination will become emasculated with the march of history. Now, it is the 'artistic' Esteban who provides the vital link between the transcendent universal Will and the multitude of human wills striving confusedly to progress. The artist alone is capable of relating 'the time of history' to 'the time of man'.

There remains, none the less, a vagueness about the link between art and history evident in the coda to the main action, where we encounter Sofía and Esteban living together in Madrid several years later but, significantly, not as lovers. Their non-sexual relationship might be taken as a sign that Carpentier could not conceive of a more positive engagement of the 'spiritual' Esteban with the 'political' Sofía beyond the passive connection already established by Esteban's earlier sacrifice of his liberty for the sake of Sofía. There is a corresponding vagueness about the ending of the novel. The two cousins melt into the crowds which take to the streets of Madrid in revolt against Napoleon's invading army – an uprising that was to trigger the revolutionary process leading to the independence of Spanish America.

However, it is left to the reader to speculate on the way the spiritual and the political might once again interact.

In this respect, the novel does not fully synthesize the contradiction between faith and rationalist humanism which was generated by Carpentier's original notion of magical realism. Still, the contradiction has been substantially mitigated – Carpentier's account of the historical process is less tormented by mutually exclusive polarities. For example, the figure of the artist is not that of the assertive Mackandal, rather he is self-denying like Esteban. Accordingly, Sofía is a dynamic actor on the historical stage and not a submissive feminine principle – previously embodied in Rosario – whom the artist must possess in order to find authenticity. Finally, 'civilized' Europe and 'barbarous' America do not collide in direct antagonism; their relations show a degree of cross-fertilization which parallels the new reciprocity between the sexes. *Explosion in a Cathedral* testifies to an internal evolution in Carpentier's thought. The desire for the marvellous remains, but it is no longer associated with the survival of primitive magic. As a result, the creation of a distinctive cultural identity for Latin America need no longer involve the total repudiation of the historical course taken by Europe.

However, it was an event external to Carpentier's artistic development that decisively transformed his ideas about magical realism and the marvellous. The success of the Cuban Revolution in 1959 was to dispel for him some of the vagueness about the connections between art and history outlined above. Returning to Cuba after having lived for fourteen years in Venezuela, Carpentier was appointed to several official positions and did not publish any major work for over a decade. The novels that appeared during the 1970s are markedly different from his previous work. Art has now yielded the initiative to revolutionary action in the struggle for wholeness and authenticity. Spiritual or transcendental preoccupations are largely irrelevant to the artist. Relations between Europe and Latin America are not determined by the civilization–barbarism opposition but by problems of economic inequality and political power. As a result, Carpentier's approach to history is relatively unproblematical – he accepts man's capacity to direct his own progress, even though he might suffer setbacks. All this suggests that Carpentier had moved very close to an orthodox Marxist position. Nevertheless, he did not sever his links with literary modernism – his fundamental interest remained the individual consciousness as opposed to social reality. In other words, his ideological proximity to dialectical materialism was not accompanied by a corresponding transformation in either form or subject matter. Instead, Marxism allowed him to see his established preoccupations in a new light.

Reasons of State (*El recurso del método*), 1974, can be read as a parody of some of his former attitudes, particularly as regards his predisposition to make a qualitative distinction between Europe and America. It is an account of a representative Latin American dictator's repeated efforts to keep his grip on power at home even though he prefers to spend his time in Paris enjoying the fruits of a European culture which he admires so much precisely because it seems to be beyond reach of his own people. Indeed, it is the dictator's excessive reverence for European civilization which provides him with a pretext for tyranny, since if his own country is condemned to barbarism, it can therefore only be ruled with a rod of iron, not by the light of reason. The dictator's attitude to power determines the historical complexion of his country: if things just go round in circles, if there appears to be no progress, it is because he believes that government is the art of putting unruly elements in their place.

The dictator, in fact, is a fairly endearing and enormously inventive old rogue with more than a touch of the Mackandal about him, for his success depends upon his ability to marvel the people with improvised myths or with virtuoso displays of virile prowess. But as with *The Lost Steps*, the structure of the narrative betrays the assumptions of the protagonist. Even though the narrative discourse remains within the ambit of the dictator's consciousness, it alternates between first- and third-person narration, thereby giving the impression that the old man's hold on things is not as thorough as he might imagine. Reflecting as it does a highly personalist conception of politics, the narrative very effectively masks from view the actual nature of the forces that eventually overthrow him. The dictator is utterly bemused by the fact that his successful opponent is a young Communist of no very obvious physical endowments. Nevertheless, the latter has few reservations about applying the European-derived method of Marxism to solve the problems that exist in the marvellous 'barbarism' of Latin America. In the end, for all his artfulness and sexual vigour, the deposed dictator finds that it is his once-despised people who possess genuine reserves of power that come from remaining true to their cultural origins – for example, his much-abused indigenous servant-mistress Elmira gains the upper hand and provides some vestiges of cultural authenticity for the old dictator in his lonely Parisian exile.

La consagración de la primavera ('Rite of Spring'), 1978, attempts to bring together, in a grand synthesis, all his major themes so as to show how they are resolved positively with the triumph of the Cuban Revolution. The movement is from alienation towards authenticity, thanks to the healing powers of revolutionary consciousness. The novel consists of interwoven experiences of two main characters: Enrique, a product of the Cuban upper class who has fought in the Spanish Civil War and remains sentimentally attached to left-wing politics, and the apolitical Vera, a Russian dancer whose family fled the 1917 Revolution and who is entirely dedicated to her art. After the defeat of the Spanish Republic, they fall in love and marry but the pointlessness of their bourgeois existence eventually drives them apart: the left-wing Enrique is unfaithful to his wife with his louche aristocratic cousin Teresa in what is portrayed as the capitalist hell-hole of New York. When Vera finds out about her husband's repeated infidelities she is crushed by his cynicism and leaves Havana for a remote corner of Cuba, abandoning her musical career altogether. Her ambition had been to create a ballet of Stravinsky's *Rite of Spring*, avoiding the 'effeminacy' of the Diaghilev-Nijinsky production by using black dancers and drawing upon the virile power she had once seen displayed at a voodoo dance. However, thanks to the success of the Cuban Revolution, husband and wife are reconciled: the *Rite of Spring* can be performed after Vera regains her respect for Enrique, who has been wounded while repelling the invaders at the Bay of Pigs. In the last chapters of the novel, Carpentier's writing essays the heroic mode in an effort to achieve that epic quality he had come to believe was still available to the Latin American narrative artist. Whether it comes off (and it has been much criticized) depends on the extent to which the reader is prepared to accept the authenticating effects of the Revolution. Just as 'the marvellous presupposes a faith', so too does the resolution of 'Rite of Spring'.

Strangely enough, there is no analysis of the forces that

made the Revolution. If in *Reasons of State*, a similar lack of analysis could be attributed to the limitations of the dictator's personalist approach to power, here the technique of the interior monologue reduces the reader to the airless confines of two middle-class·bohemian minds, rehearsing at great length and without benefit of wit, their multiple dissatisfactions with love, sex, art, music and dance under twentieth-century capitalism. The form of the novel, therefore, has an in-built bias towards subjective individualism which gives it a diffuse, idealist quality, notwithstanding the fact that the Revolution is presented as the critical agent of change. It is here that one can appreciate the extent to which Carpentier remained a modernist writer even though he had moved ideologically towards socialism.

In his last short novel, *El arpa y la sombra* ('The Harp and the Shadow'), 1979, Carpentier debunks the basic European myth about Latin America which justified the mission to 'civilize' the indigenous people of the continent – the belief that Christopher Columbus's discovery was a sign of divine favour. The novel focuses on attempts to have the Admiral canonized by the Church. Yet there is something wilfully transgressive about the humour (Columbus, for example, goes to bed with Isabella of Castile), as if Carpentier were debauching the image of the Discoverer in order to disown him as the legitimate father of Latin America. However, this is done not so much in order to clarify the actual material realities of history as to keep in place, by implication, a counter-myth created by the liberal élites after Independence – the view of America as the authentic mother whose offspring lived somehow undefiled by history, blissfully at rest in the bosom of time until ravaged by the intrusion of the Spaniards.

This profoundly unhistorical idea entails the repudiation

of Latin America's European heritage as false and alienating, and it is surprising to find Carpentier returning to such a theme after having written novels like *Explosion in a Cathedral* or *Reasons of State*. However, the idealist counter-myth may have survived so tenaciously because, in the final analysis, it sustains the intellectual construct, based on the opposition between 'authenticity' and 'alienation', which informs the whole of Carpentier's work. After all, the success of the Cuban Revolution confirmed his deeply ingrained view of history as a quest for a lost paradise, for the redemption of an essential identity in the future. In this respect, the Revolution revived in Carpentier the wish to move beyond the ironic ambiguities of the novel towards the heroic modes of epic or romance.

Alejo Carpentier's origins as a writer were in the nationalist avant-garde of the 1920s. He sought to do what had largely eluded writers since Independence, namely to contribute to the creation of an authentic cultural identity for Latin America. His fiction, therefore, records the struggle of the novelist trying to regain the faculties of myth-maker and praise-singer in the spiritual waste land of the modern world. Inevitably, he came up against some of the major cultural issues of the twentieth century and, in coming to terms with them, the native Caribbean inflections of his narrative voice were to acquire a universal resonance.

Jorge Luis Borges:
A View from the Periphery

John King

Europeans were surprised at the universality of Borges, but none of them realized that this cosmopolitanism was, and could only be, the point of view of a Latin American. The eccentricity of Latin America can be defined as a European eccentricity: I mean, it is an *other* way of being Western. A non-European way. Both inside and outside the European tradition, the Latin American can see the West as a totality, and not with the fatally provincial vision of the French, the German, the English or the Italian.[1]

In this quotation, part of a homage to Jorge Luis Borges, who died in 1986, the Mexican writer Octavio Paz stresses the importance of Borges in the development of Latin American fiction. In his view, Borges is significant, not because he has proclaimed a distinctive, nationalist, Argentine or Latin American culture, but because he stresses the advantages of the 'periphery'. To be on the periphery is to experience both a nostalgia for a centre but also the freedom of distance: inside and outside at the same time.[2] From this location, the Argentine writer can declare his patrimony to be culture of the universe, not enclosed within the narrow confines of a country or a continent.

The work of Borges is a constant provocation. In his

essays, short stories and poems, he is quietly polemical – undermining nationalism, the realist novel, philosophical rigour, the Academy, regimes and ideologies that purport to explain the world as a totality; questioning, with mock seriousness, accepted definitions and cultural codes. He explores the broadest themes, but always within the strict confines of a few pages. The rigour of his craft, the purity of his writing and the breadth of his reading – he has always declared himself to be a reader rather than a writer – have caused him to be widely recognized as the most important Latin American writer of the century. Other writers all acknowledge their debt to him. In 1969, the Mexican Carlos Fuentes stated:

> The end effect of Borges' prose, without which there simply would not be a Spanish American novel, is to attest, first of all that Latin America lacks a language and consequently that it should create one. To do this, Borges shuffles the genres, rescues all traditions, eliminates the bad habits and creates a new order of rigorousness . . . [3]

To trace the development and impact of Borges's writing, therefore, is to trace the main trends in twentieth-century Latin American fiction.

THE FAMILY CODE

Borges had British ancestors, he spoke English with a slight Northumberland accent and was also fluent in Old English. In his later years, one of his favourite tests for an English-speaking visitor requesting an interview was to see if s/he recognized the Lord's Prayer in Old English. He was brought up bilingual and there is a constant tension in his work between his Hispanic and his British antecedents – the tension between barbarism and civilization, to use a phrase made famous in mid-nineteenth-century Argentina by the writer–politician, Domingo Faustino Sarmiento, who saw the country as the site of a Manichean clash between American barbarism and European civilization. If barbarism was to be found in the streets outside his house, Borges describes his sheltered childhood as growing up in 'a garden, behind a speared railing, and in a library of unlimited English books'.[4]

The world of the library, its enclosed space, could offer the pleasures of reading in different languages and it cultivated a heterodox, independent spirit. Yet Borges was also attracted to the 'reality' of the streets outside, and would try to capture its elemental and most laconically savage details: some of his stories and poems are populated by the imagined inhabitants and atmosphere of the 'South': knife-fighters, men of courage, hoodlums, the brothels, the tango, the possibility of meeting an 'American destiny' in futile but valiant, violent death.

In the same way, Borges creates Argentine history from a pantheon of ancestral heroes. His ancestors helped to fight for Argentine Independence in the early nineteenth century against the cancer of dictatorship which Borges sees as endemic in Argentine society. In his writing, as V. S. Naipaul observes, there is a 'utopian fantasy of "republics, cavalry and morning" . . . of the battles fought, the fatherland established, the great city created and "the streets with names recurring from the past in my blood".'[5] References to these ancestors abound, a simple honourable tradition of righteous struggle. Yet Argentine history can also be shameful, since it spawns the cyclical dictatorships of the nineteenth-century Rosas, or of Perón in the twentieth century. In such conditions, as we shall see, Borges feels that it is one of the duties of the writer to 'commit' himself.

In his cultivation of Argentine history as a family affair, and in his mythologizing of the city and inhabitants of Buenos Aires, Borges constantly meditates on his responsibility as an Argentine writer. Those critics who see in Borges a precursor of structuralist, post-structuralist and deconstructionist criticism prefer to leave him in the father's library, the pure, enclosed space of fiction, of limitless texts. Such an approach is valid, but it puts to one side the complex, contradictory family references, which are socially coded.

Borges assimilated all these different experiences and readings within the rigid structures of an Edwardian childhood. He later made sense of them by adopting a technique strongly reminiscent of that favourite pastime taught by English nannies: the scrapbook. In this framework, eclectic choices could be given a new order and a new meaning. Borges would always wilfully juxtapose the most varied readings, often ignoring the canonical texts of literature in favour of his own preferences, always asserting his own traditions. Such radical 'intertextuality' – to employ a phrase that Borges would never have heard and certainly never used – would have a profound influence on subsequent generations.

THE EARLY WRITING

Borges travelled with his family to Europe in 1914, when he was fifteen, and did not return to Buenos Aires until 1921. He lived in Switzerland and Spain, he learnt Latin, French and German, became acquainted with the modernist movements in Europe and began to write. He was thus well equipped to become an active member of the literary avant-garde which emerged in Buenos Aires and in other capital cities of Latin America in the 1920s. Perry Anderson has argued that modernism in art and literature occurs at a very specific socio-political conjuncture:

> European modernism in the first years of this century thus flowered in the space between a still-usable classical past, a still indeterminate technical present and a still unpredictable political future. Or, put another way, it arose at the intersection between a semi-aristocratic ruling order, a semi-industrialized capitalist economy and a semi-emergent, or semi-insurgent labour movement.[6]

Certainly in Argentina these conditions applied. There was a cultural academy, working within an aristocratic State, against which the vanguard could react. Argentina was living a period of prosperity, one of the richest nations in the world as a result of having entered into the world division of labour as an important part of the informal British Empire. In the cultural sphere, there was a strong press, a community of writers, a consolidated reading public and an expanding university. One can also see in Argentina the beginnings of export-led industrialization and consumerism (the mirage of the American way of life and the new technologies of the second industrial revolution that so obsessed the modernists), although once again it would take until the 1960s for the marketplace to develop fully. Finally, there was the imaginative proximity of social revolution with the Mexican Revolution, student reforms in the Argentine University of Córdoba, and the attraction of Bolshevism. In 1921, a youthful Borges could be found writing poems in praise of revolution: 'Bolshevik Epic' and 'Russia'.

The vanguard movement in Buenos Aires was full of youthful iconoclasm and pastiche but it did not generate many literary works of lasting value, nor did it threaten the solid structures of Argentine society, with its climate of sexual and moral repression, its apoliticism and its powerful State. Perhaps most importantly it helped to legitimate the idea of the professional writer, not in an economic sense (it was impossible to live from writing: Borges's father paid for the publication of his early works and Borges did not even consider trying to sell any copies), but in the writer's perception of himself as a writer and of literature as a craft with its own separate rules rather than the divertissement of statesmen and politicians. The vanguard also provided Borges with opportunities to begin his life-long attack on the dogmas of the literary Academy. He began to question simple, social readings of literature, mocking the earnest pious radicals of the time (the so called Boedo group, named after a working-class district in Buenos Aires) who proclaimed an easy correspondence between literature and the social text.

Borges was frantically busy in the 1920s. He contributed to every little magazine of the period and published, up to 1930, seven books of poetry and essays. Although he later rejected these texts as naïve, they reveal the dominant obsessions of his later work: a lateral view of life and literature, perceived from 'las orillas' (the outskirts) of Buenos Aires and an analysis of the problems of authorship and of the individual consciousness. He wrote in 1925,

I'm thinking of proving that personality is a dream, created by vanity and custom, but without any metaphysical support or inner reality. I thus wish to apply to literature the consequences that follow from these premises and construct an aesthetic hostile to the psychologism that we have inherited from the previous century.[7]

Such an aesthetic would lead him away from 'realistic' description, although in the 1920s he was still interested in developing his own mythological world of Buenos Aires and its inhabitants. By 1930, he had written a biography of a popular poet, Evaristo Carriego, without ever describing the man, arguing that figures such as Carriego are merely the sum of the books written by them or about them. Similarly, the 'characters' in *The Universal History of Infamy* (*Historia universal de la infamia*), 1935 are an elaborate series of masks and disguises. His writing in this period also reveals a consistent interest in the problems of philosophy and logic.

TOWARDS A THEORY OF FANTASTIC LITERATURE

The optimism of the 1920s came to an end in Argentina with the Great Slump, a military coup and the beginnings of what has been termed the 'Infamous Decade' of Argentine history, when elections were rigged and power was maintained in a direct and brutal form. In terms of fiction, the 1930s is a somewhat barren decade throughout Spanish America, with very little relief from a dull, realistic, regionalist aesthetic. Throughout this time Borges worked quietly towards his magisterial short stories of the late 1930s and early 1940s. He wrote book reviews and short essays, for the literary magazine *Sur* – the major journal of the twentieth century in Latin America[8] – and for a time edited his own literary pages in a popular magazine *El Hogar*. It was at the end of the decade, however, that he moved quietly onto the offensive, publishing in quick succession a series of significant essays, prologues and short stories. In an Argentina influenced by clericalism, nationalism and military might, in a world held in the grip of totalitarian orders and in a literary establishment dominated by dull realist writers such as Manuel Gálvez, Borges began to undermine the foundations of such systems. In a mainly complimentary review of Luis Saslavsky's film *La Fuga* ('The Flight'), he wrote in 1937, 'To idolize a ridiculous scarecrow because it is autochthonous, to fall asleep for the fatherland, to take pleasure in tedium because it is a national product all seem absurd to me'.[9] In repeated articles he warned against the dangers of nationalist autarchy.

Borges also equated nationalism with the realist text. In the preface to a work by his close friend Adolfo Bioy Casares, *The Invention of Morel* (*La invención de Morel*), 1940, a beautifully wrought short novel about a man on a desert island who falls in love with a woman who is later revealed as a holographic image, Borges lambasts novelists and critics who uphold the tenets of the 'psychological' novel. Such a form, he states, 'would have us forget that it is a verbal artifice . . . The adventure story, on the other hand, does not propose to be a transcription of reality: it is an artifical object, no part of which lacks justification'.[10] At the same time Borges published two short stories, 'Pierre Menard, Author of the Quixote' and 'Tlön, Uqbar, Orbis Tertius', and edited with Bioy Casares and his wife Silvina Ocampo an anthology of fantastic literature. In a prologue to this anthology Bioy helps us to locate his friend's work. Borges, he argues, has created 'a new literary genre which is both essay and fiction; they are exercises of unceasing intelligence and fortunate imagination, lacking all languor, all human elements, pathetic or sentimental . . . aimed at intellectual readers, interested in philosophy and almost specialists in literature'.[11] Deliberately polemical in tone, Bioy offers the fantastic as an antidote to the realist text and sees in Borges's work a twentieth-century form of the fantastic, one in which horror and fear have been replaced by literary and metaphysical speculation. All fantastic texts question and subvert the real, the monological vision of the realist text and single or unitary ways of perceiving the world. In the nineteenth century, a gradual displacement of residual supernaturalism and magic and increasingly secularized thought produced very different interpretations of fantasy: demonology was replaced by psychology to explain 'otherness'. By the twentieth century, fantastic texts had become increasingly non-referential, concerned not so much with the relationship between language and the real world 'outside' the text, as with a quest for fictional autonomy.[12] Bioy sees Borges as in the vanguard of such a movement, which 'creates and satisfies a desire for a literature that talks about literature and abstract thought'.[13]

A form of literature particularly appropriate for an attack on the realist text is detective fiction. The detective story is a form in which the relevance or the necessity of the content should not be in doubt. Its construction is such that every presence in the book, animate or inanimate, is a clue and not an intrusion for the purposes of atmosphere or naturalism. The reader, like the detective himself, has to interpret everything as evidence, and as the amount of evidence grows, so the hypotheses accounting for it must constantly be renewed. In attacking the psychological novel, Borges reminded novelists that they had forgotten how to tell a story. He has often remarked that if one reads detective stories and then takes up novels afterwards, the latter appear shapeless.

This interest in plots and plotting is linked to literary

form, but also to Borges's view of history and of systems. Plots are seductive in themselves, they have a formal elegance which captivates the reader through the writer's skill and control. Yet at the same time Borges encourages the sceptical belief that any order is plotting and therefore contingent. In fiction, the writer may control causality, but how can we know that a God or economic forces have inscribed causality in history and in the world, especially in a world gripped by the evil plots of totalitarian regimes? It should be remembered that Borges's best-known short stories are written in the decade of the 1940s, at a moment when it appeared to him that the world had gone mad. In such a world, one response of the writer was to cultivate a radical form of 'ascesis' or withdrawal. 'I write in July 1940,' Borges declared, 'every morning reality comes closer to nightmare. All that is possible is to read pages which do not even allude to reality – cosmogonic fantasies of Olaf Stapledon, works of theology or of metaphysics, verbal discussions or frivolous problems by Ellery Queen or Nicholas Blake'.[14]

In the early 1940s, Borges wrote parodic detective stories with Bioy Casares, under the pseudonym 'Bustos Domecq'; he also edited a series of detective stories (entitled 'The Seventh Circle') for a major publisher. Detection also forms the basis of many of his stories, but unlike the certainties of an Auguste Dupin in Edgar Allan Poe's short story 'The Murders in the Rue Morgue' who can solve a bloody and baffling murder by knowing the hand-span of an orang-outang or the particular knots tied by Maltese sailors, Borges's narrators/detectives set out to decipher the universe with insufficient information, mendacious clues and without the possibility of reaching a satisfactory solution.[15] He offers a relentless critique of pure reason, but also cultivates the view that

contemporary Argentine politics. The nature of Peronism remains a widely debated issue. Certainly at the level of rhetoric, Peronism claimed for itself a new synthesis of democracy, nationalism and industrial development and railed against the undemocratic, dependent Argentine oligarchy. In this climate of populism, Borges had no doubt that Perón was a neo-fascist dictator. Dismissed from his post in the Miguel Cané library by the new regime, he spoke out in 1946: 'Dictatorships foment oppression, dictatorships foment subservience, dictatorships foment cruelty, even more abominable is the fact that they foment stupidity . . . One of the many duties of the writer is to fight against these sad monotonies'.[17] Borges wrote a number of specific anti-Peronist poems and essays. He also resurrected 'Bustos Domecq' with Adolfo Bioy Casares, and wrote two savage satires, 'Monsterfest' and 'His Son's Friend', which were circulated privately and only published with the fall of the regime. Peronism, for Borges, illustrated the gap between civilization and barbarism, élite and mass taste: civilization had to be defended in the face of chaotic, primitive and idiotic forces unleashed by the 'dictator'. When Perón fell in 1955, Borges described the regime in Manichean, culturalist terms. Peronism was quite literally bad art, a substandard music-hall act. 'There were thus two stories: one of a criminal variety made up of prisons, tortures, prostitution, robbery and fires; the other more theatrical, made up of ridiculous events and plots for the consumption of louts.'[18]

This loathing of Perón, expressed in such uncompromis-ingly dismissive and élitist terms, created a problem for socially committed critics in Argentina who might condemn the rather thuggish excesses of the regime, but who could also see that Perón had created better conditions for hitherto neglected sectors of Argentine society. The problem was to become more acute in the 1960s and early 1970s when a young generation of intellectuals committed a form of patricide (very few middle-class groups had previously supported Perón) and saw Perón as a potential leader of a national, populist revolution. These groups dismissed Borges as a tetchy reactionary. Nor did Borges endear himself to left or liberal thought in the 1960s and 1970s: opposing the Cuban revolution at a time, in the early 1960s, when nearly every Latin American intellectual supported Cuba; defending the North American invasion of Santo Domingo; writing poems in praise of the Alamo, with no awareness of the offence that this would cause in Mexico; and receiving an honorary award from Pinochet's hands when the rest of the world condemned the horrors of the coup in Chile. Such wilfulness, increasingly the quirkiness of an old man, was often interpreted quite literally in Latin America as proving Borges's anti-Latin American, anti-democratic stance, hindering an appreciation of the truly radical implications of his writing. His hatred of Perón caused him to dismiss many different mass movements, without any real understanding of the issues involved. Octavio Paz puts it well:

> He was not passionately interested in history nor was he attracted by the study of complex human societies. His political opinions were moral and even aesthetic judgements. Although he voiced them with courage and rectitude, he did so without really understanding what was going on around him.[19]

THE WRITER AS SUPERSTAR

One of the reasons why Borges upset so many people with his facile epigrams was that by the 1960s he was one of the best-known figures in Latin America and probably the most respected Latin American writer in the world. A writer who in the mid 1930s could boast ironically that he had sold thirty-seven copies of a book was, by the mid 1960s, a literary superstar. After forty years, a wide audience finally recognized the importance of his work. Ironically, fame came to him at a time when he had been forced to give up writing short stories due to increasing blindness – from 1955 to 1970, his main literary production was poetry, especially sonnets, a form that he could elaborate in his head. Already a significant figure in Latin America by the 1950s, he was awarded, with Samuel Beckett, the distinguished Formentor prize, offered by six Western publishing houses in Europe and America. This recognition, in 1961, guaranteed his translation into many different languages and from this time, the honours and critical attention grew. He now appears in every survey of twentieth-century literature, and even the cinema has begun to quote him. The computer that runs the world in Godard's *Alphaville*, 1965, has clearly read him, as has Nicolas Roeg who directed Mick Jagger in the film *Performance*. When Jagger is finally shot, a photograph of Borges explodes from his head! A homage, of sorts.

In Latin America in the 1960s Borges was recognized as the precursor of the 'boom' of Latin American fiction which is analysed elsewhere in this book in the essays on Cortázar, Fuentes, García Márquez and Vargas Llosa. In the early 1960s, it was unusual for a novel to go into more than one printing of one or two thousand copies. By the end of the decade, well-known writers sold tens of thousands of copies a year. The first publishers of García Márquez's *One Hundred Years of Solitude* were not expecting massive sales: today, the first print run of García Márquez can be up to a million copies. Such interest can be attributed to the quality of the work but also to an expanded readership, especially in urban centres, a more dynamic editorial policy and an increased attention from newspapers and newsweekly journals eager to market the national product. Borges revelled in this attention, talking to journalists about anything, '*tocando sus discos*' ('playing his records'), repeating with shifts of emphasis his own idiosyncratic view of literature and of life.

It might well have been this increased attention that took Borges back to writing fiction in the 1970s. Certainly, after so many years of relative isolation, he was aware of a new and expanding audience (however much he might protest to the contrary, as in his introduction to *The Book of Sand* in 1975). The 1970s saw two new anthologies, *Dr Brodie's Report* (*El informe de Brodie*), 1970, and *The Book of Sand* (*El libro de arena*), which Borges proclaimed as 'realist', but which are in practice just as ironic and subversive as his earlier work. In his final years he continued to write poems, articles and the occasional story. He also began to travel the world in a more relentless fashion, conscious that he had very few years to visit those places which had always populated his dreams and writings. He died in June 1986, in Geneva, the city where as an adolescent he had learnt new languages and developed his heterodox reading.

NOTES

1. Octavio Paz, 'El arquero, la flecha y el blanco', *Vuelta*, no. 117 (August 1986), pp. 26–9.
2. See Silvia Molloy, *Las letras de Borges*, Buenos Aires, 1979.
3. Carlos Fuentes, *La nueva novela hispano americana*, Mexico, 1969, p. 26.
4. *Evaristo Carriego*, Buenos Aires, 1930, p. 9.
5. V. S. Naipaul, *The Return of Eva Perón*, London, 1980, p. 129.

6. Perry Anderson, 'Modernity and Revolution', *New Left Review*, March–April 1984, pp. 96–113.
7. *Inquisiciones*, Buenos Aires, 1925, p. 84.
8. See John King, *'Sur': An Analysis of the Argentine Literary Journal and its Role in the Development of a Culture, 1931–1970*, Cambridge, 1986.
9. *'La fuga'*, *Sur* 35, August 1937, pp. 121–2 (p. 121).
10. Prologue, to A. Bioy Casares, *The Invention of Morel*, translated by Ruth Simms, Texas, 1964, pp. 5–6.
11. Prologue to *Antología de la literatura fantástica*, Buenos Aires, 1940, p. 13.
12. See Rosemary Jackson, *Fantasy: the Literature of Subversion*, London, 1981.
13. *Antología de la literatura fantástica*, p. 13.
14. Borges, 'Ellery Queen, *The New Adventures of Ellery Queen*', *Sur* 70, July 1940, pp. 61–2 (p. 62).
15. See David Gallagher's chapter on Borges in *Modern Latin American Literature*, Oxford, 1973.
16. 'Julio Cortázar en la Universidad Central de Venezuela', *Escritura* No. 1, Jan–June 1976, p. 162.
17. Borges, *Sur* 142, August 1946, pp. 114–15.
18. Borges, 'L'illusion comique', *Sur* 237, pp. 9–10 (p. 9).
19. Octavio Paz, op.cit., p. 27.

João Guimarães Rosa: An Endless Passage

Charles A. Perrone

The undisputed master of modern Brazilian narrative is
João Guimarães Rosa (1908–67). Author of seven volumes of
fiction ranging from brief sketches to an encyclopaedic
novel, Rosa traversed well-mapped literary terrain and
charted new directions for artistic expression. He defied
the frontier between 'regionalist' and 'universal'
approaches to fiction, achieved an unparalleled transformation of Brazilian literary language, and prompted ceaseless
waves of critical reaction. Terms such as experimentalism,
transrealism, transcendental or universal regionalism and
instrumentalism have been used in an effort to categorize
Rosa's singular work. His fictional world is the *sertão* of the
state of Minas Gerais, a vast and mysterious backland in the
Brazilian interior. Rosa's hinterland is home to magical
wayfarers, mythical figures and quixotic adventures; the
badlands of his *sertão* spawn epic battles between gun-
slingers and rustic philosophers. Using the peculiar linguistic varieties of the remote regions of Minas Gerais as a
base, Rosa incorporated and invented diverse elements in
the creation of a unique and highly poetic narrative prose.
Both this synthetic literary language and the speculative
ideal plane of his stories distinguish João Guimarães Rosa
in the sphere of contemporary Brazilian letters.

When Rosa published his first volume of stories, *Sagarana*, in 1946, he challenged and surpassed the mimetic

regionalism that had been dominant in Brazil. Critics recognized in this collection an inventive style and an invigorating reformulation of the art of storytelling. It was not until 1956 that Rosa published his second work, *Corpo de Baile*, often rendered as 'Corps de Ballet' in English-language commentary. Subsumed under this general title are seven narratives which further develop the stylistic idiosyncrasies of the first work. Rosa's monumental *The Devil to Pay in the Backlands (Grande Sertão: Veredas)* also appeared in 1956. Widely held to be one of the greatest Latin American novels, this vast neologistic epic was dubbed the 'first metaphysical novel of Brazilian literature'.[1] No single work has so absorbed Brazilian critics as this epoch-making novel. Rosa returned to the domain of short fiction in 1962 with the publication of *The Third Bank of the River and Other Stories (Primeiras Estórias)*, a collection of twenty-one short stories.[2] Condensation is essential in the following work *Tutaméia (Terceiras Estórias)*, ('Trifle (Third Stories)') 1967, consisting of forty brief tales and four interspersed prefaces which constitute Rosa's *ars poetica*. The posthumous work *Estas Estórias*, 1969, (These Stories) was organized before Rosa's death. The last work *Ave, Palavra*, 1970, (Hail, Word) comprises miscellanea: stories previously published in periodicals, diary entries, diverse notes, sketches, vignettes, and poetry. In the works published in his lifetime, there is a cumulative process of radicalization in Rosa's prose and approach to fiction.

Sagarana comprises a cycle of nine long stories or novellas. The title is an amalgam of the Scandinavian word '*saga*' and a Tupy (indigenous Brazilian tongue) suffix meaning 'rough, crude' or 'in the manner of'. This dual appellation prefigures the linguistic and thematic inter-relations of the series of tales. Before each story, Rosa places carefully chosen epigraphs which encode narrative formulas applied in the text and crystallize the story's 'metaphysical dimension'.[3] Each tale has one or more subplots, framed anecdotes or 'deviations' from the development of the central conflict. The significance of these 'secondary' lines is seen in relation to other stories or to the cycle as a whole; recurring structural motifs such as the personal quest, honour, love, poetry and witchcraft link narrative settings and thematic spheres. All the tales are set in the *sertão*, providing insight into the human and physical geography of the region, yet are encompassed within a broader symbolic vision of destiny and endeavour. A cogent analysis by Stephanie Merrim shows *Sagarana* to be an interwoven 'story system'. Though diverse on the surface level of action, the stories all represent transgressions of the harmony of nature and the restoration of equilibrium through man's 'merging with nature in some way'.[4] Merrim's study illustrates both the higher 'spiritual' plane of Rosa's 'regionalist' tales and their paradigmatic unity.

The first readers of *Sagarana* were struck by the novelty and power of Rosa's language. The author mixes the lexical and syntactic peculiarities of rustic *sertão* speech with other aspects of Brazilian idiomatic expression, and shapes innumerable new words. More striking is the orchestrated use of poetic devices such as onomatopoeia, alliteration, echoing, internal rhyme, rhythmic structuring and metrical patterns. Some passages comprise poetic forms rendered in consecutive prose lines. In the story 'São Marcos' ('Woodland Witchery') the narrator discovers some verses carved on bamboo stalks and responds to the unknown poet by writing the names of ten Assyrian and Babylonian kings on another stalk. These names, as Rosa's narrator says, constitute poetry in and of themselves because they have *canto e plumagem*, song and plumage. This passage is an early articulation of the author's sound-based poetic theory. While much of the poetry in Rosa's narrative prose is inevitably lost in translation, this episode comes across effectively in English. Rosa's notions of poetic prose, related to his concept of nature's purity, is perhaps most evident in *Sagarana*, but underlies all of his narrative output.

The poetic qualities in the stories of *Sagarana* clearly distinguish Rosa from the essentially realist, regionalist novelists who formed the second generation of Brazilian Modernism beginning in 1928.[5] Writers such as José Lins do Rego and Jorge Amado sought to infuse their novels with 'Brazilianness', to document the specific language, culture, and problems endemic to the North-east region. Folk speech was attributed to characters as a part of socio-historical portraits, but authors did not assume dialectal diction as their own. In the novel of the North-east, the referential function of language is dominant. The works are characteristically linear in construction, with an emphasis on exterior social reality, and are often informed by an attitude of denunciation. Rosa, on the other hand, eschews the logical and rational bias at the core of region-alist fiction and follows a more subjective fictional time. He assumes a playful stance toward language, using folk speech not just to reflect regional character but also as a point of departure for the creation of a *sui generis* literary idiolect. *Sagarana*, moreover, reveals the *sertão* both as a rural setting for the playing out of intriguing dramas and as a symbolic space to explore man's destiny and solitude.

The narratives of the voluminous *Corpo de Baile*, unavailable in English translation, are difficult to classify according to genre. The seven titles that form the collection were originally released in two volumes, subsequently in a single tome, and finally as three books. In each version, the author offers a table of contents before and after the texts; the works are alternately called 'poems', 'stories', and 'novels'. Recognizing the figurative and sonorous qualities of the prose Rosa employs in his storytelling, Jon Vincent adopts the terms 'tale' and 'proem', from the coined Portuguese critical term *prosoema*, to refer to these dense and difficult narratives.[6] The term 'narrative prosetry' might be added to the critical arsenal needed to attack Rosa's 'ballet' of prose fictions, which, like poetry, resist paraphrase.

The stylistic acrobatics initiated in *Sagarana* become more complex in *Corpo de Baile*. There is a vast array of regionalisms, obscure lexical items, syntactic inversions and rhetorical devices. Rosa's prose is convoluted, ornamental, playful – in a word, baroque. The adventures and dramas enacted in the *sertão* suggest both the medieval or feudal character of the region and the mythical quality of its tales and personages. In the individual narratives and in the series as a whole, there is a complex web of folk motifs, mythical structures, and symbologies, often associated with a pantheistic or animistic outlook. Rosa's concern with authenticity, essences, illusory appearance, psychic and psychological phenomena is evident at every turn. The polyvalent inhabitants of Rosa's fictional *sertão* are frequently marginal types, eccentrics, deranged cowboys, children or poets, who operate from unconventional perspectives.

The narrative 'Campo Geral' ('Field of the High Plain') illustrates Rosa's propensity for creating youthful characters, as well as his preoccupation with the issue of perception. The story is filtered through the eyes of Miguilim, a sensitive boy who sounds human conflicts, and attempts to unravel questions of morality, emotional loss, natural order and aesthetics. During his first venture outside his faraway corner of the *sertão*, he seeks to determine if his town is 'beautiful' or 'ugly' as different people have told him. In the final sequence of the wandering narrative, a country doctor realizes that the boy suffers from myopia. Wearing the doctor's glasses, Miguilim rediscovers the world and finds a symbolic clarity. While the boy's near-sightedness has limited his world-view, he now prepares to embark on a new life. Sharpened vision brings both solutions and new questions. The prospect of enhanced perception is sufficient to blur the difference between happiness and sadness, a seemingly clear opposition in the story until the conclusion.

In the mainstreams and tangential currents of *Corpo de Baile* Rosa introduces many of the themes and motifs that form the vertebrae of his masterpiece *The Devil to Pay in the Backlands*. The title refers, again, to the Brazilian backlands and to the streams that run through those expanses and form fertile valleys, oases in the dry, scrub brush region. The title of the English translation is closer to Rosa's subtitle, *O diabo na rua no meio do redemoinho* (The devil in the street in the middle of the whirlwind). Man's relation to the devil is one of the main thrusts of the novel. The first-person narrator is Riobaldo, a retired gunslinger who tells his gripping life story to an implied listener, a learned gentleman from the city.[7] As Riobaldo narrates his adventures with rival bands of gunmen, he reflects endlessly in an effort to determine whether, in his vengeful pursuit of a rival, he made a pact with the devil. In this sense, the novel is a reformulation of the Faust legend in the context of the Brazilian 'Wild West'. The narration involves the tracking of warring factions, the unfolding of Riobaldo's intimacy with his companion Diadorim, and accounts of amorous affairs. The profundity

122

of *The Devil to Pay in the Backlands* resides in the spheres of transformed language and philosophical speculation.

The action of the novel bears resemblance to a Western, yet it is a complex and difficult novel, even for native Brazilian readers.[8] The form of the chapterless book is not unlike the disorienting expanses of the setting itself. At the outset, a considerable span of the monological oral narration is akin to stream of consciousness. As Riobaldo evokes his earlier life, subjective time and free association dominate. He leaps forward and backward in time without contextualizing or orienting his listener. Events, descriptive passages, interpretations, and apostrophes to the interlocutor seem to be mixed indiscriminately as Riobaldo explains the mysteries of the *sertão*, the beliefs and behaviour of its strange inhabitants, his own relationships and his role in the wars of armed bands in the early twentieth century. By the time the narrator's tale assumes chronological form, all the major motifs of the novel have been introduced; with their subsequent development, multiple perspectives are generated rather than unilateral consistency.

The Devil to Pay in the Backlands is a challenging work because of its temporal dislocations, the variety of narrative constituents, and the radicalization of diction and exposition. The idiolect of Rosa's narrator here is especially distinctive, and occasionally impenetrable. Riobaldo is a native of the backlands of Minas Gerais, whose dialect is marked by regionally specific vocabulary (notably, terms for flora, fauna, and geographical accidents), anachronistic usage and grammatical deviation. While this picturesque and non-standard 'sertão-ese' is at the root of Riobaldo's speech, his tongue reflects many influences. Rosa endows his narrator with unusual mental acumen, a phenomenal memory and an alert imagination. Riobaldo has had some schooling and exposure to literature; he absorbs the linguistic practices of diverse people (ranchers, illiterate gunmen, trailblazers, educators, religious teachers, folk with non-hinterland origins); and he is a poet. These are among the many sources reflected in his oral prose. Through Riobaldo, Rosa explores and exploits the virtualities of language. Prefixes and suffixes are freely attached, often in defamiliarizing ways. There are unusual nominalizations, adjectivizings, and verbalizations. Local items and Indianisms are used alongside arcane and erudite terms, and derivations from several foreign languages (Latin, English, Oriental tongues, etc) appear. Original compound words and countless neologisms punctuate the verbal flow. Rosa's discourse is also characterized by the use of poetic devices, such as those employed in *Sagarana* and *Corpo de Baile*, and by all manner of grammatical and syntactical twists and turns.[9] In a stylistic rendering, a typical passage would look something like the following:

> Lesser, don't think that religion minishes. Think the contrary, sir. Visibly, those other times, I'd picture-chalk that caroas flock the flowers. Yep, my pasture's good . . . Youth. But youth is a task to deny later. Also, if I'd been given to think so much so vague, I'd be losing the hand-of-a-man I had to heated handling, in the middle of everyone. But, now'days, I've reasoned, a chain-gang of thoughts, ain't no reason to think lower of my competence with a firin' iron. Le'ssee. Vamoose. Bring 'em on let 'em come at me with their war, cold couriers, other laws, eyes to spare, I'll still cast the lot and set this zone on fire, if so ow ouch! It's in the barrel of a gun: it's in the rat-atat tatoo . . . And you bet all alone by myself I won't be.

Archaic language, characterization and action link *Devil to Pay in the Backlands* with medieval epic literature, many traces of which persist today in the oral and written popular literature of the Brazilian backlands. If Riobaldo is like a singer of heroic deeds, both he and his companions resemble knights errant who pursue purveyors of evil and seek to redress injustices. Descriptions of leaders are reminiscent of heroes of the *chanson de geste*, for example Charlemagne. The values, practices and behaviour of leaders and soldiers, notably trials and the code of honour, recall both the romance of chivalry and courtly literature. There are many other parallels with ancient heroic literature. These resonances fit into a larger scheme of juxtaposition and interplay.

Shifting perspectives and plurisignification are at the foundation of *Devil to Pay in the Backlands*. The narrator's use of the word *sertão* illustrates the plurality that informs the whole of the novel. The *sertão* is first characterized as an enormous geographical expanse and depicted as a stage for violence and lawlessness, where the most powerful and astute rule. At other junctures, Riobaldo uses the term metaphorically and relates it to the realm of thought and contemplation. He says, for instance, 'the *sertão* is when you least expect it', and 'the *sertão* is where our thinking becomes stronger than the power of the place'. These and other variants such as 'the *sertão* is inside of us', suggest the subjective, interpretative significance of the external space. On other occasions, Riobaldo proclaims 'the *sertão* is everywhere' and 'the *sertão* is the size of the world', implying the universal symbolic relevance of what he narrates. The scope of two other leitmotifs that punctuate Riobaldo's act of telling is also progressively expanded. The frequently repeated phrase 'living is a dangerous business' appears in the context of violent confrontations, but is also invoked in connection with the notions of human destiny and the pursuit of elusive knowledge. The related dictum 'narrating is very hard' appears as a kind of justification for the seemingly chaotic form of the story-telling. This phrase also expresses the difficulty Riobaldo experiences in his attempts to order and interpret clearly the many varied actions and reactions of so many forms and figures that cross his paths.

Ambiguity and doubt imbue the whole of Riobaldo's narration. The question of fate is of particular concern to him. Citing the seeming lack of natural vocation, he wonders whether he was 'destined' to become a sharpshooter and the leader of a gang. During his years as a roaming warrior, he wavers between courageous strength and fearfulness, grappling with a sense of guilt associated with having been an outlaw and a killer. Above all, he is preoccupied with the questions of whether the devil exists and whether he could have made a pact with him. At alternating junctures, Riobaldo seems to believe or disbelieve in the devil, yet there is no definitive resolution concerning his past and his hope for the salvation of his soul. The scene in which he supposedly made the pact is narrated in a nebulous and inconclusive fashion. Many statements suggest that Riobaldo is telling his story to persuade himself there is no demon. The role of the learned listener, who is presumably free of traditional backland superstitions, is to confirm Riobaldo's idea that the devil does not exist. At the end of his story, the narrator declares as much, but this declaration is followed by a new question and suggestions to the effect that the search for answers has not ended. Major critical studies of the novel find, in the final analysis, that Riobaldo, in his quest for transcendent knowledge, invokes the devil to resolve the mysteries of tales he has not come to terms with, that is, as a heuristic tool to represent all that cannot be explained.

All the characters of *The Devil to Pay in the Backlands* are filtered through the eyes of the lone narrator; relativity and uncertainty mark them too. Riobaldo refers often to a spiritual consultant whose advice has proved to be reliable yet insufficient. The numerous gunmen that roam the backlands, leaders and followers alike, are seen both as murderous bandits and as righteous heroes who follow a special code of honour pursuing just quests. Riobaldo even questions his own portrayal of his arch-enemy Hermógenes as the epitome of evil. The narrator is particularly concerned with his dear companion Diadorim, whom he calls 'his mist'. This central figure is responsible for Riobaldo's commitment to a band of riders. Riobaldo is tortured throughout his years as a gunman because he feels an 'impossible love' for his closest friend. At the conclusion of the definitive battle between opposing bands, Diadorim is discovered to be a woman, a revelation that haunts Riobaldo until the fictional present, the time of narration. Critics have interpreted the central figure of Diadorim in varying ways: as a guardian angel, as temptation (Eve), as an embodiment of ahistorical immanence, as a vehicle of Platonic mysticism. This critical diversity attests to the changing nature of Riobaldo's presentation of Diadorim and to the mutable outlooks of his narration.

In the construction of this monumental work, Rosa draws on numerous sources, notably Luso-Brazilian popular culture, modern and ancient European philosophy and Oriental religions. A multiplicity of elements structure Riobaldo's thinking and speaking; his narration can be put in focus via the values of Christian romance, Greek idealism, esoteric/occult arts and sciences,

Hindu enlightenment, and existentialism. Each of these varied perspectives is adopted by the pantheistic narrator in his incomplete search for truth and salvation. The plural constitution of Riobaldo's narration can be synthesized into an all-embracing duality, central to the world-view forged in *The Devil to Pay in the Backlands*. As Merrim has illustrated, the bipolarity of the narrator, 'half rational thinker, half intuitive warrior, sets off all the other ambiguities of the text'.[10] Riobaldo confronts a heterogeneous and ever-changing world-in-becoming that defies concepts of fixity or absolute truth. Using the analogy of travel, Rosa's narrator asserts that the essence of things is not in departure or arrival, but rather in the movement from one point to another. The central word and image of *The Devil to Pay in the Backlands* is *travessia*, meaning 'traversing', 'crossing', 'passage'. As the crusading gunmen ride across the vast *sertão* chasing after their enemies and their destinies, Riobaldo is in passage through an immense story in search of knowledge and spiritual insight, a crossing whose ultimate destination he does not reach. The last word of the novel is *travessia*, yet this is not the final sign: the text concludes with an infinity symbol ∞. The verbal and graphic conclusion to *The Devil to Pay in the Backlands* is the clearest sign that Riobaldo's quest continues. The end-less novel's final passage is an initiation of renewal.

The text-final infinity symbol of *The Devil to Pay in the Backlands* reappears in the table of contents of *The Third Bank of the River and Other Stories*. For each of the twenty-one stories listed there is a corresponding pictographic 'synopsis' which includes astrological, alchemic and cabalistic signs. The only story without the infinity symbol is 'Nenhum, Nenhuma', which was translated as 'No Man No Woman' but also suggests something like 'none, not any'. This titular play balances infinity with nothingness. The occult graphic presentation (omitted from the North American edition) indicates that the esoteric and symbological undercurrents of Rosa's great novel flow with continuing force through the diverse stories of this collection. There is a calculated structural balance in the organization of the volume; the middle story (Number 11) is 'The Mirror', and stories equidistant from the centrepiece reveal parallels in theme, narrative focus, and motifs.[11] Unlike the expansive and exuberant works of short fiction preceding *The Devil to Pay in the Backlands,* these later tales are condensed and oriented around single occurrences. While the stories and language are less bound to the *sertão,* Rosa's tendencies towards linguistic gamesomeness, elliptical construction and neologistic expression gain greater momentum. The author's themes, characters and prose continue to reflect and stress his unconventional approach to language and fiction.

The personages of *The Third Bank of the River and Other Stories* are almost all exceptional beings who incite or undergo experiences beyond the range of logical expectation, normality or social propriety. Most frequently Rosa paints acutely sensitive children, figures with intense fixations and madmen. The insane are not presented as clinical cases but rather as agents of change or visionaries who open access to the irrational, the unreal, the magical, the poetic. The most representative story of the collection is 'The Third Bank of the River', the tale of a man who abandons his family to spend the rest of his life in a canoe, shuffling up and down the river and between the two banks. The man's son (the retrospective narrator) is perplexed by his father's actions but eventually decides to follow the paternal example. When the moment comes to assume his place in the canoe, however, the son is overcome with fear and flees. In this story Rosa explores the psychology of family relations alongside reactions to the abnormal, fear of the unknown, estrangement and atavistic urges. One reader finds the story to be an existential allegory of man's abandonment by God.[12] From an epistemological perspective, 'The Third Bank of the River' proposes a breakdown in the patterned perceptions of binary logic. The 'third bank' remains an open symbol of creative freedom, the extra-quotidian dimension, and transcendence. Rosa's eternal river crossing (*travessia*), as in the traversing of the great *sertão*, is an all-encompassing image of human experience as flux and dialectical becoming.

The last work Rosa published in his lifetime was *Tutaméia (Terceiras Estórias)*. These 'third stories' appeared, in the author's symptomatically playful manner, without there having been any 'second'. The title word is an apocopation of a colloquial term meaning, with some authorial modesty, 'trifle', but etymologically can be construed as 'everything and a half' or 'all (that is) mine'. Many believe that this collection holds the keys to Rosa's narrative system and concepts of fiction. This belief is founded not so much on the form and content of the volume's forty micro-narratives as on the four prefaces the author strategically distributes among the stories. The first preface, 'Vermicelli and Hermeneutics', contrasts concepts of 'story' and 'anecdote'. In a mini-anthology of humorous tales, Rosa examines the value of nonsense in conjunction with philosophical categories. The forms and functions of what the author calls 'anecdotes of abstraction' are linked to the sublime and to the ontological concept of nothingness. The neologism is the subject of the second preface, as reflected in the title 'Hypotrelic'. This term is applied to a gentleman who is representative of all those who resist inventive language, which is at the core of all Rosa's writings. The third preface, 'We the Inebriated', comprises a series of drunk jokes. More than simple absurd humour, these comic episodes suggest connections between poetic transfiguration of reality and the crooked angles of perception of intoxicated people. The longest and most involved of the prefaces is the final one: 'On Toothbrushes and Doubt'. In seven sub-sections, Rosa juxtaposes 'pure' and 'engagé' writers, ponders time and the inadequacies of language, hails serendipity, assails routine and useless habits, and confronts the interplay of illusion and reality. The prefaces aim, as one of the author's epigraphs indicates, to provoke 'a suspension of judgement'. Rosa seeks to apply 'a jolt of unreality which disturbs readers' preconceived rational notions and impels them to make the crossing – the *travessia* – from one concept of reality to another'.[13] In his penetrating art of preface, Rosa effaces Cartesian coherence, linear exposition, and the controls of grammarians, radicalizing his assault on language's substance in his pursuit of the ineffable.

Each of the forty short stories of *Tutaméia* contains an appeal to scepticism and a call for the temporary suspension of the utilitarian outlook. The tales are brief and synthetic, often taking the form of a parable or expanded aphorism. While themes of separation, individualization, isolation and alienation abound, the general climate of the stories is comic. As in previous works, many of Rosa's characters are depicted on the edges or outer limits of sanity and normality. Grouped according to their prefaces, there are four narrative blocks: stories that gloss the theme of illusion versus reality, stories involving the concept of nothingness, stories featuring altered states of perception, and stories that reveal linguistic metamorphoses.

The most celebrated story of Rosa's posthumous

collection *Estas Estórias* (These Stories) is a tale of transformation. In 'Meu Tio o Iauaretê' ('My Uncle the True-Jaguar'), the narrative situation, like that of *The Devil to Pay in the Backlands*, involves a solicitous backlander who speaks uninterruptedly to an implied listener from 'civilized' Brazil. Son of a white settler and an Indian mother, the speaker tells how he was employed to rid the region of wildcats (jaguars) but came to identify with and protect them. In the course of the narration, he becomes cat-like and his Portuguese is increasingly 'contaminated' with the native Tupy tongue. By the story's end, the narrator's utterances consist of howls and growls. Rosa's search for primordial expression leads him to explore the sonority and mythical sources of Amerindian language. This jaguar-story is representative of Rosa's literary endeavours, for the zoomorphization of the narrator and the metamorphosis of his speech are processes of discovery and authentication through experimentation and returns to nature.

João Guimarães Rosa has achieved the status of a demi-god in Brazilian literature. Yet his place in the 'boom' of contemporary Latin American narrative has not received full recognition. The fervour Rosa stirs and the command he respects in Brazil have not had truly pan-American repercussions.[14] This is due, to some degree, to the lamentable separation of Spanish-American and Brazilian cultural affairs, but may also be partially attributed to Rosa's stylistic extravagance, which makes translation an unusually formidable task. Only *The Devil to Pay in the Backlands* and *The Third Bank of the River and Other Stories* exist in Spanish translation. Works of the stature of *Corpo de Baile* and *Tutaméia* have not yet been translated into English, and an ambitious 'linguistic' rendering of Rosa's cosmic novel of the Brazilian backlands would be welcome. Readers everywhere face the challenge of attaining a command of Portuguese so that they may then embark on a journey within a journey towards Rosa's 'third bank' of transcendent literary expression. *The Devil to Pay in the Backlands*, novelistic passage that concludes without end, remains a permanent critical project and is worthy of standing, alongside such works as *Don Quixote* and *Ulysses*, as a monument of universal literature. For, as Guimarães Rosa said, 'in the *sertão* the language of Goethe, Dostoevsky and Flaubert is spoken', and, as Riobaldo says, 'the *sertão* is everywhere'.

NOTES

1. José Carlos Garbuglio, quoted by Paulo Rónai, 'Trajetória de uma obra', in *Guimarães Rosa Seleta*, Rio de Janeiro, José Olympio, 1973, p. 149. The English translation of the novel is by James L. Taylor and Harriet de Onis, New York, Alfred A. Knopf, 1963. All original editions are by José Olympio Editora, Rio de Janeiro.
2. English translation by Barbara Shelby, *The Third Bank of the River and Other Stories*, New York, Alfred A. Knopf, 1968.
3. Franklin de Oliveira, preface to João Guimarães Rosa, *Sagarana*, tr. Harriet de Onis, New York, Alfred A. Knopf, 1966, p. viii.
4. Stephanie Merrim, 'Sagarana: A Story System', *Hispania*, 66:4, 1983, p. 504.
5. On the neo-realist novel of Brazilian Modernism, see Fred P. Ellison, *Brazil's New Novel – Four Northeastern Masters*, Berkeley, University of California Press, 1954.
6. Jon S. Vincent, *João Guimarães Rosa*, Boston, Twayne, 1978, p. 42. This is the best English-language introduction to Rosa's complete work and contains a valuable annotated bibliography.

7. Recent narratological criticism has focused on the importance of the interlocutor in the novel. See especially Maria Tai Wolff, 'The Telling Situation', Ph.D. dissertation, Yale University, 1985, Chapter 3, 'The Narrative In/Im Pact', and Elizabeth Lowe, 'Dialogues of *Grande Sertão: Veredas'*, *Luso Brazilian Review*, 13:2, 1976, pp. 231–44.

8. A dictionary/glossary has been compiled to assist Brazilians with the reading of *Grande Sertão: Veredas*. See Nei Leandro de Castro, *Universo e Vocabulário do Grande Sertão*, Rio de Janeiro, José Olympio, 1970. Another reading aid is Alan Viggiano *Itinerário de Riobaldo Tatarana*, Belo Horizonte, Communiçao-INL/MEC, 1974, which maps the geography and plots.

9. The most complete study of the formal aspects of Rosa's style is Mary Lou Daniel, *João Guimarães Rosa: Travessia Literária*, Rio de Janeiro, José Olympio, 1968. Jon Vincent, op.cit., pp. 71–5, discusses the implications of the formal intricacies of Rosa's prose for translators. He compares a passage of the original with the smoothed-over North American translation and with his own, more literal and, paradoxically, more faithful rendering of the same passage.

10. Stephanie Merrim, *Logos and the Word: The Novel of Language and Linguistic Motivation in* Grande Sertão: Veredas *and* Tres Tristes Tigres, New York, Peter Lang, 1983, p. 16 ff. See also Stephanie Merrim, '*Grande Sertão: Veredas*, A Mighty Maze but Not Without Plan', *Chasqui*, 13:2, Nov. 1983, pp. 32–68. Especially important in the first study is the relationship drawn between the exposition of the novel's philosophical dialectic and Rosa's transformation of language. Major Brazilian studies have used terms such as 'inside-out man', 'the reversibility of the world', the 'moving world', and the 'forms of falsity' to describe the ideological contradictions and structural ambiguities of the novel. See Jon Vincent's annotated bibliography (op.cit. note 6).

11. Consuelo Albergaria, *Bruxo da Linguagem no Grande Sertão*,

Rio de Janeiro, Tempo Brasileiro, 1977, pp. 68–9.

12. David William Foster, 'Major Figures in the Brazilian Short Story', in *The Latin American Short Story – A Critical History*, Boston, Twayne, 1983, pp. 17–19.

13. Stephanie Merrim, 'The Art of Preface in Guimarães Rosa's *Tutaméia*', *Review*, 29, 1981, pp. 10–12. Merrim's critical introduction is followed by a translation of four sub-sections of the fourth preface.

14. The late Uruguayan critic and Yale professor Emir Rodríguez Monegal was a Hispanic champion of Brazilian literature. Monegal said of Guimãraes Rosa: 'He is beyond dispute Latin America's greatest novelist.' *The Borzoi Anthology of Latin American Literature*, Vol. II, New York, Alfred A. Knopf, 1977, p. 679.

Carlos Fuentes: An Interview

John King

I interviewed Carlos Fuentes in Cambridge, November 1986. The discussion was wide-ranging but I was particularly interested in exploring Fuentes's views on the relationship between the cultures of North and South America.

John King

Question. Could you tell me about your continuing interest in North American culture? How much communication is there between North and South?

Answer. I think that there is vastly more intercommunication between the literatures of Anglo America and Ibero America today than when I was a child. I'm a special case, because I grew up in the United States. I was very close to the manifestations not only of the literature of North America, but in general of popular culture. I'm very influenced by the cinema, for example, by radio – there was no television then – by jazz. Then I discovered as a young man that all these influences on my childhood were not privy to me. You have the extraordinary influence of the cinema on Puig, Cabrera Infante and Salvador Elizondo in Mexico or the enormous influence of jazz on Cortázar. The writer I knew who was least influenced by the United States was Alejo Carpentier. In Borges, there is a great influence of Anglo-American culture, even if it is in a sense very narrow: Borges always talks of his love for Chesterton, Kipling, Stevenson.

All this was something of a one-way street. It still is, to an extent. Now that I've edited the Smollett translation of Cervantes, I find that I have brilliant North American friends who cannot read *Don Quixote*, they find it absolutely uninteresting. It's as if I say that I cannot read Chaucer, Shakespeare or John Bunyan, that they are alien to me. They are not alien to me and *Don Quixote* should not be alien to an Anglo-American reader. There is this barrier and yet we are talking about a text which is the founding novel of modern Europe, it is the novel with the most illustrious descendents, *Tristram Shandy*, Diderot, a good part of Dickens, Dostoevsky and even Jane Austen – think of Catherine Morland reading gothic romances and going bananas, just like Don Quixote. She's Don Quixote with a hoop-skirt. It's very mysterious to me why there should be these barriers, which we don't have towards your culture.

Question. You mention *Don Quixote*. You have argued in your book *Cervantes or the Critique of Reading* that this novel offers a 'critique of reading' whereas Joyce offers a 'critique of writing'. Could you expand on this insight?

Answer. I think the novel is basically a genre without genre, it cannot fit into any genre, because at that moment it fixes, solidifies and ceases to be the protean genre of genres or dialogue of genres. This comes from the fact that the novel is basically a corruption of the epic. More than from myth or from tragedy, it springs from the epic. But it also feels it has to mock what has preceded it. And I think that there is a circle that would go from Cervantes to Joyce, in which *Don Quixote* and *Ulysses* are mock epics, degraded epics, that spring from the epic, but have to deny their parenthood, from romances of chivalry or the whole epic of

Western culture, from Homer to Queen Victoria, in the case of Joyce. So there's a manner of re-reading the world in Cervantes and re-writing the world, discovering the vast palimpsest of the West in Joyce. I think that Cervantes inaugurates the modern novel and Joyce, in some ways, closes it and therefore they meet as the circle closes in a critique of a univocal, scholastic, canonical reading of the world in Cervantes and a critique of purely linear, positivist, naturalist, realist writing of the world in Joyce. They are the Alpha and Omega of the development of this genre without a genre. It is extraordinary to read *Don Quixote* today and see how modern it is and how many genres are at work in it. It is an epic, a novel of chivalry, a pastoral novel, a Byzantine novel, a story within a story, a picaresque tale; it's so many things and demands so many languages. I agree with Bakhtin who defines the modern novel as an arena characterized by the struggle of languages, the combat of all sorts of languages which is the world we are living in. So many languages are disputing our attention and disputing amongst themselves that I think it is the genius of Cervantes to have founded the novel on the premise of genres and languages in conflict, a form taken to a pitch of perception and chaos by James Joyce, in his reading of the plural languages of the world. One sentence contains a plurality of languages in conflict.

Question. What of William Faulkner, whom you have described as the 'only novelist of defeat in a country that basically has been a nation of optimism and success'?
Answer. In general, not only in literature, tragedy was banished by the modern world. It did not fit in with the optimism of Christianity or of Croeso-hedonist industrial society later. Things had to be happy: they could be redeemed in the Christian sense, or you could have

progress in the secular sense. And we forgot that history
does not guarantee happiness and the twentieth century
woke us up and told us that history does not guarantee
happiness and progress. Dostoevsky had known it, William Blake had known it as had the Marquis de Sade and
Kleist, but in the American continent which is premised
on happiness, on the idea of utopia – we were discovered
in order to make the world happy – we have great
difficulties in shedding the utopian promise and facing the
tragic possibility of humankind and I frankly think that
the only writer in the western hemisphere who has faced
up to that tragic proposition is William Faulkner. So he is
even more Latin American than most Latin Americans.
I've always said that maybe Latin America begins south of
the Mason-Dixon line, the South is in a way Latin American, as is Faulkner, if for no other reason, through his
language. In order to convey this tragic vision, he usually
has to use a language which has a great tradition amongst
us, which is the baroque. Once Allen Tate very pejora-
tively referred to Faulkner as a Dixie-Gongorist. I think it's
great praise to be compared to the poet who, along with
John Donne, is the greatest poet of the seventeenth century. Nevertheless, there is that link. When Borges trans-
lates Faulkner, he has to do no violence to the prose of
Faulkner. It comes out perhaps even better in Spanish,
because the model is there, it is called Luis de Góngora.
There is a need for a language to convey the tragic, which
is a baroque language, a language of hunger, which aims
to fill the vacuum, a language of people who are searching
for the truth. I think this fact is essential to the understanding of Faulkner. In order to be the novelist of defeat, it is
not enough to say I am from the South, the South was
defeated, it is the only region in the United States that has
been defeated, whereas the rest of the country has been

premissed on success, success, success, never learning any lessons from defeat. It is also necessary to find the appropriate language and it is curious that the language chosen had to be the baroque, which comes so much from Spain. So I feel that Faulkner had, and has, a great lesson for us and it is not only a formal lesson, of the modern use of the baroque, it is a profound historical lesson on how to face defeat, to admit the tragic possibility in history, it is also a profoundly literary lesson, which is the discovery of the novel, through the novel, the discovery of the story by telling the story, the discovery of the characters by letting the characters act, all these magnificent lessons which I think had a profound influence on the literature of Latin America. Certainly many of the more modern novelists, García Márquez, Mario Vargas Llosa, myself, were very influenced by Faulkner.

Question. Dos Passos as well?
Answer. For me the reading of Dos Passos at eighteen was an incredible event. I felt there you had many ways of chronicling the life of a city, but then I was a reader of Dos Passos and of Faulkner at the same time, so I knew that there was a difference between Dos Passos, who was recording time and Faulkner who was creating time and I tried to get both things into my first novel, *Where the Air is Clear.*

Question. Can we explore this treatment of time? You have said that in Faulkner, everything is in the chronic present. Even the remotest part is present.
Answer. Here I'm quoting Faulkner himself, something he says in *Intruder in the Dust,* which is that today began ten thousand years ago. I mean, no other modern novelist tells me so strongly what I know, what I think of time and that

is that all time is present, that we remember in the present, which is the past, and we desire in the present, which is the future. When Quentin and Shrive are sitting remembering that is when *Absalom, Absalom!* is happening. It is not happening in the 1870s in the South, it is happening in that room in Harvard, but you could also say that it *is* happening in the South in the 1870s, for that is where the room in Harvard is. This radical *present*-ation of time is more radical in Faulkner than in any other contemporary author and that is the supreme lesson of the modern novel. I don't think that anything has impressed or influenced me as much as that precise discovery that you could be the master of time in a novel, that was the glory and beauty and freedom of writing novels that you could create time instead of having time dominate you.

Question. Why does the Joycean and Faulknerian novel not get written in Latin America until the time of your generation?

Answer. For a very simple and complex reason, which has to do with time and has to do with space, so we're talking about chronotopes in the Bakhtinian sense, a Latin American chronotope, a sense of time–space continuum, which has been constantly broken up in Latin America. This continuum that comes from the origins of our history and is present in our Indian myths for example, and also very present in the world of the Renaissance – circular time, the time of simultaneity, spiral time, in the sense of Vico, who influences Joyce so much – is lost the moment we decide to enter the modern world. We enter this modern world with Independence – we have to choose what is deemed to be the modern time, which is the time of the eighteenth century, the Enlightenment, a linear, progressive time which will take us again to happiness and progress and the perfectibility of human nature and human institutions. So we embark on this linear time and it fails us completely and we write novels which are also linear novels, novels adequate to this time of progress. But this is a denial of half our being, of our past, a denial of many things that define us as a polycultural and multiracial society in Latin America. So a moment comes when the breakdown of linear, positivistic time occurs in Europe. William Faulkner is an expression of it, James Joyce is a prime expression, as are Virginia Woolf, Marcel Proust and Kafka – they're all talking about a breakdown of linear time. Time is many things: it is a Vico spiral; it is latent time, in which the past is present for Virginia Woolf; it is a subterranean time to be found in the basements of old legends and myths, Germanic and Hebrew, for Franz Kafka; it is the instant which abolishes time in Proust. And suddenly our novelists see themselves in this time which, by the way, the poets had already seen. At the same time that the European novel was discovering this sense of time, so were Gorostiza and Octavio Paz and Neruda and Lugones. So it was a double influence of the European novel and the Latin American poets that made the Latin American novelists say: what is this time Joyce and Proust are talking about? Is it my time? Yes, it is my time, for it is the time that we lived from the dawn of our history and then forgot in the nineteenth century. So we simply rediscovered our time along with the European revolution in time wrought by the novel and the poetry of the twentieth century. It is a very interesting phenomenon of cultural integration, of mutual discovery on a cultural plane. It is the closest we've ever been to the West and to Europe thanks to this cultural phenomenon.

Question. You have called this modern novel a process of *desyoización* which we might translate as 'de-I-ification'.

142

Answer. Yes, the adventure of the modern novel has been a confessional adventure, the ego has been at the centre of writing from Saint Augustine, through Montaigne and Rousseau. It is what gives relevance and thickness to most of the European novels of the eighteenth and nineteenth centuries. Then suddenly this European ego ceases to have a face and the name of that missing face is Kafka. The Prague ghost appears in the perfectly oiled machinery of the modern novel and we are terrified. I think we are faced with the breakdown of the first person singular and the great question of how to save the individual, the person, where to put him now. That is why I think that Hispanic literature has an extraordinary role to play, for there is a wonderful page in Novalis where he speaks about discovering persons in the moment when they are constituted and they still do not have a name or a face. He calls these figures. If there is a literature which has been capable of creating figures out of nothing, it is Spanish, in the three great archetypes, La Celestina, Don Juan and Don Quixote. I'm interested in this and it is something I attempted to explore in *Terra Nostra*, especially in the three young men who come onto the beach constantly and they do not have a name and they do not have a face and they have no memory: there is nothing to singularize them. This is a reflection on the problem. The great modern tragic novel has this major preoccupation of the disintegration of the human personality. Something we are seeing every day, it is mass communications, it is the atom bomb, it is AIDS, it is a million things that destroy the formal, formative bearings of the individual that is so precious a creation of Western civilization. The novel has always jumped ahead and shown its concern for this central problem.

Carlos Fuentes: An Interview

Question. In Mexico, at the time of the modernist literary revolution in Europe, you had the Revolution and a resulting body of literature. Can you talk about the importance of all this?

Answer. I think that the Mexican Revolution, whatever its political, economic and social failings, was an immensely important cultural event for Mexico and for the Americas, for it is the great occasion in which a Latin American country, after the colonial experience and after the experience of Independence, really decides to break through its veneer of Westernization and look at itself – at its plurality and traditions – straight in the face. What we see may not be very delightful, but there it is, it is probably a horrifying mask with a bleeding scar on its face, rip off that mask and you find a bleeding scar and another mask, I don't know. But the country looks at itself and the country breaks down its isolation, all these big cavalcades of the Revolution, Zapata, Villa, are the first wars in which Mexico gets to know itself and many Mexicans from the north go south and those from the east go west. There is a great creative chaos that the Revolution creates and brings out what we are today, including the novels and the novelists. So the novel of the Mexican Revolution tells us about this central fact of our history. It permits Martin Luis Guzmán to write chronicles that otherwise would not have been there because the serious Mexican politician of that time, until very recently, left nothing written down. Now politicos have become speakers, verbose even, they cackle and gossip and confess. But then, they did not. So the only chronicles you have are works such as *The Eagle and the Serpent*. Then you have a spectacularly rich and wonderful work which is Azuela. He is often seen as the novelist of only one novel, *The Underdogs*, but he actually covers about thirty years in the life of Mexico, it's our

Comédie humaine. Then you have the transformation of these given elements of the Revolution by Agustín Yáñez, who adopts modern literary techniques to break up the time of the Revolution and give us a more powerful sense of how the Revolution broke up the country and its sense of time and space. And then you have the great summit of the Revolution, which is Juan Rulfo, who presents the Revolution or the agrarian novel as a kind of naked tree with golden fruits.

Question. Could you explain this image?

Answer. Rulfo is a writer of very spare prose and very dramatic prose and the sense I get is that he has painted a very naked and black tree, with no leaves on it, but suddenly you see something shining and you come near it and there is a golden apple hanging strangely from that barren tree and you pick it and eat it and you die, maybe after having had some very interesting dreams. It is through these experiences that we could write modern novels in Mexico, that we could go on to write the novel of the Mexican city, which is something my generation started and which has been continued by the younger generation such as Sáinz, Zapata and María Luisa Puga, all basically urban novelists. In any culture you have to have a constant process of assimilation of your past, or your past will be there, inert and useless. So I'm glad we have had the novel of the Revolution, the agrarian novel, the so called *indigenista* novel, they've all had a role, so that we can go on to another stage of fictionalizing.

Question. We have talked of influences. How important do you think Faulkner is to Rulfo?

Answer. He always swore that he had not read Faulkner and that his influences were from Scandinavian literature,

writers such as Knut Hamsun. I also feel that a novel like
Pedro Páramo is close to *Wuthering Heights*, the whole
problem of *l'amour fou* and the identification of sex and
death, is both Brontë and Rulfo. But you must be very
careful with all this talk of influences. Alfonso Reyes made
a very pertinent remark when Rulfo and Arreola appeared
on the Mexican literary scene in the late 1940s. Two such
excellent writers had not been seen in Mexico for quite a
long time, probably never, such peculiarly modern writers,
bringing something absolutely new to the Mexican literary
landscape. Everyone devoted themselves to nitpicking and
finding influences and Reyes was asked what are the
influences on Rulfo and Arreola and he said two thousand
years of literature. So one can talk about Faulkner, Brontë
and Knut Hamsun. Rulfo was a voracious reader and I'm
sure he did as we all do: he accepted, he filtered, he chose
what was most convenient for his own vision.

Question. You talked earlier of the influence of popular
culture on your work. Is it important for the modern novel
to assimilate these traditions?
Answer. Yes. The Americans are good at this, but so also are
the Latin Americans, Cabrera, Puig, Vargas Llosa. I think,
for example, that Mario Vargas Llosa did a very good thing
in *Aunt Julia and the Scriptwriter*, in the sense of discovering humour in the melodrama of Latin America. One
should not, also, forget Luis Rafael Sánchez, because he is
right at the intersection, which is Puerto Rico. I'm not
afraid of popular culture, I'm not afraid of the mass media,
of entertainment. I feel that this is all grist to the mill of
literature, it always has been. There is a constant re-
elaboration of these themes which takes them, nevertheless, to another level and gives them more of an archetypal
value than they would otherwise have, and hopefully

146

wrests them from the purely entertainment value in which things would perish. Nobody's going to remember Rita Hayworth in a hundred years, except perhaps through Manuel Puig's book. He has been capable of creating an archetype out of a fluffy piece of entertainment.

Question. Rita Hayworth or, in your case, María Félix?
Answer. Yes, María Félix has meant a couple of things in Mexico. First, she is an independent woman in a country where women over the centuries were destined to be nuns or whores. She presented herself as an independent woman, who owned her own body. This I found very interesting. Of course, there's the whole problem of goddesses in Mexico, which is even stronger than the sense of the goddesses in Europe. In Europe there is a powerful sense of the function of the goddess in literature as you go from antiquity to the Middle Ages: witchcraft appears as a way, if Michelet is right, of preserving the ancient goddesses, of transforming Venus, since you do not see her in marble any more, at least into a little doll made of cloth and filled with flour, that is Venus now and it becomes an object of demonology and witchcraft. In Mexico, you descend from strange, inhuman, decapitated goddesses such as La Coatlicue (the earth goddess), who is then humanized by La Malinche, who is then divinized by the Virgin of Guadalupe, who is then humanized again by Sor Juana Inés de la Cruz or La Adelita in the Revolution, or by modern women such as Félix or Dolores del Río. All these give the contemporary image of that mother-virgin-whore figure that comes from the remote Mexican past, this impure mother who seems to be there with her tenderness and her stains throughout the history of Mexico as a counterpoint to the Father, the Montezumas, the Corteses and the presidents of Mexico. So we're dealing with our

father and mother figures. But of course some people don't recognize themselves in mothers such as María Félix, and this is the problem of *Holy Place*: is this my mother?

Question. Is it important to keep the myths alive?
Answer. Yes, why should we become impoverished? If you lose a myth you know and nourish, you can be sure that it will be sustained by another myth which will be imposed on you politically or commercially.

Question. Returning to our North–South comparisons. You said earlier that the traffic on the bridge between the cultures was largely one-way? When does this change?
Answer. Probably at the time of the so-called 'boom'. At this moment a taste for Latin American literature developed first in the United States and then in Britain. So it's much less of a one-way process now.

Question. Why did this not happen before, especially in Britain?
Answer. I don't fault the British public with lack of generosity or discrimination. The most I would fault it with would be lack of information. Now, information is better, in the universities, in the newspapers, in publishing houses. There is also the fact that in the last quarter of a century we have developed a narrative literature which is far better than anything we have done before, something that can interest a universal audience, which I don't think our nineteenth- or early twentieth-century novelists were capable of doing. They were extremely local, extremely parochial, they had an extraordinary confusion about politics and literature. They thought that you could express good politics with bad literature and it turned out to be bad literature and bad politics, which interested

nobody. You are not interested in the plight of a banana worker in Ecuador *per se*. So I think that basically the literature of Latin America assimilated these lessons and made a big leap forward, understanding that it had the enormous possibility of talking about the state of the city and the state of the art. In fact, putting these two things together made a powerful mix. Then, let us say, there has been a Latin Americanization of the world, that many of the problems we thought were particular to Latin America, turned out to be universal problems, problems of violence, of repression, of torture, of miscegenation, a million things. Suddenly you see in the streets of London, New York and Paris things which in 1930 you might have considered the exclusive preserve of backward, underdeveloped people. There is a greater universalization or Latin Americanization of the world, notably through the phenomenon of violence. In Latin America at present we're in the middle of the worst social and economic crisis probably of our history. All the structures identified with progress, the political and economic models, have cracked, fallen on their faces and the only thing that is left is the literary critique of these models. That's the only thing that has stood up. And this critique is valid not just for Latin America but for the whole world.

Question. We've talked of Faulkner and Dos Passos. Do you continue to read with pleasure modern American literature?

Answer. I've always been a great reader and admirer of the literature of the United States. I think it is an extremely vital literature and certainly today I would express a joy at reading writers such as William Styron, Philip Roth, Malamud, Mailer, Capote ... it would be quite a constellation and then younger people like Moon or Louise Erdrich or Tom McGuane, any number of writers.

Question. Do you feel the same excitement reading British literature?
Answer. No, not really, I liked Ackroyd's *Hawksmoor* very much, but not that much interests me, not much if one compares it to writing in the Americas.

Question. Why should this be?
Answer. I think that perhaps in Britain it's the sensation that everything has been said. We have the sensation of saying things for the first time, or of having to say things, for if not, they would not be said. The more important point is that when you have a very well-developed civil society as in Britain or France, you feel that society takes care of itself and you don't feel like writing about it so much, because it will appear in information, on the news or television. But that doesn't explain how a country that is suffused in information like the United States does have an interesting literature. Perhaps it is the sense of the New World and the sense of things needing to be named. I don't know. But generally for us the main motive for writing is the weakness of the civil societies. If you don't say certain things they won't be said. It is a very powerful motivation. I think that this is a generalized feeling among writers, independent of political positions.

Question. Is this a continuing need?
Answer. When you consider that the most developed civil societies of Latin America would be Uruguay, Chile, Argentina and look what they've gone through and are going through. You get Pinochet, *desaparecidos*, torture,

Answer. It will either be done through culture or it will be done through strife. I'm afraid that it will happen through strife. What we have in *The Old Gringo* is two very different civilizations facing each other. We have to recognize these differences and recognize that they translate into political differences, two visions of the world, purposes, proceedings, meanings which are different in Anglo America and Ibero America. It seems to be extremely difficult for North Americans to understand this, for they feel, to go back to Faulkner and the sense of victory and triumph, that they are the bearers of the universal truth and that what is good for them must be good for the rest of the world. Why are they God's chosen land? With all due respect to them and to their values, which are very great, it just is not so. There are other values and other ways of doing things and other purposes in life, apart from what they propose. So until they understand this, we're going to have a very difficult coexistence in the Western hemisphere. Indeed I think that one of the ways to deal with the matter is to try to communicate as much as we can with them. It's difficult because the United States is a country without memory. We have an abundance of memory in Latin America. They substitute the mass media for memory and every twenty-four hours Peter Jennings or Daniel Rather comes on television and tells you what you should remember of that day, which twenty-four hours later you should have forgotten in order to make room for the news of the next day. That is not the way our memory and our mind work and therefore dealing with each other is extremely difficult, but, of course, extremely important. I'm sure many Mexicans would like to say, I'm a ship and I cut off from this pier and off I go to Polynesia because I don't want to live next to the Americans. I'm sure many Americans would

say the same about Mexico. OK, so poor Mexico, so far
from God and so near the United States, but what about
poor Poland, so near to God and so near the Soviet Union?
We are going to have to deal with them, so we'd better get
to know them and try to get them to know us better. The
US is a democratic country in which you can speak and
communicate and filter certain ideas at least through the
élite and intelligentsia of that country. Right now, when
we're speaking in November 1986, I think that it's impossible to pretend to hold a dialogue with the American
government, when you have men such as Eliot Abrams in
the State Department or Pat Buchanan in the White House.
But they're not eternal, Reagan is not eternal.

Question. Do you find that in the cultural sphere there is a
greater understanding of Latin American fiction?
Answer. I feel that there are many different attitudes to
Latin American fiction. There is a breakdown of the
utopian illusion in most Anglo-American reviewing of the
Latin American novel and more and more a sense of
community. Also there is a sense that we're facing very
similar problems and that they cannot classify us except at
the risk of us classifying them. Increasingly there is a
danger that if they apply clichés to us, we will rebound
with clichés of our own and then both sides will be in
trouble. In other words, the way of looking at each other is
more and more serious and fraught with dangers and less
and less a frivolity. You cannot continue to adhere to
Carmen Miranda and Pancho Villa via Wallace Beery as the
image, and we cannot continue in our own stereotypes.
For example, if you see old Mexican films of the 1930s and
1940s, there are always two gringos in them. One man is
called Clifford Carr – no one has ever heard of him. He
always appeared in Mexican films as a cigar-chomping

gringo in Bermuda shorts with an Hawaiian shirt and a camera, saying dumb things. The other is a man called Charles Rooner, who appeared in Emilio Fernández films with jodhpurs, riding boots and a crop, always about to rape an innocent Indian woman. Well, we have to go beyond these two clichés and I think we are, because we are understanding more and more the stakes of living together in the western hemisphere.

Carlos Fuentes

Steven Boldy

Carlos Fuentes was born not in his own country, Mexico, but in Panama City in 1928 and indeed spent many of his formative years in foreign lands where his father was serving as a diplomat: Rio, Washington, Santiago de Chile, Buenos Aires. Initially trained as a lawyer, he held various administrative and diplomatic posts and more recently has accepted a series of teaching posts in major North American universities and at Cambridge.

An energetic cultural promoter, article writer and reviewer, he has published prolifically since his first collection of fantastic, myth-inspired short stories, *Los días enmascarados* ('The Masked Days') in 1954, which were followed by the more conventional stories of *Cantar de ciegos* ('Songs of the Blind'), 1964, and the powerful tales of labyrinthine family relations and inheritance against the background of Mexican politics and violence of *Burnt Water* (*Agua quemada*), 1981. The first novels, *Where the Air is Clear* (*La región más transparente*), 1958, *The Death of Artemio Cruz* (*La muerte de Artemio Cruz*), 1962, and *The Good Conscience* (*Las buenas conciencias*), 1959, share a basic realism which, though tempered in the first two mentioned by avant-garde technique and innovative structure, made some critics regret the apparently radical change to the oneiric and self-referential worlds of *A Change of Skin* (*Cambio de piel*) and *Holy Place* (*Zona Sagrada*), both published in 1967. Another recognizable type of fiction is constituted by *Aura*, 1962, *Cumpleaños* ('Birthday'), 1969, and *Distant Relations* (*Una familia lejana*), 1981, haunting and maze-like explorations of identity and time.

Terra Nostra (1975) is the rather self-conscious culmination and synthesis of Fuentes's novel-writing practice and thought on the identity and destiny of Spain and Latin America. Its grandeur did not lead one to expect the publication, three years later, of the political spy thriller *The Hydra Head* (*La cabeza de la hidra*). In 1985 *The Old Gringo* (*Gringo viejo*) appeared, where the arrival of a suicidal North American in the Mexican Revolution allows the identity of the two countries to come face to face. His production for the theatre consists of *Todos los gatos son pardos* ('All Cats are Grey') and *El tuerto es rey* ('The One-eyed Man is King') from 1970 and *Orquídeas a la luz de la luna* ('Orchids in the Light of the Moon'), 1982. The four collections of essays reveal a highly developed skill in literary criticism and a keen and knowledgeable grasp of issues of national identity. They are *La nueva novela hispanoamericana* ('The New Hispanic-American Novel'), 1969, the best published survey of the so-called 'boom' of Latin-American fiction; *Tiempo mexicano* ('Mexican Time') and *Casa con dos puertas* ('House with Two Doors'), 1970; and *Don Quixote or the Critique of Reading*, which offers an explanation of the poetics of *Terra Nostra* and serves as a companion volume to it.

Fuentes tells a story which serves nicely as a symbolic introduction to his work. He was a popular and integrated schoolboy in Washington DC when, in 1938, the leftist Mexican president, Cárdenas, nationalized foreign oil companies. Suddenly and simultaneously the child became consciously a Mexican and a leper, 'the other' to his companions.

To the present Fuentes has tirelessly written about the

Mexican as 'other', about a protean 'Other' which emerges as fascinating, dangerous but above all necessary. His novels, stories and theatre are a search for this other, a provocation of it and dialogue with it which often wreaks the same violence on his characters as it does on the surface of his texts. When Javier in *A Change of Skin* returns, like his author before him, from Buenos Aires to Mexico City, he finds no comfortable Ithaca, but morose and unknowable Mariachi musicians at whom he throws peanuts as a prelude to finding himself inevitably, contentedly and bloodily on the *cantina* floor.

Mexico as a complex, violent, mysterious, ugly–beautiful reality, with its subterranean forces of Indian culture, and resentment, historical traumas and contradictory masks imposed or donned over the centuries is a reality alien to much of the national bourgeoisie. Alien and yet their own in so far as Mexico is a *mestizo* country, and the bourgeoisie is *mestizo*, though often more and less than it claims. The forcible relation to this alien reality, this other without which one is not oneself, is an extreme existential situation, a national existential situation in Mexico and other Spanish-American countries: a relation which for the European, immersed largely even yet in the naturalness and homogeneity of his own culture, which any other, elsewhere, only serves to confirm, is predominantly intellectual. A passionate participant in the national tensions and contradictions, Fuentes has, over some thirty years, brought to bear his immense cultural and historical awareness and unquestionable flair to universalize the problematics of local identity to describe and forge an acute and radical modernity.

The nature of the texts, and of the man, is dialogic: Fuentes is a great interlocutor and of considerable importance and value in his dialogues with the foreign media as a voice representing Mexico. Latin American writers, through historical circumstance, have often taken on the role of national conscience and spokesman, which they often become formally: Fuentes, for example, was ambassador in Paris. Such relative power invested in the writer can encourage a prophetic or even messianic stance, as it did on occasions with the Chilean poet Pablo Neruda, but in Fuentes has manifested itself principally in the injunction to know. Not by chance does a tortured and torturing Mephistophelian presence recur in the novels, with Ixca Cienfuegos in *Where the Air is Clear* and Freddy Lambert in *A Change of Skin*, and are whole works such as *Aura* written in the second-person voice.

The injunction to know the other is to know oneself. The Old Gringo of the 1985 novel travels, perhaps a little too neatly, across the Mexican border to die, and simultaneously across the frontier of self. But there where he had expected to find the ultimate, solitary answer, 'he discovers more than ever, that he is in the company of others'.[1] The Mexican Revolution where the American, Ambrose Bierce, dies, has a double or ghost in the American Civil War about which he had written in *In the Midst of Life*. (In *The Death of Artemio Cruz* a similar role is fulfilled by Stephen Crane's *The Red Badge of Courage*.) Indeed the whole novel is a clever and revealing confrontation of the US and Mexico each as the double of the other, in their contrasting conceptions of land, tradition, legality, death and language.

The dialogue with the other occurs on many levels: Mexico with Spain and the US, Germans with Jews; man with woman, father, mother, son and God; the individual with the plural presence of the others whom he denies and the multiple possibilities which he has neglected in order to be what he is, but which still constitute him; sanity and rationalism with madness and unreason; the optimism of capitalism and Christianity with the darker wisdom of tragedy; eschatological time with cyclical mythical time; the novel with the epic; the text with its intertext: the plurality of its history which contests its univocal authority. This awareness of the other within and without is coloured by a fundamentally tragic sense of life. Well versed in the thought of Nietzsche, Domenach, Unamuno and Steiner, and a devotee and exegete of Faulkner, Fuentes seems to voice something basic to his vision in a conversation with Bill Moyers.[2] The eighteenth and nineteenth centuries, he argues, were marked by an optimism founded on notions of progress and the perfectibility of man which excluded tragedy. When excluded, tragedy returns as its opposite: the banality of evil and crime. The lack of a tragic vision in the modern world has led to Dachau, Auschwitz, the Soviet gulag, Guernica and Hiroshima. Culture has as its purpose to relate to what is different and strange, and the failure to relate produces the fatal temptation to exterminate. These comments express not pessimistic fatalism but rather imply that only by facing and integrating the other can one avoid being used by it. Without a sense of the past, and of others, he believes, there is no present, and though one may repeat the actions of others, without this despairing and hopeful action, human action would die. Oedipus and Prometheus must be reborn in every generation.

This conception of the past makes Fuentes in the widest sense an historical novelist. Not only does he come in the wake of the first major Spanish-American historical novelist, Alejo Carpentier, but he is born into a country tortured by the failure or betrayal of the 1910 Revolution. Declared by Francisco Madero against the longstanding regime of the tyrant Porfirio Díaz, the movement developed eventually into a bloody civil war between revolutionaries such as Pancho Villa and Carranza. The turmoil of these years were seen to reveal Mexico to itself in all its racial and cultural diversity. The single party which emerged, however, the PRI, is given to celebrating the continuing course and success of the Revolution in vacuous nationalistic and epic rhetoric. Fuentes's two first major works are the culmination of a tradition of novels which emerged from the Revolutionary period. From the fast-moving documentary realism of Azuela's *The Underdogs* (*Los de abajo*), based on first-hand experience and published during the Revolution, through the much wider and more reposed vision of Martín Luis Guzmán and up to the tortured, laconic and brilliant pages of Juan Rulfo's *Pedro Páramo* (1955), a fertile ambiguity is introduced into Spanish-American literature, which Fuentes will take up and exploit.

Where the Air is Clear and *The Death of Artemio Cruz* follow dramas which unfold through the generations and successive oligarchies which relay each other during the vicissitudes of the nineteenth century (the presidencies of Santa Anna from the 1830s to the 1850s with the loss of Texas, the liberalism of Juárez, interrupted by the French invasion and the empire of Maximilian, 1864–7, and the constantly renewed periods of Díaz's power from 1876) through the revolutionary years and up to the neo-capitalist regimes of the 1950s. The first of these novels, with its vast number of characters painted on a wide and open Dos Passos-like canvas, combines a polyphonic rendering of the versions of Mexico debated at the time (by the great poet Octavio Paz for example, who often stands close to Fuentes's shoulder as he writes) with an indigenous mystique not exclusive to D. H. Lawrence. *The Death of Artemio Cruz*, for many his best novel, has all the stature of *The Death of Virgil*, *Malone Dies* or *As I Lay Dying*. Both recount the story of individuals who progress from idealists to revolutionary heroes to powerful and corrupt

capitalists: who move from one to the other pole of
Fuentes's cosmos: frenzy and paralysis. To act and create,
they must survive, and in Mexico there are only dead
heroes. Heroes who survive become tyrants; or in other
words one is either *pendejo* or *chingón*, fool or fucker,
Plumed Serpent or Hernán Cortés. The protagonists live
isolated in their power, in their petrified egos which
exclude, destroy or reify whatever is not themselves:
woman, nature, God, their home and people. There is a
certain synonymity between these terms in Fuentes: to
remain with them or be drawn into them is death, madness and castration; the necessary rebellion against
them is alienation and death.

What Cruz and Robles have repressed or ceased to be
constitutes in them an absolute and irreconcilable duality.
Betrayed woman takes her revenge by denying (nature
and) man, his paternity, and becoming the Virgin Mother,
or taking the side of Nature against the patriarch by
becoming witch. In both novels a woman (Mercedes,
Catalina) condemns the man to be one thing by day,
another by night, to squander his strength in a useless
display of power. (In the two separate parts of his memory,
the central Pilgrim of the monumental *Terra Nostra* is
alternately the peaceful Plumed Serpent and the bloody-
handed conquistador Cortés.) Duality is both a curse and a
salvation: perhaps the split between body and soul of the
Judaeo-Christian tradition against the original, and vital
duality of the Mexican deities (as in complementary pairs
such as Quetzalcoatl and Xolotl, Venus as Morning and
Evening Star). At the beginning of each novel, there is a
character who is simultaneously hero and traitor in the
Revolution (as El Señor in *Terra Nostra* is defender of the
faith and heresiarch). This dilemma is inherited by the
son, or reproduced in every generation by two sons of

opposing tendencies. Through the inevitable choice-making of life, however, the determinism of history, or in narrative terms the univocal nature of the epic, only one of the two strands of life can be followed.

But the novel is neither history nor epic, though it partakes of both. By an affirmation of imagination and desire, the novel recovers not only what was, but what might have been, or rather what was and was denied as a potentiality for the future: it becomes a memory fertilized by imagination and desire. What Artemio Cruz might or should have been, a martyr faithful to his love and companions, is taken up by his son Lorenzo, who, re-enacting his father's steps one by one, is killed in that alternative to the Mexican Revolution: the Spanish Civil War, where the heroes were defeated and thus remained heroes. The death of the son, who incarnates what the father was not or destroyed, not only redeems him but recreates and renews his original duality: the duality from which another cycle can spring so that human acts do not die. The mysterious package at the end of *A Change of Skin*, associated with the death of Franz, half-human and half-animal, perhaps dog and child, and the androgyne at the end of *Terra Nostra* signal perhaps similar new beginnings.

The real passion of the son is parallel to the painful memory, the purgatory, of Cruz himself: the text of the novel, not fatal like the superficial story of his life or the official course of the Revolution, but pluralized by its narration in three alternating voices of widely varying character: third person narration in the past tense, first person in the present, and second person in the future. This triadic structure favoured by Fuentes clearly carries many connotations: Father, Son, Holy Ghost; superego, ego, subconscious; Inferno, Purgatorio, Paradiso;

memory, intelligence and providence or will. Through these voices of memory the others against whom, for whom or through whom Artemio came to be what he was (the Indians like the *yaqui* Tobías who rode with him, his 'twins' the idealist Gonzalo and the unknown soldier whom he abandons during a battle, Father Páez whom he sells for political survival and advancement at the time of the Cristero war, and his first love Regina who died for him) return to contest the inevitability of his life and the exclusive oneness of his self, recover his early love and ideals as part of his present reality and reassert the vitality of Revolution against its present sterility. Underneath the apparent determinism of the text, its multiple echoes, identifications, parallels and mirrorings assert a similar ambiguity and freedom for the reader against his initial complacent judgements. In *Where the Air is Clear* the role of the three voices as dialogue and contradiction is taken by the semi-mythical and fantastic Ixca Cienfuegos, a sort of collective double and incarnation of the activity of the narrative, who opens the novel with the statement, 'In Mexico there is no tragedy: everything becomes an insult.'[3] By being the provocative memory of the characters, Ixca opens up the tragic and fertile contradictions in them in an attempt to explode the iron grip of social, psychological and family determinism. Fascinating though obscure and obtrusive in this text, he takes the centre of the stage as Freddy Lambert in *A Change of Skin*.

Change of skin, metamorphosis, becomes a constant or temptation in Fuentes's works and forms a major link between two works centred on female characters: *Aura* and *Holy Place*. The witch Consuelo and the film actress Claudia Nervo belong to a class of woman who, according to the author, refuse any division between body and will and mortally wound the man who wishes to resemble God

in thought and the Devil in flesh.[4] Woman in her role as
Circe dissolves such alienating dualisms, and Fuentes's
men are torn between the dizzy and dangerous change of
Circe and the permanence and security of Penelope: as
was Cruz between paralysis and frenzy. The classic and
haunting novella *Aura*, though belonging to a wide and
almost explicit tradition (Michelet, James, Pushkin, *The
Bride of Corinth*) is close to some of the central obsessions
of Fuentes with woman and time in the specific if latent
evocation of the author's dual vision of Charlotte of
Mexico as beautiful young empress and mad old lady
obsessed with the presence of her dead husband Maximilian. The progressive young historian Felipe Montero is
hired by the aged señora Consuelo to edit and continue
the memoirs of her long-dead husband Llorente, a general
of Maximilian, who interestingly carries the name of a
major historian of the Spanish Inquisition. As he
immerses himself in the anachronic atmosphere of the old
lady's house, he falls in love with the young and beautiful
Aura, who is gradually revealed to be a magical creation by
Consuelo of her younger self. She is not, however, able to
maintain her eternally youthful incarnation, and Felipe
wakes one morning to find the ghastly wrinkled body of
Consuelo in bed beside him. In order to restore the unity
of Consuelo and Aura, and thus her immortality, Felipe
becomes his 'own double', Llorente, in an act of sacrileg-
ious copulation which has an analogue in various other
novels. Felipe's experience is double-edged: while he does
gain the promise of a world of sensuality preserved by the
witch from pre-Christian days, an imminence of renaissance (and Fuentes seems to follow Michelet in linking the
witch to the Renaissance), he also regresses to a period of
French imperialism over and against which modern Mexico and his own mentality were built, and imperils at least

his soul and freedom in the devouring maw of his decrepit lover's bed.

Holy Place, something of a 'happening' of a novel, and very much of the 1960s – pop, ritualistic, camp, mythical, orgiastic and cinematic – drolly combines an exploration of woman and of epic around its protagonist Claudia Nervo, modelled on the glorious and redoubtable Mexican actress María Félix. Under the constant gaze of her doting son Mito, Claudia becomes the one-dimensional replica of her silver-screen roles, which he plays over and over again in rapt fascination. This static parody of personality and the narrative which supports it is associated in one strand of the novel with Homer's epic of Ulysses. The splendid castrating figure of Claudia (Mexican womanhood's ans-wer to Pancho Villa) is here only half a person: Beauty without her other, the Beast, without which renewal is impossible. Mito as narrator (distinct from the character and in many ways his opposite) is pledged to provide that other, and rather like Felipe Montero secretes an inces-tuous *doppelgänger* in Giancarlo, the Dionysus to his Apollo. Any stability in the narrative is swept away by a vertiginous system of ritual transformations, versions and readings and the inevitable ending of the myth, the conventional narrative, psychological, cultural and histori-cal order, is dissolved. No final reading, closure, anchylo-sis of being is allowed: no return to Ithaca to an endless recounting of the same story by the patriarchal hero. Significantly, Fuentes has on occasions described various Latin American texts as 'unfinished pilgrimages'.[5] The univocal myth is liberated and pluralized by its own other: its variants, history, versions and transformations through time, and its uniqueness contaminated by combinations with mythemes from other cultural systems. To use a phrase from *Terra Nostra*, the cave of Plato is flooded by the river of Heraclitus. Against the official myth of Homer, for example, is set that of Apollodorus: Telemachus marries Circe while Telegonus, the son of Ulysses and Circe, kills his father and marries Penelope. Claudia's travelling salesman husband is spurned, ritually killed in a doll, while Giancarlo's officially dead hero father lives with a whore in Tripoli. (In *A Change of Skin* Javier similarly has a travelling salesman father exiled from the home, while in *The Old Gringo* Harriet Winslow's supposedly dead and hero father in fact lives with a mulatta in Cuba.) Giancarlo becomes the lover of Claudia while Mito looks on from the eyes of a dog.

While *Holy Place* is an entertaining and demanding literary exercise, its twin, *A Change of Skin*, published in the same year, is a major and important novel. The practice and conception of both, however, prepare for the colossally monumental *Terra Nostra*, which places Fuentes among the few Spanish-American writers seriously to have tried to come to terms with the culture of Spain, going beyond the frequently schizoid relation with the cultural father. Underneath the seemingly final cultural heritage of Spain, the selective and determining memory which spawns fanaticism and tyranny, another is discerned and wooed: the other of the official culture. This other is released and created by a literary *ars combinatoria* on a vast scale. Ranging from an apocalyptic Paris, the Spain of the Austrias and the Mexico of the Conquest, the novel tells not only what happened but what might have happened; new possibilities are created as classical literary texts are combined and characters pass from one to the other; a complex series of echoes and cross-references opens up the range of meaning even more. The plurality and excitement of the Renaissance is rescued from the limiting and univocal dogmatism of the Counter

Reformation; the unconsummated thrust of the Comunero Revolt is proposed as a heritage for America no less legitimate than the authority of Philip II, who wishes to enclose the whole of reality within the walls of his monastery-palace, El Escorial. The path from the presence of the plural voices of Mexico in the single voice of Artemio Cruz to the agile-cumbersome mechanism of *Terra Nostra* is not difficult to discern.

· *A Change of Skin* is a highly intellectual novel in conception and structure and yet contains writing of a dense and irreducible psychological realism and of an almost unbearable immediacy of the senses, place and feeling. It is a work designed almost to defy the reader or critic to say anything completely right, except perhaps about its assault on certainties and all their vehicles: moral, intellectual, literary and psychological. To this end every judgement, notion and role is accompanied somewhere by its opposite. Something else which cannot escape the attention of the most casual reader is the recurrence of cruelty and evil throughout history. The slight fabula of a trip by two couples in a VW Beetle from Mexico City to Veracruz and which ends, unfinished, in the ancient religious centre of Cholula, orchestrates visions of Aztec cruelty, the massacres of Cortés, medieval witch hunts, and the pogroms against Jews culminating in the supreme evil of the Nazi holocaust.

The main actors in the drama are the two couples, who later exchange partners: Javier, a Mexican writer, bureaucrat or teacher, his Jewish wife Elizabeth, perhaps North American, Franz, a Sudetenland Czech architect, and the young Mexican Isabel. While the couples double each other in complex and varying ways, they are all doubled by their narrator (witness or inventor), memory and interlocutor, and finally destroyer Freddy Lambert, the composite author of the tradition out of which the novel creates itself: Pirandello, Nietzsche and many others. He in turn is coryphaeus or puppet of his beatnik-exterminating angels the Monks, who parodically and grotesquely re-enact the lives of the characters in a trial after which one or some of them die or are executed in the pyramid at Cholula.

Franz and Javier are highly ambiguous doubles. Rather like Artemio Cruz and his 'twin' Gonzalo, one acts or constructs while the other does not, or does so with greater scruple. Franz uses his professional skills to build a concentration camp where his Jewish fiancée is held; Javier, while he seems at times to be seeking the ultimate Faustian truth, constructs or writes very little: partly through sterility, partly for fear of being manipulated or misunderstood, and because of what he sees as the epoch's inability to offer describable totalities. But unlike Gonzalo and other heroes, he does not die, and too is guilty. Every individual is guilty, perhaps in the light of the intuition of Vico, made his own by Fuentes, that man is responsible for making his own history. Both men come close to losing their soul for their work, but Franz, presented as a student in Prague, closer. Both are certainly responsible for the death of a child, a haunting leitmotif in the work: Franz directly, Javier in Elizabeth's abortion for the sake, she claims, of his virtually non-existent creation. His guilt is that of Jason at the death of his children by the hand of Medea, and indeed the couple follow closely the mythical relationship and its development in the tragedy of Euripides.

The disturbing juxtaposition of literature and Nazism lies at the core of *A Change of Skin*, and the roles of the two men in this context are dramatized in the final trial, modelled partly on Peter Weiss's *Marat/Sade*, where the man of action and the man of violent contemplation face each other on the stage of the lunatic asylum. The question is similar to that posed by Borges's 'Deutsches Requiem' where the highest examples of humanistic thought lead Zur Linde and Europe to its own negation in tyranny. We are not far of course from the tragic coexistence of revolution and tyranny in the earlier novels. *A Change of Skin* thus becomes a questioning of the morality and function of literature and culture in dealing with its other, that which denies it, a meditation and dramatization of themes present in all his works. The text is the impossible answer to two parallel questions. Does optimistic, Christian, humanistic rationalism spawn tyranny because it refuses to contemplate its own underbelly of madness, chaos and instinct? Or do irrationalism, as is argued by writers like Lukács, and 'heretical' writing foment the ultimate and real irrationalism? As the text puts it: 'Sade, Lautréamont, Nietzsche: firing squad commanders in Auschwitz?'

Given this problematic, the presence of the literature of the daemonic is correspondingly large in the novel. Alternately seen as a liberation of man and the apologia of Franz and his Caligari-like demiurge Herr Urs, German Romanticism takes a central place, evoking the link which Mann saw so well and dramatized in works like *Doctor Faustus* between the daemonic and Dionysiac in art and its debased explosion under Hitler. The fundamental role of German Hellenism in this context, as prefiguring the new Germany, in its dual form of classic serenity in Wickelmann and the tragic and Dionysiac in Hölderlin, Rhode and especially Nietzsche is stressed in Javier and Elizabeth's founding and possibly apocryphal stay on the Greek coast. For Javier as for Nietzsche, Greece becomes the ideal home and origin, and in a sense, the trip to Veracruz is an unfinished, unfinishable quest for that point of stability.

169

What the writer does with the other, its function and morality, is linked with the ubiquitous theme of the spectacle and its development in voyeurism: the couples watching the madmen in the asylum, the Nazis watching the Jewish choir sing their own requiem, Elizabeth's father spying through the lavatory keyholes as vigilant policeman or criminal voyeur, etc. The madmen displayed as spectacle in Charenton to reassure the Parisian bourgeoisie of their own sanity and normality is a paradigm taken from Weiss and Foucault's *Madness and Civilisation*. Is this the role or ultimate function, *malgré lui*, of any writer's dealings with the daemonic? The question echoes through the novel in the insistent parallels drawn between the lunatic asylum, the concentration camp at Treblinka, the pyramid and other forms of enclosure. The strategy of Fuentes's text against such risks is to render the stability of the relation between spectator and spectacle, between one and the other, and the comfortable voyeuristic position of the reader untenable, as roles are exchanged, madness and sanity constantly shuffled and perspective dizzyingly manipulated. Hence the use of the important model of *The Cabinet of Dr Caligari*, where the director of the lunatic asylum is either benign and maligned humanist or monstrous criminal madman. Freddy Lambert is alternately seen as sanely surveying the characters from his Lincoln convertible and narrating and inventing from his cell in the asylum: thus echoing the end of (Freddy) Nietzsche, of Balzac's Louis Lambert, and of the Oliveira of Julio Cortázar's novel *Hopscotch*, which the narrator uses as a pillow at night. Within the constant exchange and metamorphosis of the text, the security and ignorance which creates the 'temptation to exterminate' is dissolved. Literature, Fuentes seems to suggest in answer to his own questions, especially perhaps at its most extreme, knows of such dialectics; the Nazis with their rational insanity did not. Javier and Elizabeth, unlike Franz who believes that he has evaded his past, maintain and live through the hell of their lives; like the characters of the Spaniard Unamuno, those of Fuentes turn their own life into a spectacle so that it will not become one for others: 'We will defeat their collective violence with our individual violence against our minds, bodies, art, sexes, we will defeat them by defeating ourselves first.'

What emerges from this area of the novel is the practice of a reason tempered by folly, the Dionysian by the Apollonian (and vice versa of course): a tragic and ironic consciousness of the limits and interdependence of one and the other if humanity is to continue. Cervantes as tutelary spirit of the novel knows something of this as his knight sallies forth to question the world through the romances he has read, question his romances with the world. *A Change of Skin* parades its status as literature, its textuality and intertextuality to the point of becoming avowedly pastiche, palimpsest: a conjunction of texts which are different from the world and contest it while criticizing themselves. Javier and Elizabeth write themselves from the books, papers, Hollywood and German expressionist films they keep in a chest, choosing to live out the ever-changing roles of Lear, Phèdre, Medea, Ligeia, etc. and the commentaries on them. Or are they, like the Monks, the musicians and the madmen players of Weiss, simply forced to follow a script written by another? The reader of *A Change of Skin* cannot be sure or complacent about which of these ways he adopts on reading the text or living his life. 'You quote your classics, and be happy', the text insistently and ironically taunts.

Almost twenty years after the publication of *A Change of Skin*, on which I have dwelt to a certain extent out of

Julio Cortázar and the Drama of Reading

Jason Wilson

Julio Cortázar, the Argentinian writer, was born in Brussels in 1914 and brought up from the age of four in Buenos Aires. He studied briefly at university and then taught at a school and at the University of Mendoza until he clashed with Peronist authorities and resigned. He then trained as a translator and interpreter and won a scholarship to Paris where he remained until he died in 1984.

His earliest published work consisted of critical essays (on Keats, Rimbaud, Artaud), and poems under a pseudonym, 'Julio Denis'. He matured as a writer under the shadow of Jorge Luis Borges and *Sur*, the cosmopolitan literary magazine edited by Victoria Ocampo, and only relatively late found the medium for his surprising originality.

He published his first collection of finely crafted and jolting short stories the year he left for Paris and called them *Bestiary (Bestario*, 1951). He followed these with seven subsequent volumes: *Secret Weapons (Las armas secretas*, 1959), *The End of the Game and Other Stories (Final del juego*, 1965), *All Fires the Fire (Todos los fuegos el fuego*, 1966), *Octaedro* ('Octahedron'), 1974, *Alguien que anda por ahí* ('Someone Who Walks There'), 1977, *We Love Glenda So Much and Other Stories (Queremos tanto a Glenda*, 1980) and *Deshoras* ('Awkward Moments'), 1982, many ably translated into English.

Cortázar's first novel *The Winners (Los premios)* was published in 1960, followed by *Hopscotch (Rayuela*, 1963), *62: A Model Kit (62-modelo para armar*, 1968), *A Manual for Manuel (Libro de Manuel*, 1973) and *A Certain Lucas (Un tal Lucas*, 1979). His poetry first playfully appeared as *Pameos y meopas* (anagrams of the word *poemas* – poems), 1971, and recently *Salvo el crepúsculo* ('Except Dawn'), 1984. Interspersed with these are Cortázar's less classifiable, experimental works ranging from *Cronopios and Famas (Historias de cronopios y famas*, 1962) to collage books like *Around the Day in Eighty Worlds (La vuelta al día en ochenta mundos*, 1967), and *Ultimo round* ('Last Round'), 1970, or his journey down the autoroute from Paris to Marseilles *Los autonautas de la cosmopista* (a play with words: auto-car-astronauta, cosmos and autopista-autoroute), 1983. And finally his political writings have been collected under *Nicaragua tan violentamente dulce* ('Nicaragua so violently sweet'), 1984, and *Argentina: años de alambradas culturales* ('Argentina: years of cultural wire-fencing'), 1984.

Behind all his works Cortázar employs an impressive skill in engaging the reader in a world of subtle and sudden jolts. He learnt from the French Surrealists how to shake the lazy reader into an awareness that something threatens behind the conventions of everyday life without ever defining this elusive, often hostile otherness.

Behind Cortázar's multi-faceted work lies a restless youthfulness, even dissatisfaction, that invokes both intense seriousness and black humour, that refers to Zen, modern jazz and revolutionary politics in a supple prose that hints at a moral vision of the self's repressed potential, both individually and collectively. Over his later years Cortázar became more and more radical, but the turning point was undoubtedly the Cuban Revolution of 1959. He worked selflessly for the Russell Tribunal and later Sandinista Nicaragua, often giving his royalties to the causes he fought for.

Looking back over his published work a defiant integrity emerges as one of its constants. As a writer Cortázar refused to be catalogued and like a juggler combined impeccable, hypnotic short stories, novels that undermined the illusions of realism, nostalgic sonnets and whimsical surrealist collage books with earnest essays on Latin American politics. But rather than account for this exhilarating defiance through his varied books, *Rayuela* (translated as *Hopscotch*, 1967) will serve as a compendium of his ramifications. *Hopscotch* calls itself both novel and anti-novel, it has sections that read like stories, lyrical passages that approximate to poems and experimental set-pieces that mix eroticism, wordplay and black humour in debts to Jarry, Dada and Henri Michaux. *Hopscotch* is also an elegy to omnivorous reading.

As a writer Cortázar was haunted by Western culture's fascination with revolutionary change. Put as simply as possible this dilemma questions whether a person can change or escape himself and stand in somebody else's shoes, in their skin. Is freedom attainable? This quest for a radical rebirth, symptomatic of a dead-end civilization in its death throes, implies the dilemma of Otherness and how other is the other. But rather than get ensnared in generalities, let us begin with the protagonist and possible narrator of *Hopscotch*, Horacio Oliveira, and his experience of intense dissatisfaction with things as they are (the stereotypes he inherited) and the consequent trickiness of facing up to himself without self-deceit or self-justification. The novel is a mirror of his attempt to be himself and this mirror is a metaphor of self-analysis, a substitute for psychoanalysis.

But before entering the Pandora's box of *Hopscotch*, as

Carlos Fuentes once called it, a few contexts will help define Horacio Oliveira's cultural disease of self-revulsion. The crucial antecedent for Cortázar was Surrealism as a utopian praxis that set out ambitiously to change inner man and society. In 1935 André Breton prepared his speech for the Writers' Congress (which he wasn't allowed to read) with a challenge to fuse Marx's *'transformer le monde'* with Rimbaud's *'changer la vie'*. Cortázar absorbed this call but brushed Marx aside because he felt that an inner change in the individual preceded a change in the collectivity. Throughout the 1950s in Paris, while amassing the notes which ended up as *Hopscotch* Cortázar dabbled in the fashionable Zen and Vedanta which both stressed the individual's need for an inner change. But Rimbaud had become an early culture-hero. In 1941, under the pseudonym Julio Denis, Cortázar wrote an article claiming that Rimbaud's poetry and then radical change to Red Sea adventurer had become both a 'message' and a 'warning'. Reading Rimbaud had generated an inner model of a double kind of authenticity, both literary and existential which was hard to live up to. Cortázar adopted various culture-heroes, best embodied in Artaud whom he described on his death in 1948 as having attained 'the highest and most difficult grade of authenticity'; and in Charlie Parker, fictionalized in a story 'The Pursuer' ('El perseguidor') where the black alto sax player's quest for authenticity 'denounces us all'. However, what confuses Cortázar's admiration for such extremist culture-heroes is the fact that he had read (or listened to) them.

Cortázar never resolved the ambivalence he felt about reading. To Omar Prego, Cortázar described the protagonist of an early novel only published posthumously as *El examen* ('The Exam'), 1986, as autobiographically a 'super-lector' which I will interpret as the Borgesian disease of over-reading, a toxin affecting Cortázar's *Sur* magazine generation. It was reading as a child that first initiated Cortázar into the miracle of transference from his banal hometown reality in the Banfield suburb of Buenos Aires into the magic, dangerous and adventurous world of Salgari and Jules Verne. This change took place in his fertile mind as he held a book open and read; a kind of hypnosis, even brain-washing. Years later (1980) he confessed to Sara Castro-Klaren that reading still 'lifts me totally out of everyday life, my way of being and way of thinking'. In 1983, just before he died, he told Prego that he could still 'sink himself' into a book and that reading allowed him 'to change places, leave myself behind, move to another context'. But as all readers know, especially with a novel's cunning illusions of a parallel, realistic universe, there comes a moment when you have to crash out of this 'alternative' world and return to banality. Answering Prego, Cortázar remembered his rage as a nine-year-old reading his favourite novel when an aunt shouted 'Julio, your piano lesson!'. He called this return to the empiric self before the release (and relief) of reading, a bitter *disenchantment*.

Of course many other experiences shift us out of the humdrum – sex, drugs, trances, revolutionary politics – but the prime metaphor for radical change in Cortázar's case remained reading. However, the thrill of being 'elevated' into another mental realm while reading generated a counter-effect that led to a resentment at being hypnotized, for reading also smacks of escapism, privacy and élitism. So Cortázar learnt to discriminate between escapist reading and genuine reading where Rimbaud and Artaud became his way of testing other authors (and himself). Here the novel more than any other genre epitomized his ambivalence. So *Hopscotch* narrates the descent into hell

(Rimbaud's not Dante's) of a middle-aged Bohemian who discovers that the hypnosis of reading and culture is a fraud. This recasts *Don Quixote* with the bourgeois realist and psychological novel substituting the chivalry novel.

Cortázar's ambivalence about whether reading promises a revolutionary change in being points to a proviso: it depends what and how you read and whether you are a bourgeois male novel reader or not. The perplexing opening story of *The End of the Game and Other Stories (Final del juego*, 1964), called 'The Continuity of the Parks' ('La continuidad de los parques') opens with a busy man reading a novel in an armchair in his study overlooking his *estancia*, park. He loses himself in the novel's plot and characters: 'novelistic illusion wins him over completely'. Suddenly he becomes one of the characters and creeps up behind himself with a knife. Moral: it is dangerous to read novels in that way, a kind of mental suicide where fiction will revenge itself on the reader for having believed in it. Novel-reading probes the man's 'secret vice' (Rachel Billington's phrase), his unconfessed 'guilty pleasure' (Virginia Woolf in *The Second Common Reader*).

Ambiguity about reading and guilt generates many stories about doubles in Cortázar's fiction where neither has the moral superiority to exorcize his guilt. 'The Pursuer' ('El perseguidor') opposes a black musician Johnny Carter with a white French jazz critic and biographer, Bruno, in a symbiotic dance that ends with the survival of Bruno trapped in his bad faith. 'The Idol of the Cyclades' ('El ídolo de las Cícladas') opposes two kinds of archaeologist, the rational Parisian Morand and the poet-shaman from South America, Somoza: neither triumphs. 'Secret weapons' ('Las armas secretas') has Pierre (who reads Henri Michaux) possessed by his lover's guilt. In 'The Other Heaven' ('El otro cielo') the protagonist oscillates guiltily between a Paris of the 1870s and his Buenos Aires of the 1940s, trapped in both his fantasy world and in his daily life and tortured by a South American (Lautréamont, born in Montevideo) he regrets he never dared talk to. Nobody is free from guilt, especially when confronted with the likes of a Maldoror.

But Cortázar's stories are often too manipulative, too cunningly crafted to explore guilt. He followed Poe's dictum of the single effect where the reader's soul 'is at the writer's control'. His characters are not 'human' but narrative tricks, prejudices, empty names. So Cortázar turned to the novel where the economy of means does not dictate the rhythms. The novel also lies outside both Surrealism and Borges country. But most crucially the novel allowed Cortázar to combine the exploration of his own guilt through his protagonists (Medrano in *The Winners*, Oliveira, Andrés in *A Manual for Manuel*, Juan in *62: A Model Kit*), and the reader's through identification with these heroes. Cortázar devised a novel that exposes his guilt, his characters' guilt and his reader's guilt, *hypocrite lecteur, mon semblable*.

In a long essay 'La situación de la novela' (1950) Cortázar, as a reader, defines the novel as a kind of self-exploration. Only the novel integrates all the twentieth-century specializations to give an image of actual people in life. This novel is not a fiction, but a truth mirror. Indeed Cortázar has always despised the idea of literature, of being a professional writer, of writing well; 'aesthetics' is a dirty word. To write 'literature' self-consciously is to surrender to bad faith. In 1950 he categorized two kinds of reader: those who read 'to escape a certain reality', who read to kill time and those few who read to criticize reality and show it up as it is. There are novels and novels. And truth-novels can liberate and change a reader. But the

179

starting point is to begin to feel sick with shame and guilt at who and where you are (in an armchair), like Oliveira at the opening of *Hopscotch*.

So, unlike Sartre, Cortázar always held on to the idea that reading could be a revolutionary activity. Cortázar keeps his eye on his reader, he writes notes to him and offers ways of reading. In *The Winners* (1960) he still opposes two readers: those who 'escape and long to be left in peace' and those who read to 'glimpse themselves'. In *Hopscotch* these two readers are incorporated into the opening reading Instructions. All his speculations about reading within the novel take place in terms of reading as a means to radical change where art becomes a window, a bridge, a door – all favourite images – into real life.

'The Band' ('La banda') from *The End of the Game and Other Stories* illustrates the narrative problem of exploring a sudden radical change in lifestyle, a leap out of bad faith into authenticity. The commonsensical narrator explains his friend Lucio's abrupt disappearance as due to a liver attack or a woman. But we quickly see through this devious, falsely ironic narrator and realize that something intensely important happened to Lucio inside the cinema. However, even Lucio cannot squeeze his sensation of having seen the grotesque truth about his life into words. The story is realistically set in the Peronist Buenos Aires of 1947 in a cinema that existed, showing a Litvak film. But instead of the film he expected to see, Lucio witnesses a Peronist factory band play bad music: the horror of the disparity between his expectations of high art – a Litvak film – and the music so shock him that he drops everything and flees his country. What induced such a change? The narrator can only weakly hint that Lucio 'saw reality at last'. That is, not the band's fat-thighed women players, but the reality of his own inauthenticity. As readers we do not enter his mind and sudden self-revulsion. We just get a list of the perfect bourgeois life he left behind: his favourite café, his blue suit, his nights out, his girlfriend, his maturity, the day he would die. But that very list is explored through Oliveira in the novel. For example Lucio's 'girlfriend' becomes La Maga whom Oliveira drops (in case love is another fiction) and probably drives to suicide, one of the novel's main strands.

Lucio discards his old life to begin a more authentic life. But that might be an optimistic gloss, for the story is dedicated to René Crevel 'who died for something like this'. Crevel, another of Cortázar's culture-heroes (he reappears in *Hopscotch*) committed suicide in 1935, caught between loyalty to the Surrealist André Breton and his Communist Party friends. Is 'The Band' ('La banda') a story about suicide as the only moral option? Does Cortázar think that the only change a bourgeois like Lucio – intelligent enough to like Litvak – deserves is death? What suggests this, apart from the dedication, is that for nearly all Cortázar's protagonists it is harder to break out of the mould (and the past) than they think when they kick against it. Is to change and become free possibly another fiction?

For many readers *Hopscotch* was, as Cortázar conceded to Rita Guibert, 'more an experience than a book'. This unsettling, open-ended novel posed so many questions that it seemed to speak directly to its reader, without the self-conscious filter of literary artifice. The novel's basic motivations – the bankruptcy of the Western cultural tradition and Cortázar's sense of having been poisoned by this tradition – caught a 1960s spirit (Marcuse, N. O. Brown, Ivan Illich, happenings, leading up to May 1968) but this has not dated the poignancy of Cortázar's perceptions about being over-cultured.

The quickest way into this mirror-novel, which author, protagonist and reader hold up to themselves, comes from the title Cortázar gave his working notes: *Mandala*, as he told Luis Harss. Mandala, a visual aid to meditation, betrays Cortázar's own inner search during the 1950s; a mandala is a disciplined journey to enlightenment that requires a lifetime's practice. This map or guide through the labyrinth (of life, of the mind) ends, like a board game, in an often blank centre, satori. Horacio Oliveira moves through the mandala of Parisian and Buenos Airean streets, discarding friends, lovers, cities, his bookish learning, allowing unexpected things to happen *to* him as only chance corresponds to his most secret desires. A desperate attempt to find what he successively calls the Centre, the Kibbutz of Desire, the Ygdrassil dictates his journey along the bizarre passageways of this mandala. But there is an epiphany: Oliveira has been arrested drunk, just as the tramp Emmanuèle is about to suck him off. He is locked into a police van, on his way to deportation and Buenos Aires when he discovers he has no need for culturally alien meditation disciplines for the surest way to authenticity is 'a *patadas*', with a kick, 'without necessity of Vedanta or Zen' (p. 252). Being kicked up to heaven by life (in a police van, a scandal) suggests Cortázar's alternative to the mandala, a hopscotch, with the stone you kick and its reliance on chance, its heaven and the possibility of failing. On the spine of the first Argentinian edition there is a diagram of hopscotch with its numbers and its Earth and Heaven. A child's game with a deadly serious symbolism. Can Oliveira kick the stone (himself) and get to heaven? In spite of the switch in title, *Hopscotch* remains a novel about elusive salvation.

Oliveira's problem derives from the fact that adults can no longer play games with a child's nonchalance. The 'End of the Game' defines Cortázar's fictional world and implies the dull post-pubertal world of sexuality, work, loss of fantasy, self-consciousness and bad faith. To return to being a child motivates Oliveira to de-educate himself and rid his mind of the deadening bookish culture he acquired in order to become an adult intellectual, dismissing even his dream of being a poet and his belief in love. Having read too much allows Cortázar to coin his term for bad faith – the novel. His life pattern is summarized thus: 'infancy suddenly ends and we fall into novels' (pp. 251–2). The non-verbal magic of infancy leads to the Fall into the fictions of adulthood. A novel is a pre-ordained script, a congealed view of the self, a predictable life. To break free of fiction becomes the imperative for author, character and reader – within a novel. But this break is sought in relation to an inner, non-verbal, non-literary contact with 'the world under the eyelids that eyes turned inwards recognize and respect' (p. 374). The novel epitomizes bad faith because it is the bourgeois literary genre and because Cortázar, like Oliveira, had read too many, acquiring a vicarious familiarity with life. He once confessed to Luis Harss that reading 'probably denied me a good dose of vital experience'. Oliveira accuses himself of acting like a Conrad hero, like a Céline character; a friend identifies him with a phony Lautréamont, a 'Maldoror *porteño*' (A Maldoror – Lautréamont's rebel poet – from the port of Buenos Aires).

Although Cortázar sometimes rejected his novel as auto-biographical and, in interview with Picon Garfield, denounced Oliveira as a mediocre pseudo-intellectual, at this cultural disease level of over-reading we can bond Cortázar and Oliveira into a therapeutic relationship where one mirrors the other. Cortázar submitted his protagonist to his own search for some 'absolute' that would redeem him from despair and meaninglessness. Oliveira's journey through the novel mirrors Cortázar's: an exorcism of culture. Amazingly for a *porteño* intellectual, Cortázar had never been psychoanalysed – he admitted to Prego that he wrote *El examen* ('The Exam') in the late 1940s as self-analysis in conjunction with Freud's complete works in Spanish. We can make the leap that Cortázar analysed his own bad faith, his over-culturalization, through Oliveira, his doppelgänger.

In 1967 Cortázar wrote in *Around the Day in Eighty Worlds*: 'I who write this also do not know how to change my life and remain as I was before'. Yet in 1978 in an interview with González Bermejo he confirmed that he still believed in Rimbaud's 'il faut changer la vie'. Why does this change in life still defy him? Could it be that both Cortázar and Oliveira were both over forty in 1960? Part of the problem is ageing.

In order to test himself through Oliveira and see if both can 'cure themselves' (p. 249) Cortázar locates the enemy as guilt – the guilt of having read too much, of not working, of not having lived intensely enough *à la Rimbaud* – and he must exorcize it. This guilt of having wasted his life originates with his literary attraction for Paris, Mecca of Culture, from a provincial Buenos Aires. But once in Paris its dream-glamour evaporates and both author and protagonist become aliens, *métèques* in a grey city. Having seen through the veneer of Paris, Oliveira, a 'self-conscious vagrant' (p. 26), drops out and fills his days with guilty leisure; love affairs, café discussions and sauntering about the streets. But no work. Above all he *talks*; endless conversations that do not lead to a talking cure.

The novel could be narrated by Oliveira in the third person; he keeps a notebook and once wrote poems. It is as if he writes the novel as the reader reads it. But he is haunted by the authentic poets (Rimbaud, Artaud, Lautréamont) and cannot content himself with a mere novel for he is writing in order to change himself. Behind the compelling incidents and anecdotes of the first half of *Hopscotch* we can identify (or not) with a character who loathes his 'rotten measurer of a university and enlightened man' (p. 117), asphyxiated by what he calls his librarian's prejudices (p. 47). He wants to humiliate this culturalized part of himself, stub out the 'stupid pride of the intellectual who thinks himself equipped to understand' (p. 116). In order to de-sublimate himself he must turn himself inside out and look at the world through the eye of his arsehole (p. 253).

Oliveira's psychology is generated by being a self-loathing intellectual whose innate tendency has been to escape 'human filth' (p. 253) through books, 'in some metaphysical river, naturally' (p. 134). He is an idealist who has shockingly glimpsed the foul end-result in himself in the middle of his life of so much reading and talking about culture. In a discussion about *The Tibetan Book of the Dead* Oliveira quips 'the Tibetan book *for* the dead' (p. 188) but his earnest companions miss his lethal irony. For Oliveira, being an intellectual has landed him in a nightmare.

All the Club de la Serpiente discussions, all the literary quotes and allusions that froth out of Oliveira's mouth confirm how deeply Culture has poisoned Cortázar's protagonist. But in his de-education there are three escape hatches. The first is a strangely flattering view of Cortázar's 'primitive' South American roots. Oliveira, unlike his Bohemian companions, still has access to an elemental brutal life outside Europe. Secondly, the women Oliveira chooses have not been contaminated by over reading (La

Maga reads Galdós; Talita, encyclopaedias). These
women can still experience truth: 'Only Oliveira realized
that La Maga leaned out every now and then on to those
great terraces outside time that all of them had been
seeking dialectically' (p. 41). These women's perceptions
have not been codified and sullied in words, concepts and
books for the source of authenticity is a 'balbucearse'
(p. 240), a babbling, a stammering. This *balbuceo* suggests
the universal language of authenticity, a mantra or baby
talk that only authentic art taps. The third escape involves
much of the novel's realistic plot and is simply the way
Oliveira plunges into action before thought; he leaps
without thinking in order to break out of his 'paralytic's
terrible lucidity' (p. 32). Author, character and reader all
leap out of a paralysing self-consciousness in a process-
novel where nobody knows where they are going.
Oliveira's drama is cultural and historic: being stuck in
himself, unable to change; 'how tiring it is to be always
oneself. Irretrievably', everybody stuck in glass cases
(p. 122).

If Cortázar purifies his living a bad novel through his
protagonist, he also traps his readers through his skill in
writing realistic prose. He never lets his reader off the
hook. *Hopscotch* opens with a 'Tablero de dirección'
(Direction board) that with the dispensable chapters constituted the novel's experimental allure in the 1960s. He
offers two readings: he appears to despise the conventional novel reader who reads from page 1 to the end and
appeals to intellectual snobs (and literary critics) who can
follow his order, beginning with Chapter 73. But this snob
reading has been undermined because the reader cannot
get out of the novel: Chapter 131 sends you to 58 and 58 to
131, like a stuck record. Clearly Cortázar seeks a 'new'
reader who questions reading itself. How to read has

become the theme of the novel and is the same as saying, who am I? This clue is dropped by the avant-garde writer Morelli: 'My book can be read any way you like' (p. 627) which privileges the reader's *disponibilité* and suggests that a work of art's only value is its capacity to provoke whim or desire. Cortázar seeks a reader who also wants to change.

But even the reader who agrees that change is crucial is actually reluctant to set out on a reading journey into his own bad faith. When Cortázar, through Morelli, divides readers into *lectores hembras* (passive readers) and *lectores cómplices*, he intended his accomplices to suffer. For this latter reader is forced to become an accomplice to Oliveira's crime of over reading and inner death. In fact both types of reader coexist in every individual reader for he must first enjoy reading the novel as a realistic piece of fiction (i.e. confess his guilt) and then realize that fiction is a screen with an author on one side and the reader on the other, as if in analytic session. Art is not artifice but a 'living bridge between man and man' (p. 453). Real narrative first questions the author, then the reader. As Morelli wrote 'there is no message, but messengers' (p. 453). This kind of novel will be a 'coagulant of lived experiences' and will lure the reader deeper into trouble, chaos and life. The real character becomes the reader and his reluctance to change (pp. 497-8). Cortázar expressed this painful view of art in *Around the Day in Eighty Worlds*: 'What did your admiration matter to Van Gogh? What he wanted was your complicity, that you would try to look as he was looking with your eyes skinned by a Heraclitean fire'. Cortázar wants his reader to *suffer* with him; he wants to make him ill and sick up his bad faith, not sit down and lose himself in fictions.

Chapter 21 exemplifies this new way of reading.

Oliveira sits alone in a Latin-Quarter café reading René Crevel's 1929 novel *Êtes-vous fou?*. Oliveira talks to this book as if Crevel still lives. He uses Crevel to criticize himself:

> *Tu sèmes des syllabes pour récolter des étoiles* – Crevel makes fun of me.
> One does what one can – I answer. (p. 112)

Oliveira reads fiction to 'mock himself'. Crevel diagnoses his vanity: he who wanted to sow syllables and be a poet, or find stars as a symbol of wisdom and literary glory. We see that Oliveira reads prose to judge himself. It is telling that Cortázar refused to publish his own poetry 'because I feel less capable of judging myself through poetry than through prose'. Crevel winkles out his most secret vanities; that is how one becomes a *lector cómplice*. Thanks to Crevel Oliveira becomes conscious that he 'pours out his bitterness in the suburbs' (a Bohemian dropout), that he clings to stories (novels, fiction), that he hugs words (a cowardly logocentric poet). The intellectual's disease: between Oliveira and Reality 'grows a reedbed of words' (p. 115). While reading Crevel Oliveira cries out to his lover la Maga 'Ah, let me in, let me one day see what your eyes see' but he remains stuck in his *'egociencia'*, his *'conciencia'* (p. 117), terrified of changing. Reading a book has pushed Oliveira towards painful truth, 'living things' (p. 117).

Many marvellous chapters in *Hopscotch* involve the reader in Oliveira's predicament. In Chapter 23 we suffer with Oliveira as he inexplicably sits out alone the sad avant-garde parody of a concert given by Berthe Trepat, herself a grotesque double of himself; in Chapter 28 we become accomplices to Oliveira's perverse refusal to tell la

Maga that her baby is dead; we are suspended with Talita on the plank in Chapter 41 . . . but to describe the skill with which Cortázar seduces us into the realistic scenes in the novel would be to rewrite it *à la Pierre Menard*. But once we have enjoyed reading these chapters we must then submit to its 'ferocious slap in the face' (p. 250) and sink up to our necks, like Oliveira recalling Heraclitus, in our own shit (guilt) in order to 'cure ourselves'. That is why the novelist, his protagonist and the reader all end the novel sitting on the windowsill. Did Oliveira leap out, go mad, commit suicide, become a bourgeois zombie or discover his love for his friends? The real test happens off-page, the book closed. Are you still willing to remain yourself or take a leap like Cortázar into the brotherhood of politics and away from solipsism and ivory-tower culture?

In Chapter 82 Morelli defines writing as a path to salvation: 'To write is to draw my mandala and at the same time traverse it, to invent purification purifying oneself' (p. 458) where the act of writing – the verb is in the infinitive – parallels the disciplined journey along the mandala. But Morelli deflates his pedantic confession with self-irony. This is the 'task of a poor white shaman wearing nylon underpants' (p. 458). This sudden self-mocking is typically Cortázarian, so typical that this same 'Morelli' fragment appears in Cortázar's working notebook (edited by Ana María Barrenechea) in the first person as an autobiographical intention.

Fiction as a substitute for psychoanalysis? In 1983 Cortázar told Prego that Oliveira's most memorable trait is his need to 'look at himself in a mirror that reflects him as he is and not feel sorry for himself. And attack himself, directly'. After so much self-attacking does Oliveira change? Does the reader change? In one sense all great novels change the reader – art opens you out to suppressed, barely glimpsed areas of desire, hurt, jealousy, memory, dream and experience. In *Hopscotch* this kind of reading-therapy has become its theme where writing and reading are restored to activities that do not specify pre-established finalities because the truth of the self resists words and culture and speaks as a *balbuceo*. Maybe writing (and reading) a novel like *Hopscotch* retraces Freud's own experience of analysing himself?

NOTE

I have translated quotations from the following of Cortázar's works: *Rayuela*, Buenos Aires, Editorial Sudamericana, 1963; *Final del juego*, Buenos Aires, Editorial Sudamericana, 1964; *La vuelta al día en ochenta mundos*, Mexico, Siglo XXI, 1967; 'La situacion de la novela', *Cuadernos Americanos*, no. 4 (julio–agosto 1950); 'Muerte de Antonin Artaud', *Sur*, n.163, 1948; 'Rimbaud', *Huella*, n.2, 1941. I have also translated answers from the following interviews: by Sara Castro-Klaren in *Cuadernos hispanoamericanos* 364-366 (1980); Omar Prego, *La fascinación de las palabras. Conversaciones con J.C.* (1985); Luis Harss, *Los nuestros* (1966); Rita Guibert, *Seven Voices* (1973); Evelyn Picon Garfield, *Cortázar* (1978) and Ernesto González Bermejo, *Conversaciones por Cortázar* (1978). Ana María Barrenechea, 'Hopscotch and its log book', *Review* 30 (1981), publ. in facsimile as *Cuaderno de Bitácora de Rayuela*, with Ana María Barrenechea's study (1983).

Gabriel García Márquez

William Rowe

In Britain, Márquez is usually thought of as a writer of fantasy. Critics and reviewers have again and again drawn attention to the 'fantastic' and 'magical' qualities of his work, and in so doing have to an important extent obscured the principal concerns of his writing. There are cultural reasons for this emphasis on the marvellous and the exotic. Gratuitous fantasy, as in the surrealist tradition, seems particularly alien to the predominant style of literary education in Britain. A man is followed everywhere by a cloud of yellow butterflies: what is the reader supposed to do with that? Does it have a meaning, or is it just a piece of sentimental escapism, typical of a Never-Never Land? But in the same book – *One Hundred Years of Solitude* (*Cien años de soledad*) – there is a barman with a withered arm. It has become withered, we are informed, because he once raised it against his parents. Children in traditional Catholic families in Latin America are told, quite literally, if you hit your parents your arm will burn. Márquez's novel humorously takes such beliefs at their word and exposes their aim as that of duping children in order to control them.

If fantasy does not have an escapist role, does this then mean that it conveys a moral fable, as in Tolkien's *The Lord of the Rings* or, to take an earlier example, in Charles Kingsley's *The Water Babies*, a classic of Victorian fantasy literature? But fantasy in Márquez is non-allegorical:

among its attractions are gratuitousness and out-of-control exuberance. Is there perhaps some inherently magical quality in Latin American life? The idea of Latin America as a place of unbridled fantasy, larger than life, etc. is familiar. But we need to acknowledge the part played by our own escapism: a desire for the exotic, a taste for cultural tourism – or, more seriously, a search for liberation from the constraints of our own culture. Otherwise we fail to recognize that there are repressive dimensions to other cultures and see only the exuberant fantasy, not the methods for controlling everyday life. This is why Márquez has often said that what European readers think is marvellous, to Colombians is ordinary and everyday.

The image of Latin America as exotic and magical derives from a European stance. Since the Conquest, the human beings and environments of the continent, different from anything Europeans were accustomed to, have been construed as fabulous, wonderful or monstrous, which is a way of incorporating what is different and alien into one's own vision of things. Latin America as a place of fantasy and exoticism is an image of tamed otherness, much as Celticism in nineteenth-century Britain attempted to turn the Irish into harmless dreamers, the better to neutralize them and incorporate them into English culture. To the people actually living in them, the places are not exotic and marvellous. So the issue becomes, who draws the line which decides where reality ends and fantasy and magic begin? To the inhabitants of Macondo, the setting of much of Márquez's early fiction, ice, false teeth and magnifying lenses are prodigious marvels. Whereas from the viewpoint of scientific rationalism, Macondo is a fabulous and magical place. Márquez's novel laughs at the absurdity of any boundary which pretends to set up a fixed division between the real and the fantastic. Reversing the process by which the realm of fantasy is constructed in order to render things harmless, he makes fantasy challenge the rules by which reality is put together and controlled. It is therefore misleading to highlight fantasy as a special category in itself, given that it is part of something much wider: Márquez's concern is both with the rules within which social existence is established and controlled and with the possibilities of radically changing them. If we define magic as what does not fit into a narrowly scientific outlook, then the magical aspects of Márquez's work are part of his refusal to be bound by rationalism and those varieties of writing which stay within its limits. As he said to Plinio Apuleyo Mendoza, he realized he was going to be a writer when he discovered that Kafka told things in the same way as his own grandmother.[1]

His maternal grandmother, with whom he lived until he was eight years old, is a crucial source of all his writing. The endless stories he heard her tell when a child made available to him the rich oral traditions of the northern Caribbean coast of Colombia. The collision between this oral material and an aristocratic, patriarchal, written tradition is one of the most fascinating aspects of his work. The grandmother exemplified what happens when storytelling and word of mouth, as opposed to written memory, is the place where the weaving of the social fabric takes place. *One Hundred Years of Solitude* is, in this connection, an accumulation of heard stories rather than – as in the paradigm of the European novel – an assemblage of themes and characters which develop over time. Yet, despite its prodigious narrative energy, there is a feeling of relief on reaching the end of this novel. Unlike, say, *A Thousand and One Nights* – also an accumulation of stories – it is not a text whose pleasures the reader does not want to finish. There is a sadness within the constant exuberance and an

193

overall feeling of claustrophobic enclosure, arising from the uninterrupted barrage of narrative coupled with the unrelieved repetition of the characters' lives and names.

The majority of Márquez's novels are written from a place where everything has already happened. His first novel, *Leaf Storm* (*La hojarasca*), moves backwards in time from the moment of a funeral. *One Hundred Years of Solitude* includes within itself a mirror of its own production, Melquíades's room, immune from the dilapidations of time and the vagaries of weather, an entirely static place where the manuscripts, which prophesy all the events of the novel, are kept. *The Autumn of the Patriarch* (*El otoño del patriarca*), begins with the death of its protagonist, the one-hundred-and-fifty-year-old dictator, in the presidential palace now entirely invaded by nature. In *Chronicle of a Death Foretold* (*Crónica de una muerte anunciada*), the title itself indicates the certainty of the death of Santiago Nasar, described in the last sentences but experienced as imminent from the very first sentence. It is not until *Love in the Times of Cholera* ('*El amor en los tempos del cólera*'), his latest novel (published in Spanish in 1985), that the pattern changes.

This particular type of narrative structure relates to the central issue of memory, personal and social, written and oral. In his own life, Márquez underwent a series of separations from his parents, his childhood home and his native region. Until he was eight, he lived in Aracataca with his grandparents; when his grandfather died he was sent to join his mother. As an adolescent he was sent away from the tropical Caribbean region to school in Bogotá, in the cold Andean part of Colombia, where none of the exuberance and informality of Caribbean culture was available. Later he moved still further away: *No One Writes to the Colonel* (*El coronel no tiene quien le escriba*) was written in Paris and *One Hundred Years of Solitude* in Mexico. When he was twenty-one, he accompanied his mother on a journey back to Aracataca to sell the grandparents' house, an experience which was to have a crucial shaping effect on his writing. When they arrived he found everything changed: 'the houses were exactly the same, but eaten away by time and poverty, and through the windows we saw the same furniture, but fifteen years older. It was a dusty, hot town, and the midday heat was terrible, you breathed dust.' The recuperation of a past attacked by time provided Márquez with a main source of energy. But so also does a fascination with a space and time which are doomed to disappear, and with the process of decay itself.

The return to Aracataca is the recognizable source of one of his finest stories, 'Tuesday Siesta'. A woman has travelled with her young daughter to honour the grave of her son, shot dead in a suspected act of robbery. As well as the dusty midday heat, she has to face the priest's uncooperativeness and the hostile gaze of onlookers who fill the streets. Her defiance of the town is an act of personal memory, a refusal of the townspeople's social amnesia. 'Tuesday Siesta' ends with the woman walking out into the heat: the visit to the grave, which is the main event of the story, takes place in the reader's imagination. In a novel, the functioning of memory as a motive force is more complex. By what person or agency is the large accumulation of events registered? And in what medium are they inscribed? Popular, oral memory changes according to the circumstances of recall; it is continually re-actualized rather than fixed once and for all; and it takes the form of a voice heard rather than written words. Once memory becomes codified in a written form it is different: in the first place it is not open to modification. And it is no longer the property of the collectivity but is channelled through the specialized activity of priests and scribes (represented, in *One Hundred Years of Solitude*, by Melquíades). The difference between oral and written modes of inscription is marked in the first sentence of the novel: 'Many years later, as he faced the firing squad, Colonel Aureliano Buendía was to remember that distant afternoon when his father took him to discover ice.' The simple aorist of narrative ('his father took him') is placed within a future that has already happened, an operation which is only possible thanks to the fixity of writing and its complex syntax. This perspective also depends on a sense of written history, as an ordered series in time, whose later moments can be seen already written into the earlier ones. The placing of a remembered past within a future which in a sense has already happened produces the time structure of the book as a whole.

There is an episode where all the issues I have indicated are brought together and given dramatic focus: the plague of insomnia. The plague which attacks the inhabitants of Macondo produces amnesia as a side effect: people cannot remember the names of things. The contagion arose from the local Indians, an oral community, whereas the cure is brought by Melquíades, the writing-man. But before the plague is cured, José Arcadio Buendía, the patriarch of the family, invents a memory machine in order to arrest its dire effects: 'The artefact was based on the possibility of reviewing every morning, from beginning to end, the totality of knowledge acquired during one's life. He conceived of it as a spinning dictionary that a person placed on the axis could operate by means of a lever, so that in very few hours there would pass before his eyes the notions most necessary for life. He had succeeded in writing almost fourteen thousand entries . . .' It is actually a writing machine. To counteract the danger that people might forget the function of things (the humorous example given is a cow), it produces labels and definitions. But by eliminating forgetting it eliminates change: the world is subordinated to the dictionary. And given that its aim is to fill the whole of reality with words, without leaving any gaps, its circularity becomes a figure of written literature as a closed structure, admitting no modification and closed in its self-sufficiency: which is also an image of this particular novel, with its sensation of cloggedness and its machinery of inescapable fate. The material of the novel is predominantly oral, but it passes through a solidifying written form. There is a double mode of operation: on the one hand the oral stories, and on the other a fixed code of fatality, embodied in the notion of Melquíades's prophecies.

The working out of fatality is based on the Oedipal trap: incestuous desire is inherent to the Buendía family, and consummated incest is the ultimate crime, punishable by total destruction, not just of the guilty parties, but of their world. The definition of relationships through naming is crucial to incest prohibitions: without names the prohibition cannot operate, since mother, father, son, daughter etc. are a function of naming. Which is why it is so urgent to put a stop to the plague of insomnia: it could liquidate the whole Oedipal apparatus. Sophocles and Freud collide dangerously with popular rural culture.

We have moved from orality versus literacy to the control exercised by cultural codes and to Márquez's concern with the possibility of modifying the basic rules of social existence. In his Nobel Prize acceptance speech he reverses the final sentence of *One Hundred Years of Solitude* and speaks of the necessity that those condemned to one hundred years of solitude should have a second opportunity on earth. This notion of political necessity, which arises from his commitment to socialism, does not correspond with the main thrust of his fiction: the divergent paths of literary intensity and political conviction are the main contradiction of his work. The author he most admires is Sophocles, particularly the *Oedipus Rex*. In *One Hundred Years of Solitude* a soldier in the Liberal ranks declares 'we're fighting this war against the priests so that a person can marry his own mother'. Here the failure of Colombia's civil wars to bring about any radical change is placed on the same level as the impossibility of undoing Oedipal fatality: the tragic code prevails, spelling out a script beneath history which history fulfils.

The history of Colombia is marked, more than that of any other Latin American country, by constantly recurring civil wars. The worst and most recent period of civil violence, called *'la violencia'*, lasted from 1948 to 1962 and caused more than 300,000 deaths. *In Evil Hour* (*La mala hora*) and *No One Writes to the Colonel* are both set during that period. All of Márquez's other novels show the incessant invasion of everyday life by political violence, and all bear witness to the failure to achieve any significant political change. However, the patriarchal and fatalistic version of history is not the only one available in Márquez's work. It predominates in *Leaf Storm* and *One Hundred Years of Solitude*, where the viewpoint is that of the local provincial aristocracy (for example, the Buendías): the arrival of the United Fruit Company in the early twentieth century is interpreted entirely as a disaster since the social changes it brought marked the demise of this aristocracy. Nevertheless, in the latter novel, the voice of popular collective memory, with its scorn for the pretensions and distortions of official history, can be heard. As the narrator of the story 'Big Mama's Funeral' says, it's time to pull up a stool by the front door and tell the story before the historians arrive. Even the Oedipal myth itself is threatened by this comic and subversive vein of popular culture. In the naming of children, which articulates the law that must not be transgressed, patriarchal rights hold sway: family identities depend upon the male children with their repeated names. However, the only actual indication of an incestuous act is the subsequent birth of a child with a pig's tail: such proof would only be needed in a culture where a principle of uncertain paternity operates, i.e. where strict paternal rights are not observed, with the mother as the significant parent while men come and go. Such attitudes belong to peasant societies, where lineage and inherited paternal names do not matter as they do to the Buendías. Nevertheless, the mocking of the Buendías' incestuous desires does not prevent these from being the main force by which the chain of narrative time is both driven forward and, when all the gaps are finally closed, destroyed. The interlayering of popular and élitist codes produce a bifocal perspective: sometimes one, sometimes the other seems to be more prominent. Despite its surface simplicity, Márquez's writing is a complex weaving of different layers.

The potential distance between the hierarchical language of power and the voices of popular culture is at its greatest in *The Autumn of the Patriarch*. The text is narrated by a variety of voices, prominent among which are those of the common people, who finally invade the palace and put an end to the reign of the dictator. But these popular voices, which are not one but a multiplicity, do not simply express a desire to eliminate the nameless dictator; they also give him a substantiality and a presence he would otherwise lack. In other words, his being, in some measure, depends on them. The Peruvian critic, Julio Ortega, has argued that the voice of the masses in this text criticizes and deconstructs the mythology of dictatorship.[2] But it also needs to be stressed that the dictator, in so far as he can be said to have a coherent identity, is a product of the imagination of others, a construction of the multiple voices which narrate him. On the one side is the dictatorship's desire for continuity, for power in perpetuity, and on the other a heterogeneity of popular voices, in constant flux and without fixed identity. But the narrative is seamless: the gaps between the multiplicity of popular voices and the oppressive unity of dictatorship are rendered disquietingly invisible, the distance between state and popular culture becomes elusive. The responsibility for tyranny cannot finally be placed, it seems simply to be there, like the weather. By what process are the people drawn into the ambit of dictatorship so as to collude with their own oppression? The dictator's unlimited nostalgia for his mother is the main form of his desire for continuity in time; it also supplies the emotional traction in his voice which draws in and obscures the popular voices. Submission to social oppression is once again underwritten by incestuous desire, by Oedipus.

Let us return to a more general consideration of the place of fatalistic inevitability in Márquez's work. An atmosphere of enclosure and inescapability is generated in a variety of guises, including the weather, smells, the repetition of names and events, and the processes of physical and social decay. There is space here only to consider what is perhaps the most crucial level, the structure of the plots in terms of their handling of time. All of them show a fascination with the elapse of long periods of time dominated by a fatal event. In most cases, time takes the form of a postponement or a series of postponements. The history of the Buendía family, in *One Hundred Years of Solitude*, stretches to the one hundred years during which the punishment for incestuous desire is delayed. The Colonel, in *No One Writes to the Colonel*, has waited fifty-six years for his war pension, while his daily life is spent fighting off starvation. Nasar's death, in *Chronicle of a Death Foretold*, is known from the beginning: the space between its announcement and its consummation is distended by the literary device of playing off a rational investigation into the causes of his death against the townspeople's irrational desire for tragedy. Eréndira, in the story of that title, is a child subjected to endless prostitution to pay off a debt to her grandmother, whose house she accidentally set on fire. The grandmother could stand as a figure for society in Márquez, with the debts of guilt it exacts from its members. In *The Autumn of the Patriarch* what is postponed is the much-desired death of the dictator, but by the time it actually occurs, a sense of exhaustion prevails: the energies for creating a different type of political system seem drained.

Time in most of Márquez's narratives is bought at the cost of sacrifice and decay, while the possibilities of change become exhausted. Let us consider *No One Writes to the Colonel* in more detail, since it expresses the possibility of an alternative position based on sustained rebellion. Although political oppression has penetrated every crack of daily life, the colonel refuses to submit to the authoritarian discourse through which power, claiming there are no alternatives and setting out to disguise itself as part of nature, deploys itself. At every turn, with a combination of wit, humour and naïvety, the colonel undoes the pretentious language of political and existential conformity. We seem to be asked to recognize, as in Camus's *The Plague*, that there can be an act of ethical rebellion which is not sustained by any belief system but which refuses despair, finding transcendence within the ordinary and the everyday. Nevertheless, in Márquez's novel, rebellion is systematically undermined by other levels of the text. The fighting cock, symbol of political change and hope for the future, is kept alive by the colonel at the cost of sacrificing his and his wife's physical needs. As his wife says, 'an expensive illusion: when the corn is gone we'll have to feed him on our own livers'. The remark underlines the colonel's idealism but points to its cost, bringing into play the Greek myth where Prometheus is punished for stealing fire from the gods by having his liver pecked away by a vulture. Once we reclaim fire as a human invention and realize the vulture is Prometheus himself, then the myth becomes a prime instance of handing over human energy to a sacrificial structure. The cock is also the collectivity – the body politic – fed and kept alive by the sacrifice of individual people to it. The colonel, a stoic, does not touch other people, so that the moment when he touches the fighting cock has a special intensity: 'He said nothing . . . because the warm deep throbbing of the animal made him shudder. He thought that he had never had such an alive thing in his hands before.' So that we find here a notion – Christian in fact – of connecting with others through sacrifice. That dimension of the text which bears witness to radical rebellion has been played off against fatalistic and sacrificial codes.

Márquez's mastery in weaving together the different levels of a text is extraordinary. A major part of the excitement is a sense of tremendous narrative energy engaged in a struggle between liberating and enclosing forces. One of the most interesting aspects of 'Love in the Times of Cholera' is that it initiates a break with the patterns which previously dominated his writing. At first sight the plot seems to bear a familiar resemblance to the earlier ones, since the main strand is the postponement of a love affair, for no less than fifty-one years, nine months and four days. Nevertheless, there is a crucial difference.

Fermina Daza, one of the lovers, has the wisdom to let go of the past, and in particular of the allurements of nostalgia, the dominant erotic emotion of all of Márquez's previous fiction: 'The memory of the past did not redeem the future, as he insisted on believing. On the contrary: it strengthened the conviction which Fermina Daza had always had that that feverish disturbance at twenty years old had been something very noble and beautiful, but it had not been love.' What she is rejecting in particular is the version of love cultivated by Florentino Ariza as a young man: his ritual self-annihilation in the smells and tastes of love (he drinks eau-de-Cologne and eats gardenias). Love in this sense is a place of destructive self-consumption, a disease, as the title suggests metaphorically. When Florentino and Fermina finally become lovers, the equivalence of love and cholera has taken on a different meaning: now that they are both over seventy, their love is a defiance of conventions and stereotypes, and of the quarantine society imposes on those who threaten it.

Love in Márquez's novels is a place of disorder, outside rational control. For this reason it is a prime target for social control. Again and again, where structures of organization are dissolved by love, this leads merely to a recapture by fatalistic and entropic images of incestuous or otherwise unproductive desire – or at the very least by rituals of nostalgia. However, Fermina and Florentino manage to elude this process, which is not due simply to their eccentricity but to Márquez's seeking to change his source of narrative propulsion away from tragedy, sacrifice and the closed book of nostalgic memory. Florentino's fifty years of waiting have a different outcome from the colonel's stoicism, or Eréndira's endless paying off her debt, or the dictator's undying nostalgia for his mother. The place their love is consummated is a ship which carries him and Fermina up the River

Magdalena. Propelled by a different kind of time process, a non-sacrificial one, the ship is Márquez's writing machine renewed and transformed. On the way back to Cartagena, they decide to fly the quarantine flag so as to keep away passengers or cargo and remain alone with the captain and his mistress. But the authorities in Cartagena will not let the ship dock. While they wait in the estuary, Florentino finally decides the only answer is to return up-river: 'And how long do you think we can keep this bloody thing coming and going?' asks the captain. 'Florentino Ariza had had the answer ready for fifty-three years, seven months and eleven days and nights: "For the rest of our lives."'

The length of time given in Florentino's answer approximates to Márquez's age when he was writing the book, and thus the question also asks how much longer can he continue to be productive as an author. Among the obstacles to the continuing voyage are the lack of wood for the boilers (the banks of the river have been deforested) and the fear that the river will dry up and be turned into a motorway. From his first novel, Márquez had been concerned with the disappearance of the world he writes about. Here he is confident that the narrative machine can continue its journey. It needs fuel and space, but it no longer destroys the materials it uses. Only that those materials – a traditional, provincial world, before the invasion of late twentieth-century capitalism – may themselves be disappearing. This makes the question of what he will write next particularly fascinating.

NOTES

1. See *The Fragrance of Guava*, London, Verso, 1983.
2. Julio Ortega, '*The Autumn of the Patriarch*: Text and Culture' in *Poetics of Change: the New Spanish-American Narrative*, pp. 110–15.

body of fiction whose quality and range is unsurpassed in contemporary Latin American literature. Only the Colombian Nobel Prize winner, Gabriel García Márquez, and the Mexican Carlos Fuentes can be ranked with him. He has met many of the major figures of the modern world, from Fidel Castro to Margaret Thatcher, has polemicized with writers from Greene and Grass to García Márquez, has taken sides in almost every major political or literary dispute touching Latin America in the last twenty years, has been offered the premiership of Peru and has chaired Miss Universe, the International PEN Club (at the age of forty), and his own weekly television show in Lima ('The Tower of Babel', which dealt with culture in the broadest possible sense and topped the audience ratings). He has even become a regular guest on British television programmes and a familiar subject of the Sunday supplements.

Yet there is still more to Mario Vargas Llosa, as in his novels, even than meets the eye. For one so calm, urbane, well mannered – indeed, so cool and apparently rational – the Peruvian author has in his time held some disconcerting views about the daemonic function of writing (the writer seeks to avenge himself on his family, society, life and God himself; feeds on carrion, like a vulture, engaging in every form of perversion from voyeurism downwards; and is compelled to expose, exhibit, humiliate and prostitute himself like a striptease artiste for the sake of his critical mission).[2] One practical result of this improbably romantic perspective – which was, one can see in retrospect, a defensive strategy to give his essentially liberal imagination freedom to manoeuvre in a literary context dominated by socialist perspectives – is that he has converted many of the most important experiences of his life transparently (though, doubtless, misleadingly) into the subject matter of his fiction, most notoriously in the case of *The Time of the Hero* (1962), in which the military academy where he studied as a secondary school student is mercilessly depicted under its own name and in all its most secret minutiae (copies of the novel were ceremonially burned on the academy parade ground); and in *Aunt Julia and the Scriptwriter* (1977), in which his marriage to his own uncle's ex-wife is turned into a hilarious Peruvian soap opera, precipitating – not surprisingly – a lawsuit and a biographical sequel by Aunt Julia herself, who gave her own version in *What Mario Vargas Did Not Say*.[3] The novel, incidentally, had ended with the couple's inevitable separation and a further twist, in which young Mario marries his first cousin, Patricia. Which young Mario did.

Perhaps the most interesting paradox of the many which emerge from even the most casual thumb-nail sketch of Vargas Llosa contrasts the almost obsessive insistence on his own personal independence with an equally determined but much more carefully disguised, and more intriguing, need to provoke (and hence, perhaps, draw attention to himself). The explication of this paradox would surely provide a clue not only to his own public (and no doubt private) behaviour but also to the dynamic of his writing.[4] Vargas Llosa is also an adventurer, both in reality and in his imagination, fighter of demons and righter of wrongs. His enthusiasm for the medieval novels of chivalry, in particular Martorell's *Tirant lo Blanc*, is well known and perhaps betrays the boyhood reader of Dumas and Hugo. Like every male fantasist, he is sometimes the Old World knight, sometimes the New World gunfighter, and not averse, metaphorically speaking, to descending to the street brawls of his Peruvian college youth. His moral courage has never been in doubt, and he has never flinched from difficult political or literary issues, nor been a follower of intellectual fashions. But in the continent where the writer has traditionally been expected to commit himself to progressive causes, the Peruvian novelist's gradual shift to more conservative positions has brought him a succession of problems and personal antagonisms.

Up to now, indeed, Vargas Llosa's writing career has been through two quite distinct phases. Firstly, the period 1959 to 1971, in which he was universally recognized as an outstanding member of both the literary new wave and of the progressive post-Cuban Left; secondly, the period 1971 to 1984, during which he maintained his literary pre-eminence but made enemies of his former political comrades as he moved gradually ever closer to the liberal Right. Fifteen years ago, in 1971, I wrote a brief article entitled 'Mario Vargas Llosa: New Novel and Realism'.[5] Its fundamental point of view, though theoretically somewhat underdeveloped, still seems to me a valid one, despite the fact that the fifteen years since have been dominated by a titanic conflict between Marxist and structuralist criticism from whose exhaustion and mutual demise the current fad of doom-laden deconstruction emerged. In 1971 the Peruvian was already one of the 'big four' boom writers of the so-called 'New Latin American Novel' (the others were Julio Cortázar, Carlos Fuentes and Gabriel García Márquez).[6] My contention was that, despite his inclusion in this inner circle, Mario Vargas Llosa was different in literary orientation from all the other major Latin American writers of his generation, and from the new wave as a whole. The most characteristic currents in Latin American fiction at that time were a sort of labyrinthine metaphysic of fantasy mainly emanating from the River Plate cities, whose best-known exponents were Borges and Cortázar, and what might be called a tropical magical realism centred on the Caribbean zone, which was inspired by the antecedents of Asturias and Carpentier and exemplified in writers as different as Guillermo Cabrera Infante and Gabriel García Márquez. Part of my point – made before the so-called 'Padilla affair' – was that a writer who chose to be circumscribed by the actually existing circumstances of Latin America's dramatic historical reality would inevitably find it more difficult to maintain fashionable postures – whether literary or political – than the experimentalists. And so it proved.[7]

In essence what I was asserting in 1971 was that Vargas Llosa's orientation was that of the great realists of the nineteenth century (Balzac, Flaubert, Tolstoy) and their twentieth-century successors (Dos Passos, Faulkner): psychological, sociological, historical, or, in a word, critical. Needless to say, what I was not saying was that there was any positivist intention in his literary perspective. Vargas Llosa had been the most contemptuous critic of Latin America's social realist fiction of the 1920s and 1930s, and indeed his own works, like those of his mentors Flaubert and Faulkner, show an obsessive concern with form and structure. Yet, as I pointed out, whenever he was asked during that period about those stark, sober and profoundly serious works of his, he spoke in terms which suggested that what he really wanted was to be playful, whimsical and lightly fantastic like his fellow participants in the boom – as if the author of *The Time of the Hero*, *The Green House* and *Conversation in the Cathedral*, all among the greatest of Latin American novels and – I would argue – the greatest of all Latin American 'realist' novels, would rather have authored such frothy if sparkling concoctions as Cortázar's *Hopscotch* (1963), Cabrera's *Three Trapped Tigers* (1964), Fuentes's *A Change of Skin* (1966) or García Márquez's *One Hundred Years of Solitude* (1967). My point was a prophetic one. From that precise moment, which happened to coincide with Vargas Llosa's separation from the Cuban Revolution and the Latin American Left, works like *Conversation in the Cathedral* ceased to appear, and the new Vargas Llosa, playful, parodic and paternalistic (neither so young nor so angry as in his early works) emerged, a Vargas Llosa who really did belong heart and soul to the new Latin American novel, and whose over-determining literary influences, indeed, were now his own fellow Latin American writers (of course Vargas Llosa, being who and what he is, usually managed to improve on the models), and not his mortally serious, highly committed French mentors, from Flaubert to Sartre.[8]

Looking back at that early period, the work which brought him to instant celebrity was *The Time of the Hero* (*La ciudad y los perros*, 1962). This novel, which had several different titles, appeared when its author was a mere twenty-seven, at the very beginning of the boom of the new Latin American novel, and it was remarkable for its technical expertise, narrative efficiency, controlled passion and bleakness of vision. It was based on cinematic montage out of Flaubert, in the sense that it achieved density by careful cutting and cross-stitching which compressed a very long novel into the dimensions of an average-sized text. Set in the Leoncio Prado Academy which Vargas Llosa had attended, the work gives an essentially contemptuous portrayal of the Peruvian military, and a prescient one too, since it was written at a moment when the new wave of neo-fascist military regimes in Latin America had not yet struck their first blow in Brazil with the 1964 coup. It is also one of the most effective literary depictions of Latin American *machismo*, and, indeed, gives a brutal but effective insight into the effects of the ideological state apparatuses and the mass media on the consciousness of helpless adolescents in 1950s Peru, well before the New Left came to theorize such phenomena. No author had previously applied such critical realism so efficiently to Latin American society through the medium of the novel. But there was more. Formally, the narrative was structured through a ghostly architecture built on essentially Faulknerian concepts whose textual uses and strategies the author would only elaborate theoretically a decade later, in 1971, when he produced a massive critical guide to the fiction of García Márquez, at that time a close friend.[9] It is this eerie architectural programme, effortlessly organizing social space and historical time, focusing with supreme precision the novel's events and the reader's responses, which explains the impact of his early novels, a fusion of moral and aesthetic emotion rarely equalled in the history of the Latin American novel, which has excelled in many things but not in the supreme virtues of the realist text which Flaubert brought to such a fine art with *Madame Bovary*, as Vargas Llosa himself has so often pointed out.[10]

That first novel, however, had two other important features less frequently acknowledged. First, it explored the nature of fiction and the status of the novel as a historical genre. In essence, it was a murder mystery – who killed the character known as 'the Slave'? – and therefore a detective story, though as in all Vargas Llosa's works, there is no solution to the mystery and no satisfactory answer to any of the obvious questions, the book – naturally – being about something altogether different. Secondly, in addition to the self-consciousness which everywhere characterizes the work of this deceptively straightforward novelist (who uses the least 'literary' language in contemporary Latin American fiction and only rarely allows the discussion of educated 'ideas' in his texts), the work is also self-referential, not simply because all the characters are 'storytellers' in both senses of the word (narrators, liars) or because one of the two central characters, the middle-class Alberto, is called 'the Poet', but because the very last scene of the novel, a *tour de force*, is simultaneously a parody of the photo-novel approach to human reality (one of Vargas Llosa's own vices) and a spoof which satirizes the mixed motives which have led his readers through a long, sordid and frequently violent narrative which is just about to fizzle out on them like a damp squib.

The second novel, *The Green House (La Casa Verde)*, appeared in 1966, when its author was still only thirty. Astonishingly, this remains his most mature work, one of the greatest novels to have emerged from Latin America. Although the novel does not actually seem to 'say' anything (its characters manage to be both wilfully unreflexive and incorrigibly self-absorbed), it is an account of the transition from a traditional to a modern society (the development of Latin America from the nineteenth-century world it still remained in the 1920s and 1930s to the world of the 1960s when it was written),[11] and the relation between the city and the country, condensed in the juxtaposition of a series of events which take place in the Peruvian Amazon and others which occur in the coastal city of Piura. Naturally, this juxtaposition implies other contrasts, including some of the thematic mainstays of Latin American cultural history, between Europe and native America, male and female, culture and nature, calculation and spontaneity, domination and liberation, but these are for readers to trace within the interwoven forest of details and labyrinth of signs. It is disappointing that critics who have been able to respond to works more obviously typical of the new novel of the 1960s and 1970s, conceptually pretentious or metaphorically impenetrable and opaque, have sometimes failed to perceive the extraordinary richness of this vast and ambitious realist classic. Again, the text is intricately structured: it is, indeed, clearly Vargas Llosa's outstanding architectural achievement, one in which each formal device is perfectly conceived for the purpose to which it is put and in which the overall design is almost breathtaking in its simultaneous complexity and coherence. Again, too, it is self-referential: the Amazon river's shifting geography, branching its way temporally and spatially through the forest, not unlike Piura's susceptibility to envelopment in the sand drifting in from the desert, suggests the novel's knowing alternation between openness and closure, which itself reflects a text in which history has meaning for the author but almost none for the characters, for whom it is merely life, sometimes as infinitely open and mysterious as the Amazon or any other unconquered territory, sometimes as closed as the oppressive and unequal societies which have existed in Latin America since the Conquest in the sixteenth century. Written in the 1960s, when the impact of the Cuban Revolution was at its most decisive and whilst Vargas Llosa himself was exploring his own full potential as a novelist, *The Green House* represents the high point of his political radicalism, an unmistakable if not militant critique of capitalism, imperialism and patriarchy characteristic of the era.[12] It is the only work by Vargas Llosa in which women can be interpreted as triumphing over their social condition and equally the only one in which such standard New World themes as the call of the wild and indeed the primacy of nature itself seem to have much appeal as shaping concepts. Simply in terms of an achievement of the imagination, though, one must underline the fact that here for the first time in his career Vargas Llosa embarked upon the adventure of writing both about a world he only knew indirectly and about characters whom he knew hardly at all, with almost no trace of an authorial *alter ego*.

The Green House may have appeared a grim and brutal novel, but the tone of its conclusion was one of reconciliation, however arduously achieved, and there was something almost Homeric in its breadth of vision and mature wisdom. Nothing, then, prepared his readers for *Conversation in the Cathedral (Conversación en la Catedral*, 1969), which returned with a vengeance to the world Vargas Llosa himself knew so well and had already portrayed in his first major work, *The Time of the Hero. Conversation* remains one of the most bitterly pessimistic novels ever written in Latin America, yet a first reading has the shameful and almost mesmeric compulsion of our most perverse and intimate desires. No other novel about life in a twentieth-century Latin American city carries its straightforward sense of realist conviction, and although it was set in the period dominated by General Odría (1948–56), when Vargas Llosa was an adolescent, its appraisal of Peruvian society is not confined to that era but takes on a more generalized significance. It is a novel full of loathing for his country, his class and even, one senses, through the character of its protagonist Santiago Zavala, for important parts of himself.[13] It might have seemed at first sight that it was Vargas Llosa's enthusiasm for Cuban socialism and other radical political advances of the 1960s which produced this bitter settling of accounts with the past; more convincing, however, is the idea that the pessimism in the text is the symptom of Vargas Llosa finally arriving, through the act of writing it, at a full awareness of his own political scepticism: ideology henceforth suffuses the world rather than the world and its experience shaping ideology. Whatever the truth of this, most readers would agree that a novelist who had written such a novel could not take its implied trajectory much further and it is hardly surprising that from that moment he set out to distance himself through parody and gave himself over to the delights of fantasy and magical realism.

Conversation in the Cathedral is Vargas Llosa's longest and most intense novel, a work of unremitting sordidness, corruption, violence and baleful pessimism, lugubrious and nocturnal, a portrait of 'Lima the horrible' as grim as anything that had previously been written about Peru's capital city. Its central character, Santiago Zavala, a member of the Lima bourgeoisie, attends San Marcos University, engages briefly in revolutionary politics, and leaves to work as a journalist with the newspaper *La Crónica* – all experiences which Vargas Llosa himself had undergone at the same period. Santiago is sensitive, intelligent, independently minded and well-meaning but ultimately weak-willed and ineffectual. Although from the upper bourgeoisie he is the epitome of the *petit bourgeois* intellectual, despised in a whole succession of twentieth-century Latin American novels, longing to commit himself to something but incapable of believing that anything in which he is involved is of the transcendental importance which alone can justify and compel such commitment, with the result that he distances himself from everyone and everything in which he believes and usually brings about the opposite of the end that he seeks. A sophisticated innocent, Santiago progresses from one disillusionment to another, in a world of political and social perversion, until eventually he loses his own privileged place in a society which he rejects but to which he has no alternative available in this world, with the result that he loses one life but gains no other, a victim of the idealism which Lukács so relentlessly explored, the bad faith which Sartre condemned. The novel has two principal messages among many. First, the poor are superior to the rich, though only because they have more excuses for their crimes and transgressions. This theme is communicated through the story of the second major character, Ambrosio, a mulatto chauffeur who works for Santiago's wealthy socialite father; and his love for Amalia, briefly a servant in the Zavala household. This message is expected: it is a conclusion conveyed repeatedly throughout Vargas Llosa's early work. The second message is that the young are not, after all, morally superior to the old. This marks a radical change – indeed, *the* radical change signalled by *Conversation in the Cathedral* as a whole – because all the early novels and short stories (including *The Leaders*, 1959, and *The Cubs*, 1967) appear to assume that there is a natural innocence in humankind which is corrupted by the society of adults. Vargas Llosa, by this time in his thirties, had now decided that this too was a bitter illusion. When we discover that Santiago's youthful idealism is only skin-deep, like that of Alberto in *The Time of the Hero*, we note that there is no corresponding working-class youth, like Jaguar in that early novel, to offset with his passion, perseverance and – despite everything – his loyalty, the brittleness of the middle class. Ambrosio is the structural equivalent, but his moral perspective is even more opaque than that of Jaguar, and youthfulness is not one of his ingredients.

It is perhaps unsurprising that Vargas Llosa, saying farewell to his own youth, found this discovery far too serious a matter ever to write with such passionate intensity again. He had explored society and himself from within as far as he was able, mainly sociologically (that is, synchronically), ending each personal history unemphatically, at the moment where it was still not yet necessary to draw 'conclusions' about history as such.

Now such illusions would be put behind him. Instead of the youthful standpoint, 'Look how awful this is, how far below our expectations', the new perspective would be a mature, 'What else could one possibly expect?' This shift applied to human nature, socialism and almost everything else of importance. I am not sure how far Mario Vargas Llosa himself would accept this interpretation of his own history, though an analysis of his collected articles, significantly entitled *Contra viento y marea, 1962–1982* ('Against all Odds'), charts the evolution fairly ambiguously; but I believe that at that juncture, at the end of the 1960s and beginning of the 1970s, Vargas Llosa ceased to believe in the viability of exploring the realities of concrete existence through fictional form and began to explore the nature of literature and history themselves, a rather different enterprise, but one entirely characteristic of the new Latin American novel. Now the ideology is simply adjusted slightly, refocused to train on each new historical event and situation, but the historical perspective is much more inflexible.

In justice it must be frankly acknowledged that the early period itself had been infinitely more conducive to optimism and idealism, especially in Latin America, than the last fifteen years have been and that Vargas Llosa's shift is a fairly accurate reflection of everything else that has happened in between. In the 1960s, his almost geometrical approach to narrative composition, although superficially similar to the obsessive formalism of the French *nouveau roman* (dominant when he began writing), was actually the opposite. His narrative perspective, only superficially pessimistic, implied a belief that criticism was constructive and change conceivable; and the obsession with structure implied the existence of order and meaning, signifying that understanding was possible and that reason could yet prevail over the apparently inchoate material of which our world is fashioned. His technical devices were calculated to concentrate the attention of the reader-detective upon the clues so carefully concealed and so parsimoniously dosed out and therefore to increase both the enjoyment and the intensity of the text. For the most part these twin objectives were inseparable. Vargas Llosa's favourite devices were the familiar Faulknerian techniques which he calls 'Chinese boxes' and 'connecting jars', techniques which not even Faulkner had carried to such a fine art.[14] The first, simply stated, is that of the story within a story, and the second is that of juxtaposition. Both are binary phenomena, and Vargas Llosa has often emphasized the importance of the binary in terms of making the comparison and contrast which give a text narrative dynamism. Both techniques fuse for the first time in the remarkable epilogue of *The Time of the Hero*, mentioned above, where Jaguar, the real hero of the novel, tells his old friend, the thief Skinny Higueras, how he, Jaguar, got the girl. The Chinese box technique is indeed the principle on which *Conversation in the Cathedral* is constructed, since the whole story oozes out of the conversation (and the silences) between Santiago and Ambrosio in the squalid bar called the Cathedral during four hours one day in the 1960s many years after the events which form the novel's core. Similarly the device of the connecting jars is the structural principle on which *The Green House* is built, since the novel continually oscillates between the Amazon jungle and the city of Piura.

In all three novels brothels play a central role (both 'the Green House' and 'the Cathedral' are names of brothels), and we discover that these houses of shame and exploitation are actually no worse than most of the other institutions of the societies which we have constructed. But this perverse position, characteristic of naturalistic writers since Balzac, is overlaid by another still more extreme – Dostoevsky, Céline, Bataille, Genet – which appears to argue that murderers and rapists are generally no more despicable than the rest of us. The central characters of both *The Time of the Hero* and *Conversation in the Cathedral* whom the author most carefully defends (this can be demonstrated technically), Jaguar and Ambrosio, both working-class characters, are each presumptive murderers, but each remains true to his vision, to his friends and to himself, unlike the ambiguous and self-deceiving Alberto and Santiago, members of the perfidious bourgeoisie. In both cases the reader is lured into identifying himself with an attractive, and familiar, middle-class protagonist by a variety of brilliant technical devices, only to find himself defrauded and to be left at the end of the novel with the clear impression that it was his own prejudice which made him see them thus and that it is the working-class heroes, not those of his own class, who are the true moral victors. Something similar happens in *The Green House*, where three women, Chunga, Lalita and Bonifacia, despite all their initial disadvantages and all their misfortunes, triumph over the three men who have made their world, Anselmo, Fushía and Lituma. It is frankly inconceivable that Vargas Llosa could take up such an authorial perspective today.

After *Conversation in the Cathedral*, indeed, everything began to change in a quite pronounced way. The world of Vargas Llosa's novels was as oppressive as before, but it no longer troubled him as much, and his point of view began inexorably to shift. Nothing could be done about the nature of human society and thus there was no point in anguishing about it. In short, either he had changed his class perspective, or history itself – the condition of Latin

America – was changing about him, or both. The world
continued to seem as grim as before, but his own personal
position was enviable and his constitutive world – the
Peru of the late 1940s and 1950s – no longer seemed worse
than contemporary Peru as a whole, or, indeed, than any
other world past or present. His early works had seen that
Peru as repressive and morally contemptible, whilst other
possibilities (Cuba, Paris – that intoxicating alternative
for Latin Americans in the 1960s) were open and alluring.
Now, in the appalling Latin American 1970s, everything
encouraged him to undergo a change. He began to distance himself from his old allies (he was growing older
and more distant anyway, he had spent the years 1959 to
1974 largely out of Peru), began to write satires, comedies
and fantasies, and undertook the long march to the right
and to middle age along with most of the rest of the
post-Vietnam Western world.

The ironic effect of this was that his works actually
appeared more youthful, not less (many critics, indeed,
had protested at the sobriety and deadly seriousness of
the authorial persona behind the three early novels). The
first result of his ideological shift was the hilarious *Captain Pantoja and the Special Service* ('Pantaleón y las visita-
doras', 1973), the story of a captain in the Peruvian army
in 1956 who is ordered to set up a military brothel in the
Amazon jungle near Iquitos. The officer, Pantaleón Pantoja, is an unimaginative, conventional character who
simply carries out orders, however absurd. The novel is
narrated almost entirely through official documents, dialogues, letters and the night-time fantasies of Pantoja. The
humour – it had scarcely existed in Vargas Llosa's early
work – is broad but irresistible and it is frequently difficult for the reader not to laugh out loud at this satirical
assault on the military-bureaucratic mentality. The novel

is a brilliantly professional piece of writing, more serious than it appears and worth any reader's time and trouble, but hardly an important work in comparison with his earlier achievements.

His next novel, *Aunt Julia and the Scriptwriter* (*La tía Julia y el escribidor*, 1977), represented something of an apotheosis in Vargas Llosa's trajectory, because its reception by critics, especially in Europe and the United States, was almost universally warm and appreciative in the way that bestsellers are warmly and appreciatively greeted. Vargas Llosa had discarded his rather spartan and puritanical image in favour of playfulness and parody, with *Pantoja*, and this later novel remains his most lighthearted and straightforwardly entertaining work.[15] It is also, importantly, a novel which normalizes Latin American experience internationally and eschews any concessions to exotic mystery, magic or melodrama. It alternates autobiographical reminiscences – his real-life relationship with his Bolivian aunt, Julia Urquidi, and his work in a radio station – with the ludicrous soap opera stories supposedly written by the doyen of Lima scriptwriters, a dwarfish Bolivian called Pedro Camacho. The implied critical thrust of his earlier work, even of *Pantoja*, has at this point dissipated almost to the point of disappearance, as Vargas Llosa 'joins the Latin American literary party', to quote *New Republic* (from the dustjacket). The novel has obvious points of comparison with the work of the Argentine novelist Manuel Puig (author of *Kiss of the Spider Woman* and other works), except that Vargas Llosa does not in fact here give any implied critique of the effects of the mass media upon helpless individual consciousness, as Puig invariably does, but rather, in the most carefree fashion, turns his own life into a soap opera (just as the novel itself was turned into a television soap opera in Bogotá), and diffuses what was obviously a dramatic emotional experience, through the irony of his retrospective gaze, into comic melodrama.

His readers loved it (I suspect they were mainly new readers, but there were many more of them), and his next novel, *The War of the End of the World* (*La guerra del fin del mundo*, 1981), despite meeting with more serious objections if only because it was a much more serious book, was also a great and deserved success among both readers and critics. Salman Rushdie, for example, has called it a 'tragic masterpiece', fit to follow the comic masterpiece which was *Aunt Julia*.[16] It is perhaps the closest equivalent in Latin American literature to a *War and Peace*, fictionalizing as it does the tragic clash between primitive religious revivalists and republican government troops at Canudos, Brazil, in 1896–7, and thus emulating the famous socio-historical narrative *Rebellion in the Backlands* (*Os sertões*) by Euclides da Cunha at the turn of the century. Like Tolstoy, Vargas Llosa traces the paths of characters from different social backgrounds through an agonizing historical experience to draw conclusions about the relation between life and history. Interestingly, he opted to write a novel about the nineteenth century in nineteenth-century vein – an intriguing bravura gesture by the greatest technical craftsman in twentieth-century Latin American fiction. It is therefore a novel of evident classical pretensions, with no obtrusive technical devices and no attempt to divert or confuse his audience. The result is a powerful, austere and generally lucid work which nevertheless, for this reader at least, runs out of steam at the climactic moment because its internal logic requires the kind of ideological coherence which Vargas Llosa himself had so consistently rejected in earlier days – all the more ironical, this, since the conclusion of the work emphasizes the illusory nature of ideologies. The classical transparency which Vargas Llosa achieves, now that his ideology has moved to the right, here produces a kind of conceptual paralysis. His inability or unwilling-ness to end a novel, knotting the threads one section before the end and then allowing them to unravel again, more than adequate to his earlier ideology of detachment (each of the first three works had ended with a desultory conversation in a bar), now leaves him unable to 'con-clude' when he wishes and needs to do so. But if we are to take the final sections of this novel seriously, the inference is that, in an age when ends are invariably corrupted by the means employed to achieve them,[17] those who are driven by ideologies of whatever kind will die for them and take many others who are 'innocent' of ideology with them; whilst those who live for love (or sex) and life itself, whatever their class or background, deserve to endure. Whatever reservations readers may have as to this philosophical outcome, *The War of the End of the World* confirmed Vargas Llosa as a contemporary classic, Latin America's greatest living narrator on the grand scale, a novelist who might undertake almost any challenge.[18] It is a superbly structured story, narrated with clarity, effi-ciency and dynamism on a grandiose scale, and it restored its author to the ambition, the gravity of purpose, and indeed the bleakness, of his early works.[19]

His next novel was *The Real Life of Alejandro Mayta* (*Historia de Mayta*, 1984), another work set partially in the 1950s, which explores the story of a militant Trotskyist, Alejandro Mayta, who travels from Lima to Jauja in an attempt to spark a socialist revolution in the Andes in 1958. A well-known novelist, apparently Vargas Llosa himself, attempts, in an apocalyptic near future (the novel was obviously written with '1984' in mind, though set possibly in the later 1980s, just as *The War of the End of the*

World was overshadowed by the spectre of the 'final catastrophe'), to excavate the story of Mayta against a terrifying background of social dislocation at a moment where a Cuban-backed invasion army has entered Peru from Bolivia and is countered by US marines flown in to prop up the national government. (This somewhat hysterical scenario was not of course uncharacteristic of the dark years of the early 1980s.) The narrative technique employed takes us back to something close to the sort of complex montage employed in the three first novels, that is, to the style of composition with which Vargas Llosa is uniquely associated in Latin American literary history. Like those works, this assumes one of the many forms of the detective story. The effect is to produce a narrative which is hypnotic and compulsive, though, ultimately, somewhat coarser in texture than his earlier work and no more satisfactory in its conclusion than *The War of the End of the World*. Once again the message is that ideology is illusion, and an illusion which leads ultimately to catastrophe. The Left, in particular, wishes to change the world too quickly, which explains the trajectory in the novel from Mayta's absurd quixotic adventure through Hugo Blanco's 1960s movement to Sendero Luminoso in the 1980s and the clash between Communism and Capitalism which, the fictional narrator informs us, is tearing Peru apart whilst this novel is being composed. The masterstroke, perhaps inspired by his experience with the so-called Inquest in the Andes,[20] is to have this narrator, apparently Vargas Llosa himself, simultaneously inventing a fictional Mayta as he investigates the life of the 'real' Mayta, in a narrative which is in turn juxtaposed with a third Mayta, the Mayta of the novel itself. This raises a series of very interesting and subtle questions which have not, I think, been sufficiently appreciated by critics (the novel met with unusual

with his daughter is at the root of the whole affair, and as the investigation threatens to come closer to him the colonel shoots his daughter and then himself. This anecdote, characteristic of the 'red pages' of Latin American newspapers, is reminiscent of some of the material from *Conversation in the Cathedral* (itself based on Vargas Llosa's own experience as a newspaperman in Lima), or, indeed, of García Márquez's *Chronicle of a Death Foretold* (1981), which in turn signals a return to the tenor of the Colombian's own early novels from the late 1950s such as *In Evil Hour* or *No One Writes to the Colonel*. The detective story is juxtaposed with a series of amusing, and even farcical, episodes involving the two policemen, one of whom, the lieutenant, is consumed with desire for a middle-aged married woman. This strand is reminiscent of *Captain Pantoja and the Special Service*, and once again, as in all Vargas Llosa's works, the successful fulfilment of their duties sees both policemen effectively punished and demoted by transfer to inhospitable parts of the country. In a sense, like García Márquez's *Chronicle*, this is a simple story whose solution is obvious, so that the mystery lies in the telling. One thinks inevitably of Faulkner, a seminal influence on both writers, and in particular of *Sanctuary* (1929). *Palomino Molero*, then, may well be another masterpiece, although a minor one, and appears to signal a change of direction or perhaps – dare one hope? – a return to the objectivist mode of Vargas Llosa's early works. In this novel the tension perceptible in the text is once again confined to the intentions of the writing and the narrative themselves, and not distorted by the contradictions of the author. He is once more in full control not only of his materials but also of his emotions. This may be because he has returned, albeit without passion, to the perspective of his own youth, when most of what was wrong with the world was the fault of a ruthless upper class which would not make room either for the democratic evolution to opportunity of those less fortunate than themselves or for the emergence of young writers, as the novelist himself used to complain.

Vargas Llosa has never written anything that was other than a high-quality, entertaining and thought-provoking piece of writing. In purely professional terms (mastery of language, range of expression and subject matter), he is currently at the height of his powers, and one of the works from the second phase of his creation, *The War of the End of the World*, is a creation of almost Tolstoyan proportions, as I have noted. Yet I cannot be alone in thinking that neither this nor the other works written since 1970 have quite achieved that combination of rigour, emotion, artistry and significance shared by the first three major novels, one of which, *The Green House*, continues to persuade that it stands among the very greatest Latin American novels of all time. Of course Vargas Llosa is by no means close to the end of his creative cycle, but one can only regret that at this point in time the writer who, apparently alone in Latin America, seemed to have the potential to produce a Balzacian human comedy, a historical realist representation of Latin America's developing world through the particular case of Peru, has become apparently unable or unwilling to undertake such a project.

We have examined some of the possible explanations. Vargas Llosa spent a long time away from Latin America after he became a literary star in the 1960s. His long, slow gradual rejection of his intellectual inheritance as he moved to the political Right (like most other intellectuals, in Latin America and elsewhere since 1971) made his thinking, perhaps surprisingly, coarser as it became more conservative, and, more seriously for a writer of his intuition, more ideologically overt. The impulse to ideological definition, partly a defensive reaction (he became heavily attacked by the Left after the 1971 Padilla affair), partly a growing confidence and certainty, and partly the simple result of becoming apparently 'wiser' as one grows older, was prejudicial to a writer whose most important secret had been the careful balance he managed to achieve between social being and historical becoming, with the result that the later works have been more historical than sociological, more ideologically assertive than detached, more willed in advance than explored through the very practice of writing.

What is particularly ironic about this is that Vargas Llosa himself has, as we have noted, increasingly rejected ideological approaches to politics, society and literature itself. 'Against All Odds', for example, documents, in his own words, 'the myths, utopias, enthusiasms, quarrels and hopes, the fanaticism and brutality lived through by a Latin American in the sixties and seventies',[22] implying scepticism as the only rational posture. Still more ironical is his renunciation of Sartre, his first great literary-ideological hero, in favour of the more sceptical and gradualist figure of Camus. Indeed, in another depiction of 'Against All Odds', he remarks that it shows 'the itinerary of a Latin American who undertook his intellectual apprenticeship dazzled by the intelligence and dialectical twists and turns of Sartre and ended up embracing Camus' liberal reformism'.[23]

I believe, however, that Vargas Llosa is more comprehensively influenced by the interplay between the Peruvian, Latin American and international political contexts than even he is inclined to imagine. That being so, and in view of the current trends to democratization in Latin America and elsewhere, it may not be fanciful to speculate that the third phase of his literary trajectory has indeed already begun, with *Palomino Molero*, and that his almost exclusive insistence of recent years on liberal democracy and freedom of speech will now give way once more, if only in terms of emphasis, to the advocacy of social and economic justice: not least because the novels will almost certainly gain once more in range and intensity. Like the great realist narrators of the past, he is at his best when the thrust of his critical quest for truth is imbued with the passionate sincerity and idealism of the social crusader, however disenchanted. Many of his admirers must be hoping that Mario Vargas Llosa will shortly sally forth again, older but wiser, to commit his liberal imagination once more to bear witness to the urgent and dramatic realities of contemporary Latin America.

NOTES

1. The outstanding critical study of Vargas Llosa's works to date is J. M. Oviedo, *Mario Vargas Llosa, la invención de una realidad*, Barral, Barcelona, 1970, 2nd edn., 1977. See also D. Gerdes, *Mario Vargas Llosa*, Boston, 1985.

2. There is no space here to explore in detail the – remarkably coherent – evolution of VL's literary philosophy over the past twenty-five years. The interested reader can retrace the important debate between VL, Julio Cortázar and Oscar Collazos entitled *'Literatura en la revolución y revolución en la literatura'* ('Literature in the Revolution and the Revolution in Literature'), 1969–70, published by Siglo XXI, Mexico, 1970); and between VL and the great Uruguayan critic Angel Rama in 1972, following the publication of VL's *García Márquez: historia de un deicidio* ('García Márquez: History of a Deicide'), Barcelona, 1971). VL's articles are collected in his *Contra viento y marea* ('Against all Odds'), selected articles, 1962–1982, published in Barcelona, 1983. The single most important statement of VL's literary-political credo, however, remains his

'Literature is Fire' ('La literatura es fuego'), the speech he made in Caracas in 1967 on being awarded the Rómulo Gallegos Prize for *The Green House*.

3. Julia Urquidi Illanes, *Lo que Varguitas no dijo*, La Paz, Bolivia, 1983. The marriage took place in 1955 and ended in 1964. He married his cousin Patricia in May 1965. VL's justification for the writer using his or her own life or that of others as the raw material for fiction came as early as 1964 in a review of Simone de Beauvoir's *Une Mort si douce*, when he concluded that 'literature is, by definition, a shameless vocation' (reprinted in 'Against All Odds', p. 63).

4. VL's parents were separated at the time of his birth, and he was brought up by his mother in Cochabamba, Bolivia, surrounded, as he has often remarked, by adoring women who treated him effectively as if he were a girl; but without his father. One could speculate on the effect of this upon VL's psychology and on the dynamic of his writing; perhaps all the more so given VL's surprising (and rather suspicious) declaration of disappointment at the failure of Sartre (a literary idol) to throw much light on Flaubert (another, even greater idol) in *The Idiot of the Family*. That VL himself considers the years of childhood and adolescence crucially determinant is evident from his study of García Márquez or, for example, his study of 'Sebastián Salazar Bondy and the writer's vocation in Peru' (1966; in 'Against All Odds', pp. 89–113).

5. 'Vargas Llosa: nueva novela y realismo', *Norte* 12, Amsterdam, 1971, pp. 112–21.

6. Spanish American fiction has seen three major phases this century: approximately 1915 to 1940 (Azuela, A. Arguedas, Rivera, Güiraldes, Gallegos, Icaza, C. Alegría, etc.); 1945 to 1960 (Asturias, Borges, Carpentier, Marechal, Onetti, Yáñez, Rulfo, Roa Bastos, J. M. Arguedas, etc.); 1960 to 1980s (Cortázar, García Márquez, Fuentes, Vargas Llosa, Cabrera Infante, Donoso, Puig, etc.).

7. The 'affair' provoked by the imprisonment of the dissident poet Heberto Padilla in early 1971 is now one of the best-known *causes célèbres* in Latin American literary

history. VL was one of the principal movers of the protest launched by numerous European and Latin American intellectuals, which prompted a furious response from Fidel Castro and a further hardening of Cuban cultural policy. The affair also led directly to the founding in Paris of a short-lived review called *Libre (Free)* by VL and other renegades from the pro-Cuban Left such as the Spaniards Juan Goytisolo and Jorge Semprún.

8. I should perhaps point out here however that, regardless of literary differences, Sartre distanced himself from the Cuban Revolution at the same moment and, indeed, in the same letter as VL himself, following the imprisonment of Padilla in 1971. Needless to say, the assertion that moving to carnivalesque literature coincided in VL's case with a turn to the Right implies no necessary connection between these two postures in the case of other writers.

9. Vargas Llosa's mammoth work remains the most important critical study ever undertaken of García Márquez, a remarkable accolade to a fellow writer by his greatest contemporary. Unfortunately their political positions have taken them ever further apart since that time. Vargas Llosa studied for his Ph.D. in Madrid and has worked in numerous universities and research institutes, including King's College London, Cambridge University and the Wilson Center.

10. Above all in his second major critical work, *The Perpetual Orgy*, Faber and Faber, London, 1987 (La orgía perpetua: Flaubert y 'Madame Bovary', Madrid, 1975).

11. At the same time, *The Green House* is also VL's closest equivalent to the novels of chivalry, and its particular genealogy is explained in his fascinating personal account, *The Secret History of a Novel (Historia secreta de una novela*, Barcelona, 1971). In 1967, in the year following *The Green House*, his long short story, *The Cubs (Los cachorros)*, was published.

12. Perhaps the clearest implicit account of VL's own socialist ideology at the time is to be found in his important article 'Sartre y el marxismo', from 1965 ('Against All Odds', pp. 72–4).

13. Commenting on a bitter semi-autobiographical novel, *A Snakeskin* (1964), by his friend Luis Loayza, VL reflects that future generations will ask whether 'there were ever really people like that in Peru', and answers his own question thus: 'Yes, we were that emptiness, that visceral disenchantment which corrupted our every act in advance. Living contradictions, we detested our wretched little world, with its prejudice, its hypocrisy and its clear conscience, but we did nothing to break with it and, on the contrary, we studied to be good lawyers'. ('Concerning a dictator and a friend's book', 'Against All Odds', p. 65).

14. The clearest exposition is to be found in 'García Márquez: History of a Deicide', as noted above. The other main devices are the 'hidden detail', the 'extra element' and the 'qualitative leap'.

15. Its epigraph, appropriately enough, is from the Mexican Salvador Elizondo's masterpiece of writerly self-referentiality, *The Graphographer* (1972).

16. Salman Rushdie, 'A moderate goes to extremes', *Guardian*, London, 10 October 1986. This was a review of *The Real Life of Alejandro Mayta*, published by Faber and Faber in 1986.

17. A view eloquently if rather despairingly expressed in his article 'Indelicate murders' (1977), in 'Against All Odds', pp. 265-75.

18. This view was comprehensively affirmed by Angel Rama in a major review of the novel and one of the most important critical works on VL in recent years, 'A masterpiece of artistic fanaticism', *Revista de la Universidad de México*, 14 (Nueva época), June 1982, pp. 8–24.

19. 1981 also saw the publication of *The Young Lady from Tacna* (*La señorita de Tacna*, Barcelona), the first of three plays which VL has written in recent years. The others are *Kathie and the Hippopotamus* (*Kathie y el hipopótamo*, Barcelona, 1983) and *Chunga* (*La Chunga*, Barcelona, 1986).

20. 'Inquest in the Andes' was the title of an article which VL wrote in 1983 following his participation in an enquiry as to how eight Peruvian journalists were murdered in the

Andes near Ayacucho by Indian villagers at the time of the Sendero Luminoso guerrilla campaign. VL concludes that the whole affair was based on a series of tragic misunderstandings and that the Indian protagonists 'seemed to come from a Peru different from the one I lived in, an ancient, archaic Peru that has survived in these mountains despite centuries of isolation and adversity'. The article appeared in many newspapers and magazines around the world, most notably in *The New York Times* for 31 July 1983.

21. One character, Sergeant Lituma, who may or may not always be the 'same' person, appears in one of the stories in *The Leaders* (1959), in *The Green House* (1966), *Aunt Julia and the Scriptwriter* (1977), *The Real Life of Alejandro Mayta* (1984), *Who Killed Palomino Molero?* (1986) and *Chunga* (1986).
22. 'Against All Odds', p. 9.
23. 'Against All Odds', p. 11.

José Donoso: Where the Wolf Howls

Michael Wood

'History, old Marx, is not enough.'
Heberto Padilla

Modern styles are confessions of failure. It is not so much that words have failed us as that reality has come to refuse the names we used to give it, has become too vast and too brutal and too unstable for our old nouns; and our own contemporaries, adrift in the wake of the great modern writers, can't even make a style out of this dilemma, since the dilemma has already been explored, exhausted, laid low, rendered familiar. They are left with their language, which is all they have if they are writers, and a world which they can evoke or allude to but never secure with a steady, old-fashioned grasp.

José Donoso's language becomes the baffled retriever of dreams. In *The Obscene Bird of Night* (*El obsceno pájaro de la noche*), the subject disappears and the words have to follow. The task of language here is to leave the world and chase the logic of the personal nightmare. Yet there is nothing allegorical about Donoso's vision. This is not a picture of Latin America as a grotesque dream, it is the grotesque dream of a profoundly Latin American mind, something quite different.

On the strength of this book Donoso has been compared with Grass, Céline, and García Márquez, and for once such comparisons really help. Partly because Donoso clearly is a writer of the stature of the others, but also because the unreality which is his theme has a great deal in common with their demonized landscapes. All four are

234

the polar opposites of Anglo-Saxon writers, whose world is depressingly real, whose empiricism dogs them even in their furthest flights of fantasy. For what I take to be vastly dissimilar historical causes leading to similar effects, Grass's Germany, Céline's France, and the Latin America of García Márquez and Donoso (and of Borges and Carpentier and Cortázar) are the same world upside down: it is the empirical reality of things that seems incredible, that seems to require an act of faith on the part of the perceiver.

The difference between Latin America and Europe in this respect is that the condition is an ancient one there, not an accident of this century, and it is for this reason that the old school of naturalism in Latin American writing seemed such a wrong turning. How could writers devote such attention to the details of a world no one really believed was there, even when it was hitting them in the face?

Donoso invites us to watch the world become its own ghost, fade into invisibility like the old woman in the last paragraph of his book. She has been burning rags and bundles on a fire under a bridge:

> The wind disperses the smoke and the odours, and the old woman curls up on the stones to sleep. The fire burns a little while next to the shape left there like just another package of rags, then it starts to go out, the embers grow dimmer and burn out, turning to very light ashes the wind scatters. In a few minutes, there's nothing left under the bridge. Only the black smudge the fire left on the stones, and a blackish tin can with a wire handle. The wind overturns it and it rolls over the rocks into the river.

It is worth insisting on that tin can, which in most European and North American fiction would serve to remind us that the world goes on with or without the old woman. Here it first underlines the absence of human life in this scene, the only life that counts here; then it vanishes itself.

Donoso has as many styles as he has nightmares, and I can best describe his method, crudely, as part ventriloquism and part proliferation. Ventriloquism because every character who appears in the narrator's mind is quickly impersonated, is allowed his or her own voice and idioms and manners. And proliferation because the basic imaginative movement of the book is a kind of fantastic gigantism, a sort of rapid vegetable growth of every idea into monstrosity. A half-witted girl sleeps with a man who wears a giant's head made of *papier mâché* when he distributes advertising handbills. We then learn that the narrator has borrowed the giant's head in order to make love to the girl incognito. Enough? There is more. Provoked by the narrator's borrowing the head and by the money he made on the deal, the head's official user begins to loan it to anyone who wants the half-witted girl:

> They came from faraway sections of town to make love with her. Schoolboys and skilled workers were the first, then flashy types in cars. Later on, I saw gentlemen in automobiles driven by uniformed chauffeurs; diplomats in cutaways; generals with glittering epaulets; distinguished academicians with their chests covered with medals and gold braid; potbellied priests as bald as kneaded greaseballs; landowners; lawyers; senators whom, while they made love with her, made speeches about the terrible state of the nation; movie actors made up like whores; radio commentators who knew the absolute truth . . .

It is impossible to tell whether this unlikely parade takes place in the ('real') world of the novel or in the hyperactive mind of the narrator. The same is true of other proliferations: two women prepare clothes and furniture for a new baby that never appears, and as the barren months and years go by, make smaller and smaller items until they are at work on the tiniest of miniatures; the neglected old women in a home for cast-off servants go out begging, and, coughing and whimpering and wailing, soon terrify the neighbourhood by turning into bands of geriatric muggers. The book offers countless examples of this scaring, comic escalation or telescoping.

Yet Donoso's concern is not really the discrepancy between reality and frantic illusion, although his narrator does occasionally try to calm down and get things straight. A girl who was supposed to have been a witch and a saint, in that order, was perhaps neither a witch nor a saint. 'I'm sure something very simple happened.' She fell in love and got pregnant and her father put her away in a convent. The rest, her activities as a witch and the miracles she performed as a saint, is legend. But the legend is everything, and who cares, as the narrator says elsewhere, about the 'poor realistic story' of a pregnancy? Similarly, although time constantly doubles over in the novel, so that figures from the eighteenth century seem to possess people in the twentieth in order to live out once again those old configurations of dream and desire, *The Obscene Bird of Night* is not really a novel about the defeat of linear time. Witches meddle with time, certainly – old women like Peta Ponce have the power to fold time over and confuse it, they multiply and divide it – but then who imagines the witches, what needs and fears give birth to them and their brood of familiars?

Donoso's title comes from a letter from Henry James, Sr.,

to his sons, suggesting that life 'flowers and fructifies . . . out of the profoundest tragic depths of the essential dearth in which its subject's roots are plunged'. 'The natural inheritance of everyone who is capable of spiritual life,' the letter continues, 'is an unsubdued forest where the wolf howls and the obscene bird of night chatters.' The novel spells out with brilliant, lurid invention the logic that is almost hidden in those sentences. We inherit the unsubdued forest because of the essential dearth of our lives, the wolf and the bird are the legitimate children of our loneliness. This gloss brings the elder James very close to the novel's other, unmentioned patron. 'I don't want to repeat the scene, there *was* no such scene,' the narrator says of his copulation with a witch, 'it was a nightmare that produced monsters.' The phrase is too close to Goya's famous caption for the allusion to be an accident. The sleep of reason produces monsters, Goya wrote under a famous drawing, and again the logic has to be underlined. If our reason were less repressive, its sleep would engender fewer monsters.

The book does not suggest, then, that life is a dream or that reality is all in the mind. It suggests that reality can be seen as presenting such a dearth of life that our frightened, starved minds will take refuge in nightmare, indeed that nightmare will visit and infest us whether we choose it for our refuge or not. The consequent difficulty is not that we can't tell truth from fantasy, but that we lose ourselves in an infinite jungle of truthful fantasies and fantastic truths, are left a prey to the howling wolf and the chattering bird.

This novel is full of contradictory versions of single circumstances. The half-witted girl who slept with the giant is pregnant by the giant; pregnant by the narrator; or not pregnant at all. The narrator is a deaf-mute who has always lived in the Casa, a retreat house for nuns, orphans and old women; or he is a writer, the defecting secetary of the local land-owner, in hiding in the Casa, only pretending to be deaf and dumb. The land-owner himself longs for a son but never has one: or he has one, but it is a monster, and the father creates for his child a colony of mutations recruited from all over the world, housed in a spreading domain where even the statues are hunchbacked and acromegalic, so that the child will grow up believing deformity is the norm, and normality is monstrous.

Over the whole book hangs the original legend of the girl who was witch *or* saint, witch *and then* saint, who contained in one body those flanking, abnormal, exiled segments of reality. Donoso seems to suggest that if the world could reclaim both the saint and the witch, the excess of light and the excess of darkness, reconcile the figments it has banished to the right and to the left hand of its ordinary course, the nightmares would end, the monsters born of the very narrowness of our lives would cease to exact their harrowing revenge, and all the rival versions of the truth would add up.

It is an appealing thought, but Donoso must know that such schemes for the recapture of wholeness are themselves inhabitants of the sleep of reason, recurring dreams of the Western mind. And the whole force of this spectacular novel rests in the end with the anarchic old women who live in the Casa and who, even more than the narrator's fertile, restless mind, are the owners and bearers of major meanings of the work. They are the humiliated and offended of Latin America, the miserable and excluded of a whole half-continent, stealthily accumulating all the power their long submission has entitled them to. They hoard things in the Casa – 'their employer's fingernails, snot, rags, vomit, and blood-stained sanitary napkins' and they reconstruct with this filth a 'sort of photographic negative not only of the employers they robbed it from, but of the whole world'.

Donoso leads us through the looking glass into a garden of cavorting monsters. But there, at the end of the magical perspective, lurk the irreducible old women. As in Kafka, a familiar realilty waits at the end of the nightmare, and the sleep of Latin American reason producers huddled monsters that are all too easy to identify in the daylight.

In *Flaubert's Parrot*, Julian Barnes plays a game of banning various sorts of fiction. 'There shall be no more novels in which a group of people, isolated by circumstances, revert to the "natural condition" of man . . . no more novels about incest . . . a twenty-year ban on novels set in Oxford or Cambridge . . . A total ban on novels in which the main character is a journalist or a television presenter . . . 'He proposes a quota system for fiction set in South America:

> The intention is to curb the spread of package-tour baroque and heavy irony. Ah, the propinquity of cheap life and expensive principles . . . ah, the fredonna tree whose roots grow at the tips of its branches, and whose fibres assist the hunchback to impregnate by telepathy the haughty wife of the hacienda owner; ah, the opera house now overgrown by jungle.

At first sight Donoso's *Obscene Bird of Night* seems a candidate for exclusion from the quota. But Donoso is a more thoughtful writer than the game allows, and his imagination is profoundly historical, so that even his fantasies are freighted with a complicated and inextricable past. He doesn't entirely avoid the package-tour an unspecified time, but there are plenty of signs pointing to Chile, somewhere around the turn of the century. The splendid house, with its murals and stairways and terraces and peacocks and park, is built above an old salt mine, which provides endless tunnels, and secret access to the countryside. The local natives, humiliated and impoverished, mine gold and hammer it into delicate sheets which, sold in the capital, form the basis of the immense wealth and social standing of the Venturas, the family that owns the estate and the house. The mild natives are held to be cannibals who may revert at any minute, because this myth keeps the family together and permits them to picture themselves as crusaders for civilization. Cannibalism does come up in the novel in several gruesome guises, but not among the natives. At the end of the story, a group of foreigners, suspiciously resembling Americans, are planning to buy up the mines and the estate, and possibly exterminate the supposed man-eaters.

Every summer the Venturas, thirteen brothers and sisters and in-laws and thirty-three children, descend on the country house for three months, and elegantly do nothing, too caught up in their fictions about how wonderful they are even to realize they are bored. Their first commandment, we learn, is that 'under no circumstances should anyone confront anything openly, that life [is] pure allusion and ritual and symbol.' Thus Celeste, a woman of fifty-two, has long been blind but no one acknowledges this, and she elaborately decribes objects and scenes and clothes as if she could see them. Adriano, in his late forties, is thought to be crazy, and he is kept in a straitjacket and doped with laudanum. No one pays any attention to his occasional cries. A tubercular girl is prevented from coughing within earshot of the adults – or as Donoso puts it with withering sarcasm, 'she was

242

forbidden during the day to feign that absurd consumptive-heroine's cough.' The children are unloved and regimented, needed only as family ornaments; the parents in return are suspected and hated. A band of servants mediates between the two groups, ringing the great curfew bell, and administering fierce punishments to the children after dark. The place has the aura of an insane idyll, the Trianon on the eve of the Bastille's fall.

The children are already plotting. Two of them want to escape with piles of gold; others are furtively pulling up the railings of the park, they are not sure why; another waits to see which seditious band she will join; yet another plans to release his father, Adriano, and get him to lead a grand revolt. Collectively the children have managed to plant in the adults' heads the suggestion of a visit to a fabulous local site, glade and lake and waterfall, which may or may not exist, but is soon made the object of a projected day's picnic.

The adults take off on their excursion, leaving all the children behind, and what follows is perhaps predictable, and quite close to Julian Barnes's first proscription regarding isolated groups reverting to the natural condition of man. There are echoes too of *Lord of the Flies* and Buñuel's *Exterminating Angel,* those other miniature models of civilization in disarray. The children at Marulanda quarrel and panic, and some go berserk. Adriano descends from his confinement and takes command; and the natives, perfectly friendly, surround and enter the house. A commune is born, an anti-society, which is soon prey to all kinds of internal dissent and difficulty, notably between those children who relish their freedom, and those who hanker for the return of the adults – that is, between those who see the new dispensation as theirs and those who can't wait for it to sink back into the old order.

What happens next is less predictable. The adults return from their picnic? Not quite. They almost return, get wind of the rebellion, and send the servants to clean it up, while they move on to the comforts of the capital city. There is a massacre at the house, a state of emergency ruled by the servants, and then the adults return to the pacified place – but not before Adriano, three children, and many natives are dead, and other children have fled or are disfigured by torture. The adults' impressive stategy is to see none of this, and to take no notice of the ruined house and the grass-devoured park.

But I have not mentioned Donoso's most brilliant and most haunting touch. The adults have been gone for a day, but a year has passed back at the house, time enough for young girls to have children, for the seasons to turn, for crops to grow and new habits to settle. The adults stay away for another year while the servants reestablish order, and then come back pretending they have been gone only the one, initial day. The children are confused, the adults argue, they count time in strange ways. How could anyone conceive and bear a child in a single day? It's not a child, it's only a doll, all make-believe, aren't children wonderful? And the perfectly real, human baby is drowned before anyone gets a chance to look at it.

This conflict of times suggests not only the familiar gulf between generations, but a conflict of classes. What the family, the adults, want is to freeze or abolish time, to inhabit an enchanted island somewhere off history's coast. But the children are history, their time is growing time, and the natives, long exiled from history, now want to return to its forward motion. And then time and their inheritance are snatched from them by the foreigners and their cleverest ally in the family.

I don't think Donoso intends a detailed political allegory

here – although Adriano's career and death bear more than a passing resemblance to those of Salvador Allende. Donoso insists on the invented quality of his material, and scorns realism as altogether too comfortable, even when it is offering unpleasant truths. He makes a lot of fussy entrances as the self-conscious author which don't, alas, become less fussy because he knows what he is doing. His novel is an 'artifice', he says, a 'monologue'; nothing it refers to exists beyond the page. The children are boys and girls who, as in a Poussin painting, caper in the foreground, untraceable to any model because they are not portraits, their features unconstrained by any but the most formal lineaments of individuality or passion. 'I make no appeal to my readers to "believe" my characters: I would rather they were taken as emblems – as characters, I insist, not as persons – who as such live entirely in an atmosphere of words.'

Donoso is teasing us, but perhaps he also takes his quarrel with realism a little too seriously. Even emblems have to be emblems of something. What he has done in fact is to write a historical fable about a large shift of power in Latin America, about the end of an old order. And the fable works, as many fables do, by slipping in and out of allegory. At times the servants must represent the army or the police, and the children the poor or the disenfranchised. At other times they are servants and children, nothing more. But we can't hide among the words quite as easily as Donoso suggests, and no doubt he doesn't really want us to. 'I am myself,' a scheming servant says. 'I don't represent anyone' – meaning he is looking out for his own interests and not those of the ruling class he hopes to profit from. This is like Mother Courage saying she is against war, and one of the children immediately identifies the idea as preposterous. The characters may be

245

Susan Bassn.

In 1935 Victoria Ocampo, doyenne of Argenti. ature, founder of the literary review *Sur* and one of the foremost spokeswomen for Latin American writing as a whole, wrote a 'Letter to Virginia Woolf' which was published as the opening chapter of a volume of essays later in the same year. Referring to Woolf's comments on women's writing, Victoria Ocampo agrees and extends those ideas with a strong personal statement:

> My sole ambition is to one day write more or less well, more or less badly, but *like a woman*. If I could have a magic lamp like Aladdin and, by rubbing it, could have the power to write like Shakespeare, Dante, Goethe, Cervantes, or Dostoevsky, I truly would not take advantage of it. Because I believe that a woman cannot unburden herself of her thoughts and feelings in a man's style, just as she cannot speak with a man's voice.[1]

The problem of writing 'like a woman' is one which has bedevilled women writers throughout the twentieth century, but which has acquired particular prominence with the revival of feminism in the late 1960s and the emergence of different national versions of a Women's Liberation Movement. Whereas Victoria Ocampo, like Virginia

247

...ed with the problem in relative isolation, the ...wo decades have seen the emergence of a new phenomenon. Large numbers of women throughout the world have taken up the question of whether there can indeed be a specifically women's mode of writing and have begun to investigate the problem collectively. In a short article entitled 'Crear espacios propios' ('Creating your own spaces') published in *Brujas* ('Witches'), the Colombian feminist writers' journal, Margarita Baz summarizes that new collectivity:

> Creating our own spaces means, therefore, that we must plan for and take on board all those tasks which arise from our special needs, together with physical spaces where we can come together and reflect, question and help ourselves. In this way we shall be actively advancing the process of definition of a new identity and a new way of living in the world. The emergence in most countries in the world today of independent women's groups confirms the idea that the group as a unit is a historic necessity in the struggle of women for independence. We believe that only within a solid, caring, serious group structure is it possible for women to risk undermining the concrete foundations of our own personalities.[2]

The question of group solidarity, such a key feature of so much feminist thought, assumes special significance in Latin America where the ideology of *machismo* has for so long confined women to the playing of a few male-determined roles. Historians have tended to focus primarily on problems of race and class in Latin America, all too often disregarding the problem of the significance of sex roles in society, while literary critics have praised the output of male writers and until very recently have almost disregarded women writers completely. The explosion of international interest in Latin American writing that has been going on during the past decade has made García Márquez, Fuentes, Cortázar, Vargas Llosa, etc. familiar household names for European and North American readers, but nothing comparable has happened with women writers. At best, one or two names are cited as examples of great exceptions to the belief that the majority of Latin American writers have been male – names like those of Sor Juana Inés de la Cruz in the seventeenth century, writing poetry in her convent, Victoria Ocampo and Gabriela Mistral, the first Latin American writer to receive the Nobel Prize for literature. Such isolated examples can hardly be said to constitute either a group or a tradition, and in this way literary history reinforces the notion of the woman writer as an exception. In her book, *How to Suppress Women's Writing*, Joanna Russ gives a cogent account of the strategies that have evolved which marginalize or exclude women's writing, thus creating the perspective that denies their very existence in history. But she also points out that the existence of an ongoing body of writing by women is the only logical explanation for the apparently extraordinary arrival on the literary scene of 'great exceptions': 'Again and again women burst into the official canon as if from nowhere – eccentric, peculiar, with techniques that look odd and preoccupations that don't "fit".'[3] A typical example of the strategy of exclusion can be found in Roberto Fernández Retamar's essay 'Intercommunication and New Literature', where he examines the relations between leading contemporary male novelists in Latin America. He points out that: 'What Martí said in 1893 about the Modernists may be said today about these novelists: "It is like a family in America."'[4] A family it may be, but a family made up entirely of fathers, brothers and sons.

Reading the works of writers like Vargas Llosa or García Márquez, one finds a variety of women in all kinds of roles. *One Hundred Years of Solitude* offers a whole range of women, with the indomitable Ursula as the matriarch. And indeed, one of the traditional defences of *machismo* is that the power of women within the domestic world more than compensates for their lack of power in the world outside the home. The old male myth of women being somehow 'really' in charge despite their physical and economic weakness results in the family being seen as the repository of all values and the mother is perceived as a figure to be adored even though she is simultaneously despised for her femininity. If we consider the arenas of possible power open to women in colonial Latin America, there were only three possibilities – the home, with its caste system of discrimination against younger or lower-class women, the convent and the brothel. And whatever power women may have been able to exert in these closed spaces, their lack of power in the world outside these boundaries remained as firmly fixed as ever.

Consideration of the contribution of Latin American women writers to literature has increased considerably since the advent of feminist criticism. The early period of feminist criticism, in the late 1960s, focused on redis-covering the writing of women who had been forgotten by literary historians and in that process of recovery questions were raised about the fundamental premises on which any established canon of 'great' writing is based. A re-evaluation of the work of North American women prose writers, for example, has resulted in a changed perspective of American literary history and the same has begun to happen in Latin America too. Moreover, once the process of rediscovery is under way, attention can be given to the works themselves, to determine whether there are specifically feminine themes for example, or styles of writing, or patterns of imagery. Much of this work is still in its early stages, but what does seem clear is that throughout the ages, from Sappho onwards, women have contributed from outside the literary establishment rather than from inside, a position which has caused much of their work to be neglected or overlooked entirely, but which has also enabled them to innovate and experiment with new kinds of writing. The avant-garde has never come from the established centre but always from the despised margins; women who have been for so long relegated to marginal positions in society have therefore been in a position from which to write in new ways, unfettered by the pressures exerted on those writers who 'belong' to a mainstream.

In the 1980s attention has finally begun to focus on the contribution of the many Latin American women writers who have until now been largely ignored. Victoria and Silvina Ocampo, Elena Poniatowska, Lydia Cabrera, Rosario Castellanos, Alejandra Pizarnik, Clarice Lispector, Luisa Valenzuela – all these writers are gaining ground among Spanish and Portuguese language readers and have also begun to be translated and so acquire an international reputation as well. The family of male writers has started to realize that it has sisters, daughters and mothers who are emerging from their attic rooms and speaking in voices loud enough to be heard by all.

One of the success stories of fiction writing of the mid 1980s is Isabel Allende's *The House of the Spirits* (*La casa de los espíritus*). Superficially it has some resemblance to *One Hundred Years of Solitude* – the family chronicle spanning several generations, the fusion of everyday reality and otherworldliness, the recounting of private dramas against a background of historical change, the panoply of grotesque-realist characters. But despite these similarities, the tone, scope and focus of both books is quite different. Isabel Allende's novel is essentially the story of women's emergence in contemporary Latin American society. Nívea, the first of the line, is an early suffragette who takes her daughter Clara with her to 'stand on soapboxes and make speeches', despite having given birth to fifteen children. Clara, the child with supernatural powers (Clara the Clairvoyante), has a good relationship with her mother, but cannot take her politics seriously:

> Despite her tender age and complete ignorance of matters of this world, Clara grasped the absurdity of the situation and wrote in her notebook about the contrast of her mother and her friends, in their fur coats and suede boots, speaking of oppression, equality and rights to a sad resigned group of hard-working women in denim aprons, their hands red with chilblains.[5]

Clara chooses another path, that of the writer, who prefers to work on her notebooks or to exercise her ability to contact the spirit world rather than to live the life of a middle-class wife. Yet it is the spirit of Clara who comes to her granddaughter Alba in prison where she is being tortured after a right-wing coup to encourage her not to give up: 'You have a lot to do, so stop feeling sorry for yourself, drink some water, and start writing,' Clara told her granddaughter before disappearing the same way she had come.[6] The sense of solidarity between the women is a dynamic force for survival, and the books ends on a note of hope as Alba prepares to go on living in the same fascist society and to welcome her own child into the world: 'the daughter of so many rapes or perhaps of Miguel, but above all, my own daughter.'[7]

There are three categories of women who advance the narrative, and all three typify aspects of universal womanhood. The line from Nívea, down through Clara, Blanca and finally Alba narrates the story of the middle-class woman's emergence as a political animal, aware of her public role and determined to take an active part in the way the world is run. The line from Pancha García, the illiterate peasant girl raped by Clara's husband Esteban Trueba, is the line that results in the horrific figure of Esteban García, secret-police chief and self-made tyrant. The passivity of the grandmother before the power of the master sows the seeds of hatred that finally result in fascism. And the third line is personified by Tránsito Soto, the whore who rises through the skilful use of her own body and her wits to the ultimate ironic position of being the only person who can arrange for Alba to be released from the torture chambers of Esteban García.

The novel is written in the third person, except for those sections narrated in the first person by Esteban Trueba. The development of his character is closely followed by this device of using both the third- and the first-person narrative, and we see him develop from his beginnings as *petit bourgeois* son of an invalid mother, with a spinster sister, to become the land-owner who rapes his peasant women, whilst carefully planning to create the model farm for his workers, until he marries Clara. The marriage finally forces him to see his own limitations, as it becomes increasingly clear that his wife does not love him despite his passion for her and he fails to make contact with his own children. Increasingly frustrated, tormented by his daughter Blanca's love affair with a man who is both a peasant and a revolutionary, he becomes a Conservative senator and when the Left win the elections, he is instrumental in the conspiracy to undermine the government and bring about a counter-coup. The portrait of Esteban Trueba is the portait of a man who lacks vision and who falls prey to right-wing ideologies in large part because of the inadequacies of his own upbringing. Very early in the novel, in a bitter discussion with his sister Férula about his decision to go away and live in the country, he expresses his feelings in terms of hatred of women:

> 'I would like to have been born a man, so I could leave too,' she said full of hatred.
> 'And I would not have liked to be a woman,' he said.[8]

By the end, he has changed completely. His whole world has collapsed when he realizes the horror of the military takeover of his country and is forced to beg Tránsito Soto to save his granddaughter, the only person he cares for in the world. In the final chapter of the book, written in the first person but this time narrated by a woman, Alba, who has taken over the dominant I-form, she relates how her grandfather has suggested that they write down their story, and how he has saved her guerrilla lover and finally atoned for his own past. When he dies, he is reconciled to the spirit of his dead wife and slowly loses 'the rage that had tormented him all his life'. The message of *The House of the Spirits* is one of affirmation – the human being can survive even the worst of horrors and even the most entrenched reactionary can change and find peace. As she reveals herself as the storyteller, Alba reflects on the need for writing as a means of making sense of the world. Piecing together her own past, recognizing the links in the chain, the inexorable turning of the world that means that 'the grandson of the woman who was raped repeats the gesture with the granddaughter of the rapist', Alba recognizes the need to know that history in order to be able to break the power of past hatreds. Writing is therefore an act of love; in writing is coherence and through writing comes release from the bonds of generations of pain and loathing. It is this very positive double statement – that change *is* possible both within the consciousness of the individual and within society and that writing is a means of shaping and coming to terms with pain – that makes *The House of the Spirits* a feminist novel.

The device of shifting between third- and first-person narrative and the story line that follows the lives of women against a background of social change are also used in Rosario Castellanos's *The Nine Guardians (Balún-Canán)*, but in very different ways. Written some thirty years before *The House of the Spirits*, the novel recounts the gradual disintegration of a wealthy land-owning family in Mexico as their Indian peasants slowly assert their legal rights and acquire education and self-respect. But whereas Isabel Allende's female protagonists enter into the public world of politics and stand alongside their male counterparts, the women in Rosario Castellanos's novel are locked into a dark world of family pride, intrigue and superstition. Dona Zoraida, the mother who values her male child, Mario, at the expense of her female child, the I-narrator, is a proud, selfish woman who clings to her social status as her one means of self-assertion. Predictions of Mario's death, by Nana, the Indian nurse who has looked after the children all their lives, and by the crippled woman that Zoraida has professed to care for bring out the latent violence in Zoraida, but even the religion she professes cannot save him. He dies, and the child narrator is left with the burden of guilt because she feels responsible for her brother's death, having stolen the chapel key and

class hatred that has led to the death of Mario is stronger
than she is; when she sees her old nurse Nana in the
street, there is no longer a possibility of contact:

> On the opposite pavement an Indian woman is walking
> by. As soon as I see her I let go of Amalia's hand and
> run toward her with open arms. It's my Nana! But the
> Indian watches me quite impassively, making no wel-
> coming sign. I slow up – slower and slower till I stop. I
> let my arms drop, altogether discouraged. Even if I see
> her, I'll never recognize her now. It's so long since
> we've been parted. Besides, all Indians look alike.[10]

The Nine Guardians is a novel about oppression and
repression, and the dominant emotion throughout the
book is rage. The suppressed rage of the women who are
dominated by social convention and by their husbands
and fathers has its counterpart in the suppressed rage of
the peasants. Sometimes that rage explodes into the open,
as in the case of Matilde, the woman who shames her
family and destroys herself, or when the Indians burn the
sugar mill. But essentially it is a rage that is not understood
and so cannot be dealt with. The characters in the novel are
doomed to continue in the cycle that Isabel Allende's
heroine is trying to break. The child narrator in *The Nine
Guardians* loses her innocence, but learns instead about her
class position. Her remark about all Indians looking alike
returns us to the opening paragraphs of the novel, where
that same child is explaining to her brother that Columbus
discovered America, ignoring the heritage of the Indians
completely. Like *The House of the Spirits*, the novel concludes with the protagonist writing, but Rosario Castellanos's heroine can only write her brother's name 'on the
garden bricks . . . on the veranda wall . . . in the pages of

my copybook'. That name is a sign of the guilt she has inherited and it will eventually destroy her with the class to which she belongs.

Rosario Castellanos wrote her novel before the advent of the women's movement, before the changed ideological context of the 1960s. Isabel Allende, writing several years after Pinochet's coup in Chile in 1973, which appears in barely disguised form in the novel, was therefore looking at the world with the eyes of another generation. Nevertheless, both writers have in common the fact that they focus on women and use the condition of women's lives as a means of writing about social oppression in general. It is a device that has been used by women novelists since Aphra Behn wrote *Oroonoko* in 1688 and compared the oppression of slavery with the oppression of women in the marriage market. The image both writers create of women is completely different from the often stereotyped images that recur in so many novels by male writers.

In *The Labyrinth of Solitude* (*El laberinto de la soledad*), Octavio Paz attempts a definition of the Mexican woman, a definition that can be extended outwards beyond Mexico and read as an assessment of the *machista* view of woman in general. Discussing the two types of woman, the good and the bad, Paz offers a perspective that derives in part from an extreme Catholic position and in part from an Existentialist position in which Woman is viewed as the Other. Woman is essentially passive, in his view:

She is an answer rather than a question, a vibrant and easily worked material that is shaped by the imagination and sensuality of the male. In other countries women are active, attempting to attract men through the agility of their minds or the seductivity of their bodies, but the Mexican woman has a sort of hieratic calm, a tranquillity made up of both hope and contempt.[11]

The image of woman as passive, as secretive, as closed is a very powerful one in Latin American literature, along with the image of woman as rapacious, sensual and devouring. But a consideration of the work of women writers gives a very different view. Rejecting the traditional role of woman as listener, as receiver of men's ideas and feelings, Luisa Valenzuela argues that women have finally come to recognize the power of writing and are beginning to use it:

> There's a very Argentinian phrase: 'Agarra los libros, que no muerden'. For example, you might say that to a child so they will go and study. It's a saying completely opposed to the famous Peronist phrase, which was 'Shoes yes, books no'. But in the end books *do* bite.[12]

The power of the book extends out into the world of the readers, just as the outside world intrudes into the consciousness of the writer. Luisa Valenzuela is not a gentle writer and her works reflect the horrors of torture, death and pain because she believes that a writer cannot remain unaligned. Violence for her is a theme that is imposed on her by the world; as a way of coping with it she can use the medium of the pen and try to maintain a sense of humour, but ultimately she has no choice but to confront atrocity because it is part of life.

One of the most extraordinary investigations of violence and horror by a woman is a story of Alejandra Pizarnik, another Argentine writer best known for her poetry. *The Bloody Countess* (1968) is an essay-story about the Countess Bathory, the legendary sixteenth-century Hungarian beauty who tortured hundreds of young girls to death in her isolated castle and is said to have bathed in their blood to restore her youth. Alejandra Pizarnik recounts the monstrous pleasures of the Countess Bathory in a style that is both lyrical and at times child-like, using the device of the fairy tale to shock the reader but at the same time to compel that reader to go on to the end. The beauty of horror expands before us, and when the narrator intervenes with a comment it is almost to invite our sympathy for the depraved woman with her white dresses stained with blood and her 'terrible eroticism of stone, snow and walls':

> The melancholic soul sees Time as suspended before and after the fatally ephemeral violence. And yet the truth is that time is never suspended, but it grows as slowly as the fingernails of the dead. Between two silences or two deaths, the prodigious, brief moment of speed takes on the various forms of lust: from an innocent intoxication to sexual perversions and even murder. I think of Erzebet Bathory and her nights whose rhythms are measured by the cries of adolescent girls. I see a portrait of the Countess: the sombre and beautiful lady resembles the allegories of Melancholia represented in old engravings. I also recall that in her time, a melancholic person was a person possessed by the Devil.[13]

By exploring the atrocities committed by a woman, atrocities as great as those of the Marquis de Sade or Gilles de Rais, Alejandra Pizarnik gives the lie to Octavio Paz's concept of woman. Woman as torturer of other women, described in a lyrical narrative by yet another woman is a long way from Paz's vision of woman as idol or as carer.

Alejandra Pizarnik invites us to reconsider all our assumptions about womanhood in this story, and also invites us to reconsider our aesthetic assumptions about beauty. Her story is intensely literary – it begins with a quotation from Sartre and the whole is framed by a reference to a book by Valentine Penrose, the Surrealist writer, about the Countess Bathory. It is precisely Valentine Penrose's treatment of the Countess that Alejandra Pizarnik finds so fascinating; she disregards the sexual perversion and madness as too 'obvious' and 'concentrates instead on the convulsive beauty of the character'. In Alejandra Pizarnik's version, the Countess becomes symbolic of a drive for some kind of ultimate freedom, a freedom that is beyond law, beyond convention and beyond morality. Describing her death, walled up alive within the walls of her own castle, Alejandra Pizarnik stresses the simplicity of horror:

> She was never afraid, she never trembled. And no compassion, no sympathy or admiration may be felt for her. Only a certain astonishment at the enormity of the horror, a fascination with a white dress that turns red, with the idea of total laceration, with the imagination of a silence starred with cries in which everything reflects an unacceptable beauty.

The bloodstained dress of the sadistic Countess is an extreme image, but an important one. A recurring fascination for Surrealist writers in the 1920s and 1930s was the horror of unlimited freedom, and after the rise of European Fascism and the discovery of the death camps, the same question became a fascination for Existentialist writers of the 1940s and 1950s. What Alejandra Pizarnik does is to offer a woman's perspective on the question, and in doing so she extends the boundaries of the fundamental moral issues. With such a story, any last doubts about whether women writers can dare to handle the same material as men are swept away. Virginia Woolf wrote that there were two crucial phases for a woman writer to pass through: first, to kill off the Angel of the House, that gentle, caring, motherly creature of men's imaginations and, second, to tell the truth about one's own experiences as a body.[14] Her dichotomy is another (female) version of Paz's dichotomy. Virginia Woolf suggests that it is easiest to kill the image of the adored woman, whereas the 'mala mujer' who speaks a language of physical experience is far harder to bring into existence. *The Bloody Countess* succeeds even in this second task where Virginia Woolf herself felt she had not yet succeeded.

Violence and death recur in the writings of many Latin American women novelists. Rape, torture, murder, infanticide as experienced by women appear in stories and novels with enormous power and assault the reader. It might be possible to generalize and to suggest that the history of women's repression has resulted in a revolution of writing, so that what may have once been deemed subjects that were not to be spoken of are now transformed into the savage material of fiction. All that rage, the frustrated creativity of generations of women has begun at last to find a voice in the twentieth century.

Explicit violence can at times be less terrifying than implicit violence. The work of writers like Silvina Ocampo and Clarice Lispector plays with the horror of the concealed, the non-explicit, the suggested. Silvina Ocampo disturbs the reader, frequently employing the device of the unreliable narrator and destroying the reader's place of safety. So in her story, 'Las esclavas de las criadas' ('The Servants' Slaves'), we enter casually into an account of the relationship between Herminia, the servant described as

262

'una perla' and her invalid mistress. Both adore one another, though other women try to entice Herminia away from her mistress because she is such an ideal servant. As the story progresses, such women die mysteriously in unexpected ways, and the mistress miraculously seems healthier than ever and set to go on living for a record number of years:

> In fact it seemed as though her life were going to go on for ever and that one day the papers would carry a story like the ones about those ladies who reach the age of a hundred and ten or a hundred and twenty and there are photographs with little biographies about how they managed to stay so healthy to such an advanced age, what sort of food they eat, what kind of water they drink, how long they sleep or play cards. And this miracle of her longevity was due she felt to Herminia, or so she told the newspapermen:
>
> May God grant Herminia everything she desires. She is a treasure. She has prolonged my life.[15]

The hidden clues in the narrative point to a supernatural vampire power of the servant, who maintains her mistress's life in ways not unlike the blood-baths of the Countess Bathory. But in this story, nothing is made explicit. The almost childlike simplicity of the narrative conceals something dark and unexplained. The two women, mistress and servant are linked in some mysterious manner that gives life through the deaths of those who try to intrude.

Isolation, separateness, the split between the public face seen by the outside world and the private face of the individual are principal themes in the work of Clarice Lispector, the Brazilian writer who has recently been rediscovered abroad. The powerful but frustrated women in her narratives often turn in on themselves rather than attempting to speak out. In the world of Clarice Lispector, madness runs as an undercurrent, threatening women whom the world fails to understand or help. One of her most powerful stories, 'The Buffalo', recounts how a woman in love with a man who does not love her goes to the zoo to study the animals in an attempt to learn how to hate. She passes lions with their mates, families of monkeys, elephants with the power to crush but too meek to do so, camels with endless patience until she finds a solitary buffalo. She tries to attract its attention, first by throwing pebbles, then when it turns to look at her, with words:

> 'I love you,' she said, out of hatred then for the man whose great and unpunishable crime was not loving her. 'I hate you,' she said, imploring love from the buffalo.
>
> Provoked at last, the great buffalo approached without haste.[16]

Speaking the forbidden words, telling the truth about her own feelings is the trigger which rouses the beast. The story concludes with the meeting between the two creatures, buffalo and woman, where the force of hatred is more than she can bear. The climax is typical of Clarice Lispector's lush style of writing, the careful crafting of words that lulls the reader with its elaborateness but still allows the poisoned sting to strike:

> And the eyes of the buffalo – his eyes met her eyes. And a pallor so deep was exchanged that, drowsily, the woman grew numb. She was on her feet but in a trance. Small, crimson eyes watched her. The eyes of the

buffalo. The woman staggered in amazement and slowly shook her head. The buffalo remained calm. The woman slowly shook her head, terrified by the hatred with which the buffalo, tranquil with hatred, watched her. Almost feigning innocence, she stood shaking her head in disbelief, her mouth ajar. Innocent, inquisitive, entering ever more into those eyes that fixed her without haste, ingenuous, wearily sighing, without wishing nor being able to escape, she was caught in mutual assassination. Caught – as if her hand had fastened forever to the dagger that she herself had thrust. Caught, as she slipped spellbound along the railings – overcome by such giddiness that, before her body toppled gently to the ground, the woman saw the entire sky and a buffalo.

Breaking the boundaries of womanly behaviour, speaking the magic words of hatred releases a spell. The woman looks into the eyes of the buffalo and sees all the hatred of creation reflected back at her. In such a moment of truth woman is not the object but the subject and it is this process, of rejecting the objectification of woman that has been so much a part of men's writing, that characterizes the work of the many different Latin American women novelists today. The differences between these many writers are immense, differences of style, subject and ideology. Likewise, the difference between the traditions from which they come are equally immense. The very use of a term such as 'Latin American women writers' is so general as to be almost absurd; the history of women in Mexico, for example, or Argentina is completely different from the history of women in the Andean countries which is different yet again from the history of women in Brazil. But just as it is possible, since the advent of feminist literary criticism, to discuss women's writing in terms that encompass many different categories of work with the link being a commonality of sex-based experience, so it is possible to see the writing of Latin American women today as a mass of linked threads leading through a labyrinth. In the version of the myth that has come down to us, Theseus was able to enter the labyrinth and kill the Minotaur thanks to Ariadne who showed him how to use a ball of string to find his way out again. Once back among men and treated as a conquering hero, Theseus abandoned Ariadne and sailed off to find new adventures. The myth has reflected the condition of women in literary history for generations; they provided the necessary thread, gave advice, welcomed back the hero and were then abandoned when he grew tired of them. Now, in another age, that myth is being rewritten. The new Ariadnes use the thread themselves, go into the labyrinth, prepared to kill if necessary and come out independent. Victoria Ocampo's shocking statement of fifty years ago has proved to be prophetic. The women writing in their many different ways in Latin America since then are not writing like the great masters of the past but expressing their own womanly feelings and perceptions in a new woman's way.

NOTES

1. Victoria Ocampo, 'Carta a Virginia Woolf', quoted in D. Meyer, *Victoria Ocampo*, New York, Braziller, 1979, p. 127.
2. Margarita Baz, 'Crear espacios propios' in *Brujas. Las mujeres escriben*, Medellín, April 1984, pp. 67–74.
3. Joanna Russ, *How to Suppress Women's Writing*, London, The Women's Press, 1984, p. 122.
4. Roberto Fernández Retamar, 'Intercommunication and New Literature', in C. F. Moreno (ed.), *Latin America in its Literature*, New York, Holmes and Meier, pp. 245–59.

5. Isabel Allende, *The House of the Spirits*, London, Black Swan, 1985, p. 101.
6. Isabel Allende, op. cit., p. 470.
7. Isabel Allende, op. cit., p. 491.
8. Isabel Allende, op. cit., p. 60.
9. Rosario Castellanos, *The Nine Guardians*, New York, The Vanguard Press, 1960, p. 259.
10. Rosario Castellanos, op. cit., p. 271.
11. Octavio Paz, *The Labyrinth of Solitude*, New York, Grove Press, 1961, p. 37.
12. Montserrat Ordoñez, 'Máscaras de Espejos, Un Juego Especular'. Entrevista-asociaciones con la escritora argentina Luisa Valenzuela', in *Revista Iberoamericana*, No. 132–133, July–Dec., 1985, pp. 511–19.
13. Alejandra Pizarnik, 'The Bloody Countess', in A. Manguel (ed.), *Other Fires*, London, Picador, 1986, pp. 70–87.
14. Virginia Woolf, *Women and Writing*, London, The Women's Press, 1979, p. 62.
15. Silvina Ocampo, 'La esclavas de las criadas', in *Los días de la noche*, Madrid, Alianza, 1970, p. 67.
16. Clarice Lispector, 'The Buffalo' in *Family Ties*, trans. G. Pontiero, Manchester, Carcanet, 1985, p. 122–31.

Bridging the Gap: Freud and Film in Guillermo Cabrera Infante's *Three Trapped Tigers* and Manuel Puig's *Kiss of the Spider Woman*

Stephanie Merrim

Who is Corín Tellado? Perhaps the most popular (in both senses of the word) of modern Hispanic authors, the Barbara Cartland of the *novela rosa*, that is, the Latin American equivalent of the Harlequin Romance. *Where is* Corín Tellado and her *novela rosa* – as well as the *foto-novela*, the soap opera, the tango, the grade B-movie, and all the other manifestations of the popular culture which so forms and deforms the modern Latin American mind – to be found within the new Latin American novel? Neo-baroque, Menippean satire: these are the tags most commonly attached to the well-nigh élitist novels of the 'boom'. 'The Menippean satirist,' it has been said, 'dealing with intellectual themes and attitudes, shows his exuberance in intellectual ways, by piling up an enormous mass of erudition about his theme.'[1] Thus, a complex intellectual scaffolding drawn from the Olympian heights of universal culture over the centuries, underwrites the almost fearsomely difficult novels of José Lezama Lima, Alejo Carpentier, Julio Cortázar and Carlos Fuentes, to mention but a few.

Yet Jorge Luis Borges, founding father of the new Latin American novel, inscribes his metaphysical fictions within the humble generic structures of the detective story and the Western. The works of the 'Brazilian Joyce', João Guimarães Rosa, hinge at their most crucial points on the folk wisdom of popular songs (*cantigas*) and draw their structure from the traditional stories-on-a-string (the *literatura de cordel*) sold in marketplaces. Severo Sarduy, scion of the neo-baroque, inserts his deconsecrated Christ in the comic opera in *From Cuba with a Song* (*De donde son los cantantes*). And both Manuel Puig and Guillermo Cabrera Infante, the subjects of this essay, seduce the reader into their movie-ridden and -written texts. Though far from a literature of the masses, we see that the Latin American novel can and does accommodate the culture of the masses.

What are the implications and effects of such a conjunction of unlikely bedfellows, the élitist and the 'vulgar'? Let us turn to our celluloid texts and to Guillermo Cabrera Infante's notion of *lo vulgar* (the vulgar, in the sense of *vulgate*, of the people). Discussing his novel, *Infante's Inferno*, the author has said, 'It is with the movies, of course, with their raucous vitality, with their endless dynamism, with their popular taste . . . that I want my brute of a book to be associated.'[2] *Infante's Inferno* (*La Habana para un infante difunto*), Cabrera Infante's monumental foray into sexology, both proposes and embodies a theory of the 'vulgar novel' which, defiantly eschewing the intellectual models which so configure other modern novels, patterns itself on the movies. Seamless, transparent, all (sensuous) surface, *Infante's Inferno* recalls that other novel of celluloid, Puig's *Kiss of the Spider Woman*[3] (*El beso de la mujer araña*), which flowed so easily from the pen that its author thought, 'it must be as transparent as an ordinary piece of tracing paper'.[4] The ease of reading the two-dimensional movie stories which comprise *Spider Woman* parallels the facility with which it ostensibly was written. But beware, there is a certain 'spider strategem' at work in these cross-bred novels. 'Nothing vulgar can be divine,' Cabrera admits, 'but everything vulgar is human.'[5] The transparency of the narration seduces the reader into works which, far from being made of celluloid, turn out to be ever thicker webs into which are woven the most profound – indeed, the most unconscious – human concerns.

The nature and function of filmic references in Cabrera's previous novel, *Three Trapped Tigers*[6] (*Tres tristes tigres*), will give us an idea of how so radical an act of 'plotting' can be achieved. Particularly in 'Bachata', the last and most metaphysical section of the novel, references to B-horror films abound. Why B-films, one might first ask? Uncomplicated entertainments, lacking artistic pretensions, the B-films were intended to engage the widest possible audience.[7] The camp vulgarity for which the B-films are notorious, then, only indicates their most attractive feature: their appeal to the vulgate, their mass popularity. To ensure this popularity, B-films often gravitated towards the extremes of human actions (romance, adventure), generating extreme reactions (love, hate, fear, suspense) in their viewers. Through their melodramatism they thus fulfil the classical function of catharsis by articulating – furnishing a set of images for – emotions that otherwise might have remained repressed. Or, as Parker Tyler wrote in 1947 about horror films: 'Whether it be Gargantuan ape, as in the entertaining *King Kong*, or some variety of synthetic man, the creature whose destiny it is to frighten everyone in the movie, is really only a symbol of the unconscious life, rendered titillatingly subconscious by the screen images.'[8] In performing this delicate psychological service, as well as in their mass appeal, grade B-movies serve as a model of, rather than as a reproach to, Hollywood cinema.

Cabrera openly admires B-films and capitalizes on the psychological dimension of the movies, such as *Cat People, Count Dracula, The Leopard Man, I Walked with a Zombie*, and so on, which he cites in and endows with a function essential to the novel's finale, 'Bachata'. Both thematically and stylistically, the huge spree of 'Bachata' represents one last celebration of the waning game- or nightworld which the characters of *Three Trapped Tigers* have constructed to keep the outside reality of violence, political repression and responsibility at bay. According to the rules of the night-world, any threat to its existence must either be deflected or turned into a joke. In 'Bachata' the negative elements press in on the nightworld from all sides: Bustrófedon is dead; Silvestre may be going blind; their camaraderie at an end, Cué contemplates joining Fidel, and Silvestre, marry-ing Laura. As reality closes in, Silvestre increasingly copes with his fears by displacing them onto the movies to which he alludes or whose stories he tells. In other words, he displaces his fears onto an acceptable medium and retells them to himself as fictions. Hence, Silvestre portrays Cué the *poseur* as a pod from *The Body Snatchers* and the political *desaparecidos* as zombies, while images of vampires, under-water creatures, martians and panther women proliferate.

The true pathos of the act of displacement, however, comes out in the double sign – both bitter and sweet – under which movies appear in *Three Trapped Tigers*. Silvestre contrasts the delights of the patently false and collectively shared movie horror of *Cat People*: 'united by the delights of the ready-made terror of the movies', with the all too imposing and untempered horror of *The Thing from Another World*: 'but it was a different terror that I felt . . . a terror which I now know is not just an atavistic terror, but a real, almost political terror' (p. 366). Yet potent as the movie-inspired horror may be, it wards off an even greater *metaphysical* horror: the novel ends with Silvestre standing on his balcony looking out over the water and wondering where, if anywhere at all, his dead friend Bustrófedon has ended up:

> feeling a Pascalian ver . . . tigo which was will be more
> terrifying even than the idea of the Martians infiltrating
> my own body, carrying the vampire in my blood vessels
> or nursing in my body an unknown microbe, which
> was the fear that in reality there are not Martians, that
> there is simply nothing or perhaps only nothing-
> ness . . . (p. 481)

In other words, the fierce movie images provides an almost
metaphysical solace by giving a form and content to the
beyond which, if it is not these various martians or
vampires, may just be a void – la Nada, the greatest
philosophical chiller of all.

The use of movies as a language for repressed fears we
discover in *Three Trapped Tigers* becomes the determining
factor in *Spider Woman*, where it forms part of a whole
cluster of elements which depend from an analogy
between movies and dreams. The six B-movies narrated in
Spider Woman reflect Puig's literal and analytical reading of
the aphorism which regards Hollywood as a dream
machine, or, in the author's words, a 'dream factory'.[9] But
of course Puig is not the first person to draw such an
analogy, and critic Michael Wood's comments on movies
as a dream language 'preview' the shape of our argument:
'The business of films is the business of dreams, as
Nathaniel West said, but then dreams are scrambled
messages from waking life.'[10]

As do dreams in psychoanalysis, the movie stories in
Spider Woman touch off discussion of concerns central to
the characters, for the emotions and circumstances from
their present and pasts, as we shall see, provide the
scaffolding of the films narrated. But first these elements
must pass through something akin to what Freud called
the 'censor'. Similar to press censorship, the dream censor

constitutes a barrier which the raw dream-thoughts of repressed instincts and emotions must traverse to either be deemed or made acceptable to the dream content. Now, the oppression – or repression – of Argentine society under the military government which imprisoned the homosexual Molina and the revolutionary Valentín permeates every corner of the cell and comprises the censor which disallows the direct expression of truths.[11] In reaction to this system of oppression, as do the inhabitants of the nightworld, Molina and Valentín evolve a counter-system, or society apart, of the cell ('we can shape our relationship into whatever we want', p. 202 [my translation]) in which the movies play a determining role. 'And they lived happily ever after', the traditional ending of fairy tales, closes two of the movie stories produced under this system of censorship: as in a fairy tale, the 'message' has been passed through some censor and projected onto an acceptable language, of the frilly and harmless B-films, in whose unreality lies their essential truth. Their real referents replaced with a neutral set of fictional referents, the concerns of the characters both receive expression and are neutralized in the film stories.

That Molina, unwitting instrument of the censor, so significantly rewrites the movies he tells as to become their author is evident to anyone who has seen the actual films on which three of the movie stories are based (*Cat People*, *The Enchanted Cottage, I Walked with a Zombie*).[12] Even if not, the text of each movie clearly bears the traces of his intervention in the lacunae and resequencing that result from failure, as well as in the *modus operandi* chosen by Molina for the telling of the tales: at night, in instalments, to heighten the suspense. Moreover, each movie is transformed into a showcase for Molina's sensibility, of absolute beauty passed through a romantic kitsch aesthetic. Molina 'reads' and rewrites all the movies through a haze of Hollywoodesque rhetoric and optics.

That Molina actively (if unconsciously) transforms the movies in accordance with his literary and artistic tastes is plain to see. But to understand that Puig, ostensibly through Molina, follows a textual process analogous to dreamwork, we must first discuss that Freudian construct.

Rather than simply eliminating the offensive material, the censor in dreams functions as something of a translator, who changes the shape of the dream thoughts. The censor's work, known as the dreamwork, consists of a variety of transformations and serves the basic needs of the dream, which are to gather up repressed recent and infantile material and to present it to the dreamer, providing the fulfilment of a wish. Before letting the dream thoughts go, as is well known, the censor deforms them, primarily by the techniques of condensation and displacement. Displacement, of the psychic accent onto a more innocuous element, can also perform the very cinematic function of exchanging 'a colourless and abstract expression of the dream thought . . . for one that is pictorial and concrete', since 'whatever is pictorial is capable of representation in dreams'.[13] A final, equally cinematic, transformation, which Freud called 'secondary elaboration'[14] moulds the assorted dream thoughts into the semblance of a story.

The above description of dreamwork entails so accurate a picture of the process which we shall call 'encoding' in *Spider Woman* precisely because, as he admits, Puig has ciphered the novel through a code analogous to the language of dreams: 'Everything in the novel is mediated', and 'the dialogue tries not to say things straight out. What is not said is perhaps more important, more suggestive.'[15] Different aspects of the process of encoding, which is the translation of life into art (high or low) and dreams, play a central role in Puig's works;[16] yet only in *Spider Woman* (and *Pubis angelical*) does the code become the novel, whose greatest challenge lies in deciphering, first of all, the information taken from the characters' personal situations which Molina, in rewriting the movies, builds into them.[17]

As in dreams, which are always egotistical, the impetus and apparent substance of *Spider Woman*'s movie stories derive from the characters' circumstances both inside and outside the cell. We witness the process of encoding most clearly when details from the cell pass directly into the movie stories: among many such cases, Molina's depression is passed cathartically on to his *alter ego*, the little servant in *The Enchanted Cottage*: 'and the maid's sadness, sum of two sadnesses' (p. 104, [my translation]). At a further remove, acts of betrayal, betraying in palimpsest Molina's own betrayal of Valentín, compulsively shape the denouement of each movie. Since Molina always identifies with the heroine ('I'm always for the heroine', p. 25, [my translation]), the protagonist is invariably the guilty party. In addition to such displacement, circumstances in the cell receive compensatory treatment in the movie stories: as when Molina, in a fit of pique against Valentín's revolutionary fervour and atheism, portrays Nazism in the 'Adventure' film as a specifically anti-Marxist movement, glorifying Hitler as its deity. On a much larger scale, elements from the characters' previous lives actually determine the choice and plot of the movies. The rosy *Enchanted Cottage*, with its tale of a miraculous transformation through love, reflects and writes a happy ending on to Molina's relationship with the waiter Gabriel, whom love might, with luck, possibly transform into a homosexual. A transparent act of wish fulfilment, the movie signals the connection with Gabriel by applying a Freudian *double entendre*, 'un muchacho buen mozo' (*mozo* meaning both 'youth' and 'waiter'), to the film's protagonist. Finally, a curiously dense act of encoding takes place when Molina, as a penance for his betrayal, creates an adventure movie for Valentín which obliquely exposes the latter's conflict between his bourgeois origins and revolutionary ideals. Halfway through the movie story, we are shown how Valentín's dream or delirium thoughts, the passages in italics, personalize the movies: appropriating it as a means of telling his own, most intimate, autobiography, Valentín plots or re-encodes himself back into the movie.

The most striking feature, however, of the movie webs is the degree to which their elements, like the images which reach the dream content, are *over-determined*: they not only radiate laterally from the characters' concurrent lives, but also vertically, onto an 'allegorical' plane. Analogous to dreams, which draw their material from both recent events and infantile – often sexual – neuroses, when subjected to a close reading these film stories emerge as psychosexual moral tales, the locus of personal and supra-personal forces. While the characters themselves supposedly encode the films with their personal circumstances, the author has built an extra dimension into each film which addresses matters of homosexuality, sex roles, repression, and so on.

Our first indication of this extra dimension, as well as the first of a series of scholia to the films, comes with Valentín's Freudian reading of Jacques Tourneur's *Cat People*.[18] Valentín, who identifies with the analyst in the film, sets the path for similar readings of other films with his interpretation of *Cat People* as an allegory of sexual fears: 'But you know what I like about it? That it's just like an allegory, and really clear, too, of the woman's fear of giving in to a man, because by completely giving in to sex

276

she reverts a little to an animal.' (p. 31). The importance of the somewhat distracting footnotes detailing theories of homosexuality, which begin with the second movie and assume the same function of scholium, for this reason cannot be overestimated. Though the notes seem to turn up at odd moments in the text, they invariably suggest a psychological reading – generally, a Freudian analysis – of those or subsequent pages. At times the connection is patent: a note on repression accompanies Molina's first meeting with the prison director; or, the peripatetic heroics of the adventure movie, with the son betraying first his father then his mother, only make sense in light of the Oedipus and Electra complexes described in the footnotes. Often, the more oblique the dialogue between the text and notes, the more telling: while they seem to refer only to Molina and Gabriel, the theories of the physical origins of homosexuality cut in between two instalments of the Nazi propaganda film also constitute an ironic comment on the Nazis' racial theories.

By virtue of its doubly encoded nature, the final film story holds the key to both Molina and Valentín's love affair and to the larger message of the book. On the surface, the Mexican picture recounts an act of liberation as a young woman frees herself from the tyranny of the magnate to pursue her true love. In reality, she has only entered into another bondage: a slave of love, she sacrifices career, comfort and dignity, ultimately prostituting herself to save her gravely ill lover. Her gilded zombiedom reaches its peak when her love dies, leaving her to gaze into the water, still transported by the joys of having truly loved someone. Both Molina and Valentín consider this 'enigmatic ending' (p. 285 [my translation]) the best part of the movie – and well they might, because it is their story, in code, that the movie has told. Liberated from the tyranny of social prohibitions, in sexually consummating their relationship Molina and Valentín accede to a space beyond social repression. As they themselves remark ('It's as if we were on some desert island ... because, well, outside of this cell we may have our oppressors, yes, but not inside. Here, no one oppresses the other ...' p. 202), the two men believe that they have escaped the system of oppression.

There is, unfortunately, compelling evidence to the contrary. The day after their first sexual encounter, Molina and Valentín assume stereotypical male–female attitudes towards each other, with Molina waiting on Valentín and Valentín insistent upon maintaining a romantic atmosphere at all costs ('Goddamn it! I said there's not going to be any unhappy feelings today, so there's not going to be any.' p. 233). Nothing, though, is as telling as the two characters' fates. Molina, not a revolutionary but a slave of love, as Valentín realizes, dies trying to live out his B-movie fantasies: 'for a just cause? hmm ... I think he let himself be killed because that way he could die like some heroine in a movie, and none of that business about a just cause' (p. 279). And from Valentín's delirious thoughts we gather that the greatest effect this process has wrought in him is the acceptance, less of homosexuality than of his own bourgeois nature:[19] he reveals his repugnance for the spider woman, and the novel ends with his first declaration of love to the middle-class Marta. Valentín, it would appear, has trapped Molina in a web of his own, a web of exploitation.

As this 'enigmatic ending' indicates, there may well have been no conversion of homosexual to revolutionary and vice versa: the characters remain unwitting victims of oppression, of the web which only the footnotes, and hence the 'allegorical' dimension of the last movie, elucidate. The final set of footnotes to the previous film called for the liberation of homosexuals, with heterosexuals to follow their lead. At the same time, they note the great difficulty of finding a 'third way', that is, for homosexuals to break away from the oppressor–oppressed model of sex roles. Viewed in relation to these footnotes – for the Mexican movie has none of its own – the incredible romantic *cursilería* or kitschiness of the last film seems to constitute an ironic and definitively negative response to the call for a new way. The heroine's attempted liberation, only to be shackled by a conventional notion of love, therefore corresponds on the psychoanalytical plane to the characters' inability to escape established sex roles.

Why are Puig's characters unable to escape the spider woman's web? What holds them prisoner and makes them zombies of sorts? The personal and 'psychoanalytical' messages encoded in the last film dovetail precisely because the same force of mass culture is responsible for both, parallel, phenomena. And part of that force, sadly, are the movies that so mould our thinking. Particularly the romantic, convention-bound B-films with their strong silent heroes and wilting heroines which lock in our notions of masculine and feminine. Here the theme of betrayal attains its final definition for, as Puig has stated, 'the characters aren't entirely responsible for their own actions. They are products of their environment. The most oppressive part is their inability to think for themselves, to be original'.[20] Thus viewed as a weapon of cultural brain-washing, Puig's motives unite Freud and film, operating under the same double sign as those of Cabrera: bitter and sweet, repository of the unspeakable, vehicle for what would otherwise remain unsaid.

NOTES

1. Northrop Frye, *Anatomy of Criticism*, Princeton, Princeton University Press, 1957, p. 311.
2. Guillermo Cabrera Infante, lecture delivered at the University of Virginia, Charlottesville, 1978.
3. Manuel Puig, *Kiss of the Spider Woman*, trans. Thomas Colchie, New York, Random House, 1978. All citations are from this edition and appear in the text of the study. Though at times I have retranslated passages somewhat more literally, for my purposes, page numbers still refer to this edition.
4. Marcelo Coddou, 'Seis preguntas a Manuel Puig sobre su última novela, *El beso de la mujer araña*', *The American Hispanist*, II, 18, May 1977, p. 12.
5. Ibid., p. 530. I reveal the 'spider strategem' at work in *Infante's Inferno* in my *La Habana para un infante difunto* y su teoría topográfica de las formas', *Revista Iberoamericana*, 118–19, Jan.–June, pp.403–13.
6. Guillermo Cabrera Infante, *Three Trapped Tigers*, trans. Donald Gardner and Suzanne Jill Levine, New York, Harper and Row, 1971. Citations are from this edition and appear in the text of the study.
7. Don Miller, *"B" Movies*, New York, Curtis Books, 1973, p. 37.
8. Parker Tyler, *Magic and Myth of the Movies*, New York, Simon and Schuster, 1947, reprinted 1970, p. 76.
9. Manuel Puig, *Pubis angelical*, Barcelona, Seix Barral, 1979, p. 132, my translation.
10. Michael Wood, *America in the Movies*, New York, Basic Books, 1975, p. 16.
11. I refer the reader to Prof. Alicia Borinsky's excellent discussion of *Spider Woman* in chapter 2 of her *Ver y ser visto*, Barcelona, Antonio Bosch, 1978, where she argues that everything in the cell is determined by the system of oppression.
12. Of the six movie stories narrated, three are based on real films and three are composites of several films: (in order of

their appearance in the novel) *Cat People*, dir. Jacques
Tourneur (1942); the invented Nazi propaganda film
called *Destiny* (the film narrated in the movie *Kiss of the
Spider Woman*); *The Enchanted Cottage*, dir. John
Cromwell (1946); what we will call the 'Adventure'
film; *I Walked with a Zombie*, dir. Jacques Tourneur
(1943); what we will call the 'Mexican' film.

13. Sigmund Freud, *The Interpretation of Dreams* in *The Basic
Writings of Freud*, ed. A. A. Brill, New York, Random
House, 1938, p. 361.

14. Ibid., pp. 445 ff.

15. Danubio Torres Fiero, 'Conversación con Manuel Puig: la
redención de la cursilería', *Eco* 28, 173, March 1975, p. 507.

16. As I argue elsewhere, *Betrayed by Rita Hayworth* and
Heartbreak Tango examine the impact of culture on the
individual's consciousness, while the dreams, stream of
consciousness and clinical narration of *The Buenos Aires
Affair* comprise a psychosexual case history of its
protagonists. Like *Spider Woman*, *Pubis angelical*, the
ultimate psychological novel, gives us a graphic
illustration of how the unconscious encodes the real data
presented to it. See my 'For a New (Psychological) Novel
in the Works of Manuel Puig', *Novel*, 17, 2, Winter 1984,
pp. 141–57.

17. I examine more specifically the process of encoding in
'Through the Film Darkly: Grade "B" Movies and
Dreamwork in *Tres tristes tigres* and *El beso de la mujer
araña*', *Modern Language Studies*, XVI, 4, Fall 1985, pp.
300–12, of which this essay is a revised version. José
Miguel Oviedo also discusses the mediated signifying
system in his 'La doble expresión de Manuel Puig', *Eco*, 31,
192, Oct. 1977, p. 675.

18. The original *Cat People*, which featured quotations from
Freud and Donne as its epigraphs, certainly lends itself to
such a reading. It has been described by Joel E. Siegel, in
his *Val Lewton: The Reality of Terror*, New York, Viking,
1973, p. 102, as a movie containing 'suggestions of sexual
anxiety, antagonism, the identification of physical passion

with destruction, and overtones of lesbianism'.

19. I again refer the reader to Alicia Borinsky's discussion of the novel, and particularly to pp. 59 ff. Prof. Borinsky sees Molina and Valentín as 'the same person, in a relationship of doubles' (p. 60), and their relationship as a web which 'has annulled the differences between the lovers' (p. 60). The two men, she writes, 'have reconstructed – in a fascist jail cell – the sexuality of the society which has imprisoned them. (p. 62, [my translation]).

20. Danubio Torres Fiero, op. cit., p. 509.

of Cinecittà itself. The pantheon of gods I worshipped when I arrived there was highly inappropriate: Von Sternberg, Frank Borzage, the great stars: Greta, Marlene, Michèle Morgan; the poet Prévert. We were in 1956, and the reigning ideology was neo-realism. The school was dominated by two seemingly opposed kinds of oppression, which were basically akin to each other. This was a state-run school, and the Christian Democrats were in government. Consequently, the director and the administration were ultra-Catholic, of the kind still common in the 1950s, puritanical to an extent that would be laughable today. For example, they would object to actresses' necklines, they insisted on 'decorum', and any hint of sexual activity was considered an offence. This was the asceticism of a convent. Right-wing oppression by the administrators was in theory countered by the neo-realism of the teaching staff, who were all followers of this movement, begun shortly after the war with *auteur* films such as Rossellini's *Rome, Open City*, De Sica's *Shoe-shine boy*, and Visconti's *Terra Trema*. Unfortunately in Italy a number of critics and theorists of the cinema had tried to construct dogma from these films, a series of principles which they used as a bludgeon against any sort of cinema which differed from that espoused by Zavattini and his followers. They were seeking, above all, and quite rightly, to get away from Hollywood formulas, to experiment with a more enquiring cinema. They wanted an intelligent, thought-provoking cinema of social protest. But this determination led them into a grave mistake: one of Hollywood's chief concerns had always been to construct a solid plot, but since, according to the neo-realists, all Hollywood was synonymous with reactionary cinema, the ability to tell a story also became a reactionary characteristic. Any attempt to give a film a dramatic structure was dismissed as cheap melodrama or *pièces-à-ficelles*. I can recall an example of 'pure cinema' dreamt up by Zavattini: a working woman leaves her house to go shopping: she looks in shop windows, compares prices, buys shoes for her children; and all this in the real time such actions would take, so that the typical ninety minutes of screening time would easily be filled. And, of course, the director's own vision was to be kept strictly out of it: it was a mortal sin if the director were to be suspected of guiding things subjectively. The cold, impersonal, but revealing camera was their answer to everything. Exactly what did the camera reveal? In all probability, only a photographic, superficial reality. Obviously, not only was the art of narration reactionary, but the director's art as well. A movement which had grown out of the work of *auteurs* such as Rossellini and De Sica ended by establishing an *anti-auteur* theory.

I should add that 1956 was a year of deepest crisis for the neo-realist critics. The cinema public was shrinking and this, instead of making the critics stop and think, merely reinforced the rigidity of their concepts. 1956 saw the launch of De Sica's *Il Tetto,* filmed under Zavattini's reign of terror, which failed both with audiences and at the international film festivals. The only people who defended it were the neo-realist critics, because it had been made in strict accordance with their house style: which almost succeeded in stifling even De Sica's creative spirit. What was the final outcome of all this? The producers refused to back any serious efforts, and that was the end of what had started, ten years earlier, as a brilliant crusade led by directors rather than critics. Why did the producers withdraw? Because the public was voting with its feet: this cinema of political protest had become so purist, so rarefied, that only an élite could follow it. The mass audience, the lower or working classes who in Italy have a real passion for the cinema, could not understand this kind of film, though it was supposedly aimed at them. It may well be that all aesthetic theories tend to the extreme and at some point become oppressive; in this particular case, the neo-realist dogma went so far as to deny validity to anything that did not fit its own canons.

Even after so many years, it is this desire to exclude which I find the most alarming of critical phenomena. At the time I was immensely shocked to find this act of castration being carried out in the name of the Left. I was from a country where repression invariably came from the Right. Furthermore, these critics were highly refined, and met in the most expensive cafés. They were nothing like my hybrid pampa-MGM view of what Bohemia should be.

Emotionally, I was split. On the one hand, a popular cinema of protest appealed to me; but on the other, I also liked cinema with a story, and this apparently classed me as a diehard reactionary. In the midst of all this, I was struggling with my first screenplays, which were little more than imitations of old Hollywood films. I got enthusiastic while writing them, but this feeling vanished once I had finished them. I was fascinated by the possibility of re-creating moments of being a child cocooned in his cinema seat, but awakening from that brought no pleasure. The dream itself did, but not the waking. I finally thought it might be more interesting to explore the anecdotal possibilities of my own reality, so I set about writing a film script which inevitably turned into a novel. Why *inevitably?* I did not consciously decide to switch from a film to a novel. I was roughing out a scene in the script in which the off-screen voice of an aunt of mine was introducing the action in the laundry room of a typical Argentine house. Though her voice was supposed to take up at most three lines of dialogue, she went on without stopping for thirty pages or more. There was no way I could shut her up. Everything she said was banal, but it seemed to me that the accumulation of these banalities lent a special meaning to what she was saying.

It was one day in March 1962 that this accident of thirty pages of banalities happened. I think it was my desire for more narrative space which led me to change my medium of expression. Once I had managed to face reality, after so many years escaping from it into films, I was keen to explore and scrutinize it as deeply as possible in order to try to understand it. The traditional ninety minutes offered by films was simply not enough. The cinema requires synthesis, whereas my themes needed the opposite: they called for analysis, the accumulation of details.

After that first novel, I went on to write two more, convinced that I had said goodbye to the cinema. However, in 1973 the Argentine director Leopoldo Torre Nilsson wanted to buy the film rights to *Heartbreak Tango* (*Boquitas Pintadas*), which, after much hesitation, I accepted, also agreeing to adapt the book myself. As producer and director, Torre Nilsson gave me complete creative freedom, but this work of adaptation didn't feel right! I had to follow the opposite process to the one which had helped free me. I had to compress and cut the novel, to find ways of making a synthesis of all that had originally been set out analytically. Once the script was finished, I returned with a sigh of relief to writing novels, and began *Kiss of the Spider Woman*.

Four years later, I had another call from the world of cinema. From Mexico, the director Arturo Ripstein asked me to adapt José Donoso's novella *El lugar sin límites* (*Hell Has No Limits*). At first I said no, but Ripstein insisted, so I read the book again. It was more of a long short story than a novel, so in this case the problem was to add material to round out the script. I enjoyed this far more, and my good working relationship with Ripstein led to another project, which I myself suggested: the adaptation of a story by the Argentine writer Silvina Ocampo, *El impostor* ('The Imposter'), which meant a return to the cinema for the producer Barbachano Ponce. What did *El lugar sin límites* and *El impostor* have in common? On the surface, only their length: they were both short novels, or long short stories. But, once I had finished this third adaptation, I could see another obvious common denominator. Both stories were allegories, poetic in tone, without any claims to realism, even though basically they dealt with well-defined human problems.

My novels, on the other hand, always aim for a direct reconstruction of reality; this led to their – for me, essential – analytic nature. Synthesis is best expressed in allegory or dreams. What better example of synthesis is there than our dreams every night? Cinema needs this spirit of synthesis, and so it is ideally suited to allegories and dreams. Which leads me to another hypothesis: can this be why the cinema of the 1930s and 1940s has lasted so well? They really were dreams displayed in images. To take two examples, both drawn from Hollywood: an unpretentious B-movie like *Seven Sinners*, directed by Tay Garnett, and *The Best Years of Our Lives*, directed by William Wyler, a 'serious' spectacular which won a clutch of Oscars and was seen as an honour for the cinema.

Forty years on, what has happened to these two films? *Seven Sinners* laid no claim to reflect real life. It was an unbiased look at power and established values, a very light-weight allegory on this theme. *The Best Years of Our Lives* by contrast, was intended as a realistic portrait of US soldiers returning from the Second World War. And as such, it was successful. But, after all these years, all that can be said of this film is that it is a valid period piece, whereas *Seven Sinners* can be seen as a work of art. When I look at what survives of the history of cinema, I find increasing evidence of what little can be salvaged from all the attempts at realism, where the camera appears to slide across the surface, unable to discover the missing third dimension beyond two-dimensional photographic realism. This superficiality seems, strangely enough, to coincide with the absence of an *auteur* behind the camera. That is to say, of a director with a personal viewpoint.

Having outlined the differences I think I can discern between cinema and literature, I should like to turn to a question that is often asked nowadays: do the cinema and television mean the end of literature, or more specifically of narrative? I'm inclined to say no, that this is impossible, because the two involve different kinds of reading. In films, one's attention is attracted by so many different points of interest that it is very difficult, if not impossible, to concentrate on a complicated conceptual discourse. In the cinema, one's attention is split between the image, the dialogue, and the background music. Also, the demands made by the moving image are especially important. This is not the same as the demands made by looking at a painting, in which the image remains static. Because of the greater attention that can be focused on the written page, the narrator there has the possibility for another kind of discourse, which can be more complex conceptually. Moreover, a book can wait, its reader can stop to think; this does not apply to images in a film.

To conclude: some kinds of stories can only be dealt with in literature, because of the limits of the reader's attention. It is the human capacity for attention which decides the matter in the end. There are definite limits: one can focus on so much material, and no more. Beyond that, one grows tired: so, one can take in more from the written page than one finds possible on the screen. I myself had a curious experience in this respect. About three years ago, I saw an Italian film: *Il sospetto*, by Maselli. It has a very complicated political plot, and is very well made. Half way through the screening I began to grow alarmed: I simply could not follow the story. The characters were raising questions whose importance I could not grasp. I guessed that if they had been written down, those same chunks of dialogue would have been more comprehensible. Or would they? What was going on? Was it all nonsense, or was it merely that the spectator's attention could not grasp all that was being presented? I was intrigued, and through my publisher in Rome I got hold of the original film script. I read it through, and understood everything perfectly. There were one or two somewhat obscure passages, but they became clear on a second reading. This of course had been impossible in the cinema. There is no way of turning back the projector.

This all goes to explain why I think that the 'reading' a cinema spectator makes is different from that performed by the reader of a novel, and that the former, while it does relate to a literary reading, is also closely akin to looking at a painting. This would mean that it involves a third kind of reading which, while encompassing some of the characteristics of 'reading' literature and works of art, is distinct from both of them.

Translated by Nick Caistor

Augusto Roa Bastos: An Introduction

John King

In April 1982, Augusto Roa Bastos returned to Paraguay on a rare visit to his native country: he had been in exile since 1947. He went back to register his son as a Paraguayan citizen and to make contact with young writers. He was to launch a book of poetry by a fellow Paraguayan, Jorge Canese, but just before the launch, he was expelled from the country as a 'Marxist subversive' and Canese's book *Paloma blanca, paloma negra* ('White Dove, Black Dove') was seized and destroyed by order of the government.

The furore grew when, to justify their accusation, the authorities a few months later published a hitherto secret document supplied to them by the US Embassy. This listed Roa among a number of Paraguayans said to have visited Soviet bloc countries, in his case Cuba, where he was supposed to have been twice in the 1960s. In fact, Roa has never belonged to any political party, nor has he ever been to Cuba, always refusing invitations to do so precisely because of the danger of this kind of charge. Unlike other Latin American intellectuals he has had no trouble obtaining visas to the US, and is not considered a Communist by the US immigration authorities. As US officials reacted angrily to the publication of the document, the Paraguayan opposition voiced its suspicions that it was the fruit of collaboration between Paraguayan and local

US security services in order to discredit General Stroessner's opponents.

This incident was a further chapter in the violent social and cultural repression which has characterized Paraguay in the twentieth century. Roa has always been acutely aware of these problems and one cannot understand his work without reference to the formative events of Paraguayan history. The writer himself would unquestionably prefer a 'profile' which did not privilege a writer's own experiences and views, for he has stated that 'in my opinion it is superfluous and even shocking to privilege personal opinions, especially of writers who work in the field of fiction'. For him, the intellectual will always play an ambiguous and minor role in the necessary struggle for social justice in Paraguay.

The history of Paraguay after independence in 1811 was initially shaped by a remarkable ruler, Dr José Gaspar Rodriguez de Francia, who established himself as the Perpetual Dictator of the Republic until his death in 1840. Francia is the subject of Roa's most recent novel, *I The Supreme (Yo el Supremo)*, 1974, one of the most important works to have been written in Latin America. Francia inherited a divided and anarchic country, and by systematic ruthlessness, he forged an independent republic. He destroyed the power of the Creole élite, the Spanish merchants and the independence of the Church, built up and strictly controlled an army, directed education, expropriated land for the national patrimony, fostered a process of miscegenation through enlightened racial laws, and created an egalitarian rural-based society. He limited foreign trade and encouraged economic self-sufficiency at a time when other republics were becoming dependent on the advancing British Empire, and maintained the nation's boundaries despite the incursions of neighbouring Argentina and Brazil. Francia does not conform to our present-day stereotype of the cruel, selfish dictator: he was an extremely popular figure known in Guaraní as the *Karai-Guasú* (the 'great lord'). His heir Carlos Antonio Solano López developed his policies, and by the 1860s, Paraguay was a relatively advanced, independent nation.

This development was destroyed by the War of the Triple Alliance (1865–70) in which Paraguay was defeated by Brazil, Argentina and Uruguay, backed by British commercial interests. The war devastated the country. Paraguay lost half its pre-war territory to its neighbours, the population was reduced by more than half, and the young men in particular died in hundreds of thousands. As Roa has said, 'Amid the rubble left smoking for a century, lay the ruins of a people. Paraguay became a land without men and of men without land.' A local élite, allied to foreign capital, ruled the country between 1870 and 1940, fighting over control of lucrative foreign trade. A moderate, nationalist coalition did emerge at the time of the Chaco War with Bolivia in the mid 1930s, but these brief moments of political debate were finally suppressed in a bloody civil war in 1947, in which the centre and left parties were decimated. After the war, the first mass exodus from Paraguay occurred, and Roa was one of many that took refuge in Argentina. It is estimated that by 1979, almost a third of Paraguay's two million inhabitants were living outside the country. Out of the war, General Alfredo Stroessner gradually emerged as military leader and head of an authoritarian single party. Like Francia, he has developed the personality cult – unlike Francia, he has invited massive foreign investment benefiting a small, corrupt élite, allowed Brazil to make further incursions into the country, waged war against the native Indian population, and increased an unequal system of land tenure. The country is controlled by fear, torture, imprisonment, and ruthless suppression of political opposition.

The problem of exile is a dominant theme in Roa's work. The word exile has many connotations. It refers most explicitly to Roa's own life as a writer 'who has written nearly all of his work in the alienating and obsessive atmosphere of exile, in the unreal reality of his lost land and the sorrowful knowledge that it has all been an "absentee's" biography'. Many Paraguayans live abroad, but for those that remain the situation is perhaps even worse: 'The brutality of force, the contempt for the spirit and for moral dignity have invaded the air that they breathe, poisoning their thoughts even before they are formed . . . In this asphyxiating atmosphere, all possibility of communication seemed reduced to nothing. Why write? For whom?' The problem of an audience is acute. How to write for a people who are largely illiterate and whose culture is mainly oral? Even the language a writer uses cannot be neutral. Paraguay is perhaps the most completely bilingual nation in Latin America. Thanks mainly to the work of the Jesuit missions, the native Indian language Guaraní has survived and is in common usage. In a tragic paradox, the writer must choose Spanish, the language of the colonizer, yet 'the moment he writes in Spanish, he feels that he is performing a partial translation of the split linguistic choice, in which he himself is split by the fact of this choice'. Speakers of Guaraní mistrust written texts, a feature of an oral tradition based on speaking and listening. In this context, according to Roa, the Paraguayan writer must create works that go beyond literature and express this linguistic split, must write the 'absent texts' that would fuse Spanish and Guaraní. He himself wrestles with this problem in all his works.

Roa learned to speak both Spanish and Guaraní as part of a rural upbringing in the Guirá region of Paraguay. He was born in 1917 and lived close to a sugar plantation where his father worked as an administrator. He thus witnessed first-hand the difficult conditions and poverty of plantation life, which later became a central motif in his stories, and also the independence of the Indian community, in particular the *carpincho* ('rodent') hunters, who maintained a spirit of freedom in these brutal conditions. He went to military school, fought in the Chaco War against Bolivia, became a journalist and travelled widely in the *yerbales,* the maté-tea plantations of northern Paraguay, documenting the exploitation of these workers. He travelled briefly in Europe and spent several months in England immediately after the war, where he was impressed by the reconstruction work. In 1947 he was forced into exile. He moved to Buenos Aires, and has written all his major works of fiction there, whilst working in a number of occupations – as a journalist, teacher, and screenwriter. Like many intellectuals he was forced to leave Buenos Aires during the tragic confusion and violence of the mid-1970s, which led to a brutal military coup in 1976, and he now teaches at Toulouse University in France.

His earliest collection of short stories, *El trueno entre las hojas* ('Thunder Among the Leaves', 1953) is an angry denunciation of the conditions of the Paraguayan people, exploited in the *yerbales* and the sugar plantations, prey to corrupt foreign and domestic owners. Some hope is to be found in those that rebel against this system, though they become sacrificial victims of the regime. In his first novel *Son of Man* (*Hijo de hombre*), 1960, the theme of messianic social protest is fused with an analysis of the gap between the intellectual and the people; between theory and practice. It is set in the *yerbales* and culminates in the Chaco War, an ambiguous time in Paraguayan history, which generated a great deal of nationalist sentiment and enthusiasm but which was ultimately futile and wasteful of life. The main protagonist, Miguel Vera (whose biography is largely modelled on Roa's own life), is a middle-class intellectual, romantically attached to the idea of revolution but incapable of action. He eventually betrays the peasants and seeks refuge 'in despair and in symbols' *(Son of Man,* p. 225). The writer-traitor is contrasted to a number of ordinary, working men, the most important of whom is Cristóbal Jara, who sacrifices himself without intellectual anguish. In a materialist reading of Christianity, he is the true 'Son of Man', and the people themselves venerate a Christ-like figure, roughly hewn by one of them, a leper: 'a redeemer as ragged as themselves who, like them, has been constantly mocked and ridiculed and persecuted ever since the world began' (p. 9). Redemption is seen as possible through popular struggle. With this analysis, Roa can be seen as having anticipated the 'theology of liberation' movement, which became important in the Latin American Catholic Church in the 1960s.

In the 1960s Roa produced several anthologies of short stories which deal with similar themes and looked, in particular, at the nature of exile in Buenos Aires, but his second novel, *I The Supreme,* represented a major development. In this work, Roa positions himself as a 'compiler' of texts that deal with Dr Francia. With this device he seeks to 'deny the author as an entity who can work in complete autonomy, unconnected to reality and to those that forge that reality. That is why I speak of books written by the people, made up of all voices, cultured and uncultured.' The novel is a dialectic between the words that make up the title: *Yo* (the first person, Francia, the writer) *el* (the third person, the audience, the people) and *Supremo* (the supreme power, of law and of imagination). For the most part, the dictator is dictating to his scribe and to his people. He is in charge of the word, of law, and of history. By appropriating language, by narrating his own story, he can appropriate history. He attempts to fuse within himself theory and practice, necessary to preserve the independence and increase the prosperity of Paraguay. It is impossible to summarize this extraordinary novel in a few lines. It incorporates the latest developments in linguistic theory and practice, talks of the arbitrariness and unreliability of language which purports to describe reality, rereads and comments upon the various histories and travellers' accounts of Paraguay, ranges across the breadth of Latin American history, implicitly condemning Stroessner and debating with Fidel Castro, and exploring once again the gap between writer and reader. In the end, Francia's task is doomed: the supreme imagination of one man must be fused with the aspirations of the people who cannot be treated as passive recipients. One comment in the margin of the Dictator's discourse states: 'You believed that Revolution is the work of one man – in himself; one is always wrong, the truth begins with two or more.' The final anguish of the dictator is also the anguish of Roa, the compiler: how to write a message that can be received, how to fuse one's commitment to material reality and avoid being a mere *'escri-vano'* ('a vain scribe').

Roa promises two further novels in the near future. His work is exemplary in the field of Latin American fiction. There has been talk of a 'boom' in the popularity of Latin American fiction, and many authors have found favour in the market-place and cosmopolitan success. Roa's task is more solitary and he has never been tempted by the game of fiction, mere revolutions in words. He cannot play

Writing: A Metaphor of Exile

Augusto Roa Bastos

The political, social and cultural panorama in Paraguay today, under the longest dictatorship on the Latin American continent, provides a striking picture of the devastation such oppression causes to the whole range of its sources of creativity. The phenomenon of exile in this backward country seemingly forever saddled with the 'continuing hallucination of its history' that is the culmination of a century of those recurring, endemic dictatorships which beset the land like tropical fevers, has become an integral part of its nature and destiny.

The exile, first and foremost, of the country itself, in its landlocked inaccessibility, characterized by territorial segregation, internal migrations, emigration, and mass exoduses: with among the latter, that of its indigenous people, the first to take place after the expulsion of the Jesuits in 1767 which, in turn, was the first example of the forced exile of foreigners seen in colonial Paraguay. Once it had won independence from Spain, however, it managed, despite the isolation, to become the most materially and culturally developed nation in Spanish America. Under the rule of the famous Doctor Francia, who founded the Republic and built the nation state according to the principles of the Englightenment and the French Revolution, Paraguay conducted the first experiment in real autonomy and independence ever seen in the history of

Latin America, something not even the liberators had been able to achieve in the battles for liberation. Economic interests, chiefly the penetration and dominance of the British empire in the region, could not permit this dangerous precedent of self-determination to set a bad example in this tiny, out-of-the-way, landlocked country. At Britain's instigation and with its support, the financial centres of the Brazilian empire, together with the Río de la Plata oligarchies who depended on Britain, concocted what became known as the War of the Triple Alliance (1865–70). Paraguay was destroyed. Two-thirds of its inhabitants were killed, half its territory lost. Nothing was left but ruins. All that survived of the unfortunate nation was a 'vast catastrophe of memories' with at its centre a delirious reality that flung handfuls of its history into the faces of the survivors, as the Spaniard Rafael Barret wrote at the beginning of this century.

This emptying of its past, combined with its isolation and the lack of contact with the outside world and the pressure of neo-colonial interests to prevent this island surrounded by land, turned inwards on its own disasters, from receiving so much as the echoes of the cultural innovations that were transforming the ideas, arts, and literature of the rest of Latin America. Moreover, the double seclusion of its bilingual culture also has to be taken into account. Paraguay is the only entirely bilingual country in Latin America: Guaraní, the autochthonous spoken language is the true language of its people. It provides the *mestizo* cultural space in which for over four centuries orality has converted the written language into an absent text: the root metaphor of exile.

This cultural and linguistic exile compounds from within the other forms of alienation created by internal exile, since it implies the destruction of the final freedom, in the inflections and modulations of verbal expression. It is well known that a piece of literature owes its value not to its good intentions but to the resonance of its internal structure and the instinctive force it generates through the workings of 'an art which while being conscience is in search of a form that is not conscious of itself', something which, though not itself ideology, cannot escape ideology.

In this account of the kinds of exile the Paraguayan writer faces (external, internal, the loss of unlived life, the alienation of the still-unformed work, the split from reality, the impossibility those forced to live abroad have of making contact with their national public, and conversely the lack of communication with these writers which those suffering internal exile feel) linguistic exile represents the paradigm, the basic metaphor of this reality become unreal.

The dilemma of the bi-polarity between Spanish and Guaraní is at the heart of this sort of linguistic schizo-phrenia. Which of these two languages is a Paraguayan writer to choose? If at bottom literature is a linguistic act, and as such an act of communication, then the choice would seem obvious: Spanish. But when he uses Spanish, the Paraguayan writer, and above all the writer of fiction, experiences his most heartfelt alienation, that of linguistic exile. Can he ever limit this distancing from that part of his reality and the life of his community which finds expression in Guaraní, from Paraguayan culture as a whole, since it is so indelibly marked by the sign of orality, by its original mythical thinking? As soon as he starts to write in Spanish, the writer feels he is carrying out a partial translation from the severed linguistic context. In so doing, he is splitting himself. There will always be something he cannot express. This creates a need for the Paraguayan writer to construct a literature which goes beyond litera-ture, to speak against words, write against writing, invent (his)stories which counter the official history, to undermine in his subversive, demythifying writing the language built on the ideology of domination. It is in this sense that the new generations of storytellers and poets are dedicating themselves to the task of forging a *literature without a past*, born of a past without literature, of bringing it to expression in their own language.

According to Guaraní cosmogony, human language was seen as the foundation of the cosmos, man's original state. At the heart of this basic myth is the esoteric, untranslatable *ayvú rapytá* o *ñe'eng mbyte rá*, the kernel of the word-soul: the *ayvú* of the dawn of time. It is a noise or sound imbued with all the wisdom of nature and the cosmos, brought into existence by the austere, melodious Father of the beginning and end, inspirer of the founding word. A secret word, never uttered in the presence of strangers, which together with *tataendy* (flame of the sacred fire) and *tatachiná* (mist of the creative power) makes up the three original elements of the ancient Guaraní cosmology. Their founding divinities did not decree laws of retribution against anyone who aspired to knowledge. Instead, they agreed on the communion between knowing and doing, between oneness and plurality, between life and death. Every human being was God on the path towards purification, and God – or rather the many gods of their theogony – was the first and the last man. They did not cast anyone out, but spoke of the peregrination of the person–multitude in search of *land-without-evil* which everyone both carried within themselves and shared with everyone else.

In today's Paraguay, distorted by oppression, even this ancestral voice has been silenced, this final language in which a threatened, persecuted people could find refuge. This language without writing, which in earlier times encapsulated the essence of the word-soul, the seed of all that is human and sacred, is now obliged to seek a space for its message, for the illumination of reality through the unreality of signs.

Contemporary Paraguayan writers are aware of finding themselves at one extreme of the historical process. This makes them enormously sensitive to the problems not only of their society but of their own artistic labours. Those writers forced to live in internal exile share with those living outside the country a sense that the task of literature is once again to embody a destiny; their task to plunge themselves into the living reality of a community – their own – to draw sustenance from its deepest essences and hopes, in a way that will also embrace the universality of man.

These tellers of stories understand that, by their very nature, such feats can only be achieved on the aesthetic level, on the level of language and writing, in the idea of narration itself, which is not, as is commonly thought, the art of describing reality in words, but the art of making the word itself real.

The writer's task is to penetrate as deeply as possible beneath the surface of human destiny, to create the most complete picture possible of both individual and society, one that is most closely linked to the vital and spiritual experience of present-day mankind. Thus it is, that, by allying personal subjectivity to a historical and social awareness, creative imagination to moral passion, Paraguayan writers can overcome their tragic confinement and isolation and play a full part in literature in the Spanish language.

Translated by Nick Caistor

Guillermo Cabrera Infante:
An Interview in a summer manner

Jason Wilson

The interview began over the telephone.

'I understand you like written questions.'

'What I like is written answers but they don't come easy.'

'I'll bring the questions over and drop them in your mailbox.'

'My mailbox or my female box?'

'You tell me.'

'Join us. It's a big box.'

'I'm afraid I'll interrupt your work.'

'I welcome interruptions. They're the best excuse for not working. You know the difference between a journalist and a writer?'

'I'm afraid I don't.'

'Are you always so afraid? Never mind that. Here's my version of Auntie and the grasshopper. The journalist works hard but makes everybody believe he doesn't work at all. The writer is the other way round. He works hard at making believe he is working when he's not. Take a look at Truman Capote or closer to us at William Gerhardie. They toiled for years like peasants by Millet and they left nothing behind but empty furrows on their agents' foreheads. Or take a look at Hemingway . . .'

'Then I'll see you later.'

'Abyssinia.'

Question. Could you open by outlining the genesis and background to your fiction beginning with the realist stories of *Así en la paz como en la guerra* (1960)?

Answer. I disowned *Así en la paz como en la guerra (In Peace as it is in War)* because it's worse than a realist book: it's a Sartrean disaster. *Un desastre de Sartre.* There are some short stories that are salvageable, though. But that's not the genesis of a book. Nor anything except the urge to publish.

My first true book is my second book, which should be considered first. It's called *Un oficio del siglo XX.* It can be translated as *A Twentieth-Century Job* to create a confusion between job and Job. It's my job, but the reader should be a true Job. Apparently it's a collection of my movie reviews, written from 1954 to 1960, but it actually is the fictionalized biography of a movie buff off the cuff. It is encapsuled in a prologue, an intermission (as in the phrase 'Now there will be a short intermission. To cater for our patrons there is in the foyer a portrait of Charles Boyer' . . . more later) and an epilogue. When the book begins the reviewer (like all reviewers he thinks he is a critic), called G. Cain, is about to die because his days of *cine* and reviews are over. His farewell is some sort of, as he is not alone, *morituri te salutant.* They, a lot of dead film stars, salute me because I'm going to write Cain's bio.

Cain must die *cine die.* His critical body is his corpse and I must write his biography over his dead corpus. The book is rather confusing because Cain dies more than once and keeps coming back in all the old familiar places. As a matter of film, he is a familiar: just an oldie reprised over and over. He is the biographee and I'm the biographer and it all happens as in any 'Biography' of the mind. Confusion creates its masterpiece at the end. Or as in a cast *after* the

end. There is an index (called 'Index Gelardino' in honour
of another film buff) where you mustn't expect to find any
directions as to the content of the book. My index, like so
much flattery, will lead you nowhere. It is in fact a guide to
mislead you. In other words, it is a labyrinth. Be that as it
maze, the book can be funny and can be fact. It is now a
cult book and a generation of film critics everywhere in the
Spanish-speaking world has bought or borrowed it. They
have also borrowed from it. It's a book I like, which is
more than I can say of many books.

Question. With *Tres tristes tigres* (*Three Trapped Tigers*, 1967)
your style seemed to change radically?
Answer. If you read *Un oficio del siglo XX* you'll know
where *TTT* began. To help your readers I make a tongue-
twister into a voiceless stop. By the way, did you know
that the 'T' is the twentieth letter of the English alphabet
and the symbol of perfection? My book should suit my
reader to a T. (Think about it.) There is no literary
revolution, rather an evolution. Or, as Ben Jonson called
tobacco, a Havannah ebullition. A sudden outburst, for
the book was partially written in Havana, Brussels and
Madrid: from Fidel to Franco and under the spraying
Manneken Pis. In the novel there are several human
versions of the boy peeing in the rain.

Question. Tell me about the prize you won and why
publication was delayed.
Answer. The prize was the prestigious Spanish prize (all
prizes are prestigious: it must be the Homeric tradition)
and publication was delayed because of a case of persistent censorship. Though no worse than in my country:
twenty years after publication *TTT* is a *liber non grato* in
Cuba! All my books have become samizdat in my home-
land that is not my homebase. I had to rewrite the book,

change its title and pray a little. The Spanish censor was more moronic than malignant. For instance, every time I wrote 'tit' the censor, who knew I didn't mean a bird, changed it to breast or chest. Though 'tit', *teta*, is in the dictionary of the Royal Academy and in every Spanish dictionary. It means 'teat', as in English. So much tit for teat. In one of the parodies of Trotsky's assassination I wrote 'the assassin employed a deicide weapon'. It was deicide with a small d. Well, the censor crossed it out. Obviously he thought that to kill a god is to kill God. A Nietzschean censor no doubt. All in all he made twenty-two cuts in the new version of the book! Some of them were long, others longer. For him it was a case of *ars brevis, forfex longa*. But he had a major contribution to make. At the end, there is a long monologue of a madwoman in a park. She rants about the Catholics, laying it very, very thick. The contributing censor cut some sixteen lines of what the madwoman had to say about the Catholics and their church. But he stopped, I swear, at this line: 'Can't go no further.' That's where the book ends! Next question please.

Question. I have read about some of the problems you encountered translating *TTT*. Could you say how you worked and collaborated with your translators?

Answer. The problems were many in English, in French, in Italian and now in German, a totally mad language of which I know nothing. But I know my book. I should know it by now. In all these languages I found very good translators. The formidable Albert Bensoussan, a professor of Spanish at the University of Rennes, was the first to translate the book. Like all Frenchmen he had an obsession with French. To every other pun he objected with a vigorous 'C'est pas français'. Until I convinced him that

the original wasn't precisely Spanish. He did a great job
and the book got le prix du Meilleur Livre Etranger in 1970.
Then came English. Jonathan Cape, who wanted to publish the book then, chose a poet to translate it. First
mistake. The poet came riding on a bike: second mistake.
And, third mistake, the poet didn't know any Spanish. I
helped him. I helped a lot. Until one evening he called it a
day. I couldn't do the translation myself, among other
things because I was writing a screenplay titled *Vanishing
Point* and helping to make it into a movie, which is like
making war in peacetime. I did my best but it wasn't
enough. Along came Suzanne Jill Levine. She offered to
help me. She was still studying Spanish or had just
graduated. Anyway, she had that kind of Marxist upbringing that I love (by Marx I mean Groucho of course). We got
along swimmingly: I had a finger in every page. Anybody
who can read English can see that. I even delivered the
final draft to my American publishers, Harper and Row
(which I never pronounce to rhyme with bow). Jill helped.
As Humphrey Bogart says of Lauren Bacall, 'She's good.
She's very good'. Of course my authority on these translations comes from the fact that I am the author. I believe,
firmly, that translators fear to tread where writers rush in.

The main problem with *TTT* was not the wordplay, that
is puns and facetiae. I had my share of those in Spanish
but English is the *lingua mirabilis* for puns, the punster's
paradise. As a matter of fact England can be called Paro-
nom Asia. And that can take care of that. The awful truth is
that *Three Trapped Tigers* is fifty pages longer than *Tres
tristes tigres*. All of them full of puns! That's how the
jackass crossed the bridge: on a *puns asinorum*. There were
so many puns that I even rewrote one or two already
written by more prestigious punsters, like Lewis Carroll
and Vladimir Nabokov. A recent book called *Puns*, whose

author by the way has a pun for a name in Spanish: Walter Redfern (red fern is *helecho rojo* and it can easily become *el lecho rojo* or the red bed and no reds under the bed please) let me know that two of my favourite puns in *TTT*, *Crime and Puns*, the well-known novel, and an inversion, diaper/ repaid, must be credited to Vlad the Imp. But my foolish art reminds me of Joyce. Mad thematics. As the Manneken says, *tant pis!* But my book, besides the puns, was a gallery of voices . . . and that you cannot translate. You can translate texts but not voices. Not even in music, and *TTT* had not only a lot of voices but a lot of singing as well. In spite of my close attention to the translation of that book it has not been truly translated. On the other hand, it has never been traduced. *TTT* is a version and sometimes a perversion. All in the name of art, which can be read as o fart! Or as the MGM lion roared, *'Arse gratia artis'*. I've suffered enough!

Question. Do you view *La Habana para un Infante difunto* (*Infante's Inferno*), 1979, as an autobiographical fiction? An anti-Casanova's memoirs? A tribute to women?

Answer. La Habana is the biography of a city that perhaps never was. I have a lot of respect for Casanova. He was making love when everybody around him was only making hate or making war. Arthur Machen has turned his memoirs into a masterpiece. I'm glad that I never read Casanova in Spanish and as he wrote his *Memoirs* in French there's no Italian love lost between him and me. No, *La Habana*, if anything, is my version of the Don Juan myth, with Havana playing the part of Seville, the river made into an ocean and the stone guest is Ovid who in Spanish mirrorese is *divo*. For many years I wanted to write a Cuban version of Don Juan, the Zorilla comic drama rather than Tirso's tragedy. All of a sudden, at the very end of *La Habana*, I discovered that my book had accomplished what I never could. Of course there is a writer called Red Witt Hindsight who writes masterpieces after the fact. It's a tribute to the tribe. I mean, all the women in the book are Cuban. There's an old Cuban song written by a composer (he appeared in *TTT* and George Gershwin paid him homage by stealing a tune from him, believing that it belonged to folklore!) when he was in New York for a recording in 1930. The plot (songs used to have plots then) is that he sees a bosomy woman walking down Broadway and he instantly knows she is Cuban. The composer accosts this pretty pedestrian with twins, Lo and Behold. She is Cuban all right. Now he sings:

> Those who don't mince their steps,
> they are not Cuban.
> Those who don't have a wasp waist,
> they are not Cuban, etc., etc.

The song ends with:

> Cuban girls are the pearls of Paradise!

Pretty, ain't it?

Question. Did the translation into English (*Infante's Inferno*, 1985) involve you in the same way as translating *TTT*?
Answer. I took command of the book, as Dante would say, *da capo*. Starting from the title (what translator would have thought of such irreverence?) *Infante's Inferno* is all mine or all a mine, as the title might mean. All the women I once cared for are there, even my mother. Though sometimes I stab at mater. Some others are dull adults' dolls. I'm a base West Indian who throws pearls of paradise to swine. One

311

of the pearls is an island richer than all its tribes. In a summer manner I can say breezily that Havana is bigger in my books than she is in memory. She was bigger in reality because she was life. But there's a lot of prosaic acid in life. In my books there is poetic jest. Here stiffs say things off the cough because they died tubercular. They can say, 'I'll have coffee in the coffin, Cuffs' because it isn't they talking: language talks for them. Or, 'A grim ace', played with a grimace. Or having Conrad leaving a brothel and crying out loud, 'The whorerror! The whorerror of it!' Or of a lost lover to say that she was Eloise hoisted by her Abelard. That's in English but it can be worse in Spanish or in a French parody: a musing scene, miss sans scene, a miss en scene. All this was culled here and there from future fictions. Desdemona dressed to be killed because Othello suspected her of some hanky-panties. A Hamlet versed only in the martial arts answering Polonius's question, 'Swords, swords, swords'. I recently saw a garage near Oklahoma City called Onan. It was of course a self-service. All you had to do was to produce the hose. My host, a poet, thought that my Onanist connection was a blow below the Bible Belt. Finally we were onanimous.

Question. What happened to your announced novel *Cuerpos divinos?*

Answer. Cuerpos divinos (it means Divine Bodies!) is not just a pretty title. I have completed the first book (there are going to be three of those) and an epic logue, which is a fourth book. In this book, literally, nothing happens. It is only the recorded shit chat of three characters, one the everlasting narrator, and two minor characters who become major out of resilience and into the night. One of them speaks English only, for he considers Spanish a dead tongue. The conversations begin long before the Revolution and last until the main character in this dialogue leaves Cuba to settle in California. His name is Walter Ego and when he reaches his destination he sends his friends a cable which says: *'Et in arcadia'*. Signed, Ego. That's the beginning and the end of it. All I need now is what in the War-in-the-Pacific movies was called 'to fill the Japs'. That's all the method there is in my writing madness. I've been introducing lately an extraordinary moviemaker called Henri d'Abbadie d'Arrast (he was a French Basque) called in Hollywood in the 1920s Harry D'Arrast. I wrote a long article about him; I'll present him at the Barcelona Film Festival, as I did at the Miami Film Festival. My presentation was a single sentence: 'D'Arrast is silence'.

Question. Could you say something about how as a Cuban you relate to Hispanic culture?
Answer. There is a mutual magma, the Spanish language. I've been constantly opposed to the tag 'Latin American', mostly because it's used politically. Imagine, just imagine, a country ruled by a totalitarian dictator. Let's say this country is an island not entirely of itself. There is a geopolitical law that rules that all islands tend to govern the nearby continent. Suppose that a continent and a half (Mexico, Central and South America) becomes an enormous island. There you have Latin America. It's easier to rule over an island, no matter how big (look at Australia) than over many countries with many names and many identities. But if there is a reason to talk of Latin America, this a language reason, mostly the Spanish language. There is, no doubt about that, a continuum that runs from the Pyrenees to Patagonia. This set of elements is the Spanish language. I'm being read in Spain as I once was in

Cuba. Sometimes, though, I wonder if what they read is what I wrote. That's, of course, a risk all writers must take.

Question. You once said that between Quevedo and Borges there is nobody. Could you say something about Borges?

Answer. I've seen Borges become more and more a great writer, from the time I first read him in 1947 to today. I once told him in Brown's Hotel, apropos of the Nobel Prize, that he was the only writer writing in Spanish now, that is then, that would be read in 2085. He laughed it off but there was joy, not Joyce, in his laughter. Borges has also become something of a sage and that's quite a feat these days. It also is quite a feast. Borges is a joy to all readers but to the Spanish reader he was, first of all, quite a revolutionary writer. Not only for what he wrote about but for the way he wrote. The way he places an adjective (as you know this is a decision before the noun in Spanish, where *el gran hombre* and *el hombre grande* mean very different things) and the adjectives he chose, or perhaps invented, were a very new thing circa the late 1930s. He was a fearless man and a fearless writer. One must be very humble before *Hombre de la esquina rosada*. He dared disown that story and that language. Though he was right most of the time one should say that he was right even when he was wrong. As he said of Quevedo, Borges is not a writer but a literature.

Question. In your fiction written in exile you have lovingly and wittily detailed Cuban life, its voices, places, rhythms, etc., so that your work seems a kind of 'A la recherche du temps cubain'. Do you see yourself as the only real chronicler of Cuban life?

Answer. Not the only one but the best, and as Margot Kidder likes to say, I'm not kidding. Let's consider three

314

major Cuban writers this century: Alejo Carpentier,
Lezama Lima and Virgilio Piñera. Virgilio is closer to me
because he was a dear friend, he was a joyful gay but he is
the lesser of the three. He wrote mostly short stories, you
see, and his novels were not good. He was an original (he
wrote a story of the absurd long before it was done in
Paris) but something is wrong with his writing, a certain
weakness, a surfeit of catch phrases and a carelessness
about language. His Havana is never there, for he lives in
the land of whimsy. Lezama Lima, in his only novel
Paradiso, his Havana is suffering from the Bloch syndrome.
Remember Bloch, the elephantine pedant in *A la recherche*?
I've never been able to read this monstrous novel, defeated
by a prose thicker than water but not of my blood. He is a
considerable poet but his *Paradiso* is Havana as Hell.
Carpentier is the best writer of them all. He was stingy
with me as with everybody, but I can afford to be gen-
erous. The only Cuban book that comes close to my
Havana books is a novel by Carpentier called *El acoso*
(Manhunt). Like many novels it is actually a thriller, part
Liam O'Flaherty's *The Informer*, part Malraux's *La Condition humaine*. Here you have Havana in a nutshell. My
Havana is in expansion, a universe that began with a
whimper and will end in a big bang. With Carpentier you
have that breaking point when knowledge is about to
become pedantry but doesn't. Besides, Havana comes off
much better than O'Flaherty's Dublin, even when dreamt
by John Ford. Instead of my set of songs you have
Beethoven, a symphony orchestra and the collision of
culture and violence. The hunted man is a terrorist super-
grass at large. He finds shelter next to a theatre where an
orchestra is rehearsing *L'Eroica*. The constant repetitions
of the symphony are more overpowering than the
squealer's fear. In a true *coup de théâtre* he is killed in the

empty orchestra pit. This is a double *tour de force*, where the writing is like music and the plot a true melodrama. But it is also a driller, what with the rehearsing and the purple patches.

There is a fourth writer, Lino Novas Calvo. He has written beautifully about Havana in the 1930s, which he knew well. He never wrote a novel and as you know the short story is a limited, limiting form. Erskine Caldwell, John O'Hara and John Cheever were trapped in it, in spite of their novels. Novas Calvo, by the way, wrote a masterpiece called 'The Night of Ramón Yendía', a short story about an informer driver who, after the fall of Dictator Machado, believes he has blown his cover. The story is about what happens to him in the last twenty-four hours of his life. Doesn't it sound as familiar as a symphony?

Question. The Hispanic tradition is poor in a special kind of word-play epitomized by the pun. Do you feel more in tune with a Sterne, a Joyce, a Lewis Carroll or a Nabokov than any of your contemporary Latin American writers?
Answer. Joyce, Lewis Carroll and Nabokov, but Flann O'Brien also. He is a punster extraordinary.

Question. Did the so-called 'boom' help you as a writer?
Answer. Except for Borges, I don't see I have much in common with the so-called Boom, which was a political club of writers. I've always felt more comfortable, as a reader and as a writer, with Severo Sarduy and Manuel Puig. I rejoice in every new book by them, I reread their old books, especially *Heartbreak Tango* and *From Cuba with a Song* and of course the masterpiece *Kiss of the Spider Woman*. We have a lot in common, especially a firm belief that high culture is *haute couture*, but that there are *prêt-à-porters* and ready-mades and jumble sales and even

the old rags man. We understand each other and we believe that literature is everything that you can read, that you can write, including graffiti on a wall and those moving shadows on a screen called the movies. The other writers from that continent called Mongrelia (there is Inner Mongrelia and Outer Mongrelia) are simply too busy reading slogans on placards. You see, they are perched on hustings waving buntings and listening to the bunkum and hokum of *supremos* and *máximos*. Severo is made of the stuff of literature; Manuel is an avid collector of movies on tape. When they talk shop, if they do, I never forget that that's my shop too.

Question. I have read some of your work first in English (on W. H. Hudson, on Padilla and *Holy Smoke*). Could you say something about writing in another language? Do you feel any affinities with a Conrad or a Nabokov or a Joyce because of this and your exile? Have they been examples, influences or simply pleasures to read?

Answer. Language is a river but we are the river. This is a paraphrase of Borges paraphrasing Herakleitos on the river of time. The Greek wrote that song, 'Take me to the temple on time'. He was a barrister who said this to a cabbie, with the barrier of English between them. The cabbie hit the horse and the road and soon they, speaking different dialects, joined the morning traffic. *Sic transit.* Language can be a river and traffic and whatnot but the cabbie and his passenger are different travellers on the same vehicle. One can swim across the river, one can bathe in the river, one can watch the current and sometimes even see an Oxford professor floating downstream like a dead admiral: quiet flows the don. If you are Christian enough you could watch an emaciated dark man in a long white robe walking on the river. That man has all the time in the world (he is, in fact, eternal) and he speaks in tongues, while Herakleitos spoke tongues in Greek.

I'm convinced that if you can write in one language, you can write in all of them, including Swahili. Hemingway, for instance, spoke Swahili very well. He could read Spanish if he wanted too but he never wrote in Spanish because, simply, he didn't need to. I write in English because I want to, because I like the language, because there are two or three writers I consider not only masters of the language but masters of language as well. I wanted to belong in that old time relation. I had four years of English school in Cuba and I lived three years in Belgium, where I learnt French with Flemish masters. I'm convinced that if I had gone to Paris instead of London I'd be writing in French now – with the temptation of Spanish lurking in my mind.

Since I first came to England, even before moving to London from Madrid, I was writing filmscripts: *El Máximo* and then *Wonderwall, The Jam* and later *Vanishing Point*. You can correct me and say that screenwriting is no writing at all and I'll stand corrected. But I also wrote bits and pieces for American magazines and later a very long piece on Cuban culture for the *London Review of Books* and a long short story for an anthology, *London Tales*. My story is called 'The Phantom of the Essoldo' and it is my version of the *Phantom of the Opera* or *PhO*, as I called him long before Weber or Webern ruined it. I enjoyed writing it and I enjoyed even more writing 'Bites from the Bearded Crocodile'. But as Ronald Reagan said, after crying out loud 'Where's the rest of me?' when he saw he didn't have any legs, that's no feat. A true feat is Joyce getting up in the morning and treating English as if it were an alien tongue. Datsa feat. No wonder the Joyces spoke Italian at home. Nabokov spoke Russian with his wife Vera, which means true in Italian. Meanwhile, back on his ship, Conrad spoke Polish to himself. After having Polish you can have whatever you want. Conrad to my chagrin (that's how I call my grin: cha is short for chachachá) had no humour or a sense of poshlost when all was lost. Yes, I feel a close affinity with Nabokov, though he shunned vulgarity. Fortunately, the man between, James Joyce, was very vulgar. Though I found his excremental excesses distasteful. He mixes the ordinary with the extraordinary and sometimes what he gets is the ordurenary. But he can be very funny. Especially after *Portrait of the Artist,* a pedantic book, and just before *Finnegans Wake,* its pendant. I am an exile but I'm never silent and seldom cunning. He has been, indeed, an influence, an example, and a pleasure to read, especially *Dubliners* and *Ulysses* and fragments of the *Wake* before I fall asleep.

Question. Some of your non-fiction has a 'J'accuse' quality. What is your view about the writer and politics and those in power?
Answer. But not, I hope, Zola's *bute.* You know the song of course, 'Whatever Zola writes, Zola wets'? *Yo no acuso,* I simply point. I don't indict, I indicate. And those who have ears (van Gogh, for example, would be halfway through) let them hear. I wrote my first tract against Fidel Castro (and I've never been a one-tract man) in 1968. It was in fact the first public accusation (without drinking 'J'Accuse' Potion) of his regime by a writer of some consequence, who had been with the Revolution even before it triumphed and had been its propagandist and barely three years before, a diplomat for both regime and revolution. This caused a scandal but there was no success: nobody listened for they had vowed to be Semper Fidelis and bestowed on Castro the order of Defensor Fidei,

which ironically means that he should defend himself. Those writers had no Latin but Castro had. They mounted a campaign against me, which was a destroy-and-then-search operation. I survived because survival is my business and my business then was making movies. But my books became all of a sudden out of print: my stories were never published in anthologies where, as they say in Spanish, even the cat was admitted, and I began losing weight and friends. This didn't happen in Cuba but abroad for, as George Orwell says, you don't have to live in a tyranny to be a tyrant's subject.

Question. Do you read contemporary English and American novels?

Answer. I read English fiction and American faction. England is where it's all happening again. The American scene, on yet another hand, is like the prairie in the moonlight: immense but empty. The Americans have developed a huge politically guilty conscience with blacks, browns and beiges. Instead of phonetics they have fanatics: they hear themselves speak but cannot listen to other voices, other booms.

Question. Can you name names?

Answer. Peter Ackroyd is the author of a posthumous pastiche, *The Testament of Oscar Wilde.* Here you see, and above all you hear, Oscar giving away his precious words for free: pearls to pigs. You can even feel how Wilde thinks. Julian Barnes, like Ackroyd, is a master of parody and pastiche. Ackroyd's words are Wilde's. Barnes built his house of words with bricks-à-Braque. His ace in the whole is a trump-l'oeil. The Flaubert in the fabric dies in the wool before the book begins. Flaubert is dead, Wilde is dying: these are postmortems as autopsies. Both books are brilliant.

Question. Can you say a bit about Hemingway?
Answer. Joyce had the first and last word about Hemingway. He said that he was a *naïf*. He didn't say a naive writer, just a *naïf*. Hemingway pronounced it knife.

Question. Can you say something about your work in the cinema? Has writing film scripts like *Vanishing Point* affected your writing of novels? Are you still a film-goer? Could you return to being a film critic?
Answer. The last screenplay I wrote was based on *Under the Volcano* and it sent me, literally, to a lunatic asylum. It was written for Joseph Losey but he didn't own the property. That's a book in Hollywoodese. Losey, a fine man (and that rarest of things in the movies, an intelligent man), not only lost his battle to John Huston (who, typically, after professing a love for the book for years, proceeded to make a turd of it – what's amazing is that some reviewers saw the turd as an urbane turkey) but lost his life. Luckier, I only lost my reason. Miriam Gomez took me to a posh loony bin (yet a bin) and when I came to, after many a summer song, I heard lions roaring. I said to myself: 'If this were a movie it would be an MGM movie.' A few days later I knew better: reality had crept back into my bed. The asylum was behind the Regent's Park Zoo. A fine madness was mine!

What I've done with the scripts I wrote (as with my lectures: travels with my cant) is to subsidize my writing. Not with my serious writing, for all I write is jokes, but with the writing I publish in book form. This is being said in a summer manner, that is to say, breezily. The scripts crept into my consciousness. But I never was a turd man.

And I never was caught chewing Gomez. To slip into something more Freudian, I was born with a silver screen in my mouth but I'm no longer a film-goer: movies come to me from behind the television set and sideways from two video recorders. I don't have to fly down to Rio any more. As you see, with me puns are a *tic douloureux*. I suffer from the grimace but you have the pun. No, no, never! I quit after five years in the stalls. Never again!

Question. Can your books be bought and read in Cuba today? Are you an underground author? Have you been censored in any other country?

Answer. My books are not allowed in Cuba at all. Since 1979 I've tried to have a copy sent to my father, to no avail. My Spanish publishers sent different copies from different places, even Mexico, and they never arrived. You know that *TTT* and *Infante's Inferno* are totally apolitical books. Not even *Holy Smoke* reached my farther father. But my books are read, a paradox, like printed samizdat. Not only that, the younger generation doesn't write like Lezama or Carpentier or even Piñera: they are all being clones together of *TTT*. Twenty years later. A recent novel by a young commissar is like three tigers trapped in a time warp. This seems ungracious of me, but I must tell you the truth, warps and all. Almost twenty years ago, my Uruguayan publisher sent copies of *Así en la paz* to Argentina. All copies were confiscated by the authorities (a cool, calm and collecting name for a collective office), judged subversive and burnt accordingly. It's a pity it didn't happen with *Holy Smoke:* my book turned to ash, like a cigar should. Otherwise my books have suffered more under the hideous regimes of pirates. Piracy and piranhas being the wolf-bane of writers in South America.

322

Question. You have part translated your own work as well as Joyce's *Dubliners:* do you enjoy translating? Can you say something about how you translate?

Answer I do enjoy translating. I enjoyed translating *Dubliners.* Joyce's short stories, though shamelessly naturalistic, are exacting and precise: every word counts. In my translation some words count down. I paid homage to his catalepsy in *Infante's Inferno*, as read in *The Dead.* In Havana it rains where it snows in Ireland. When we were correcting proofs and Miriam Gomez, as usual, helped me by reading from the original and, when we reached the snow-covered tomb of Michael Furey, she burst out crying. I cried too. I don't advise crying over a split infinitive as a method of translating anything. The book sold very well in Spain and was successfully pirated in South America. So some books need crying out loud to be translated. As to my own books, I followed only one rule: when in doubt bring in two puns of Attic salt, stir slowly, to be damned before publishing. Facetious but not facile. Nevertheless, to translate into English is a pleasure to behold. Not only because of the pluperfect passion of the language but because you are writing for a public whose culture is where I'm heading. Of course you will have the nightmares of Kew dreamt by a Jew, but that means youth in a very old system of signs. Salt and saltus is my recipe.

Question. As a Cuban who has lived through a revolution, do you still today see history as a 'parade of fashions'?

Answer Fortunately I don't see history any more, much less History. For me, history is just a book with the title of history. Of course there is natural history and the history of literature but neither determines anything. Reading Herodotus you can see how pretentiously crazy is a phrase like 'History will absolve me' as uttered by Fidel Castro sometime in 1953. Later, when he was in power, a journalist friend once wrote, 'History can absolve you, no doubt. But what about geography?' The journalist, friend made foe by decree, had to seek asylum in an embassy and later flee Cuba. History is writing with hindsight; history is the leftovers of a banquet on power; history is, finally, just gossip.

Question. Could you say, that is write down, why you prefer to write answers to an interview?

Answer. It all began when I started giving interviews left, right and centre in 1968. *TTT* was out in Spain and becoming some sort of best seller and I was asked for interviews that were mostly political. I was in a difficult political position then because I never asked for asylum in England or took refuge in Spain. Technically, I was just a Cuban abroad. Suddenly there was an Argentine interviewer from a very popular news magazine south of the border who wanted me to talk of exile and exiledoms by the sea. I asked him to write down the questions, which he did, and I promised that my answers would be forthcoming, which they were. Since then I've become addicted to the written interview: written questions, written answers. I have more control of what I say. As Humpty-Dumpty says, it's all a question of who's going to be boss: who asks the questions and who answers them. I deplore the young reporter armed with pad and pencil. Even more so when he props himself up with a tiny tape-recorder that doesn't work most of the time or what is worse, he doesn't even know how to start it! Then the interviewer takes a bow and disappears with a sheepish smile on his wan face. But the question, not the answer, lingers: who's to tape, who's to type? Some interviews! Read later in a newspaper called *The Herald of Calahorra* or *The Pocahontas Inquirer* (interview

taped by one John Smith) or *The Gay Desperado*, a rather
sad sheet. In any of those publications I read with
amazement a maze of answers I never gave to questions
nobody asked me! Why? It's not for me to reason why.

Question. I once read your *(C)ave Attemptor* in English, but
this self-chronology stopped in 1965. I know you have
updated this as 'Breaking the noise barrier'. Has this
updating been translated? Would you contemplate translating this as the last question and bring it up to 1978?
Answer. Not in a million years! By that time I'll be needing
a new chronology. Did you know that the first (unreliable)
chronologies were established by Plutarch, the historian as
gossip? He is the one who said 'Bad news travels far'. Was
he talking about interviews? *Plutarch plus tard.*

Bibliography

PRIMARY SOURCES

This section lists the English translations of the main texts discussed in this volume. The dates of publication in Britain refer, whenever possible, to the most recent paperback edition.

Ciro Alegría, *Broad and Alien is the World,* New York, Farrar and Reinhart, 1941; London, Merlin, 1984

Isabel Allende, *The House of the Spirits,* New York, Knopf, 1985; London, Black Swan, 1986

Jorge Amado, *The Violent Land,* New York, Knopf, 1965.

– *Gabriela, Clove and Cinnamon,* New York, Knopf, 1972; London, Souvenir, 1983

– *Home is the Sailor,* New York, Knopf, 1964; London, Chatto and Windus, 1964

– *Dona Flor and her Two Husbands,* New York, Knopf, 1969; London, Weidenfeld and Nicolson, 1970

– *Tent of Miracles,* New York, Knopf, 1971

– *Tereza Batista, Home from the Wars,* New York, Knopf 1974; London, Souvenir, 1982

– *Tieta,* New York, Knopf, 1979

– *Jubiabá,* New York, Avon Books, 1984

– *Sea of Death,* New York, Avon Books, 1984

– *Pen, Sword, Camisole: A Fable to Kindle a Hope,* New York, Avon Books, 1986

Mário de Andrade, *Macunaíma,* New York, Random House, 1984; London, Quartet, 1984

Bibliography

Oswald de Andrade *Seraphim Grosse Pointe*, Austin, Nefertiti Head Press, 1979

Ivan Angelo, *A Celebration*, New York, Avon, 1982

– *The Tower of Glass*, New York, Avon, 1986

José María Arguedas, *Yawar Fiesta*, Austin, University of Texas Press, 1985; London, Quartet, 1985

– *Deep Rivers*, Austin, University of Texas Press, 1986

Miguel Angel Asturias, *The President*, New York, Atheneum, 1964; London, Penguin, 1972

– *Men of Maize*, Boston, Delacorte, 1975

– *The Mulatta and Mr Fly*, Boston, Delacorte, 1967; London, Penguin, 1984

– *The Cyclone*, London, Peter Owen, 1967

– *Strong Wind*, Boston, Delacorte, 1968

– *The Green Pope*, Boston, Delacorte, 1971; London, Cape, 1971

– *The Eyes of the Interred*, New York, Delacorte, 1973

Lima Barretto, *The Patriot*, London, Rex Collings, 1978

Adolfo Bioy Casares, *The Invention of Morel and Other Stories*, Austin, University of Texas Press, 1986

Jorge Luis Borges, *A Universal History of Infamy*, New York, Dutton, 1972; London, Penguin, 1975

– *Labyrinths: Selected Stories and Other Writings*, New York, New Directions, 1964; London, Penguin, 1982

– *The Aleph and Other Stories, 1933–1969*, New York, Dutton, 1970; London, Picador, 1973

– *A Personal Anthology*, New York, Grove Press, 1967; London, Picador, 1968

– *The Book of Imaginary Beings*, New York, Dutton, 1969; London, Penguin, 1984

– *Dr Brodie's Report*, New York, Dutton, 1971; London, Penguin, 1981

– *The Book of Sand*, New York, Dutton, 1977; London, Penguin, 1982

– *Dreamtigers*, Austin, University of Texas Press, 1964

– *Other Inquisitions, 1937–1952*, Austin, University of Texas Press, 1964

- with A. Bioy Casares, *Chronicles of Bustos Domecq*, New York, Dutton, 1976

Guillermo Cabrera Infante, *Three Trapped Tigers*, New York, Harper and Row, 1971; London, Picador, 1980
- *View of Dawn in the Tropics*, New York, Harper and Row, 1978; London, Faber and Faber, 1988
- *Infante's Inferno*, New York, Harper and Row, 1984; London, Faber and Faber, 1984
- *Holy Smoke*, New York, Harper and Row, 1985; London, Faber and Faber, 1985

Alejo Carpentier, *The Lost Steps*, New York, Knopf, 1956; London, Penguin, 1980
- *The Kingdom of This World*, New York, Knopf, 1957; London, Penguin, 1980
- *Explosion in a Cathedral*, Boston, Little Brown, 1963; London, Penguin, 1971
- *The War of Time*, New York, Knopf, 1970; London, Gollancz, 1970
- *Reasons of State*, New York, Knopf, 1976; London, Writers' and Readers', 1978

Rosario Castellanos, *The Nine Guardians*, New York, Vanguard, 1970

Julio Cortázar, *The Winners*, New York, Pantheon, 1965; London, Allison and Busby, 1986
- *Hopscotch*, New York, Pantheon, 1966; London, Collins, 1967
- *End of the Game and Other Stories*, New York, Pantheon, 1967; London, Collins, 1968
- *Blow-up and Other Stories*, New York, Collier, 1968
- *Cronopios and Famas*, New York, Pantheon, 1969; London, Marion Boyars, 1978
- *62: A Model Kit*, New York, Pantheon, 1972; London, Marion Boyars, 1977
- *All Fires the Fire and Other Stories*, New York, Pantheon, 1973; London, Marion Boyars, 1979
- *A Manual for Manuel*, New York, Pantheon, 1978
- *We Love Glenda so much and Other Stories*, New York, Knopf, 1983; London, Harvill, 1984

– *A Change of Light and Other Stories*, New York, Knopf, 1980; London, Arena, 1987

Euclides da Cunha, *Rebellion in the Backlands*, Chicago, University of Chicago Press, 1967

José Donoso, *Coronation*, New York, Knopf, 1965; London, Bodley Head, 1965

– *This Sunday*, New York, Knopf, 1967; London, Bodley Head, 1968

– *The Obscene Bird of Night*, New York, Knopf, 1973; London, Cape, 1974

– *Sacred Families*, New York, Knopf, 1977; London, Gollancz, 1978

– *Charleston and Other Stories*, Boston, David Godine, 1977

– *A House in the Country*, New York, Knopf, 1984; London, Penguin, 1985

Autran Dourado, *The Voices of the Dead*, New York, Tapingler, 1981; London, Peter Owen, 1980

Gilberto Freye, *The Masters and the Slaves: A Study in the Development of Brazilian Civilization*, New York, Knopf, 1946

Carlos Fuentes, *Where the Air is Clear*, New York, Ivan Obolensky, 1960; London, André Deutsch, 1986

– *The Good Conscience*, New York, Ivan Obolensky, 1961; London, André Deutsch, 1986

– *The Death of Artemio Cruz*, New York, Ivan Obolensky, 1964; London, Penguin, 1979

– *Aura*, Bilingual edition, New York, Farrar, Straus and Giroux, 1968

– *A Change of Skin*, New York, Farrar, Straus and Giroux, 1968; London, André Deutsch, 1987

– *Holy Place* in *Triple Cross*, New York, E.P. Dutton, 1972

– *Terra Nostra*, New York, Farrar, Straus and Giroux, 1976; London, Penguin, 1978

– *The Hydra Head*, New York, Farrar, Straus and Giroux, 1978; London, Secker and Warburg, 1978

– *Burnt Water*, New York, Farrar, Straus and Giroux, 1980; London, Secker and Warburg, 1981

– *Distant Relations*, New York, Farrar, Straus and Giroux, 1982; London, Abacus, 1984

- *The Old Gringo,* New York, Farrar, Straus and Giroux, 1986; London, Picador, 1987

Gabriel García Márquez, *No One Writes to the Colonel and Other Stories,* New York, Harper and Row, 1968; London, Picador, 1983

- *One Hundred Years of Solitude,* New York, Harper and Row, 1970; London, Picador, 1983
- *Leafstorm and Other Stories,* New York, Harper and Row, 1972; London, Picador, 1983
- *The Autumn of the Patriarch,* New York, Harper and Row, 1976; London, Picador, 1983
- *In Evil Hour,* New York, Avon Bard, 1979; London, Picador, 1983
- *Innocent Eréndira and Other Stories,* New York, Harper Colophon Books, 1979; London, Picador, 1983
- *Chronicle of a Death Foretold,* New York, Knopf, 1982; London, Picador, 1983
- *Story of a Shipwrecked Sailor,* New York, Knopf, 1986; London, Cape, 1986

José Lins do Rego, *Plantation Boy,* New York, Knopf, 1966

Clarice Lispector, *Family Ties,* Austin, University of Texas, 1972; Manchester, Carcanet, 1985

- *The Foreign Legion,* Manchester, Carcanet, 1986
- *The Apple in the Dark,* New York, Knopf, 1967; London, Virago, 1983
- *The Hour of the Star,* Manchester, Carcanet, 1986
- *An Apprenticeship or the Book of Delights,* Austin, University of Texas, 1986

Machado de Assis, *Epitaph of a Small Winner,* New York, Noonday Press, 1956; London, Hogarth Press, 1984

- *The Heritage of Quincas Borba,* London, W. H. Allen, 1954; The New York edition (Noonday Press, 1954) has the title *Philosopher or Dog?*
- *Dom Casmurro,* New York, Noonday Press, 1953; London, W. H. Allen, 1953
- *Counselor Ayres' Memorial,* Berkeley, University of California Press, 1972

Bibliography

- *The Psychiatrist and Other Stories*, Berkeley, University of California Press, 1963; London, Peter Owen, 1963
- *The Devil's Church and Other Stories*, Austin, University of Texas Press, 1977; Manchester, Carcanet, 1985
- *Helena*, Berkeley, University of California Press, 1984
- *Yayá García*, Lexington, University Press of Kentucky, 1977; London, Peter Owen, 1976

Alberto Manguel, ed., *Other Fires: Stories from the Women of Latin America*, New Jersey, Crown Publishers, 1986; London, Picador, 1986

Elena Poniatowska, *Dear Diego*, New York, Pantheon, 1986; London, Faber and Faber, forthcoming

Manuel Puig, *Betrayed by Rita Hayworth*, New York, Dutton, 1971; London, Arena, 1984
- *Heartbreak Tango*, New York, Dutton, 1973; London, Arena, 1987
- *The Buenos Aires Affair*, New York, Dutton, 1976
- *Kiss of the Spider Woman*, New York, Knopf, 1979; London, Arena, 1984
- *Eternal Curse on the Reader of These Pages*, New York, Random House 1982; London, Arena, 1985
- *Blood of Unrequited Love*, New York, Random House, 1984
- *Pubis Angelical*, New York, Random House, 1986; London, Faber and Faber, 1987

Graciliano Ramos, *São Bernardo*, London, Peter Owen, 1975
- *Barren Lives*, Austin, University of Texas Press, 1961
- *Childhood*, London, Peter Owen, 1979

Darcy Ribeiro, *Maíra*, New York, Random House, 1984; London, Picador, 1984

João Ubaldo Ribeiro, *Sergeant Getúlio*, Boston, Houghton Mifflin, 1978; London, Faber and Faber, 1986

Augusto Roa Bastos, *Son of Man*, London, Gollancz, 1965
- *I The Supreme*, New York, Knopf, 1986; London, Faber and Faber, 1987

João Guimarães Rosa, *The Third Bank of the River and Other Stories*, New York, Knopf, 1968
- *Sagarana*, New York, Knopf, 1966
- *The Devil to Pay in the Backlands*, New York, Knopf, 1963

Bibliography

Luisa Valenzuela, *The Lizard's Tail*, New York, Farrar, Straus and Giroux, 1983; London, Serpent's Tail, 1987

Mario Vargas Llosa, *The Time of the Hero*, New York, Grove Press, 1966; London, Picador, 1986

- *The Green House*, New York, Harper and Row, 1968; London, Picador, 1986

- *The Cubs and Other Stories*, New York, Harper and Row, 1979

- *Conversation in the Cathedral*, New York, Harper and Row, 1975

- *Captain Pantoja and the Special Service*, New York, Harper and Row, 1978; London, Faber and Faber, 1987

- *Aunt Julia and the Scriptwriter*, New York, Farrar, Straus and Giroux, 1982; London, Picador, 1984

- *The War of the End of the World*, New York, Farrar, Straus and Giroux, 1984; London, Faber and Faber, 1984

- *The Real Life of Alejandro Mayta*, New York, Farrar, Straus and Giroux; London, Faber and Faber, 1986

- *The Perpetual Orgy*, New York, Farrar, Straus and Giroux, 1986; London, Faber and Faber, 1987

- *Who Killed Palomino Molero?*, New York, Farrar, Straus and Giroux, 1987; London, Faber and Faber, 1988

SECONDARY SOURCES

A selective bibliography of criticism on Latin American fiction in English.

P. Apuleyo Mendoza and G. García Márquez, *The Fragrance of Guava*, London, Verso, 1982

S. Bacarisse, ed., *Contemporary Latin American Fiction*, Edinburgh, Scottish Academic Press, 1980

S. Boldy, *The Novels of Julio Cortázar*, Cambridge, Cambridge University Press, 1980

R. Brody and C. Rossman, eds., *Carlos Fuentes: A Critical View*, Austin, University of Texas Press, 1982

G. Brotherston, *The Emergence of the Latin American Novel*, Cambridge, Cambridge University Press, 1977

Bibliography

- *Image of the New World: The American Continent Portrayed in Native Texts*, London, Thames and Hudson, 1979
- J. Brushwood, *The Spanish American Novel: A Twentieth-Century Survey*, Austin, University of Texas Press, 1975
- J. Donoso, *The Boom in Spanish-American Literature: A Personal History*, New York, Columbia University Press, 1977
- G. Duran, *The Archetypes of Carlos Fuentes: From Witch to Androgyne*, Connecticut, Archon Books, 1980
- W. Farris, *Carlos Fuentes*, New York, Frederick Ungar, 1983
- J. Franco, *The Modern Culture of Latin America*, London, Penguin, 1970
- *An Introduction to Spanish American Literature*, Cambridge, Cambridge University Press, 1971
- *Spanish American Literature since Independence*, London, Ernest Benn, 1973
- D. Gallagher, *Modern Latin American Literature*, Oxford, Oxford University Press, 1973
- E. Picon Garfield, *Women's Voices from Latin America: Interviews with Six Contemporary Authors*, Detroit, Wayne State University Press, 1985
- J. Gledson, *The Deceptive Realism of Machado de Assis*, Liverpool, Francis Cairns, 1984
- R. González Echevarría, *Alejo Carpentier: The Pilgrim at Home*, Ithaca, Cornell University Press, 1977
- *Voices of the Masters: Writing and Authority in Modern Latin American Literature*, Austin, University of Texas Press, 1985
- D. Haberly, *Three Sad Races: Racial Identity and National Consciousness in Brazil*, Cambridge, Cambridge University Press, 1983
- L. Harss, B. Dohmann, eds., *Into the Mainstream: Conversations with Latin American Writers*, New York, Harper and Row, 1968
- J. King, *'Sur': An Analysis of the Argentine Literary Journal and its Role in the Development of a Culture, 1931–1970*, Cambridge, Cambridge University Press, 1986
- A. J. MacAdam, *Modern Latin American Narrative: The Dreams of Reason*, Chicago, University of Chicago Press, 1977
- *Textual Confrontations – Comparative Readings in Latin*

American Literature, Chicago, University of Chicago Press, 1987

S. Magnarelli, *The Lost Rib: Female Characters in the Spanish American Novel*, Lewisburg, Bucknell University Press, 1985

S. Menton, *Prose Fiction of the Cuban Revolution*, Austin, University of Texas Press, 1975

S. Merrim, *Logos and the word: The Novel of Language and Linguistic Motivation in 'Grande Sertão: Veredas' and 'Tres tristes tigres'*, New York, Peter Lang, 1983

S. Minta, *Gabriel García Márquez*, London, Cape, 1987

J. Ortega, *Poetics of Change: The New Spanish American Narrative*, Austin, University of Texas Press, 1984

D. Patai, *Myth and Ideology in Contemporary Brazilian Fiction*, Rutherford and London, Associated University Presses, 1983

E. Rodríguez Monegal, *Jorge Luis Borges: A Literary Biography*, New York, Dutton, 1978

J. Sommers, *After the Storm: Landmarks of the Modern Mexican Novel*, New Mexico, University of New Mexico Press, 1968

R. Souza, *Major Cuban Novelists: Tradition and Innovation*, Columbia, University of Missouri Press, 1976

D. Shaw, *Alejo Carpentier*, Boston, Twayne, 1982

J. Sturrock, *Paper Tigers: The Ideal Fictions of Jorge Luis Borges*, Oxford, Oxford University Press, 1977

J. S. Vincent, *João Guimarães Rosa*, Boston, Twayne, 1978

R. J. Williams, *Gabriel García Márquez*, Boston, Twayne, 1984

– *Mario Vargas Llosa*, New York, Ungar, 1986

Critical Guides to Spanish Texts, Grant and Cutler, London
Relevant titles include:

D. L. Shaw, *Borges: 'Ficciones'*, 1976

R. Brody, *Cortázar: 'Rayuela'*, 1976

P. Standish, *Vargas Llosa: 'La ciudad y los perros'*, 1982

V. Smith, *Carpentier: 'Los pasos perdidos'*, 1983

R. Young, *Carpentier: 'El reino de este mundo'*, 1983

List of Contributors

Susan Bassnett is senior lecturer in comparative literature at the University of Warwick. She is author of several books, most recently *Feminist Experiences: The Women's Movement in Four Cultures* (1986) and *Sylvia Plath* (1987).

Steven Boldy is lecturer in Latin American literature at Cambridge University. He is author of a book on Julio Cortázar, and of articles on Isaacs, Rulfo, Carpentier, Fuentes and others.

Gordon Brotherston is professor of literature at the University of Essex. He has written books on contemporary Latin American literature, and on native American culture.

John Gledson is senior lecturer in Hispanic Studies at the University of Liverpool. He has published books on Carlos Drummond de Andrade and Machado de Assis, and articles on other aspects of Brazilian literature.

Randal Johnson is associate professor of Brazilian literature and film at the University of Florida. He has published several books on Brazilian cinema and a comparative work on literature and cinema.

John King teaches Latin American cultural history at the University of Warwick. He has written two books on Argentine cultural history, and articles on Latin American literature.

Gerald Martin is professor of Latin American Studies at

Portsmouth Polytechnic. He has published books and numerous articles on Latin American literature and is currently writing a history of Latin American fiction for the *Cambridge History of Latin America*.

Stephanie Merrim teaches Latin American literature at Princeton University. She has written widely on modern and colonial topics.

Charles Perrone is assistant professor of Brazilian literature at the University of Florida, specializing in contemporary poetry and song. He has a book forthcoming on popular music in Brazil.

William Rowe is reader in Latin American literature at Kings College, University of London. He is author of a book on Arguedas and has written widely on modern Latin American literature and culture.

Edwin Williamson teaches Spanish and Spanish-American literature at Birkbeck College, University of London. His book *The Half-Way House of Fiction: 'Don Quixote' and Arthurian Romance* was published in 1984. He is currently writing a general and cultural history of Latin America.

Jason Wilson teaches Spanish and Latin American Literature at University College, London. He is author of two books on Octavio Paz and has published widely in the field of Spanish American literature and cultural history.

Michael Wood is professor of English at the University of Exeter. He is the author of *Stendhal* and *America in the Movies* and is a regular contributor to *The New York Review of Books*.